The Carrington Duet

Age Gap Forbidden Dark Mafia Romance

The Carrington Cartel Series

Chiquita Dennie

304 Publishing Company

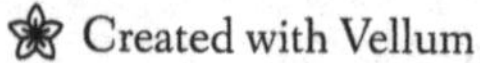 Created with Vellum

Torn

A Forbidden Age Gap Dark Mafia
Romance

Disclaimer

This work of fiction contains strong language, graphic violence, and explicit sexual content and is only intended for mature readers. The story may contain unconventional situations, verbal abuse, grief, and encounters that may offend some readers. Please consider carefully before reading or try my contemporary romance work instead. Intended for mature readers (18+).

Introduction

Grab some wine and get ready for more spicy, sinful, sexy suspense.

Are you signed up for my newsletter?

Join today and find out all the latest in new releases, contests, giveaways, sneak peeks, and more.

www.chiquitadennie.com

The Carrington Cartel Series

Welcome to the Carrington Cartel, a duet series that features characters from Stuck in Love, and Fuertes Cartel. Gigi, Laurent, and Axel briefly appear in the Struck in Love series as an introduction. You do not have to read the entire series, but spoilers are included in this new series. If you want the entire reading order of Struck in Love Universe, check the next page.

Struck In Love Universe

https://books2read.com/u/49Zjnw
Ruthless Struck in Love Book 1
https://books2read.com/u/4AxKLo
Savage Struck in Love Book 2
https://books2read.com/u/bpED6g
Beast Struck in Love Book 3
https://books2read.com/u/3LpgdJ
Janice and Carlo Captivated by His Love
https://books2read.com/u/b6je6M
Brutal Struck in Love Book 4
https://books2read.com/u/4NQyE9
Stolen-The Fuertes Cartel Book 1
https://books2read.com/u/mvZlgV
Saved-The Fuertes Cartel Book 2
https://books2read.com/u/4DWwLd
Redemption Struck in Love Book 5
https://books2read.com/u/b5kZ8O
Betrayed-The Fuertes Cartel Book 3

https://books2read.com/u/4A5LGp
Torn: The Carrington Cartel Book 1
https://books2read.com/u/mqXare
Claim: The Carrington Cartel Book 2

Latest Releases from Chiquita Dennie

The Early Years-A Prequel Short Story
    Ruthless: Struck in Love 1
    Savage: Struck in Love 2
    Beast: Struck in Love 3
    Brutal: Struck In Love 4
    Redemption: Struck In Love 5
    Broken Book 1 (Emery & Jackson)
    Heart Of Stone Book 1.5 Emery &Jackson A Valentine's
Day Short
    Janice and Carlo: Captivated By His Love
    Rebirth Book 2 (Jordan and Damon)
    Temptation
    Reveal Book 3 (Angela and Brent)
    Cocky Catcher
    Bossy Billionaire
    Bottoms Up Heart of Stone, Book 3.5 (Jessica and Joseph
Short
    Love Shorts: A Collection of Short Stories
    Stolen: Fuertes Mafia Cartel Book 1

Exposed (Salvation Society Novel)
Saved: Fuertes Mafia Cartel Book 2
Refuel (A Driven World Novel)
Pressure (A Driven World Novel)
Until Serena (HEA World Novel)
Renew Book 4 (Jessica and Joseph)
She's All I Need
Red Light District (A Fantasy Romance Short)
The Carrington Cartel Book 1
Betrayed: Fuertes Mafia Cartel Book 3
Something Gained (A Romantic Comedy Book 1)
Upcoming Releases (2023/2024):
The Carrington Cartel Book 2
Fall For You (Satin Hill Book 1)
Bronx
Unveiled (Achille Cartel Book 1)
Nicco: TN Seal Security Book 3

Synopsis

When a cartel princess breaks a longstanding promise – her life isn't the only one in danger

Gigi has always known what her future holds. Marry into the Ramini family, strengthen the cartel and obey her father.

That was until her father assigned Axel as her personal protector.

A trusted associate of her father and a high-ranking member of the cartel, Axel is everything Gigi knows to avoid, instead she finds herself drawn to him.

Their desire for each other is danger, more dangerous than the cartel itself.

Because if anyone learns the truth, the consequences will be dire.

Chapter 1

Gigi

"Rise and shine, Gigi!" Aurora, our housekeeper, drew the curtains in my room.

The bright sunlight made me groan. I didn't feel like dealing with anything or anyone today. I was still dealing with a hangover from the party my father made me go to with him to meet Joaquin Fuertes. Too many times, I'd pretended to be sick. My excuses had run out, and time was ticking for me to finally step up as the leader of the cartel. Unlike most families led by men, my parents only had me, and being the daughter of one of the top families in Italy, I had no choice but to follow in the family's footsteps.

"Ugh. No, Aurora." I groaned, tightening the covers around my body. I heard her chuckles inside the room.

"Gigi, you know your father wants to have breakfast with you."

"So?" I tossed the covers back and sat up against my bronze monogrammed headboard.

"How was the party?" Aurora bent to pick up my dress and shoes off the floor.

I complained to her all the time about picking up behind me. I was a grown woman, yet she still treated me like a little girl. A smile remained on her face as she grabbed more of my clothes off the floor.

I shrugged and stretched my arms before lifting my cell phone from the night table. "It was boring as usual." I tapped on my messages, seeing I had lots from my best friend, Ginerva.

"Did you meet anyone?" Aurora walked into the bathroom as I lay across the bed, texting Ginerva.

"I met Sofia Fuertes and a few other mob wives." I stared at the photo of me getting out of the limo with Axel standing off to the side, watching.

Me: *Where did you get these?*

Ginerva: *Baby, you're plastered on all the papers.*

Me: *Fuck.*

Ginerva: *You can't panic, Gigi. This is your life.*

Me: *I know. I wish they'd leave me alone.*

"Oh, is she nice? I've seen a few of her movies." Aurora came out of my bathroom carrying the trash bag.

I closed out my message, jumped off the bed, and took it out of her hands. "Aurora, I told you to stop cleaning my room. You need to relax and go on vacation."

She waved me off and reached for the trash. Although she was in her early sixties, Aurora looked no older than forty. She always kept her gray hair in a bun and wore heels all day long, no matter the season. Aurora had been with my family since before I was born, and from the stories I'd been told, her husband was killed years ago. He worked for my father, so he brought her on staff when she needed a place to live. My mother wasn't fond of her because my father and I loved her and treated her like family. In Rosa's eyes, Aurora was the help who needed to stay in her place. I thought of Aurora as more of a parent than Rosa.

"One day." Aurora kissed me on the cheek and pulled the bag out of my hand. Her golden-brown cheeks rose in a smile, and I rolled my eyes.

"Gigi, time for breakfast!" Rosa shouted.

I grunted, walking toward the bathroom.

Aurora smacked me on the butt, then cupped my cheek. She had a gentle, wise, and beautiful spirit. "Be a nice little girl."

The warmth of her touch on my chin calmed me down. "Yes, ma'am."

"Who were you texting with?" Aurora pointed to my phone.

"Ginerva."

Aurora started to make my bed. "It's early for her to be texting. Everything okay?"

I walked into my bathroom, turned on the shower, and checked the temperature. "Yeah, she sent photos of me at the party last night," I yelled from the bathroom, preparing for my facial routine and gathering all my products.

"You looked beautiful last night." Aurora stood at the door of the bathroom.

I nodded and winked at her through the mirror as I brushed my teeth, and she shook her head.

"What is taking so long for you to come downstairs?" My mother burst into my room.

Aurora hurriedly shut my bathroom door, and I locked it. Removing my nightshirt and shorts, I hopped in the shower before she could come in and bug me. I was twenty-two, and she still treated me like I was five, wanting to dictate everything I did and who I saw. Arranged marriages were a well-known tradition in the cartel lifestyle, and she was all about pushing me into the Ramini family. Something I refused.

"Hurry up, Gigi!" I heard banging on my door.

"Coming, Rosa!" I yelled.

"Keep disrespecting me, Gigi," Rosa shouted from the other side of the door.

"Keep disrespecting me, Gigi." I mimicked, lifting the lavender body wash and towel and lathering them across my arms and legs.

Rosa was the definition of a kept wife, one who only wanted to shop and throw parties. The goal of my marrying Dario Ramini was so he could form a cohesive unit with our gun business, ultimately signifying a stronger hold on all of Italy. My mother and Dario didn't understand that the De Luca Cartel would never relinquish or fold their power. Dario was an egomaniac, a pompous asshole, and a womanizer who only wanted to fuck me so he could tell his friends. He was twenty-five, the eldest of Ramini's sons, and power-hungry like his father. Edmundo Ramini trained his son to be like him regarding women, which meant treating them like objects instead of someone you loved.

I turned off the water, slid the door open, and grabbed the towel on the island near my vanity mirror. My father agreed to redo my room and bathroom if I went on a date with Dario and attended the party last night. I'd learned that to get anything out of him, I needed to show I wasn't weak.

Drying off, I removed my wrap and let my soft curls fall against my back, nearly to my ass. I turned, looking at the stretch marks on my thick curvy figure. Rosa constantly complained that I needed to lose weight before the wedding, but I loved my curves and thick frame. Not obese or stick thin, in the middle, with thighs, hips, and plump breasts women paid to get.

Coming from a mixed background, I inherited my mother's tawny skin and my father's green eyes, thin nose, and short height of five-six. I thanked my mom for giving me her beauty, even though she was evil on the inside ninety percent of the time. She acted like she'd never had a privileged life outside of my father's money, despite her family coming from a political background. Her father was a retired congressman, and when she met my father during his visit to America for a business meeting, it was arranged that she would marry him, and her life was uprooted to Italy.

Unlocking my bathroom door, I was met by my mother sitting on the edge of the bed. I tightened the towel around me and smiled sweetly.

"Morning, Mommy." I strode toward her, leaned down, and kissed her cheek.

She gripped my chin, forcing me to look at her. "Why do you insist on pissing me off, Gigi? Huh?"

I jerked out of her hold and stomped to the dresser drawer to grab a bra and panties, ignoring her fussing. "I don't know what you're talking about."

I scanned through my wardrobe, wondering what I was in the mood to wear and what would piss my parents off even more. Having a walk-in closet that expanded into another room was the best idea I ever had. I ran a hand across the dresses and shoes hanging in a color-coded sequence. The walls were painted a light cream to match my bedroom color scheme of cream and silver. The two-thousand–square-foot room was my safe haven when I needed to be alone, including a couch nook for reading and doing my class work.

"One of these days, you're going to piss me off too much, and your father won't save you." Mother stalked into my closet, standing with her hands on her hips. Her hair was pulled to the side, her face all made up, and her eyes dipped low in slits.

"Why are you in my room?" I pulled down a pair of black leggings, a white crop top, and flat sandals.

Stepping around her, I moved back into the bathroom and started to close the door, but she blocked me.

"This is my house, and you will follow my rules." Mother's mouth thinned with displeasure.

I opened my mouth to respond, and she held her palm up, stopping me. Closing my eyes, I took a deep breath to control my emotions before we got into another shouting match. "I need to get dressed."

A muscle flicked angrily in her jaw. She glared and finally moved out of the way.

I closed the door, locking it for good measure.

"Breakfast is getting cold," she called from the stairs.

Breakfast is getting cold... pfff.

I removed the bra I had just donned and replaced it with nipple tape, then threw my shirt on and slid my legs into the leggings. I grabbed my brush to comb my hair into a ponytail, then dabbed on a little lip gloss and eyeliner.

"Ready for the show." My mouth took on an unpleasant twist.

Leaving the bathroom, I grabbed my phone, shut the door, and trod down the spiral stairs, checking for missed calls or messages. I scrolled past the calls from Dario and tapped on Ginerva's message.

Ginerva: *Gigi, call me*

Me: *Sorry. Rosa started with me again.*

Ginerva: *Girl, you better stop calling her Rosa.*

Me: *She'll be fine.*

I stepped into the massive dining room with its twenty-seat table, million-dollar chandelier, and family portraits on the wall. Growing up, I thought we lived in a museum with the amount of artwork and statues lying around.

"My little girl finally graced me with her presence," Dad stated.

I smiled, heading toward him and kissing his cheek.

He grasped my hand, shaking his head at the leggings and crop top I wore. "Why do you continue to dress like this, Gigi?" He waved for me to take a seat at the table.

Aurora came in with a plate of food and laid it in front of me.

"Laurent, I think it's time she married Dario," Mother muttered, enjoying the gentle sparring for my father's attention.

I glared at her and jumped up from my chair.

"Sit!" Dad yelled, pointing at me.

"You promised I could finish school." A tremor touched my lips.

Mother's eyes were sharp and assessing. "Promises are meant to be broken," she said, sipping her morning drink of orange juice and vodka—more vodka than juice, I assumed.

"Listen to me, Gigi. You know I'm retiring, and we need protection." My father leaned back, his eyes cold.

Dario was only interested in using me as a trophy on his arm and trying to get in my pants. I'd prided myself on remaining a virgin and refused to lose it to a man like Dario.

My father's hand came down on the table. "The deal we have is not a hundred percent secure, and having the Ramini family—"

"I don't care about the Raminis!" I whirled to leave the room.

"Stop! Come sit back down." Father stopped me with a raised hand.

Tears welled in my eyes. I wiped them away and sat

down with my arms crossed. One day, I wanted to open an antique shop and graduate with a degree in business. I loved finding out where things came from and how they were built.

I shook my head. "Dario is not a good man."

"He's the eldest boy of a great family, and your father made a good choice," Mother explained.

"Then you marry him," I mumbled.

"Do you think someone magically created all of this? You have to make a sacrifice like the rest of us," Mother chastised. She threw her napkin on the table, rose out of her chair, and left the room with her drink.

"She's right, Gigi. You're our *neonata*." Father smoothed my hair.

As usual, I became their baby girl in Italian when they wanted to manipulate me into doing what they wanted. I knew this was all a ploy to keep me under their thumbs and from leaving home.

"If you love me, don't make me marry Dario." I cradled my head.

"The decision has been made." Father slammed one fist against the table.

It wasn't often he was so upset with me, but I had to get out of this arrangement. "You want this life. I don't." The last thing I wanted to do was sit down with Dario today.

"She's right here, Dario," Mother stated, re-entering the room. She was smirking with her arm looped through his.

I almost gagged at the fakeness as he kissed her hand and came over to me, trying to kiss me on the lips. I turned my head away.

"Gigi." My father warned.

Dario raised his hand. "It's fine, Laurent. In time, she'll fall in line." Dario pinched my cheek.

"Why is he here?" I questioned, ignoring his presence.

"Your fiancé wanted to see you today and take you out on a date," Mother informed me.

I shook my head. "Not happening." I moved away.

"It *is* happening. You want to move to America, correct?" Dad reminded me about the negotiation we made a year ago. If I married Dario and took over the family business, I could move to America. Even though I grew up in Italy, I was familiar with the lifestyle, having traveled occasionally and visited my mother's family.

"And you want someone to take over this business. Put Dario in charge and leave me out of this," I spat, renewing my efforts to leave.

Dario grasped my wrist. "I love you, Gigi," he said, taunting me.

"Let me go," I gritted through clenched teeth.

"Gigi, Ginerva is here," Aurora blessedly interrupted.

I nodded, and Dario removed his hold. I rolled my eyes at him, stomping out of the room.

* * *

As soon as I walked into the living room, I saw Ginerva sitting on the couch, typing away on her phone. I plopped down next to her and groaned in annoyance.

She closed the phone and sat up to stare at me, pulling her feet underneath her. "Aurora called me."

I removed my arm from over my eyes and smiled. Aurora was the only one who knew me and protected my sanity. "Were you in class?"

"No, I was shopping." Ginerva grinned.

I chuckled, knowing how she loved to spend her father's

money. Ginerva Pauduano's family wasn't in the business directly like my father. Her mother, Piera, was a retired school teacher and her father, Marcuello, was a police officer. He was on my father's payroll, but treated Ginerva way better. She wanted to move to America, and he was fine with letting her live her life as a beautician. Her mom encouraged her to be independent and not become someone's wife without exploring the world first.

"Dario's here," I scoffed, lifting a hand to my forehead.

"Oh. You want me to put a hit out on him?" She bit her lip to stifle her grin.

"If that's all it took, I would say yes. But we both know my parents will find another family to ship me off to." My tongue nervously moistened my dry lips.

"You never told me how the party went." The warmth of her smile echoed in her voice.

I shrugged my shoulders and started to speak when a throat cleared behind me.

"Dario." Ginerva kissed her teeth.

"Ginerva." His smile was without humor.

They hated each other ever since Ginerva caught him having sex with another woman at our joined family dinner. I told her I wasn't bothered since I knew it came with the territory, but when we were alone in the limo, I tried to scratch Dario's eyes out for embarrassing me in public.

His long-time mistress was a girl we went to school with before she dropped out after having a baby. Rumor said it was his baby, but he refused to claim the child since it was a girl. The old rules of having a child out of wedlock mattered to our parents more than anything, and it would bring shame upon our families if he let her take his last name.

"Dario, leave me alone." I stood up to leave, get some fresh air, go shopping, anywhere.

"We have to talk at some point, Gigi." Dario followed, approaching me with a smirk.

"No, we don't." I tried to move around him to head out of the living room.

He grabbed my elbow, spinning me around. His expression was stony. "We're getting married, and you *will* be my wife."

I wanted to smack him. "Get your hands off me."

"That mouth of yours is going to get you into trouble." He thought I would obey him because he got along with my father.

"You heard what my best friend said." Ginerva cocked her head to the side, standing beside me with her arms crossed.

Dario glanced from me to her and back with a smile. Removing his hand, he raised it in surrender.

"How long have we known each other?" Dario slid his hands into his pockets.

"Too long," I replied, resigned.

He chortled. "Since you were twelve, and I was fifteen. It's always been understood our bloodline would connect in marriage."

"You don't own me, Dario," I voiced firmly.

He leaned in closer, with his face only a few inches from mine. "Think again, my love. Once we get married, all of you will belong to me." Dario ran the back of his hand across my cheek.

I didn't miss the lust in his eyes. I slapped his hand down. "Understand something, Dario. I might be quiet and reserved, but you need my family's money more than we need you."

"Are you threatening me?" Dario snapped, his voice cold.

"Stay out of my way." I smiled, grabbed Ginerva's hand, along with my purse and phone, and left the house.

Despite living in Sicily all my life on my family's sprawling estate, it could be suffocating, with all the bodyguards and people who showed up for meetings with my father, forcing me to be the dutiful daughter.

Chapter 2

Axel

I stamped my foot into the man's chest, with no regret at his screams. People never learned. I was the last face they saw as they took their last breath. Like this guy. The minute Laurent agreed to a deal with him—and gave an extension—he thought it would be a good idea to leave town. When I had to chase, I made the pain even worse. Time I felt was wasted because they thought I wouldn't catch them.

I cracked my neck, wiping the sweat off my brow as I slammed my foot into his chest again.

"Please don't kill me." He coughed as blood seeped down his nose, placing a hand on his stomach.

I took my lit cigar and twisted it into his forehead. "Shut the fuck up!" I yelled in a harsh, raw voice.

People like Kiran pissed me off when they interrupted my schedule. I had plans to check in on a big shipment Laurent wanted me to ensure would arrive on time after weeks of delays. And here I was because no one else could be trusted to get rid of this piece of shit.

"Hold his leg out."

My crew grabbed both legs and held them together as Kiran squirmed.

I removed my gun and placed it on his kneecap. My voice dropped in volume. "Where's the money?"

He closed his eyes, tears squeezing out as his lips trembled.

"Speak," I hissed.

He tensed. "I will get his money, I promise you."

My voice was icy. "Too late for that. Laurent saved you more than once."

"Come on, Axel. I just need a little time." His mind was languid, without hope.

"Time, huh?" Men like him would never learn—same excuses every time.

I fired the gun.

"Argh!" he screamed, gripping his left knee.

"Why should I let you live?" Their answer never mattered to me, but I allowed them to feel comfortable enough to think I wouldn't kill them.

Kiran groaned in pain.

My phone buzzed in my pocket, and I answered it, staring at the blood on the ground.

"Is it done?" Laurent asked.

I glanced at Kiran, pointed the gun at his head, and fired. "It's done." My skin grew hot, and my jaw clenched.

"Come to my office." Laurent didn't wait for me to agree before hanging up.

When I took on the role of enforcer, I made sure the disposal of bodies wouldn't fall back on the cartel or me. We had our hands in real estate and owned locations like this where situations would never be questioned.

"Clean this up." I pointed at Kiran's wallet on the floor.

"His family?" Lazaro asked.

"If they question his whereabouts, kill them."

He hesitated. "The women..."

Many would consider me evil for hurting women and children. I paused at the door. "Make the consequences clear if they go to the police."

"Understood." The words caught in his throat.

"Check his home for the money. If it's not there, burn it down," I instructed.

I exited the back of the room and jogged outside, climbing into the passenger seat of the chauffeured car Laurent expected his team to travel in when doing business. Most of the time I drove, but I'd had to get my hands dirty tonight and didn't have time to go home and change.

I reached down and picked up the clean shirt and jacket. "Take me to Laurent's."

"Yes, sir."

The car ride was silent while I looked out into the streets. I haven't slept for the last few days because of repeated nightmares. One of the reasons I did business at night was to keep my mind off what would otherwise creep into my thoughts. Laurent needed me to handle another situation, but I might be late with his last-minute call.

We arrived at his home a few minutes later, and I jumped out. "Keep the car running."

I removed my gun and checked the chamber, placing it back in my holster and walking up the stairs to knock.

"He's expecting you," Butler remarked.

I headed toward his office and lightly knocked before pushing the door open.

"Sit," Laurent said.

"What's this about?" I brushed a hand through my hair.

"How are you?" He eyed me up and down.

My brows scrunched in confusion. "Is there a reason for the visit?"

Laurent huffed. "Still the same Axel."

"How else should I be?" I looked at the clock on the wall.

"Did you get the money?"

My phone vibrated. I pulled it out, seeing a message from the team.

Lazaro: *Got it.*

"We have the money." I pocketed the phone.

Laurent's mouth thinned. "More business is coming our way."

"Okay."

"Things are going to change and get busier for you and me." His mouth hardened.

"Busier, how?"

"A few businesses I want to expand. With the upcoming marriage of my daughter and Dario, I think we'll be in a good place."

I paused at the mention of Dario and the deal Laurent made. "Anything else?"

"Are you sleeping at night?" he asked somberly.

My face wrinkled in contempt. "We're not talking about my personal life."

He reached for a cigar. "The anger you hold inside won't just go away."

My face grew warm with shame. "Unless you need anything else—"

A knock at the door interrupted me, and I turned to see the one person who never failed to piss me off.

"Oh, sorry. I thought you were alone," Gigi said, glancing from her father to me.

I looked away, leaning back in the chair.

"Give me a minute, and I'll be out," Laurent replied.

"Excuse me." She pulled the door closed.

"That girl will drive me to an early grave," Laurent complained.

I stood, finally ready to get back to what I loved most.

"I got word you killed some of Casella's men," Laurent stated.

"My job." Color stained my cheeks. I didn't like being questioned about my moves.

"A truce is in place for a reason."

"Then remind his people," I stated, leaving the office and shutting the door behind me.

Marching down the hall, I passed the kitchen, glimpsing Gigi laughing with Ginerva. She caught my stare and quickly turned away.

As soon as I got home, I poured a drink and lit a cigar to ease the adrenaline from the day.

* * *

"Axel, you need to eat your vegetables," Mother complained.

I laughed when my dad made a funny face behind her. "Leave the boy alone," he responded, brushing his lips against her cheek.

"He's spoiled because of you." Mother looked up at him with slight surprise in her eyes.

All eyes moved to the front door as someone knocked. My father rose out of his seat and answered with a nervous smile.

"Mr. Carrington," Father greeted, stepping to the side to allow the man entry.

At ten, I didn't understand what business needed to be conducted at eight at night, but Laurent Carrington was in my home. My father introduced him to my mother, then me, before motioning him to the back office.

My mother snapped her fingers to stop me from staring at the large men in suits standing outside the door. "Finish eating, Axel."

"I'm full. Can I go to my room?" I rubbed my eyes sleepily.

"Fine, but take your bath and go straight to bed."

She picked up my plate, sauntering to the kitchen. I slid out of my seat and plodded down the hall, staring up at each man. Neither said a word, but I heard whispering from the office.

"I can't do that. You're putting too much in without a trail," Father said.

I wondered what he was talking about.

"You can. I believe you're the best. Think about what I said." The door opened, and Laurent looked down at me and smiled. "I'll see you soon," he said, marching out of the house.

"Shit!"

I woke to another reminder from the past I couldn't forget.

I pushed the covers back, stumbled from the bed, and picked up my watch from the nightstand. It was two a.m. I strolled into the bathroom, reached for the light, and splashed water on my face. Seeing the bruises on my knuckles, I clenched and unclenched my fingers to ease the soreness. I popped open the medicine cabinet and took two Advil.

Banging at the front door instantly had me on red alert.

"The fuck?" I stomped out of the bathroom and snatched my gun off the dresser. In only my boxers, I yanked open the door with my gun raised.

"I tried to call but didn't get an answer." Fulgenzio studied my face, then the gun in my hand.

I set the gun on my front counter near the closet. "What are you doing here?"

"One of Laurent's businesses got hit."

Nerves rippled low in my stomach. "Which one?"

"The warehouse where he keeps some of the guns."

I raised a hand and stroked my jaw. "How much did they take?"

"Not sure. Laurent is pissed, and most of the team is there."

"You need to get back to the house. I'll drive myself."

"Yes, sir." He stepped back.

I shut the door and headed to the bedroom. I grabbed a pair of pants and a shirt before hopping in the shower.

Less than thirty minutes later, I arrived out front of the Temple—a nightclub owned by Laurent. He'd built storage units underground to make it easier to transport our merchandise.

Some of his men stood out front, stepping aside as I walked into the deserted club. I noticed Laurent yelling on the phone.

Lamberto took a shot from the bartender. "What do you know?"

I scanned around the room; it felt rigid. "I just got here." Anger wedged in my throat. Laurent expected me to be ten steps ahead. "Is this the best time to drink?"

Emotion flickered in Lamberto's eyes. I was the only one to get away with questioning him. "It helps calm my nerves. Who do you think hit us?"

His face darkened as he searched the room. His men never saw him agitated. He endeavored to be in control at all times—like me.

"Too early to tell," I answered.

"You tell me the second something is found." Lamberto slammed the glass on the bar.

I scanned the room, picking up a single screw from the

dismantled floorthey'd left behind. "Soon as we get the surveillance, we'll have a better idea."

"How much was taken?" Lamberto questioned.

"Laurent doesn't keep a lot here. Only enough for a quick sale," one of the guards said.

"From now on, we need to have extra men on sales," I replied.

"I agree, but Laurent only listens to you," Lamberto commented.

I looked behind as Dario came through the door. "How did this happen?" he demanded.

I shrugged. "I just got the message to come here tonight."

"So you didn't have people at the door?" Dario quizzed.

"That's not my job." I didn't run the day-to-day operations of the club.

Dario huffed, considering my comment. "Laurent is always bringing outside people around."

I clenched my fist.

"Dario, not now," Lamberto replied, clutching his elbow.

"He's the enforcer, right? So enforce security around here. When I take over, this won't happen," Dario emphasized, waving his hands dramatically.

"If that time ever comes, we can have a conversation." I ignored his vile stare at my statement.

"Look, they say it was only a hundred grand, plus a crate of guns," Lamberto said as the door opened to Laurent and his guards.

"Update me with better news," Laurent snapped, folding his arms.

"Fulgenzio told me we got hit, and Lamberto confirmed a crate of AK-47s and a hundred grand."

Laurent glared at Lamberto. "Any idea on who was in charge of the exchange?"

"Dario, you handle the clubs," Lamberto hinted.

Dario glared at him in humiliation. "I put Lazaro to monitor the exchange."

"Lazaro," Laurent responded, glancing at me for confirmation.

I nodded. "He was with me earlier."

Lamberto and Dario had harsh expressions.

"So he didn't come directly here to handle the exchange?" Dario inquired.

I observed the room, noticing the bottles of liquor arranged on the floor exactly where they should be after being brought in, and only a select few had access. "Nothing looks tampered with. If Lazaro is behind anything, I'll catch him."

"Bring him to me now," Laurent demanded, his brows pulling together in a frown.

"I can handle him, Laurent," Dario countered.

That suggestion piqued my curiosity. Lazaro took orders from me on a daily basis unless Laurent specifically gave a direction.

Laurent agreed and faced me. "Get reliable people down here, and I want the footage brought to me only."

Laurent turned and left the room.

"I'll send you the footage," Dario spoke over his shoulder.

Lamberto left the room, and I touched the hardwood floor where the crates were kept. Dario was jealous that Laurent always listened to my advice, and our first meeting had determined the outcome of our relationship.

"Axel, I want you to meet my future son-in-law, Dario Ramini," Laurent introduced.

I nodded in acknowledgment and focused on the meeting. I'd never been a friendly man and wouldn't start now.

Dario dropped his hand, and a few men chuckled at the situation.

"Gigi always talks about the help around the house," Dario taunted, arching a black brow.

Laurent interrupted the unspoken tension between us. "Gentlemen, we have some decisions that need to be made, and I wanted Dario here."

I listened as he paced the office.

"As you all know, Dario is marrying my daughter in the future, which means he will have a position in the family. He comes from a fine family. Edmundo Ramini is a longtime friend and business partner," Laurent explained.

"She's going to be the perfect wife and mother," Dario bragged.

"I want a grandbaby soon." Laurent laughed, causing some of his men to chuckle in response.

I grew bored at Dario kissing ass; most men came in by working hard and building respect. Dario was trying to get into a top position without earning respect from Laurent's team.

"Anything new we need to be discussing?" I broke up the conversation.

"Axel, always about business. The main reason I requested this meeting was to introduce Dario as an adviser and as the Boss once he marries my daughter. I have a few deals coming up soon with the Casella family." Laurent paused and turned his head.

"They're not reliable, Boss," I said.

"Orson has always been on time with my father," Dario stated, a vein throbbing in his forehead.

"We're talking about the Carrington's. No offense, but your family doesn't have the reach that Laurent is capable of." Dario's eyes darted around the room.

"If you go in with Orson, you have to know the risks," I countered.

"Orson is well known in Italy. We could take the entire area, plus more if we work with Orson," Dario chimed in excitedly.

Laurent sat back in thought.

"Friends end up with more problems that turn into foes. I hate to kill unnecessary things," I mentioned, continuing to take in the conversations around me.

Since that day, Dario and I had been cordial but nothing more, and we hated each other's guts. Laurent was a smart man, but even he had to know that marrying Gigi off to Dario would result in more issues.

When I needed peace and clarity, I visited my parents' gravesite. That was the only place where I could cope with the grief that continued tormenting me after their deaths. It was paralyzing how little things reminded me of their laughs or the times I got into trouble.

I closed my eyes and took in the night air. "I bet you're pissed I came here again after what I've done."

People always said it got better with time, but each day, I grew angrier. Family tried to talk me into speaking with someone, but I felt no one could understand how this world worked. When you lived within the mob, you knew your time could be up at any moment, but I hated it came for my parents. All I had left of them were pictures and a gravesite.

After an hour of staring at their names, I hopped in my car and drove home. My phone rang as soon as I tossed my keys down and removed my jacket. Laurent's name popped up on the screen. Out of respect, I answered immediately and listened to Laurent explain he needed me to check in with Fulgenzio and stay close to the family. Threats had increased against the family, and he didn't want Gigi in harm's way.

I rubbed my forehead to relieve the stress. "I've checked in with Fulgenzio, and he says she only goes to class and hangs with Ginerva."

"She drives me crazy, like her mother."

I put the phone on speaker, removed my watch, and left my shoes at the door. I angled toward the kitchen and lifted a glass, pouring the rest of my brandy. "Boss, I don't trust Lamberto and Dario."

"Do you think I'm stupid?" Laurent probed.

"No." My mouth hardened.

"Good. I have my eyes open, Axel. Never fail to know that I see everything."

I placed the glass in the sink and left the kitchen. "I'll have the footage sent over to you."

"The wedding is coming soon. I need you on top of her security at all times."

I stalked down the hall to my bedroom. "Of course."

I ended the call, placed the phone on the bedside table, and removed my shirt and pants. Shower, then sleep.

Chapter 3

Gigi

A week later.

Ginerva spilled to me about her latest argument with her parents as I walked out of the school building. Everybody was used to the two guards who followed alongside me every day. I watched people, noting the normalcy of folks my age—cuddled up couples in love, doing the usual college routine—made me long for a simpler life.

"Are you done with class now?" Ginerva interrupted my thoughts at the end of the phone.

"Yes, thank God. Do you want to meet for lunch?" I let my guard open my door when we arrived at the car.

"How long will it take? My parents have plans and want me to join," Ginerva whispered.

Fulgenzio turned onto the road, and I put my books down, sliding the seat belt over my shoulder. I noticed a few girls laughing together, and a shot of envy ran through me.

"Hmmm..." I checked my watch. "Maybe twenty minutes if you want to meet at Capri Cafe."

"I think I can pull that off," Ginerva answered.

My phone beeped with an incoming call. "Hold on, Ginerva."

I pulled the phone from my ear and clicked over to my mother's call.

"Hello," she answered.

"Yes, Mother," I responded, checking my nails.

"I need you to meet me somewhere," my mother commanded, trying to run my life as usual.

"Where?"

She hesitated. "Fulgenzio has the address."

I groaned, looking up at him with desperate eyes. "What is going on?"

Often she'd inconvenience me by "bonding" through shared interests, but it was all for her ego. She wanted to be seen as the perfect mother in front of other people.

"Something I should have set up sooner." Her tone seemed truthful.

"I made plans with Ginerva." No matter my excuses, it never changed her mind. My heart beat faster.

Rosa said, "She can come too. I'll send her mother the address."

"Wait! Where is this place?" If Aurora was there, I knew she would tell me to give her a chance to show me her mothering skills.

"Keep an open mind, Gigi."

"That doesn't sound good."

"I'll pretend you didn't say that, but you'll have fun."

I exhaled heavily after she got off the phone. "Where are we going, Fulgenzio?"

He looked at his phone. "The address is a boutique."

"Shopping?" I asked nervously. Mother was judgmental about my clothes.

"Yes, Miss Carrington." Fulgenzio responded.

I relaxed a little. "I told you to call me Gigi."

He grinned and made a turn at the light. "Gigi."

"I'll tip you if we head to Capri's instead." Fulgenzio would never take a bribe from me, but I'd offered many times.

He chuckled. "Sorry. Mrs. Carrington wants me to bring you here."

I sat back in a daze while he passed through long lines of traffic. Mother sets up a situation to blindside me at the worst times to show off in front of her high-profile friends. So many dinners I've had to attend and act like the perfect daughter of Laurent and Rosa Carrington.

We stopped in front of a wedding dress shop, and my brows dropped when I saw my mother wave and open the door.

Rosa's smile was fake. "Hurry up, Gigi."

Fulgenzio started to get out of the car, and I motioned for him to stop. "Stay. I might need you to keep the car running."

He laughed, and Rosa glared at him, which caused him to stop.

I stomped toward the store, and my mouth dropped open as I saw a few cousins and friends sitting with champagne glasses. "What is this?" I motioned with my hand.

"Dress fitting," Mother answered.

A few family members whispered amongst themselves. "Mother—"

"Stop worrying. You'll fit in everything or lose a few pounds," Rosa said, nudging me forward.

"I had plans." I forced a smile on my lips for appearances.

"Your plans can wait. We need to pick out a dress for your wedding." Rosa swept my hair off my shoulders.

The sales associate walked over to us with a tray of champagne, and I thanked her as I took one. My stomach was in knots at the thought of trying on gowns for a wedding I had no intention of fulfilling.

A rack of gowns came out from the back, and Mother pointed at what she wanted me to try on first. "Here, make sure you suck in your stomach."

I gave her my glass and took the dress out of her hands, heading to the dressing room to change.

"Can we get some more gowns wider in the hip section?" I heard my mother's request.

A few minutes passed before I emerged from the room, maneuvering the long sequined gown with a train and pearls embedded on the sleeves and corset.

A smile spread across my mother's lips. "You look beautiful, but maybe if you lose two or three pounds." She came to stand beside me and held out the train, staring at it with a perplexed look.

"I don't need to lose weight."

"Women in our business have to look a certain way, Gigi. Hold in your stomach." She tapped me on the hip.

"Seriously. I can't do this with you."

"The dress costs seventy thousand, not including the veil and shoes. If you think I'm going to have people talk negatively about how you look in pictures, you've lost your mind," she spat.

"We could try the off-shoulder silk gown," a sales associate suggested.

"How about we don't," I quipped.

Mother glared. "How about we try it on and see?"

I whipped around and went back to change.

The bell rang over the door, and I glanced behind me to see Dario entering.

"Gigi. Mrs. Carrington. Glad to see my soon-to-be bride

is close to finding her gown. You look amazing, Gigi," Dario said as he shut the door.

His mother hugged me, then approached Rosa. "Gigi, I must say, my son is going to be very proud to walk down the aisle with you," Mrs. Ramini commented.

I bit the inside of my lip to avoid expressing my disgust. "Don't you know you're not supposed to see the bride in her gown before the wedding?" I snapped.

Dario covered his snarl with a smirk and reached out to hug me. "Behave," he whispered in my ear, pinching my side.

"She's technically right, but he brought his mother, and I didn't think it would hurt," Mother said, patting him on the arm.

"How many times do I have to tell you to stay out of my affairs?" A flame rose in my stomach.

My mother frowned. "Gigi, not today. You're standing in the middle of a dress shop in a gown. It should be a fun day."

"Yeah, fun." I grabbed the train and turned to change into the next prison apparel.

* * *

Mother picked out her favorites and told them I would lose three pounds in time for the wedding. Dario promised to help me lose the weight. I wanted to scream for everybody to leave me alone, but I played nice long enough to get out of there. I put my shades on and left with Dario on my heels.

"Slow down." Dario gripped my elbow, but I snatched it away.

"You can stop pretending to be nice. They're still inside gossiping." I turned, falling into a hard chest.

"Sorry." I glanced up into Axel's sharp, cold eyes.

"You all right?" His warm hand touched my hip.

I looked down at his hand, and he removed it swiftly.

"Why wouldn't she be?" Dario extended a hand around my waist.

"I don't know what to do with her." My mother's voice pulled me from my daze, and I stepped out of Dario's grasp.

"I can say the same," I mumbled under my breath. I went to the car and pulled out my phone to call Ginerva.

"Bored already?" Ginerva laughed on the phone.

I watched through the window as Dario and his mother talked with Axel. "Beyond bored. Guess where I am and who showed up?"

"Who?"

"Dress fitting for the wedding, and Dario brought his mother."

"Maybe you should try to make the best of things," Ginerva said.

I balked at the statement. "So, give up?"

"Not give up, but see if you can have input in what you want for the wedding and marriage."

"We're talking about Rosa Carrington."

Dario hugged my mother and opened the car door to speak to me.

"Hold on." I covered the phone with my hand.

"I want to take you to lunch tomorrow," Dario stated in a silky tone.

"I'm busy." I turned away.

"Gigi, either way, I'll see you tomorrow. Did you forget I practically grew up around your family, and your mother likes to impress?" Dario taunted.

My cheeks burned as his eyes swept over me. "Visit if you want. Doesn't mean I'll be there."

Ginerva giggled in my ear.

"Who are you talking to on the phone?" Dario asked.

"We're not married yet. You don't need to screen my calls," I snapped.

Dario moved back to let my mother get in the car.

"See you soon!" Mother waved at them.

"Yeah, Ginerva." I ignored my mother.

"Tell Ginerva you'll call her back," Mother said, turning to face me.

"Can't this wait for when we get home?"

Her brow wrinkled. "No."

"Talk to her," Ginerva suggested.

"Tomorrow. Don't forget." I reminded her.

I finished the call and stared off into the traffic. A headache was forming and would only worsen the longer I was in my mother's presence.

Mother turned up her nose. "You've embarrassed me, Gigi. I wish you would understand your place."

I pointed at myself. "My place?"

"As a mother and a wife, I am expected to teach you how to raise your household."

My next words spilled from my lips. "Aurora did that."

Mother shook her head. "School was a mistake. I might have to talk to your father."

She would use anything she could to manipulate me, like throwing school in my face. "You wouldn't dare."

"Give me a reason I should keep letting you slide."

"Mother—"

"Oh, *now* I'm 'mother?' What happened to Rosa?"

I sighed and caved to her ego. "I liked the silk gown with the ruffles.".

She grinned. "Good. That was my favorite." She lifted my chin and stared into my eyes.

"We still have time to change our minds, but you need to lose a little weight."

"I'd planned to go to lunch with Ginerva, but she's busy. Do you want to come with me instead?" I asked, playing into her hands. She hated when I gave others more attention than her, especially my loyalty to Ginerva and the number of secrets I dumped on her instead of my mother.

"Lunch would be good. My treat." Mother stretched her arm around my shoulder.

"You mean Dad's treat."

We burst into laughter. While the moment was nice, I thought back to when I was younger and tried to ask my mother about her life growing up in America. We rarely saw her family. I had memories of her flying back and forth and a few brief phone calls, but my father mentioned the deep hatred some felt at the marriage. If I'd grown up during their time, would I have had the courage to make those same decisions?

Chapter 4

Axel

The following day.

I pushed my sleeve back to check the time on my watch. It was unbearable dealing with Gigi when she was in her shopping mood. We'd spend all day going from one store to the next, carrying multiple bags.

Laurent Carrington elected me as the enforcer of the Carrington Cartel a few years ago when he caught me stealing from one of his men. I was nineteen, and trying to get money to survive after my parents died in a car crash. Well, that's what I was told, but I knew it was a mob hit.

The door opened, and Gigi walked out with Dario behind her. The soon-to-be-married couple clearly weren't on the same page.

I thought we would have a drama-free day without problems, but then I saw Dario grab her arm. She tried to smack him, and he caught her wrist. Gigi had her faults, but no one put their hands on her.

I started to get out of the car when the door opened and Gigi's friend came out. Dario released her wrist and stepped back, allowing them to come down the stairs before he got in a separate car. Dario pulled off while I held the door open for Gigi. Our eyes connected, and she briefly smiled.

I shut the door, then came around to get in the front passenger seat. Fulgenzio, her driver, started the car, heading out of the compound. I respected Laurent because he'd saved me and put me in a position to become my own man. Some of his men hated me, along with a few rival families, because I could have become the Underboss at thirty-four. But I liked not having to deal with the politics of the cartel world. My goal as enforcer was to make things go away without leaving a trace. I was good at that.

I glanced in the rearview mirror and saw Gigi and Ginerva whispering back and forth. Gigi still had a lot to learn, and it didn't help that she rebelled against her family's rules.

"Maybe you should tell your mother," Ginerva stated.

Gigi shook her head. "Be for real, Ginerva. My mother would throw me under the bus."

I could relate to being an only child, but how she handled her parents would never have been tolerated by mine. My father was strict but had an open-door policy that I could come to him about anything. Plus, my mother was my best friend.

"Either you speak up now, or you're walking down the aisle with that scumbag, Dario," Ginerva stated.

Fulgenzio approached a red light, and I turned in my seat to pause their conversation. "When we get in the store, try not to spend all day. I have another appointment I have to handle."

"Don't you work for me?" Gigi tilted her head and smirked.

I pulled my shades down slightly to make eye contact. "I

work for no one, Gigi." I slid them back up to cover my eyes and turned to face forward.

"That's what you get." Ginerva giggled and poked Gigi in the arm, who swatted her hand away.

I smirked in satisfaction. We usually kept things light between us. She knew not to pull that Carrington Boss role on me. All the other men cowered, but I pushed back. One reason could be her intimidating beauty. I found her exquisite, with her deep-set, concrete-green eyes, catlike facial structure, and tawny skin.

"The engagement dinner is soon, right? You might as well force their hand." Ginerva drew my focus away from Gigi.

"I don't know. It's like suddenly, what I want in my life doesn't matter. My father's making me do this."

We arrived at the mall, and I stepped out to open their door, helping them out. Gigi swished into the mall, with Fulgenzio in the front, while I stayed back. We constantly told Laurent that having detail stationed at locations would be better. I greeted our men with a nod, and they tipped their chins up in acknowledgment.

Gigi laughed about something, bringing my focus back to the women.

"And it's only pissing me off even more because they know this isn't what I want. I need to talk to him again," Gigi stated, entering the Louis Vuitton store.

A sales associate came around the counter, extending a tray of champagne for Gigi and Ginerva. "Miss Carrington, nice to see you again."

Gigi took the glass off the tray. "Miccuia, nice to see you again. Did you get my message about pulling some looks for me?"

"Yes, we have everything in the dressing room for you." Miccuia turned and placed the tray on the table.

"Ginerva, are you getting anything?"

"Probably. I have to pick something for my date next week," she responded, standing and following Gigi to the dressing room.

"Follow them," I commanded, sliding my hand into my pocket to take out my phone.

"Hopefully, she won't keep us here all day. Boss has a meeting tonight," Fulgenzio said, marching to the dressing room.

I scanned the text message from Mr. Carrington.

Boss: *Axel, make sure Gigi doesn't cause any problems. We don't need any bad press before the announcement.*

Me: *Gigi plays by her rules, but I'll try.*

Boss: *My daughter is special but extremely spoiled.*

Me: *You created a monster.*

Boss: *That I did.*

The dressing room door opened, and I lifted my head to see Gigi stroll in wearing a long silk ball gown. I didn't know all the different styles of dresses, but this one caused a flutter in my chest. Something about the curves of her hips and the sway of her arms when she planted them on her small waist. She was only five foot five compared to my six-one height, and it could be said she would bring any man to his knees with her full lips, voluptuous curves, and plump breasts. It would never work between us; not only was she Laurent's daughter, but she was young and had goals of living in America and seeing the world. I was there to protect—at all times—the Carrington Cartel. I would never hold her back from her future, and I refused to give up the pledge I made to Laurent and the cartel, but I knew she and I had a connection.

Gigi turned left to right in front of me as she posed. "Do you think it's too much?"

My eyes locked on her delicate, manicured hands.

"Hello, Axel?" Gigi waved a hand in my face.

"Yeah, what was that?" I cleared my throat, not up to holding a long conversation after another sleepless night.

Gigi looked confused. "I said, do you think it's too much?"

She turned around to show the back, and she was bare from the top of her shoulders to the curve of her plush ass.

It annoyed me that another man would see her in the dress, but I quickly reigned in my thoughts. "Only you can make that determination."

There was an excited catch in her voice. "But I want a guy's opinion."

I knew what she was doing. "If you were mine, I would say yes; it's too much."

"Really? You don't think I look cute in the dress?" As usual, she fished for compliments from me to prolong a conversation.

"I think you need Ginerva's opinion more than mine."

Gigi sauntered over to me, closing the distance. "I want your opinion," she muttered, staring into my eyes.

She often tried to challenge me, and I ignored her little flirtations.

"Gigi, what do you—" Ginerva interrupted, breaking our intense gaze as we turned to look at her.

"Ginerva, do you think this is too much?" Gigi spun around, posing for her.

Ginerva looked from Gigi to me.

"It looks good on you, but your father will have a heart attack." Ginerva glanced at me as Gigi walked away to change.

"You're right. I have to be prim and proper." Gigi lifted the bottom of the gown, sauntering off.

"She's about to be engaged," Ginerva said.

My head whipped around to face her. "Very aware, Ginerva." I was unsure if she'd fabricated something between Gigi and me, but she was my boss's daughter and nothing more.

Ginerva smiled. Without hesitation, she said, "You like her?"

"She's the daughter of my boss. Not having this conversation."

"If it matters, I think Dario is only using her." Ginerva looked over her shoulder, then back at me.

"Not my business."

Ginerva shrugged and went back to the dressing room.

* * *

People murmured around the table, and laughter and shouts from some family members greeted Laurent and his wife. After a mundane afternoon of Gigi having us go in and out of four different stores, she finally picked a dress suitable for the evening that wouldn't cause an argument between her parents.

I stood next to Laurent, observing the crowd that included a few familiar faces. He'd told me to sit and relax for the night, but there was no time clock in my job. Loyalty was something I would give willingly to Laurent, and that meant always being vigilant.

Tonight's celebration with Dario and Gigi seemed extremely fake. She sat beside him but kept her body turned toward her mother or talked to Ginerva. Every time Dario took her hand, she swiftly moved it out of his reach.

Dario and I didn't get along because I knew what kind of snake he was and how he was only doing this to become the

Boss of all the families. Laurent was too blind to see Dario's intent to change his plans and put Ramini as the top family in charge once he retired.

Candles flickered on the tables, and the lighting was dim. A few servers arrived with food for the table, and Laurent stood up with a glass in his hand to make a toast.

"Everyone, I would like to say a few words," he said, reaching down to cup Gigi's chin.

She smiled, but it didn't reach her eyes. I clenched my teeth and felt a hand on my shoulder. I turned to see the Underboss, Lamberto.

"Come with me," Lamberto commanded.

I glanced back at the table, motioning for Fulgenzio to take my spot. We walked to the back of the restaurant, through the kitchen, and into the manager's office.

"What's wrong?" I crossed my arms over my chest.

"The delay in the shipment tonight. We need you to go check and make sure nothing is hindering," Lamberto said.

"Now?" My brow spiked at the statement.

"Laurent only trusts you, and I agree. This is a delicate situation." Lamberto fixed his eyes around the room and never on me.

"Why not send Lazaro or Sandro?" Some of our foot soldiers could check into something this small.

"They are there already, but if our shipment gets stolen, Laurent will be pissed," Lamberto said, his voice holding an edge.

I blew out a breath, running a hand through my hair. It was getting longer and would fall in my eyes if I didn't get it cut. "All right. I need to let Laurent know."

"I can do that," Lamberto replied.

"As Laurent's enforcer, I want to ensure he's protected at all times."

Lamberto held his hands up in surrender. Most times, I wouldn't push back on other people doing recon for situations like this, but Lamberto and I weren't on the best of terms. He'd wanted to be the Boss after his father retired and thought Laurent wouldn't last as long as he had in the position as the Don of the family. They were cousins, but not as close as regular family members.

I marched out of the office and back to the table, where everybody cheered Dario and Gigi while he held her hand up with the engagement ring.

Laurent kissed his wife, then grabbed her palm and kissed the back of her hand.

I bent down to whisper in his ear. "Lamberto told me about the issue. I have someone covering me while I check on the shipment."

Laurent nodded and clapped me on the back. "I trust you to ensure we are on the right track, Axel."

"Always, Boss." I stood to leave and caught Gigi's stare.

My commitment was to the family, and I couldn't abandon it for anyone—including her. Once a man fell in love, his senses betrayed him, and he was vulnerable to his enemies. We both knew she shouldn't stay with Dario, but he was a safer bet compared to the unpredictability of my life.

"Do you need backup?" Laurent asked.

I shook my head. "Lamberto told me Lazaro and Sandro are there."

I headed out of the restaurant, hopped in the awaiting Jaguar, and pulled a cigar out of my pocket.

"Those things will kill you." Turin flicked the lighter, and I puffed on the cigar, exhaling the stress away.

"Better than someone," I responded, checking to see if I had a text message from Lazaro.

"So, what are we supposed to be doing?"

Turin was the only person I could call a friend and brother throughout my time in the cartel. Many times we'd battled for survival and won to make it to the top. As soon as I came up, I brought him with me as my right hand. He was the one who brought me back from the edge whenever we needed to get rid of someone—a job that always unleashed my bloodlust. Where Turin was a straight shooter, I gave people false hope, thinking they would live until that last second—and then I slit their throat.

"Lamberto said something is up with the shipment."

"Does Laurent know?" Turin was the type to investigate every angle before attacking.

"He was the one that wanted us to check it out."

"Lamberto told you that?" Turin asked.

I rubbed my chin, puffing on the cigar again. "What are you saying?"

"Nothing. Lamberto hates us, so I'm surprised he even talked to you."

In Lamberto's eyes, Turin and I should be replaced because Laurent trusted us too much.

"Laurent probably told him to pull his panties out of his ass." I chuckled.

Turin laughed and sped up. It was only nine at night, so most of the streets were empty. Thirty minutes later, we reached the abandoned building Laurent bought a few years back. I went to open the door, but my phone rang. I put it on silent, slid it into my pocket, and shut the door after me. Lifting my gun from the holster, I double-checked the clip as Lazaro and Sandro approached.

"How's it going?" Lazaro asked, tugging at his beard.

"You tell me. Lamberto said you two were fucking up." I held my gun at my side.

"Axel, we just got the information," Lazaro replied.

"Which is?" I challenged.

A few rumors had circulated that Lazaro had gotten too high with power.

"Fifty caseloads of weapons should be here, and the guys who came only brought twenty," Lazaro pointed out.

"Whose job was it to double-check the order?" I glanced from Lazaro to Sandro.

"Lamberto told us it was fine," Sandero informed me.

My brow hiked at his answer.

"Lamberto told you to take whatever they gave you?" Turin repeated.

"Yeah, we were told to wait here," Sandro said.

"By Lamberto?" Turin was good at sniffing out liars. He'd rub his chin while he smiled at them to make them feel comfortable. Right now, he seemed relaxed, with no alarm bells, so I positioned my gun back in my holster.

"Are the men still here?" I queried, walking toward the building.

The place displayed a meat packing sign, the front for his money laundering. The land it sat on covered two acres and had mostly abandoned homes nearby. Turin opened the door, and Lazaro and Sandro came in behind us as we stared at our guys packing the guns.

"Stop what you're doing!" I demanded.

All voices quieted as I looked around the room from the doorway.

"Who are you?" responded a tall man with a large, round gut spilling over his pants.

I wanted to bust him in the mouth. "I ask the questions. My guys say you're short by thirty crates."

"I brought what I was told to bring," the fat fuck responded, waving me off.

I hated being ignored or dismissed. My response to their disrespect crept into my voice. "By whom, exactly?"

"Lamberto. It's all laid out in my form." His hand went into his pocket, and my men pulled out their guns.

His hands rose in the air. "Hold on, fellas. Let me grab the order sheet."

I motioned for my men to stand down. "What's your name?"

"Alvar. I work for the Casella family."

Alvar passed the paper to me. I looked it over and saw exactly twenty meat orders to be delivered.

"What does it say?" Turin asked.

"Lamberto and Laurent, what are you up to?" I muttered to myself. It wasn't like Laurent to go along with something Lamberto cooked up.

"Are we good?" Alvar asked.

I grinned, folding the sheet and giving it back to him. I clapped him on the back. "We're always good, Alvar."

He turned away, and I reached into my holster, cocked my gun, and shot him in the back of the head.

"What the fuck?" Lazaro shouted, jumping back.

"Pack up everything, and we will meet tomorrow," I instructed.

I stomped out of the warehouse, pissed because someone was lying to me, and I didn't know why. Patience was something I didn't have, thanks to the constant dreams every other night. Laurent was probably too full of excitement over the wedding to talk business right now.

I slammed the car door and Turin hopped in the driver's seat.

"Did you have to kill him?" Turin asked, shaking his head.

A van pulled up to the back of the door to dispose of anything left behind.

"*Merda!*" I cursed, slamming my hand on the window.

"Casella's family will want answers about Alvar," Turin pointed out.

"He's worthless to them."

"Axel Bresciani, you need to focus. We have enough problems with the other families trying to take Laurent's position when he retires." Turin said, his expression disgruntled. He backed up out of the gravel, turned the radio down, and sped away.

"I think something is going on and they want me here." I settled in my seat, recalling the last few meetings in my head as Turin hit the gas.

"Have you been sleeping?"

I ignored his question. "When we get back to the restaurant, I need to talk to Laurent." I took out my phone and turned it back on to see multiple missed calls and text messages. "Something happened." I clicked on Gigi's voice message.

Turin continued out of the area to get us back to the restaurant.

Gigi's screamed message came through the phone. "Axel, where are you? They shot at my dad and we're on our way to the hospital."

I quickly dialed her number.

Gigi picked up right away. "Something's happened to my dad."

I slammed my hand on the dashboard. "Fuck! Are you hurt?"

"No! I don't give a fuck... It's my phone," Gigi argued with someone. The phone call ended abruptly.

"Gigi! Gigi!" I tried redialing her number, but it went straight to voicemail.

"What happened?" Turin asked grimly.

Everybody was on my distrust list now. "Someone took a shot at Laurent."

"What! They know it's a death sentence to go after the boss," Turin spat.

My hand was itching to kill everyone. "Just hurry and get us to the hospital."

Turin fought through traffic, while my mind replayed the fear in Gigi's at the thought of her father getting hurt. Gigi was headstrong, spoiled, and opinionated, but she loved her parents. I prayed he pulled through because there would be hell to pay otherwise. The streets loved Laurent more than any Don we'd had in the past. No matter the deaths he'd sanctioned, people respected him.

Despite the back-and-forth between Gigi and me, she knew I was the only person she could rely on to handle this discreetly. Laurent had embedded the idea that I wasn't a lost cause after my parents were gone. He gave his time and advice freely, pushing me to look into a legit life. I'd always made it known he had my full loyalty wherever I was in life. Besides Turin, Laurent was the only other person who knew about my sleepless nights and graveyard visits.

Chapter 5

Gigi

One hour earlier.

After my father's toast, I held a fake smile on my face and grinned as people came up to us to extend congratulations on the engagement. Dario ate it up and ensured I played my role. Anytime I didn't speak or give him attention, he squeezed my thigh or hand under the table.

Like right now. As my father sat down to talk to my mother, Dario leaned over to cup my hand, and I moved it out of his reach. The public perception was that we were in love and happy, but behind closed doors, I couldn't stand the man. If I could get away with killing him before the wedding, I would. Everybody knew Dario was trying to position himself as Boss once my father retired. Many times he'd said it would be in my best interest to go along with the wedding because marriage wasn't about love but a partnership to get to the top.

I examined the guests and my eyes fell on *him* again, standing behind my dad as his protector and guard. Axel Bresciani was a six-foot-one, sexy asshole with a god complex I hated but loved at the same time. In the beginning, when my father brought him around, I was young and still in high school and had no business crushing on my dad's henchman. One look at Axel and all of his rules went out the window. I tried to always be in his presence, and he stared at me when he thought I wasn't looking. Whenever his eyes were on me, my heart pounded and butterflies erupted in my stomach. If Dario was around, Axel's mouth always curled in disgust. I never said anything and thought his jealousy was cute. But when I tried to flirt, he shot me down. I was younger at twenty-two, but I was also the daughter of his boss and technically untouchable. That only fueled my desire and need for him. I had a plan tonight to get him alone for a few minutes, but Lamberto approached and tapped him on the shoulder.

I sat back in my chair and played with my food.

"You can at least look happy," Mother whispered.

"I am happy. See?" I put on a fake smile, cupping my chin with both hands.

"Soon as this wedding is over, you'll thank me," Mother said, rubbing my arm.

"Doubt it," I mumbled, despite my best efforts not to bitch.

"Ladies and gentlemen, I'd like to make a toast." Dario rose out of his seat and knew more bullshit was about to come out of his mouth.

I would respect him more if he'd do like other husbands and stay away from the wives. Every other day, his mother planned something for us to do as a couple. I explained I had a life outside of her son, but she always called me a silly young girl.

"Laurent and Rosa, I truly want to thank you for creating a beautiful woman because my future wife is gorgeous, smart, and caring. I hope our life reflects the love our parents have." Dario smiled and raised his glass, and everybody clapped and cheered.

My mother jumped up in excitement and pulled me up by my arm to nudge me toward him.

"Don't make me look ridiculous. Kiss me," Dario growled in my ear.

I grinned, pecking him on the lips, and he gripped the back of my head to force his tongue down my throat.

"That's my boy!" Edmundo Ramini yelled loudly and whistled at us.

"Save it for the honeymoon, son," Father teased.

I jerked away, reaching for my purse to go to the restroom.

Dario gripped my elbow, turning me around to face him. "Where are you going?"

"To the bathroom. Is that okay, Sir?" I challenged. He knew I didn't like to be manhandled or treated like some dutiful wife. I wasn't married to his ass yet.

Dario smiled. "Of course, dear. Take my mother with you."

"I don't need a babysitter."

"Either she goes or you don't." Dario glared at me.

"Fine, I'll sit back down." I huffed, plopping down in my seat.

"More wine for everyone!" Father shouted.

"Laurent!" a gravelly voice shouted right before all hell broke loose.

Gunshots rang out and the guests screamed, running for safety. All I could do was watch as bullets tore through my father's chest and he fell backward. Someone grabbed my arm and pulled me to the ground.

"My father! Let me go!" I screamed, trying to get up to help him.

"Gigi! Shut up! We're under attack." Dario tried to soothe me as more gunshots echoed around the room.

"Get away from me! I want my mom and dad." I tried to push him off me, but he wouldn't budge.

Babies cried and women yelled for help. Time stood still until the gunshots stopped.

"Move! I want to see my dad."

"Your place is at my side," Dario said in a menacing tone.

* * *

When I came up from behind the table, I crawled toward my father. His eyes looked lifeless and tears stained his cheeks. There was so much blood that I didn't know how many times he was shot. I glanced around the room and couldn't see Axel, so I knew something was off about this hit.

Dario wouldn't let me ride in the ambulance. My mother agreed I should ride with him and show that our union was solid. The last thing on my mind was Dario or the public's awareness of how in love we were—which was a load of shit.

The nurses and doctors were taking forever to come and tell us what was going on with my dad. Dario's mother and father sat with my mom while we waited, and most of our family and friends were there.

Dario got in my face as I tried to call Axel. I ignored him until he snatched my phone from my hands.

"Give me back my phone." I tried to grab it out of his hand, but he slid it into his pocket.

Dario stood in front of me with his arm around my waist to show he was comforting me. "Who were you on the phone with?"

"None of your business."

"My love, do you really think you're smarter than me?" he challenged.

Our eyes connected.

If he wasn't so evil, he'd be a good catch.

There was a devil behind those crystal blue eyes; everything revolved around him and if you challenged him, you were an enemy.

I frowned uneasily. "I was talking to Ginerva."

A devilish smirk tugged at the corner of his stern mouth. "You expect me to believe that?"

"I don't care what you believe," I snapped

"Keep your voice down," he commanded.

"My father is fighting for his life and you want me to play along with your little game?" I glowered at him.

"As the future wife of the Ramini family, I expect you to do what I say," he said with his trademark haughty grin.

"Whatever, Dario." I walked around him and went to sit beside my mother.

"If anything happened to him, it would be all over the news," Mother muttered.

I wiped the tears off my face and rested my head on her shoulder.

"What were you talking with Dario about?" she queried.

"Nothing."

"You should be over there with him. It will look better to be near your fiancé," Mother preached. "As our daughter, your life is mapped out for you."

"We need to focus on Father right now."

"Dario is your future husband."

"I don't love him." Arranged marriages were outdated to my generation.

She lifted my chin. "Gigi, you need to be in his arms for comfort. You have to show a

united front."

"I'm not going over there. Besides, he's probably talking about who's responsible for this hit."

Suddenly, butterflies swarmed in my stomach. I looked up and there he was. Dario didn't have one-tenth of his looks.

Axel was here.

I wanted to run to him. Have him hold me in his arms, but I knew that would look suspicious, and not only because we weren't in a relationship. I was the daughter of the mob boss, and Alex was the enforcer. It was all kinds of wrong.

"Oh, there's Axel," Mother said.

Sweat formed on my palms, and my stomach knotted.

Axel walked over and bent to cup Mother's hands, his attention fixed on her. "What happened?"

That was the million-dollar question.

His eyes flickered from my mother to me. My mouth opened and closed. I wanted so badly to touch him, to be in his arms. He reached out and grabbed my hand.

I closed my eyes as a tear rolled down my cheek. "I don't know. We were all eating and laughing. Suddenly, a man called out Laurent's name and shots were fired."

"Axel, find out what happened," my mother demanded.

He responded, "I will."

"This can't be seen as a weakness for our family." Mother narrowed her eyes at Axel.

His stare was intense. "You don't have to worry, Mrs. Carrington. I'll take care of this personally."

I felt like I couldn't breathe. Nothing made sense without my father.

"Gigi, how are you?" Axel asked gently.

My gaze fixed on him. "I'm not handling it very well."

"Mrs. Carrington."

We all looked at Doctor Zappa as he approached us. My heart beat fast and I tried to steady my breathing, leaning into my mother.

"Is my father okay?"

All the family waited in anticipation.

The doctor shook his head and lowered his eyes. "I'm sorry, Mrs. Carrington. We tried everything we could, but one bullet hit his heart."

She froze. "What do you mean?"

I gripped her hand tight and shoved him back. "Where's my father?"

"We can speak privately." He gestured toward the hallway leading to his office.

"Get back there. Right now," I demanded. "You can still save him."

"I'm sorry. We did everything we could, but there was too much blood loss," he said.

I shook my head. "No, I don't believe you."

He slid his hands in his pockets, then sighed.

The doctor was wrong. "Do you know who my father is?"

"Miss Carrington. My team—"

"Do you?" I cut him off.

Seconds ticked by before he responded. "We tried everything." Doctor Zappa raked his eyes from my mother, then toward me.

Before I realized what I was doing, I swiped my hand across his face. "Get back there and save him or I swear to God, you will find out what the Carringtons can do."

The room went silent.

"Gigi, stop it." A look of embarrassment crossed Mother's face as she pinned me with a glare.

My head whipped around to avoid her eyes. She'd pay him off and have a new wing opened up at the hospital to make my outburst go away.

"Doctor, we understand. You did everything you could.

Please excuse my daughter's behavior," Mother pleaded, walking away with him.

I jumped in front of her. "Are you crazy?"

"We're in public, so please be respectful," she murmured.

"Your husband is dead," I argued, close to dropping into a ball on the floor and crying in pain.

"Honey, these are the best doctors in the world."

"This is a serious matter, don't you think?" I probed.

"Gigi, I did not mean it that way. It's not okay for you to threaten people."

I pointed at the doctor. "My father is still alive. Do your job. Go back and help him," I screamed, shoving him in the arm.

The waiting room full of people hung on his next words. "Miss Carrington, there's nothing else we could do. Again, I'm sorry for your loss."

"Thank you," Mother whispered.

My shoulders dropped in agony. "Can I see his body?"

The doctor looked at my mother, then at me.

"There's no need for you to see him. Remember your father the way he was." Mother rubbed my back.

"I want to see him."

"I'm his wife. I say leave it alone," Mother remarked, folding her arms.

"No."

My head whipped back as she slapped me. "Are you out of your mind?" I gasped, covering my cheek.

The entire room went silent.

"Rest is what you need. You'll be driven home by Axel," my mother told me, wiping her nose with the Kleenex.

"You're unbelievable!" I snatched my arm out of her hold.

"I'll take her," Axel said in a raspy voice.

"I don't need your help," I snapped, stomping out of the hospital.

I pointedly ignored Dario and his parents. Seeing Fulgenzio near the entrance, I marched over and demanded to leave.

Fulgenzio blinked in confusion, his eyebrows bunched together. "Miss Carrington, we need to wait for—"

"I'm giving you an order. Follow it, or I'll fire you," I hissed, slamming my hand on the window.

I felt his presence behind me before he reached to open the passenger side door. Breathing became difficult. I shook my hands, rubbing each wrist, and closed my eyes, opening them after a few minutes.

Axel leaned around me and pulled the door open further.

I looked over my shoulder.

His eyes stayed on me. "I'm taking you home."

I nodded and climbed inside.

Axel shut the door, coming around to the driver's side. Fulgenzio greeted him briefly, they shook hands, and he walked into the hospital.

Axel got in the driver's side and shut the door.

I tugged on my seat belt. "What about Turin?"

He put the key in the ignition, ignoring my question. "Tell me exactly what you remember."

Nervousness clouded my mind. "Everything happened so fast. One minute, people were laughing and excited. Next minute, the whole place was blazing with gunshots."

He pinched the bridge of his nose. "I'll find out what happened."

I cleared my throat. "Where are you taking me?"

"Home," he replied, avoiding my eyes.

When Fulgenzio drove me around, we talked, or he listened to me gripe about my parents. Whenever I was around Axel, his presence stunned me to where he rendered me mute.

My lip trembled. "I want to go with you."

"No."

"Axel, I'm not a child."

He pulled over to the side of the road, parked the car, and turned in his seat to face me. I blinked several times as I contemplated what to say. In my heart, I knew he thought I wasn't the right person to look into my father's death.

"Understand me clearly. You're engaged." His words stung.

"I'm not marrying him."

"You have to. It's the life you're meant to have." His eyes darted around the area.

"Fuck you, Axel!"

When I raised my hand to smack him, he grabbed it, pulling me close to his chest. He stared at my lips, then my eyes. Was he going to kiss me? Caught in his intense gaze, I felt tempted to close the gap between us. I knew he knew what I wanted, and while my feelings were coming at a difficult time after receiving news of my father's death, I sought comfort from him. Our connection was unaffected by the passing cars and the flashing lights of the second guard car behind us.

"Axel."

My phone vibrated, but I ignored the call. Whether it was my mother or Ginerva, this was the first time I'd been alone with Axel in a long time.

Chapter 6

Axel

I couldn't deny my attraction to her, but I would no longer be objective the moment we went there. I would become possessive of her.

"*Splendida donna*," I mumbled under my breath in thick Italian.

My parents raised me to speak both my native Italian and English. I spent time in America and made friends, plus some enemies. When Laurent had Gigi go alone to Joaquin and Sofia's party, I was able to catch up with Joaquin. He was a friend before and after my parents died. We'd worked together on some deals that needed a special touch.

Once my parents died, I pushed everyone away and became hollow and bitter. The *policia* didn't work hard enough to discover why someone wanted to kill my parents, and I'd struggled to find the answers alone.

So I raised myself not to get close to people, and I respected Laurent when he didn't kill me after I was caught snooping around his business. He brought me in and molded me to work alongside him, to be his eyes and ears when he couldn't see the enemy coming.

I could sense my actions confused Gigi. She was a gorgeous woman and always brought out the beast in me, to where I started talking in my native tongue.

"I'm taking you home. Extra men will be on guard to keep watch. It's the only way to keep you safe until we find out everything."

I turned around, putting the car in drive to head home.

"Either you take me with you, or I'll sneak out. I have my ways, Axel," she sassed.

"Do you talk to your fiancé like this?" The word fiancé made her wince, and I wanted to take it back, but she pushed my buttons.

"He's not my fiancé. You know I don't love him."

"Gigi, you know we can't be together." I focused on the men behind us to avoid being distracted. Turin and I would need to rehash with Rosa what she saw tonight.

"Why? I see how you look at me. It's not a one-way attraction."

Laurent had my loyalty, but falling in love with a woman would never happen. I lacked any meaningful emotions beyond my job as an enforcer. A relationship would demand too much of me. I couldn't imagine being vulnerable, showing someone I cared, and then losing it all.

"I work for your father. The entire family and Carrington organization would have me killed if I touched you."

"If you're too chickenshit to give into your feelings, that's on you. You're older than me, and yet you act like a child. I guess I expected more from you."

I parked the car as we arrived at the family estate. "My only job is to protect you and find out what happened to your father. That's it."

Gigi didn't respond. She shoved the door open and jumped out before I could catch her.

I slammed my hand against the steering wheel. "Fuck!"

I wanted to chase after her, but I needed to focus. It wasn't long before the car behind me honked to see what I was planning to do next, but I couldn't focus on anything but Gigi's angry outburst.

I ran a hand through my hair. "Fuck! Fuck!"

My phone rang, and I removed it from my jacket. "Yeah."

"Where are you?" Turin asked.

"I just dropped Gigi at home." I glanced around the massive yard. Laurent and Rosa updated the place recently to include a small pond near the guard gate.

"Are we meeting?"

"Gather all the men at headquarters and find out where Lamberto is. He never showed up at the hospital." We couldn't go back to the crime scene. It would still be fresh. Police on our payroll should give up some information.

"I'm on it," Turin replied.

I looked toward the house, my eyes trailing to the third level of the sprawling estate. A light came on in her room that faced the front of the house. My distraction was cut short when car lights flashed behind me.

Mrs. Carrington briefly talked to Fulgenzio, and I took that as the moment to leave and meet Turin and the team.

Thirty minutes later, I pulled up to the Carrington office building. I jumped out, raced inside, and headed toward the executive suite. Laurent had some legit businesses, and one was real estate. It wouldn't be too obvious with us meeting here at night because his team often worked long hours.

My eyes were drawn to the conference room once I left the elevator. Several of his men were gathered around Lazaro and Sandro, who were seated. Anyone who looked away from me told me something. I had a strong sense that this was an inside job.

When I saw Dario sitting at the table, I paused. "What are you doing here?"

The question brought a smirk to his lips. "I thought it was important that I sat in on this meeting." He leaned back in his chair like he needed to ensure I knew how to do my job.

"Mrs. Carrington told you to come." I never needed guidance on how to do my job when I received an assignment.

"Laurent meant a lot to me. He was like a father. Gigi is worried. Now I want to make sure we find the people who did this," Dario remarked.

I studied him as I listened to his words. Something told me it was all for show. I cleared my throat and pushed my hands into my pockets to control the urge to hurt him. I couldn't react in haste.

"Tell me what happened. What did you see, Dario?"

"Not much. I was talking to my father and Gigi when everything went crazy, I covered Gigi."

His words played over in my head. "Why wasn't he protected? I left my men with him," I challenged to see if anyone would come forward.

"That's a good question, Axel. Since you're an enforcer, you're in charge. Why weren't your men trained up? I know everything that's going on. Once I take over, we're going to do some reshuffling," Dario said, trying to intimidate me in front of my men.

Laurent explained a while back that Dario and Gigi's relationship was purely business. Yes, he loved his daughter, but she needed to marry into another family to continue their legacy.

"The Carrington and Ramini family are coming together as one," Dario preached.

Suddenly, the door opened. Lamberto entered the room with his guards and took a seat .

"You're late." I was the only one that could get away with questioning him.

Lamberto was the Underboss. If I discovered he was behind the shooting, there would be hell to pay.

"I just came from the hospital. Rosa is distraught, and Gigi is crying. It was awful. We need to find out who did this for Laurent's legacy. I will step into his shoes until Dario marries Gigi," Lamberto assured the guys.

I shot daggers at him. That was the second lie he'd told tonight. I'd dropped Gigi off at home. On top of the gun shortage, he was lying about being at the hospital.

Dario caught my eye, and a crooked smirk appeared on his face.

"All right. We need to figure out who the shooter is and why he struck tonight at your engagement dinner," I started the conversation.

"I have a few contacts to check phone records," Turin said, leaning forward.

I looked at Lamberto. "Alvar told me you put in the request for only thirty packages."

Lamberto froze. "What are you talking about?"

I held his gaze. "Explain to me why there was a shortage of guns. On the same night Laurent was shot."

"Are you accusing me of something?" He cocked his head arrogantly as he challenged me.

"Don't hide now that Laurent isn't here to overlook your movements," I prodded, pushing his buttons.

"I'm not hiding!" he said thunderously.

"Why did you send me on a dummy mission the night Laurent was shot and killed?"

"I don't know what you're talking about," Lamberto

blustered.

"I think you do. Lazaro and Sandro said you sent them over to wait for us to get there.

"They aren't in a position to know if something is wrong with a shipment," he spat.

"You told me there were supposed to be fifty guns. Something's not adding up, Lamberto."

A tense silence enveloped the room. "An accusation like that will get your tongue cut out," Lamberto barked.

"As enforcer, Laurent put me in charge to protect the family and the legacy. If you know anything, if you're behind any of this, I suggest you confess now because when I get through with whoever took the hit—"

"I know. They won't even be able to recognize his body," Lamberto recited, rubbing his forehead. He bit his lips nervously before changing the subject. "The funeral will need to be sped up to avoid Rosa and Gigi having to suffer."

"Gigi wants to see his body." Despite what I wanted, she was his daughter.

"I can speak for my fiancée, and she doesn't need to see it. That will only bring her nightmares," Dario stated.

I clenched my fists.

"I decide what she can and cannot do," Dario declared, staring at me.

"She's Laurent's daughter, and until you marry, she can make her own decisions," I argued.

"Gentlemen, this is up to Rosa as the mother and wife. She will decide," Lamberto remarked.

"I know she wants to have it taken care of quickly," Dario said.

"She's setting up a meeting with the lawyer soon. The family is still in shock, but we have to continue with business," Lamberto reminded everyone.

"We need answers about what happened. It's gonna be all over the media tomorrow. And our enemies will think we can be touched," Dario insisted.

"Dario will take his place immediately after the wedding, and it will be like nothing ever happened," Lamberto said.

Everyone stood and shook hands. Lamberto and Dario stood in the corner near the window, grinning as they talked quietly. He didn't look too upset for a guy whose fiancée was devastated by the death of his future father-in-law.

Turin and I made eye contact. If either of us found out they'd had anything to do with Laurent's death, they would discover what hell was like.

*** * ***

A few days later, I sat opposite Rosa, Gigi, and Aurora in the back of the limo procession, heading to the funeral. Mrs. Carrington had a closed casket and asked for the body to be immediately delivered to the funeral home.

Gigi hadn't talked to anyone since her father died. She'd locked herself in her room, and even Aurora had a hard time getting her to come out and eat. Ginerva came to visit, but she turned her away.

Dario rode in the car with his parents, and Lamberto was in the other limo as the police escorted us through the streets of Italy. The Carrington family was loved by some and hated by many. After the funeral, I had a meeting with Casella's family. They were worried now that Laurent was gone. Things could get sticky if Dario didn't take his position. Plus, the family lawyer was meeting at the house tomorrow to go through Laurent's will.

Mrs. Carrington was drinking more than usual and putting even more pressure on Gigi to marry right after the funeral. If it were up to me, she'd move to America, leave everything behind her, and live her life. The limo stopped in front of the church, where the family had been longtime members since before Gigi was born.

"Gigi, please be respectful when we get out of the car, for your father's sake," Rosa said.

Gigi's head whipped around. "I'm not the one who ordered cameras to be at the funeral."

"Your father is known all over the world. It would be foolish not to broadcast it," Rosa defended.

I stopped Gigi as she reached for the door handle. "Let me."

I helped her out, and she adjusted her shades. Dario approached and bent to kiss her on the cheek, but she moved away. Embarrassed, he reached for her hand, but she sauntered around him. Rosa whispered something in his ear, and he nodded.

After Aurora got out of the car, I shut the door and strolled to the steps, catching up to Gigi. "You can't run off."

"He's pathetic," Gigi mumbled, watching her and Dario's mother hug.

"He'll be the leader of the family."

"I don't care." Gigi started to walk inside.

I extended a hand, cupping her shoulder. "Think of your father."

Although she wore shades, I knew her gaze was on me as I spoke about her father.

"Miss Carrington, what do you have to say about your father's death?" A reporter pointed a camera in her face.

"Get that camera out of my face!" Gigi snapped.

I pushed him back and ushered Gigi into the church. Rosa had the church put up a picture of Laurent from when he was younger, and the podium held a backdrop of the family. I escorted Gigi to the front row reserved for family before positioning myself in the corner of the church with a visual of the entrance and exit.

"What took you so long?" Gigi hissed at her mother.

"I needed to do damage control with the reporter from your little outburst," Rosa spat.

"Never should have invited them," Gigi argued.

"Gigi, I'm trying to do the best I can." Rosa blew out a breath and wiped her cheek with the handkerchief.

"Papa wouldn't want all this." Gigi waved her hand at the large crowd filling the church.

I had to agree with her because it seemed more like a TV event than a funeral. As enforcer, it wasn't my place to question her mother, but she appeared to do things to satisfy her own needs.

Forty minutes later, Gigi didn't want to see her father go into the ground, so I had Fulgenzio drive us home.

"Can we go to the beach for a minute?" Gigi asked.

I looked at her, then at Fulgenzio, and nodded. He drove to the ferry and paid. Hopefully, the time away would help her grieve.

"Laurent talked about taking you to the beach when you were younger."

"Growing up in Rome, he made it a point to give me somewhat of a normal childhood, even with all the guards. Marina Grande was our special place we visited together." Gigi sniffed, remaining motionless for a moment.

I slid my hand into my pocket and removed my handkerchief, passing it to her.

"Thank you." Gigi wiped her nose and hugged her arms around herself.

"It's going to take time, but the pain will ease."

"I must look like a fool to you," she commented faintly.

I cupped her chin and turned her head in my direction. "You look like a woman who lost her father."

She opened and closed her mouth, placing her hand on my leg.

I released her chin. "Have you eaten?"

Gigi sat up straight and looked out of the window. "I'm not hungry."

I recognized her grief. She wanted to be alone and avoid people. My mouth thinned with displeasure. "You have to eat something."

"I don't love Dario," she blurted.

I sighed, planting my hands on the seat. "I know."

She swiveled quickly. "Then you'll help me convince my mother."

My expression stilled and grew serious. "Gigi—"

"Axel, please." She pressed her hand against mine.

I lifted her hand to kiss her palm as the ferry arrived at the port. "You eat something after the beach, and I'll think about how we can convince your mother."

She grinned and climbed out of the car. Fulgenzio stood by the car with the captain. Gigi slipped off her heels, and I carried them while we walked down to the water. There were only a few people out during the afternoon, so we'd have enough privacy. She let my hand go and removed her shades, walking further into the water.

"Gigi," I warned in a gentle tone.

"Don't worry, Axel. I'm fine." She ran down the beach and paddled in the water.

I watched as she picked up a rock before throwing it further out. Suddenly, she dragged her dress off and dove into the water in her bra and panties. My head whirled to check if anyone had seen her, but we were alone.

"Come get in the water, Axel!" Gigi requested matter-of-factly.

"You shouldn't be in there."

She smirked, throwing her head back in the water. "My dad taught me to swim."

"He told me." I stood in the sand near the water's edge.

"Do you care about me, Axel?" she asked huskily.

"Of course, I care about your family." I valued Laurent and his family's support, but I knew her question went deeper.

"I know you're loyal to our family, but do you care about me?" She pointed at herself.

I gazed into her eyes. "We have to get going."

Gigi played in the water, "It's fine. You don't have to answer. Maybe I *should* marry Dario."

My thoughts went to a cold and dark place. "Fuck Dario."

"He's already talked about how he can't wait to be my first." Gigi searched my face.

I was surprised at her announcement. "You're a virgin?"

She nodded. Reaching behind her, she unhooked her bra and tossed it away.

"What are you doing?"

"Living life. My father is no longer here, and my mother doesn't care about me. I may as well enjoy my last days of freedom before I become Dario's wife." A wicked laugh erupted from her mouth.

She shouldn't be out here naked. "Get out of the water, Gigi."

"Come and get me."

She was the Don's daughter. Acting on our attraction would be perilous.

Chapter 7

Gigi

My intention when we came to the beach wasn't to hurt myself; hell, I thought I could sneak off with no one finding me, but Axel had increased the number of guards to protect my mother and me.

When the funeral was over, I explained we needed some space from everyone. Our family and friends pretended to care about us when all they wanted was money. As soon as the lawyer read the will, we wouldn't see them or their fake sympathies.

As a child, my father took me to the beach at least once a month, maybe more if I was good. Being Laurent's daughter was a curse, but also a blessing when Axel came around. Either the man was honorable or an idiot, but he never made a pass at me, no matter how many times I flirted with him. I guess I grew on him after I tried to sneak out one night, and he caught me when he arrived late to talk to my father. We argued, then talked, and I got to know him as more than the enforcer of our family...

"What are you doing?" Axel demanded.

Holding my heels and purse, I looked behind me. "Umm, nothing."

Axel's steady gaze bore into mine in silence. His broad shoulders were intimidating, and something in me wanted to submit. A strange expression flashed across his face. "Does your father know you're sneaking out?"

"He's out with my mother," I lied.

"Funny, I just called him and he answered."

"Well, they're not here." There was an open challenge on would break eye contact.

"How old are you?"

The same tired question his guards used to put me in my place like I was a child. As an adult, I could come and go as I pleased without a curfew.

"Old enough." I huffed, placing a hand on my hip.

"If that's true, you wouldn't be sneaking out."

Today was supposed to be me kicking it with my friends after a long day in class, but he wanted to play judge and jury for my father.

When I stepped around him, he grabbed my elbow and pulled me into his chest.

"I'm not a child. Move out of my way."

His mouth spread in a faint smile. "I don't take orders from you."

His accent made my stomach flutter. My breath caught in my throat as my eyes locked on his lips.

"How old are you now?" He caught the attention I paid to his lips.

"Eighteen," I answered in a whisper.

Axel shook his head, releasing me. "A baby."

His smile sent a spark up my spine. "How old are you?" I wasn't worried if he was a year or two older than me.

"Thirty."

"Oh." He was way older than I thought.

Axel quirked his brow.

"How long have you worked for my family? I can't imagine my father had just anyone come to our home."

"Since I was nineteen."

I learned at a young age that my father was powerful, but he never took me around his men besides the guards assigned to my mother and me. A few times, I'd had a crush on some of them, and when he noticed, they were reassigned and never heard from again.

"Why am I just now seeing you?" I wanted to know everything about him. Ginerva called me nosy, but I'd picked up a few things as the daughter of a kingpin.

"Because your father kept you away from his business."

I wanted to keep him here longer talking to me. "I know what he does as the Boss of the cartel."

"Keep that to yourself." He turned to leave.

I caught him with a hand on his shoulder. "Are you going to rat me out?" I quickly removed my hand and broke into a grin.

He smirked. "What would I get out of ratting you out to your father?"

"You must be high up in the family if you're here." I wanted to run my hand through his beard. His smile was magnetic.

"I take care of business for your father."

As expected, he didn't give an exact answer, and I commended him because you never knew who was listening.

"What about your parents?" I probed. This stranger made me feel comfortable enough to want to do a deep dive into his life.

A cloud fell over his face. "They were killed when I was younger."

"Sorry to hear that." The mood shifted, and our flirty banter now felt awkward.

"You should get inside." He gestured toward the house, and a light came on downstairs.

"Shit, that's my father," I hissed, taking a deep breath and scanning the yard to see where I could hide.

"Thought you said your parents weren't home." He tilted his head and stared at me.

"Okay, I lied, but can you distract them until I get back in the house?" I begged, placing my hands together in prayer.

Axel folded his arms. "Now, why would I do that?" His eyes grew openly amused.

"Because I'll be your best friend." I smiled, sticking my hand out for a shake.

After he grinned, my heart skipped a beat. The door opened, and I raced to the side of the house, my back pressed against the wall and my eyes closed tight.

I heard my father speak. "Axel."

"Mr. Carrington," he answered.

"Did you take care of that problem?"

I wondered what problems Axel had "taken care of."

There was a pause, and Axel's gaze drifted toward me. "I did."

"Good. You didn't leave any evidence from the bomb, did you?"

At my father's words, I almost gasped in shock. The look on Axel's face was intense.

"Is something wrong?" Father asked.

Axel turned to face him. "Everything went according to plan, Mr. Carrington."

That was four years ago when Axel and I became familiar with each other. Right after, my father cracked down on me going out. I ended up with Axel as my guard, even though he was the enforcer for the family. Father put him in place to watch over me because I ditched all the other guards he tried to put on me.

Axel hated whenever I went shopping, especially with Ginerva. So again, we were back in each other's orbit based on my father. But I was no longer that young girl sneaking out of the house. Despite my love for the man, I wondered whether he loved me too, regardless of how forbidden it seemed to the outside world.

"Axel!" I yelled.

"What?"

"Put me down!" I fussed, wiggling in his arms.

Smack!

"Axel," I whined, rubbing my butt.

He carried me up the stairs to the car. The moment I'd removed my bra and refused to get out of the water, he'd jumped in and carried me out.

"Obviously, you wanted my attention," Axel growled, rubbing the sting away.

"Please put me down," I pleaded sweetly.

He let me slide down his body and it was clear he was aroused. I felt his thickness pressing against my stomach.

"Somebody needs to get that under control." I pointed at his pants.

"Shut up and get in the car." He was unmoved by my humor.

I started to remove the jacket he'd draped over my shoulders, but he shook his head. He held my dress, which I'd refused to put back on. "You're going to get sick. Keep the jacket on."

"What if I want you to take care of me?" My mouth lifted in invitation.

"We have a nurse on call."

I rolled my eyes. The ferry started back to the mainland, and Fulgenzio unlocked the car door. I slid in and grabbed my purse, removing my phone. I checked the time and noticed I had a few missed calls. The burial should've been over, so hopefully, I could go home to peace and quiet.

"I'm going to America," I announced, crossing my legs. I'd slipped my dress back on and removed Axel's jacket.

"Good idea."

I combed my hand through my hair. "Do you even care?"

Axel stopped and inhaled a breath. "Gigi, you know I care."

"Then kiss me." I turned to face him.

He closed his eyes, biting his bottom lip. "We can't."

The two words I always got from him. *We can't.*

"Then I guess Dario will get his wish."

"Is that supposed to make me jealous?" He chuckled as he rubbed his beard.

"I might be young, but I'm not stupid, Axel."

My phone rang, and I put it to my ear.

"Where are you?" Dario growled.

He was taking his role as my future husband too seriously and consistently tried to boss me around, but I wasn't like those weak females he was used to dating.

"Out." I glanced at Axel. Either I took the chance and tested Axel while I was on the phone, or I cursed Dario out even more.

"With whom? I shouldn't hear from your mother that my fiancée is missing," Dario argued. He was more worrisome than my mother.

"I'm not missing. My guards are with me," I taunted as I stared at Axel.

"I expect you to check in with me," Dario said.

Axel stared at his phone, trying to ignore our call.

"Dario, I buried my father today. I'm sorry if I forgot to cover all the steps of being a fiancée."

Axel had said he wouldn't date me, and I needed a distraction from the pain.

Dario released a breath. "You're right. We had to bury your father and my mentor. I understand you need time for yourself, but you could still be a target."

He was right. I needed to stop being reckless. "I apologize," I said, and for a split second, I felt bad for going back and forth with him.

"Your mother has arranged dinner for our family at your home," Dario confirmed.

"I'll be there soon."

"I love you."

I cringed at his words. A part of me didn't know if I should believe him or not because of the way we'd been fighting.

"I know," I responded, ending the call.

"Make sure next time you take his calls away from me," Axel muttered.

I wanted to say something back, but it was torture being in the middle of my father's rules—that no one could date me who worked for him—and Axel's nonchalant behavior. I wondered if he genuinely cared or if he liked to toy with me because I was young.

"Dario's at the house." Suddenly, I felt like I had cheated on him, which was stupid since we weren't together.

"Good, he can help you during this time." Axel stretched his long legs and bumped into mine.

I studied his side profile, his strong chin and the line of his nose. I could almost hear his whispers as he kissed my neck and cheek.

"Do you have any leads about who did the shooting?"

Axel took a second to look at me. "I have Turin looking into some things."

The car approached the gate of our compound. Fulgenzio checked in with the guards before they opened for him, and he drove the spiral driveway to our home.

My mother loved this place and wanted me to keep it for my future children. I didn't have the heart to tell her I would be living in America for good when I got the chance. Now my father was gone, I had no reason to return to this place. She could sell it, and I'd be happy to find another home in Italy as my second place when I visited. Our extended family was spread out all over Italy and America.

I turned to Axel as Fulgenzio jumped out of the car and opened the door for me. "I want to be there when you get the information."

"Gigi, for the last time, you are not getting involved. It's too dangerous," Axel replied, standing on the other side of the car.

The front door opened, and my mother's brows dipped in confusion. I lowered my head, ready for the bashing to begin.

"What happened to your dress and hair?" Rosa questioned, tugging on the end of my dress. Her face filled with bitterness before she looked away.

"I went to the beach." I moved away.

She glanced from me to Axel, then Fulgenzio. "You ask to be alone, and this is what you come back looking like? A homeless person?"

"I'm going to my room."

She blocked me with her hand on my chest as I went to walk away. "No, I have guests, and you will come and sit."

"I don't want to sit and listen to a bunch of people tell me how much they loved my father when they probably had something to do with his death," I barked.

My mother's palm cracked across my face. "Gigi, baby, I'm sorry!" She reached to grasp my hand.

I yanked my hand out of her hold. "I'm going to my room." I hated Axel seeing me punished like a child.

I stepped inside and sprinted up the stairs to my bedroom. Aurora came out of my bathroom, and I lunged into her arms and cried.

"I hate her," I sobbed, burying my head in her chest while she rubbed my back.

Aurora kissed my forehead. "Shush, it's going to be okay, Gigi."

I shook my head and stepped back. "She never wanted me, Aurora, just the name of Carrington."

"Honey, you know better than to think like that." Aurora put her arm around my shoulder, squeezing me tight as we sauntered into my room.

I dropped my purse and phone on the bed and removed my dress. I remembered I needed to get my shoes, which were in the car. Stepping into my closet, I grabbed a pair of leggings and a T-shirt to prepare for a bath.

"I'm leaving for America after the reading of my father's will." My relationship with my mother couldn't be repaired after today.

Aurora looked sad. "When was this decided?"

My mother entered my room without knocking. "Can you knock before entering my room?"

"No one tells me where to go in my own home," she retorted, keenly aware I hated her now that all we had in this world was each other.

Her guests could wait while I changed my clothes. I didn't care how long it took. "Father would have respected my privacy."

Mother turned to Aurora. "I have guests coming for

dinner. Can you please go downstairs? I like to be prepared."

"Aurora is helping me," I replied.

Mother glared at me as she spoke to Aurora. "Aurora, can you make sure dinner is ready?"

I was surprised she hadn't fired Aurora now that my father was gone. She'd always complained about my father and me spoiling her. I didn't want Aurora to lose her job, even though I planned to leave tonight.

I wrinkled my nose and shook my head. "No, she stays."

Our gazes clashed.

"Aurora," Mother warned.

Aurora nodded her head and left.

"Go ahead and say what you have to say."

"What has gotten into you today?" Rosa snatched my wrist.

"Nothing besides my father being killed, my mother slapping me, and being forced to marry a man I can't stand." I counted each situation on my fingers.

"Give me some respect. I'm still your mother, Gigi."

"Dario is using us for our money. He's probably planning to lock me away." I tugged my hand from her grasp and spun around to grab clean panties from my dresser.

Mother watched me move around the room and plop down on the bed. "Why must you act this way?" she asked, sitting by the headboard.

I gestured at myself. "Me?"

"Everything I do for you gets thrown back in my face." Rosa had a way of playing victim and villain at the same time.

"It's hard to believe."

She moved closer to me. "Who is getting in your head?"

"No one." I swallowed hard and squared my shoulders.

"Why do you believe all these lies? I've worked hard for this family," she said, placing her hand on my knee.

"Did you love my father?" It was a question I'd pondered for a long time.

"What kind of question is that? Of course, I loved your father. We were married years before you were born."

I'd held so much within me for years, and now I was battling a situation I knew couldn't be undone. "Feels like... It doesn't... You know it doesn't matter anymore."

"Say what you want to say." Mother clamped her jaw tight and watched me.

"I don't want to marry him," I made the plea with my eyes low and sorrowful. The thought of throwing me away for money seemed like a death sentence. Although I didn't think my mother had deep compassion for me, I kept trying to reach her.

"Gigi, we are not having this conversation again," she groaned.

"There you go again, not having my back." I threw my hands in the air.

"You're being a spoiled little brat." She pointed a finger in my face.

"I'm old enough to make my own decisions."

"The wedding is moving ahead." Her dark eyes were fixed on mine.

"I don't want to have an arranged marriage like you."

"Don't you dare talk about your father and me. I loved your father. Yes, it was set up by our families in the beginning, but he was a charmer and made me feel like the luckiest woman in the world." Raw hurt glittered in her eyes.

"There must have been something you wanted out of life or someone you desired more than anything, who took your breath away with just one glance." I was practically begging not to be pushed into a cruel marriage.

"We grew to love each other," she said, a satisfied light in her eyes.

"I don't doubt you cared about Dad, but you were never there for me the way a mom should be."

"In what sense? I fed you, clothed you, and sent you to the best schools!" she shouted, lacking any sensitivity to my pain.

"Seems like you want to pawn me off to another man to take care of me. I'm supposed to just go along with it? Give up my dreams and goals for America? What about my school?" I scoffed.

"You are being dramatic, Gigi," she mocked.

"What about my friends?"

"You can have all those things, Gigi."

"Not if I'm supposed to be some dutiful wife without a brain or a voice." My words were playful, but the meaning was not.

Over the last few years, I'd seen the same Stepford wife amongst their friends too often. Throughout history, women had allowed men to cheat on them, beat them, and force them into having children they never truly cared about, getting nothing apart from spending money and beginning the next generation of cartels. I wanted more for myself than the title of a trophy wife.

"Is that what you think of me?" she quizzed.

"No," I mumbled.

She rubbed my cheek. "Please understand, you can continue with your school. I'll make sure of it with Dario."

"What if I promise to date a few people you've always wanted me to date?" I bargained.

"Dario is expecting you. No more talk. Ramini and Carrington will become one big family and bring immense fortunes to you. Future grandkids. Think about how happy he'll make you."

If my father was alive, he would tell us both to stop talking, go to our neutral corners, and relax. "What if I'm in love with someone else?"

"No more talking. Come downstairs now." Mother was clearly over my tantrum.

"All right." I gave up.

"We're having a few people who were close to your father for dinner. Be respectful. Dario and his parents are here." Her annoyance at my detachment from the conversation showed on her face.

"I'm not hungry."

"Do this for me, all right?" A small smile appeared briefly.

"Okay," I answered.

She kissed me on the forehead before walking out of my room.

A frustrated breath blew from my lips as I sat back on the bed, gazing up at the ceiling. "Daddy, if you can hear me, please tell me what to do." My tears escaped before I could grab a napkin. "Should I go through with this wedding? What about my dreams of moving to America?"

I got up, locked the door, strolled to my dresser, and picked up the family photo of me with my parents at a party they'd thrown for me. I was around ten or eleven, and I'd asked for a princess-themed party. My father had spared no expense.

Fighting back more tears, I put it back on the dresser and sauntered into the bathroom to look at the crease lines underneath my eyes. I would need more makeup to cover my swollen eyes.

I pinned up my hair and got into the shower, turning it to the hottest temperature.

Chapter 8

Axel

Gigi looked annoyed by everyone at the table tonight. She barely touched her food, and as soon as her in-laws approached and hugged her, I could tell she'd completely checked out of the conversations. Almost defeated.

Her father put me in charge to keep her safe, but he never told me how to guard her heart against pain. All the "sorry for your loss" and statements of support seemed to cause her whole world to crash down around her.

She sat next to Dario, and I sat across from him. Mrs. Carrington was at the head of the table where her husband used to sit. Tomorrow, we had the reading of the will. Then Lamberto wanted to meet to discuss our potential movements on the people who killed Laurent.

Dario stood with a smug grin on his face. "Everyone, I want to make an announcement,"

Dario disgusted me. He'd had everything handed to him. Never worked a day in his life. Gigi was spoiled, but they were totally different in how they conducted themselves. I had no respect for Dario.

"In light of the fatal shooting of Laurent, and after approval from Mrs. Carrington, and with my mother's blessing..." Dario smirked, shooting a cynical glare my way.

I shifted in my seat, ready to bust my gun over his head if he disrespected Gigi.

Why do I care if he disrespects Gigi?

I shook the thought out of my head.

"... instead of the planned six months to get married, we moved it up to one month," Dario finished, captivating the room with his statement. He sat down with a tight grin on his face. His father patted him on the back, and his mother hugged him.

"*What?*" Gigi hissed.

"I thought you'd be happy about the date moving up." Rosa sat composed.

Darion nodded. "Especially with how hurt and distraught you've been since your father's passing—"

"His murder," Gigi snapped.

"Gigi, stop it," Rosa muttered as a war of emotions spilled over the table.

Gigi shook her head. "No, this is crazy."

"I know I should have talked to you beforehand, but I spoke with your mother, and she thought it was best." Dario thought he could control Gigi with an abrupt announcement.

"You agree with this?" Gigi asked, her gaze unwavering on her mother.

"A wedding is a beautiful thing," Rosa declared, too concerned with appearances.

"Without talking to me first," Gigi accused.

"Gigi, we think it is for the best," Dario said.

"I can't believe you. What about our discussion in my room?"

"Dear, we can talk about that later." Her mother grabbed her drink and smiled at Dario.

Gigi tossed her napkin on the table, jumped out of her seat, and ran from the dining room. Dario did the same as I stood to go after her.

"I got her," I said with mixed feelings.

"That's my future wife. I can handle her."

My head swirled. "You still have a month before that happens."

We exchanged a long, hard stare, silently challenging the other to break eye contact first.

"Dario, sit. Don't worry about Gigi. Axel will handle it. He speaks her language." Rosa rolled her eyes, gulping the rest of her wine.

Dario sat back down as I made my way out of the dining room. I noticed the front door was open. She would inevitably end up in her favorite place when she was angry with her parents.

I walked around the side of the house to the backyard, down the ravine to the gazebo facing the lake. I slid my hands into my pockets and watched her for a few moments as she sat and stared up at the moon.

"You can't keep running off," I finally murmured.

Gigi shrugged. "Do you want me to marry him?"

"That's not up to me," I replied coolly when I wanted to say, "Fuck, no." If I could kill him without causing a mob war, I would.

Gigi sighed in irritation. "That's not what I asked you. Do you want me to marry him?" She turned her head to look at me.

The question was a stab in the heart. I took a step up the

stairs, facing her with my back against the pole. The moon shined down on the lake, and the night air was crisp. "How many times have I explained? You know the rules of the cartel."

Pain flickered across her face. "I don't care about the rules."

"Gigi, this is my life. I owe everything to your father." Any falter on my part would have a ripple effect on the cartel.

"Axel, you act like I'm not a part of this world. I know the risk."

"I'm not good for you," I answered truthfully.

I couldn't lose another person because of my connections to the mob lifestyle. Dario wouldn't be my first choice, but at least he was in a position to take over the cartel and keep her secure, away from the damage I might bring to her from my unstable living. Turin had commented many times about how I lived on the edge, not caring if I died because I had no one to grieve for me.

"I'm living this cartel life. I lost my father because of his choices. With him gone, we can make new rules." Gigi always banked on simple solutions.

A strange surge of affection rose inside me, frightening me. "Do you know what I always promised your father?"

"No," she responded, returning her gaze to the lake. Being here brought peace for her to clear her mind.

"That no matter if he were here or not, I'd protect you. And that includes from myself." The thought tore at my heart.

"Do you think I'm some naïve little girl with a crush? I love you, and I know you love me."

My heart pounded at her words. "We're not having this conversation."

She pulled her legs up to her chest. "Remember what you did after your parents died?"

I clenched my fists. "Beat the shit out of somebody."

She chuckled. "That's what I feel like doing right now."

My mouth twitched. "That's what you have me for."

"So if I give an order to kick someone's ass, you'd go do it for me?" Gigi looked around as if someone was lurking.

Darkness had always lived within me. "Is that what you want?"

Our eyes fixed on each other. My soul was like a mirror to her eyes.

"I can't ask you to do that. My mother will ignore me from this point forward."

"What makes you think that?"

"She has money involved with this sham marriage."

"Rosa is many things, but I know she loves you." Rosa and I never had more than a surface relationship. Laurent never complained about his wife in my presence, but I knew from overhearing their arguments that she was demanding.

"I can't believe she's forcing me to marry him in a month. This can't be my life." She brushed her hand across the furniture.

"None of us can see how our lives will end up."

"Dario is not my choice. I want a choice in my life decisions. If you weren't working for my family, would we have had a chance?"

"Don't ask that question." I bent over and lifted her chin, and she smiled at me.

It was then I heard a throat clear. I looked over my shoulder and saw Dario with a smug look on his face. Gigi narrowed her eyes, and I stood back to give her space.

"What's going on here?" he asked.

Gigi jumped up and wiped off her legs. "Nothing. I needed some fresh air."

He walked toward her, keeping his eyes trained on me. "My mother wants to talk about wedding plans, and I like to have my bride next to me."

Dario took her by the hand, and a long brittle silence stretched between us.

"I need to meet up with Turin," I finally said.

Gigi watched me as she spoke. "Guess I'll start my first night as a dutiful bride-to-be."

"Just be quiet, nod, and agree to everything," Dario jested, pulling her close to his side.

I wanted to pull off each of his fingernails one by one. Another man touching her was not acceptable. But I knew that giving in to my feelings would destroy both of our lives.

To monitor them, I stayed a few feet behind. There was a moment when I didn't know if she was acting or if he said something funny to make her laugh. In the past, she laughed at me when she tried to teach me about celebrity gossip or those *Housewives* shows.

They walked hand in hand back into the house. A voice whispered in my head, warning me to leave her alone for good.

My phone rang, and I took it out to see Turin's name. "What do you have?"

"You aren't going to believe this, even when I show you."

"Send it to my phone, and I'll meet you at the bar."

I looked back at the house for a second, staring up at Gigi's room as the curtains closed. Letting Dario take on the responsibility of Gigi was for the best, while I focused on finding out who killed her father. She and her mother would probably fight about the wedding for the rest of the night.

* * *

Turin passed me a cigar, and the server smiled at him as she left him a glass of Don Julio.

I grabbed the bottle of water. To keep my mind clear, I avoided sex and alcohol whenever I needed to focus. "Tell me."

"They know Alvar's wife is gone."

"What do you mean?"

Turin gestured across his throat. "Dead. Orson's people have pinpointed it at us."

"Someone set us up. Probably thought we got close and found out too much, so they made a bigger play to put it on the Carrington Cartel."

Turin nodded. "Right after Laurent was killed, Alvar's wife was found in his home with a slit throat."

Alarm bells went off. "Casella hit?"

"Not sure. Why would they take out their own?"

"To cause confusion. We've secretly been at war for years."

Cautious was the state of play between all three factions —the Carrington, Ramini, and Casella families. If one could test the other without making a sound, they would.

Turin sat in the chair with a pensive glare. "But they need us more than we need them."

"Doesn't matter. Power makes anyone take the first shot." I puffed on the cigar and focused on the other couples in the bar.

"Casella would be an idiot to go against us."

What Turin said was true, but if word was back on Alvar, we needed to be prepared for anything.

"Might think we're weak because of Laurent. I would."

Old play, to hit while the Don is gone and a new replacement is yet to be named.

"How's Gigi?"

My head turned at her name being mentioned. "Why?"

He downed the rest of his drink, slamming the empty glass on the table. "She's your weakness."

I scoffed. "I don't have weaknesses."

"You're defensive at the mention of her name."

"Because she just lost her father."

"He was a father figure to you as well. Have you processed that he's gone?"

I glared at Turin for trying to be my therapist. "I'm fine," I answered, blowing out more smoke.

I was used to death. It surrounded me constantly and losing my parents taught me that life was short and you couldn't get attached.

Born and raised in Rome, Italy, I was the only child of Antonella and Gaspare Bresciani. My mother stayed at home while my father worked in accounting—or so I thought. It was accounting, but he was doing the numbers for the Carrington family.

Our lifestyle came with many perks, but it ultimately killed my family. People wondered why I came to trust Laurent, and it was because he never wavered in his loyalty. I had recurring visions of our last evening as a family. My parents went out for dinner and left me alone. A few hours later, I got a call about their death.

Turin's demeanor shifted. "We need you to be a hundred percent now that Alvar and his wife are dead."

The hothead in me knew I shouldn't have killed him. I had a short temper. "That means we can't verify the information with Lamberto and Dario."

Turin chuckled. "Correct. You were rash in your response."

"Maybe we don't need him."

Turin waved his glass at the bartender. "What do you mean?"

An idea formed in my head. "Can you get all the records from the past twelve months?"

His eyes flashed with recognition at my request. "Possibly, if I can get into the office computer."

"That might be a problem if Lamberto and Dario are around."

Turin reminded me, "They won't always be around when the wedding comes up."

A vicious guilt stabbed at my chest. "True."

"So you think if Lamberto has done this before by faking the numbers, we might have something?" Turin picked up his fresh drink from the bar.

"Not sure, but Lamberto is too quiet for me, and the way he sent Lazaro and Sandro on that dummy mission..." Again I was pissed about the last-minute run I'd had to make.

"The same night Laurent gets clipped." Turin and I were on the same page.

Inner torment gnawed at me. "Can we go to war with our own people?"

"We might not have a choice, especially if Dario takes over," Turin responded.

A few girls came over, and Turin grinned.

"Saw you two and thought you could use some company," the blonde in a short red dress and red lipstick stated. The low V-neck of her dress exposed her breasts.

"I'm not interested," I replied, and her friend looked surprised.

"Sorry, ladies, my brother's in a mood," Turin smirked.

I snorted as I stood, removed some money from my wallet, and left it for the bottle girl.

Turin frowned. "Where are you going?"

"I need to see Orson." I buttoned my jacket.

"Tonight?" Turin pushed the brunette off his lap.

"Just a quick catch-up." I turned and marched out of the bar, tossing the cigar to the ground.

"Not by yourself." Turin caught up to me at the front entrance.

I unlocked the doors, hopped inside, and turned the window down. "Leave your car here," I directed, sliding the key in the ignition.

Turin climbed as I pulled into traffic. "Promise you won't kill him?"

I looked in the rearview mirror as we stopped at a red light and noticed a car on my bumper. "Check the glove compartment."

"What for?"

"I think I'm being followed."

"Who would be stupid enough to follow you?" Turin removed a Glock and turned to look out the back window.

I lifted the console to take out my pistol. "Good question. We're going to find out right now."

The light turned green, and I sped away from the crowded streets. I came around Via Condotti, and the car stayed right behind us. Turin slid the gun up, ready to shoot, as I stomped on the brakes. The car behind me also hit the brakes, stopping an inch from my bumper.

I pushed the car door open, gun in hand. Turin threw open the passenger door, and we started shooting as they reversed. I gritted my teeth and watched the car leave down another alleyway.

"We need to get out of here," Turin stated.

"If Lamberto is behind this, I'm killing him," I promised as we jumped back in the car and headed to Casella's.

We arrived at Orson's brothel thirty minutes later. I paused in the car, watching the men standing outside. It was late, and Orson had the place surrounded by his men and some police he'd paid off for coverage.

"Are we going in?" Turin asked.

"If we do, I need to know you're prepared not to leave." I glanced at him.

"Brothers, no matter what," he answered.

"Let's go." I secured my gun and stepped out of the car.

The men turned their heads as I slammed the door, their glares hard as I approached.

"What can we do for you?" the guard questioned.

"Need to see Orson."

"He's not here," the stocky guard replied, bracing his hands on his hips. I guess that was his way of trying to intimidate me.

"Tell him Axel is outside, and we send our regards about Alvar."

His upper lip twitched at my comment. Then he looked at the other man and nodded to let us go through.

The music blasted as we entered the club. Orson constructed the place with a bar in the corner, a few couches spread out, and a TV in the opposite corner playing porn. Orson made his money any way he wanted off the backs of naïve women.

A woman stood at the bar wearing a black corset, fishnet stockings, and a thong. She grinned and blew me a kiss as we approached.

"Where's Orson?" I asked.

She placed the tip of her finger in her mouth. "In his

office. Can I help you with something?" She planted her hand on my chest.

I grasped her hand and turned her, placing my gun on her back. "If you want to make it out of here tonight, take me to him and be quiet." I rubbed my nose against her ear.

"Please don't kill me."

I stroked her hair. "Shush... show us to his office."

She nodded and led us through the crowd of people drinking and making out.

"What's your name?"

"Andrea," she murmured.

"Don't worry, Andrea, you're doing fine."

We moved along a hallway, hearing moans from each room we passed. Andrea pointed at a door, and I moved her behind me before knocking.

"I'm busy!"

I knocked again.

"Ugh, fuck!" he groaned.

I raised my leg and kicked the door open.

A woman screamed, and Orson jumped, trying to reach for his gun, but I leveled my weapon at him. Orson was only five foot six and in his late fifties, but he looked older because all he did was drink, smoke, and sleep with girls barely in their twenties.

I pointed at the chair. "Take a seat, Orson."

"Leave." Turin motioned at the woman.

"Come on, Axel, this is a bad move," Orson remarked bitterly.

Turin shut the door and locked it after she left.

"Have a seat," I directed again, standing beside his desk.

Orson lit a cigarette and blew out smoke. "What do you want?"

"Did you kill Laurent?"

A glimpse of a smile flashed before he answered. "No."

It was senseless to lie to me. "I don't believe you."

Back in the early days of the Casella reign, Orson had a lot of people scared and wanted to be a faction, but his greed became too much. It wasn't well known, but some of his right-hand men dipped into hard drugs and screwed him over. Once Laurent made people aware of who ran all of Italy and how Orson couldn't take land that didn't belong to him, jealousy became the biggest issue, plus a rumor spread that Orson tried to sleep with Rosa.

"I have no reason to lie." Orson coughed and took a sip of his drink.

"Did you ever hear from Alvar?" I taunted.

"I know you had something to do with him going missing." Orson stared at me.

I chuckled. "I had nothing to do with that."

"All I can tell you is that your home may not be so clean," Orson said.

"If you know something, it would be in your best interest to tell me."

"Axel, I know you think you're untouchable, but don't threaten me," Orson grumbled.

"As the Boss of the Casella family, we know you're in a position of influence," Turin said, switching to persuasive tactics. He had the patience I lacked and charmed people into opening up before I made a move.

"I don't know anything," he responded.

Orson's eyes darted from Turin to me, and I could tell he was covering for someone.

"I gave you a chance." I turned to leave while Orson yelled behind our backs. This game required more self-control from me than anyone else. Once I learned who killed Laurent, I'd proceed to what happened to my parents.

Chapter 9

Gigi

Our family attorney, Cyrus Pappalardo, was two-thirds done reading my father's will. His office was large scale and *grande* with old Italian paintings, furniture, and Italian pride. From what my mother said, he'd been around before I was born. Both families had been in each other's life since my christening. His daughter was also a lawyer and visited our home during the holidays. It was interesting how he tried to make it seem like I didn't know my father was into illegal business, but I knew everything about my dad. The man he was in the public eye never came home to my mother and me.

Cyrus cleared his throat, took a gulp of water, and read on. Axel stood off in the corner, while my mother and I sat at the end of the table, with Dario beside me. At first, I was shocked when we walked in and he was there. Then my mother explained that he wanted to be there for support.

"What was that last part, Cryus?" Mother brought me out of my daze.

I looked from the scowl on her face to Dario's dark eyes.

Cyrus repeated his words. "His last will and testament state Gigi is to be the new boss."

"There must be some mistake," Mother snidely remarked.

"Gigi is not running anything," Dario barked.

Cyrus held the papers up, pointing the pen to the circled section. "Mrs. Carrington, it's here in plain black and white."

My mouth was dry. I picked up the glass of water and gulped it down. "I don't understand."

"Laurent left you fifty million in a trust. He left your mother the house, cars, and a monthly stipend until her death."

"A stipend! I've worked too hard to be on a budget," Mother argued. Her usual poise and dignity were absent as she jumped out of her seat.

Cyrus's face was bleak. "I promise it's not a small budget."

"When did he put her in charge?" Dario demanded. "It was always going to be me."

Dario pissed me off with his condescending tone. "Dario, I can speak for myself,"

I spat, straightening in my seat.

"About five years ago, he came to me to change his will," Cyrus replied. "Gigi has to get married to run the family business, or it will be split among the other cartels."

Mother replied, "That can't happen. Dario is going to run the business soon as they get married."

Cyrus fixed his glasses. "Until she hits twenty-five, Mrs. Carrington will control her trust fund."

I slammed my hand on the table. "But that makes no sense. I won't control my life. Either my mother runs me until I'm twenty-five or I get married and have a husband control me."

"Do not embarrass me here," Dario whispered in my ear.

I jerked away from him. "You embarrass yourself." I turned my gaze to Cyrus. "Please continue?"

"As the only child, Gigi will be the new boss once she marries. That is worth a billion dollars.," Cyrus reminded.

"So, as her husband, I will be in charge?" Dario prodded.

Cyrus glanced at the document again. "He specifically stated Gigi."

"She's preparing to become my wife. I will not have her in that type of business," Dario objected.

"That's up to Gigi. I'm only the messenger," Cyrus said.

"I'm an adult. I shouldn't have to jump through these hoops," I grumbled.

"Please understand your father loved you, Gigi, and wanted the best," Cyrus reiterated.

"Can I think about it?" I questioned.

"You're not taking over anything," Dario stated.

I stood and grabbed my purse, leaving the office as Axel, Dario, and my mother rushed to catch up. The elevator doors opened, and Dario and Axel stood on either side of me, with my mother in front. I had knots in my stomach thinking about what I had to do. I wanted to move my hand an inch and touch Axel.

The doors closed, and I caught Axel's reflection staring back at me. I dropped my shoulders and shifted on my feet as I accidentally bumped into him.

The elevator dinged and Mother stormed off with Dario behind her. Axel waited for me to leave, and we headed for the car. I started to open the car door when someone grabbed my arm, and I whirled to see an angry Dario.

"Laurent was probably drunk when he made those changes. You're not taking over."

"This is not your business. It's my family," I said.

"My family will be your family, or did you forget? Get it through your head." Dario poked me in the forehead.

I looked at my mother, and she turned away. Axel started toward us, and I held my hand up to stop him.

"Gigi, didn't you say traveling and school are more important?" Mother asked.

I had a sinking feeling. "It is."

Rosa took a deep breath. "Then sign over leadership to Dario."

"That makes sense," Dario agreed.

It seemed pointless to fight them both. Maybe it was the best way for me to get out of everything. "What about the marriage?" I lacked trust when it came to Dario and his intentions. He had no morals. All he wanted was to break me down into someone else rather than who I was.

"We can talk about divorce when we've been married for ten years," Dario answered.

"This family doesn't believe in divorce," Mother answered.

My phone rang, and I released a breath. "Hello."

"Gigi, this is Cyrus."

At the mention of his name, I turned and walked a few steps away. "Yes?"

"Who are you talking to?" Dario snapped, trying to snatch my phone.

"Hey!" Axel stepped in between Dario and me.

"Axel, this is between Gigi and Dario," Mother intervened. "They need to get on the same page."

"I'm sorry, are you busy?" Cyrus queried.

I took a deep breath. "No, but I wanted to tell you I'm taking over the business."

A loud gasp could be heard behind me.

Dario's forehead creased and his eyes narrowed.

Cyrus broke into our stare-off. "And you understand the stipulations?"

A smirk creased my lips. "I do."

"All right. I'll have the papers drawn up," Cyrus responded.

I gulped. "Thank you."

"Also, your father bought a home in America and put it in your name. He knew it was your dream."

My face lit up. "Seriously?"

"So if you want the information—"

"Yes, please send me the details."

"Good. You'll do just fine, Gigi," Cyrus replied.

"He trusted me, and I'm willing to keep his legacy alive." I smirked at Dario as I ended the call, sticking the phone in my pocket.

"They'll never listen to you," Dario pointed out.

I shrugged. "Then they'll be my enemy."

Dario stomped to his car and my smile dropped. I was terrified about what I'd agreed to.

The car started and Fulgenzio turned into traffic. Mother and I sat across from each other in the back seat.

"You are not doing this, Gigi."

"Based on the will, I am."

She grabbed my elbow and pulled me face-to-face with her.

"I suggest you listen to me. You are to be married and focused on a family."

Out of the corner of my eye, I could see Axel observing our conversation.

"If you want to continue to get Father's money, this is the only way."

"Are you threatening me?" Rosa snapped.

"I want you to be on my side for once!" I shoved her hand away.

"I'm always on your side!"

A mother and daughter should have an unbreakable bond, but Rosa made it almost impossible with her lack of compassion and support. Her entire life was about picking at me—how I should sit, dress, look, and act.

I inhaled a breath, staring out the window and wondering how much longer we'd fight as enemies.

* * *

A week later, I was still in a state of shock. Tonight, I was going out with Ginerva to relax and get Dario and my mother off my mind. They'd been in my ear about doing the right thing and letting Dario take control. Now we'd buried my father, I had to go back to school, try to figure out how to get out of a wedding, and run a billion-dollar cartel ring.

We'd finished dinner, and I changed into a black leather bodice dress which showed a little cleavage and strappy heels. My hair flowed down my back in waves with golden highlights. Axel saw me step out of the house and did a double take. I knew he'd be watching me all night, and I wanted to give him a show.

When we pulled up at the venue, I rolled on the nude lipstick, placed it in my clutch, and reached a hand out of the car into Axel's. The movement forced me close to his chest, and he slid his hand down to my waist.

An intense sensation coursed through my veins.

"I know what you're doing."

I angled my head and grinned. "What am I doing?"

"Playing games."

"For whom?"

"You'll get yourself in trouble." Axel tapped me on the thigh.

"That's the plan." I seductively strolled away, holding Ginerva's hand while Axel directed us inside to our reserved VIP section at La Cabala. They held stunning views and had the best food and bar in the world. People waved and greeted us as we moved through the crowd.

The guard stepped aside to allow us to sit. It was just past midnight, champagne was flowing, and dance music from Drake to Dua Lipa thrummed through the club.

"So happy to be out for once." I picked up the bottle and glass.

"How did you get out of the house without crazy security?" Ginerva took the glass from me and I poured another one.

"Axel has sharpshooters everywhere, and he only allowed me to come because I said I was going to sneak out." I laughed.

"What about your mother?" Ginerva snapped her fingers and tapped her feet to the beat.

"A long story, but she's out somewhere."

"How are you two holding up?"

A bitter agony popped into my head. "Honestly, my father was the glue that kept us together."

"Hello, ladies! Would you like complimentary shots on the house?" Bottle service approached with tequila and lime shots.

"I plan on getting wasted tonight." I grabbed the glass off the tray.

"Drunk Gigi is the best." Ginerva laughed.

"Here's to new memories!" I held the shot up and took it straight, chasing it with lime.

"That was strong." Ginerva patted her chest.

"I want to dance." I snapped my fingers.

"Well, before you do, you might want to look over there." Ginerva gestured at the front entrance of our booth.

Dario stood there with his men.

He had a way of making my day even worse. "Fuck! Not in the mood for him."

"What happened at the reading?" Ginerva asked.

"Let's dance first." I took another shot and jumped up, pulling her with me to the dance floor.

Dario looked at me, and I rolled my eyes. Axel stood with Fulgenzio and Turin at the bar as we danced. I rolled my hips and raised my hands in the air.

Ginerva got in front of me and snapped her fingers. "Go, Gigi!" she encouraged and bounced to the beat of Lizzo.

For once, I felt like a normal girl, and I let all my inhibitions go, blocking out all my problems. I smiled as strong hands planted on my waist and masculine cologne wafted through the air.

"I can't wait to marry you," Dario whispered in my ear.

I jerked as I realized who was behind me. I turned to free myself from his hold, looking around the club to find Axel, but he wasn't next to Turin.

"Don't touch me!" I shouted, pushing his hands away.

"We are in public. Do not embarrass me," Dario seethed.

"We're not married yet."

He raised his hand, but was held up in a chokehold by Axel.

"What the fuck!" Dario shouted.

"Axel!" I screamed.

Dario's men jumped in, and Fulgenzio pulled his gun out. Tonight was about Ginerva and me having fun, and now a brawl was breaking out.

"Keep your filthy hands off her," Axel growled.

"Oh, shit," Ginerva muttered.

"Axel, I'm fine," I pleaded.

A hint of hurt appeared in his eyes.

"Are you sleeping with him?" Dario barked.

"Shut up!" Again, he made it about Axel and me sleeping together when nothing was further from the truth.

"You expect to continue working as the enforcer after this? You can kiss your life goodbye," Dario threatened.

Axel yanked his arm, and Dario cried out in pain. I worried Axel would kill him in front of everyone and go to jail. Both men had a lot at stake if something went wrong.

Suddenly I felt sick to my stomach. I wanted to go home and forget the night ever happened. "Axel, please let him go."

He looked at me.

The hurt lingered in my stomach. "I'm fine. He didn't hurt me."

"As soon as we get married, you're cutting ties with this family," Dario promised.

My brow dipped in annoyance. "I don't take orders from you."

Axel released him, and Dario straightened up. Axel grasped my hand and pulled me off the dance floor and through the hallway.

"What was that back there?" I questioned.

He pushed me up against the wall and then his mouth was on mine.

I groaned and wrapped my hands around his neck. "Axel..." I moaned as his warm hands gripped my waist. And then he stepped back abruptly. I looked from left to right to see if Dario was near. "You kissed me..."

He ran a hand down his face, letting out a frustrated breath. "I apologize. I wasn't thinking."

A part of me wanted to continue kissing, but I was worried Dario or one of his men would see us.

I closed my eyes and touched my lips. "No, you can't kiss me like that and pretend it meant nothing."

"You're getting married," he reminded me.

"Yeah, but he didn't say to whom," I jested, placing my hands on his chest.

He shook his head. "It would never work."

"Why do you keep fighting what we both want?" I stepped into his space.

"Because this will end badly for both of us." Axel rested his hands on my hips.

I ran a finger across his bottom lip. "That's if you don't fight for what you want."

"And what do you want?"

I looked into his eyes. "You."

Axel was the guy parents warned you to stay away from, but I knew the real man behind the killer. He wouldn't admit it to himself, but he was sensitive and compassionate toward me and the people he cared about. Dario hadn't once tried to talk and get to know the real me outside of our parents pushing us together.

He groaned. "I'm not good for you."

"Why do you keep saying that? Do I look like a little girl to you?" I grabbed his chin to face me.

"Did you forget you're my new boss and I'm older than you?"

"So, that only means we can have more time together and my parents are an example of a couple with an age difference."

"It would put you in a bad position with the other families."

"Fuck them."

"Gigi." Axel's mind was made up.

I turned my head to see Ginerva, and I stepped back from Axel. "Um, we were just talking."

"Dario left already. You don't have to hide." Ginerva softly smiled on her approach.

Secrets between best friends had a limit. Ginerva knew how I felt about Axel and encouraged me to date other people as a distraction. At one time, I talked to other guys, but nothing transpired because they all lacked passion.

"I need to get you both home," Axel announced and started to walk out of the hallway.

"Not ready to leave," I informed him.

"Did you forget about business?" Axel asked.

I swallowed down the despair and forced a reply. "I need to coordinate my school schedule."

"Shit. I forgot." Axel pushed a hand through his hair.

"I can handle both."

He chuckled. "This is crazy. Laurent put you in charge."

"So you don't believe I can run things like Dario said?"

He glared at me. "Never compare me to him."

"Just take me home." I stomped away.

* * *

"I think he has something to do with my father's killing." Ginerva and I were in the kitchen in our pajamas. Even though our night was cut short, I was happy that Axel finally let go and made a move. My mind still swirled from the kiss and Dario's actions at the club.

Ginerva grabbed the sandwich I made for her and took a bite.

"Promise me, Ginerva."

She swallowed before she spoke. "Anything."

"If something happens to me, you'll make sure to get the truth out."

"Gigi, don't talk like that." Ginerva pouted.

Dario had a plan, and I needed to find out what he was up to and put a stop to it before it created trouble for my friends and family. "Only way to get through this marriage is to find a loophole."

Ginerva had a big heart and wanted the best for me. "Give up the business and run away like you wanted."

"And let my father's legacy go up in smoke?" He would be so disappointed in me.

"Then you have to marry Dario." Ginerva took another bite.

I wrapped up the bread and put the knife in the sink. "My life can't be this complicated."

She picked up the bowl of chips and popped some in her mouth. Axel went home for the night and most of the staff were asleep. My mother hadn't called, so I wondered if she'd spend the night out. If I found out she had a new man within a month of my father's death, I'd lose my shit on her and move out.

"Maybe Dario isn't that bad." Ginerva looked away hastily, taking a sip of her drink.

I sat on top of the counter and kicked my legs back and forth. "He's worse and I won't take him as a husband."

I grabbed some chips and crunched on them before I hopped down and headed for my bedroom. The will stipulated that I needed to get married, but it never specified Dario. If I had my choice, Axel would take his place as my husband and business partner in the cartel.

Ginerva grabbed her things and followed me. Aurora passed by us on her way to bed. We waved and said good night. Ginerva closed the door behind us, and I turned on the TV to find a movie for us to watch.

"Something funny or scary tonight?" Ginerva kicked her feet up on the bed.

"Anything to avoid my life."

Ginerva rubbed my back, and I pulled the covers over my knees, listening to her complain about the latest issues with her parents.

Chapter 10

Axel

Two days ago, I kissed her. Now I stood beside her at the table before all of our men. My chest was tight with pride, but I was nervous about how the men would challenge her today. Women in charge were rare in the mafia world, and Gigi was so young. When Cyrus read out Laurent's wishes, I was as shocked as everyone else. It would be dangerous for her to step into this position. By the hard expressions on the face of every man in the room, she wouldn't get out of this alive.

"As you all know, I called this meeting because I was named as the replacement in my father's will." Gigi had her hair pulled into a low bun and her curvy frame was shown to perfection in a black pantsuit. I hated that the other men in the room got to be near her and see what I saw.

Dario continued to glare at me following the incident at the club. We hadn't said two words, and I was sure he knew I had feelings for Gigi.

"Wait a minute. You're in charge and not Dario?" Lamberto asked.

Gigi cleared her throat. "Yes, that's true."

"We're still getting married, and I'm going to take over," Dario interrupted, a warning in his voice.

"Actually, Dario, that's *not* true," Gigi said.

The room erupted in confused conversation.

"Gigi, we talked about everything already," Dario said, becoming increasingly uneasy.

"We did, and I've decided," Gigi answered.

"You can't make a decision without your mother or me," Dario reminded her.

All eyes bounced from her to Dario.

"Sorry to inform you so late, but I already had it drawn up with Cyrus," Gigi responded.

I was perplexed by the time frame since I knew her schedule.

"Does your mother know?" Dario probed.

Gigi looked at her watch. "She will, right about... now."

Her phone rang on the table and she picked it up. "I'm getting married, but not to Dario."

"Bitc—" Dario caught himself as I moved toward him.

Gigi held me back. "It's okay, Axel. His pride is hurt. Anyway, gentlemen... We have a lot

to talk about. I know taking orders from me will take time, but I learn quickly. Plus, I'll have the help of my husband to guide me if I stumble."

"Bringing in an outsider is not how things are done, Gigi," Lamberto said.

For all of his faults, I had to agree with him.

"He's not an outsider. Axel and I are getting married," Gigi announced.

Every mouth in the room dropped in surprise.

"You stupid bitch!" Dario leaped over the table.

I shoved Gigi behind me and pulled out my gun.

"Dario, I wanted to avoid any problems, but if you call me out again..."

"This isn't over," Dario barked as Lazardo held him back.

"I need to talk to you," I whispered in her ear.

"Can it wait?" She licked her lower lip.

I got distracted for a moment. "No, now." I gestured for her to step into the hallway. We walked out of the room, and I closed the door behind us.

Anger crept in at being left out of the plan. "Is this your plan? To lie to everybody?"

"Do you want Dario to be my husband? To force himself on me, possibly beat me in order to get my father's business."

"I would never let that happen." For her to think I would allow such a thing was disrespectful. Women weren't taken to my bed by force, and I would never let that happen to her or any woman.

She waved toward the door. "I believe he's responsible for my father's death."

"He wouldn't do something that stupid."

"Then help me prove it." Gigi was furious and couldn't see the implications of her actions.

"A fake marriage?"

"Who says it has to be fake?" The rebellion in her peeked out. Gigi had a way of getting under my skin, and I tried my best to reject her at every turn.

I sighed. "Gigi—"

She grabbed my face and put her lips against mine.

I instinctively wrapped my arms around her and pulled her closer. "You're dangerous," I mumbled, sucking on her bottom lip.

"Dangerous, but smart."

"What makes you think I want to get married?"

"Look me in the eye and tell me you would rather I marry Dario and I'll leave you alone forever," she muttered.

I thought about not having her in my life. Her slightest touch did something to me that no other woman could.

The door swung open, and we broke apart.

"The guys want answers," Turin remarked.

I nodded. "On our way."

Gigi squeezed my hand. "I'll handle my mother."

"If Dario was involved, I'll find out," I promised.

"And I'll be the woman who takes his last breath away." Gigi sauntered back into the conference room.

"The other bosses won't like this," Lamberto announced upon our reentry.

"That's understandable, but I assure you, it's a done deal. As of right now, I will keep things as they are, but make no mistake. I am my father's daughter. I won't allow betrayal and dishonesty to go blind," Gigi responded.

My mouth twitched with a smile.

"Lamberto, this will not stand," Dario argued.

Lamberto looked at Dario, defeated.

"Dario, I'd like for you to address all concerns to me from now on," Gigi directed.

My dick hardened as she "Bossed" him.

"Gigi, we all know you as Laurent's daughter, so you have to give us time to get used to this new look," Lamberto said.

Gigi sat down with crossed legs and folded arms, looking at each man in the room. "Lamberto, I doubt you were told this when you joined the cartel, so I'd like you all to understand. I give respect when respect is given to me. Carrington Cartel is my family name, and Carrington blood runs through my veins. No one can deny that truth."

* * *

One year ago.

"What did you get me?" Gigi stuck her hand out and wiggled it at me.

"Nothing big, but I thought of you when I saw it in the store." I removed my hands from behind my back and placed the long, thin box in her hand.

She smiled, unwrapping the gift, and something in her eyes sparkled. "So you listen to me when I talk."

Tonight she was going out with Ginerva for her twenty-first birthday and I promised Laurent I'd make sure protection was tripled.

"A gold necklace with a symbol of the world."

"I know you want to travel when you're finished with school." Something she'd said during our many nightly conversations when she sneaked off to the gazebo.

Gigi bit her bottom lip. "Can you put it on, please?" She held the box up.

Lifting it out, I turned her around, pulled her hair to the side, and locked it around her neck.

"Thank you, Axel."

"You're welcome."

She stood on her tippy-toes and kissed me on the check. "The best birthday present."

"Your father got you a new car. My gift doesn't compare."

"Your gift is more valuable because you listened to me."

I released the magazine clip and removed my goggles, staring at the remains of my target sheet.

The meeting with Gigi had everything jumbled in my mind and I needed to think and get clarity on what she wanted me to do. A fake marriage could only backfire on her and possibly cause us both to be killed.

I watched her with the instructor as she planted her feet

before giggling loudly. I didn't know what was so funny, but I had to break up this little moment.

"You broke up with your fiancé, proposed to me, and now you're flirting?"

The guy stepped back and Gigi moved the gun around without thinking.

I took it out of her hand. "You need more practice."

"Sorry, but I wasn't flirting," Gigi said.

"Yeah, right. Tell me anything to distract from the meeting."

She watched me lift the gun and release the clip. "My plan can work."

"Gigi, it would put us both in danger." Her life was dangerous, and her new role would only make it more so, possibly changing her for the worse.

Gigi expected me to always have the answers, but I'd lost my trust with Laurent's death. If she got a hint that I had doubts about her safety, she might not take the role and then marry Dario.

She stepped forward, pressing her breasts up against me. "When has danger scared you?"

I ran a hand over her hair, looking up to see the instructor staring at us. "Can I help you?"

He motioned in surrender and walked off.

Gigi giggled. "You're already behaving like a jealous husband."

"That's not a good thing." I shook my head. "I have to show you the warehouse."

"Where my father's business is based?"

I rubbed the necklace around her neck. "Yeah."

She covered my hand with her palm. "I never take it off."

We held hands. "Twenty-first birthday."

"A gift I sleep with at night."

"Do your parents know where it came from?" Not once did I think to ask if they knew I'd bought her gifts. When kids grew up in this business, each family would gift money. I'd given her jewelry.

She shook her head. "No. I don't plan on ever telling her."

"After we return from the farm, I think you should talk with Rosa."

"She's going to try to talk me out of the wedding to you, and I refuse."

"Gigi, I live alone in a condo. Are you willing to give up a massive estate for my place?"

She paused for a moment. "No."

"I didn't think so." My eyes roamed over her figure. Money was never a problem for me. I had plenty, but living in a massive home when it was only me didn't sound appealing.

"My father bought me a home in America. I want us to move."

I groaned, released my hold on her, and stepped back in frustration.

Her lids lowered, flickering her thick black lashes. "Why not?"

"My life is here."

"Can we talk about this later? I need to know every aspect of the business before Dario tries something."

"I don't want you digging into anything that has Dario coming after you," I said as we walked back to the car.

"Too late. I know he's behind my father's death."

"What do you remember about that night?"

Her phone rang, and she turned it off. "I haven't talked to my mother, and she's been blowing up my phone."

"Does she know about your marriage idea?"

"No, but I don't need her permission."

I unlocked the car door and helped her into the passenger side of my Lamborghini.

Fulgenzio motioned he was ready and started his car to escort us away.

When I reached the driver's door, I climbed in and slid the key into the ignition. "We'll swing by the farm first. What are you doing about school?"

"I can see about moving online if things get hectic, but I like the in-person experience. If we move to America, I could find a university."

"You have it all planned out."

She grinned, patting my knee.

* * *

The cartel's main facility for guns was housed on over thirty-four acres of land that Laurent held in his family for many years. It was reached by a winding road and only certain people got to come up here to work. Casella's primary goal had always been to get ownership over this land, and if Dario was behind anything, or wanted to marry Gigi to get control, it made sense. This place was a gold mine, and I rarely came here unless Laurent needed me to handle business personally. The Tuscany property housed about five bedrooms, with a wine cellar with a basement.

"Looks like a normal home," Gigi commented, shutting the door.

"That's the idea."

I took her hand, escorting her inside. A few men stood around the property with guns for security. The door opened, and Turin stuck his hand out for a shake.

"Turin, how long have you known about this place?" Gigi asked.

"Since I started working for your father," he answered.

"Weapons are housed here only?"

Turin and I looked at each other.

"Drugs come in and out sometimes," I responded.

Gigi continued to walk through the home. "This is the main house."

"We have people sleeping here twenty-four seven. Plus guards outside," I explained.

"Dario knows about this place?"

"He does."

Lamberto and Dario knew many Carrington family secrets; she could change up some of the setup, but it mostly was managed by them. Laurent allowed Lamberto to have a lot of freedom while he focused on his other businesses. Gigi would need to understand what came with trying to take things back.

"I don't want him to have access," Gigi voiced.

"Lamberto is the Underboss. He sets up the drop-off schedules," Turin informed her.

"Then I want you to take over that position." Gigi countered.

"Gigi, Turin can't do that."

"Why not? I'm the Boss of the cartel and I want him to monitor the shipments," Gigi demanded.

"We can discuss it more later."

She turned toward the window, looking out at our men loading up trucks. "Can we see the product?"

"Sure." Turin directed us to follow him to the shed at the back of the property. Guns were being loaded into crates as we walked through.

"Do you trust them?" Gigi waved at the men packing up the crates.

"They've been here from the beginning with Laurent," I replied.

"So tell me why that one over there is whispering to his friend." Gigi pointed at Gasto and Diego in the back of the assembly line. "Turin, bring them here."

Turin looked at Gigi, then at me for approval, and I nodded.

"What are you going to do?"

"Give me your gun." She extended her hand.

Killing our men in front of the crew wouldn't bring loyalty. "Gigi." I shot her a look.

She wiggled her hand at me. "Axel, give me your gun."

I removed it from my holster and checked the bullets, making sure the safety was on.

"Miss Carrington," Gasto said, wiping the sweat from his brow.

"You know who I am?" Gigi asked.

He hesitated briefly. "Um, ye-yes," he stuttered.

"Good, because I'll never forget your face from my father's dinner." Gigi raised her gun and pointed at his head.

"Gigi!" I warned gruffly.

She raised her hand to stop me. I knew she was hurting from her father's death. Hell, I still had nightmares, but to make a statement like this in front of her men without major proof would not look good for the other families.

"Gasto, tell me why I shouldn't kill you," Gigi demanded.

"Ma'am, I don't know what you're talking about," Gasto pleaded.

"When they brought my father out on the stretcher, I remember you and Dario talking."

My brow cocked up at that statement. She never told me this information from that night.

"Gigi, give me the gun." I covered her hand with mine and took the gun. I looked at Turin. "Take him," I said.

Turin directed Gasto to the basement.

"Where are you taking him?" Gigi asked.

"Nowhere you need to worry about. I need to get you out of here."

"Axel, I'm not a little girl. I understand what that means, and if you keep me away from how things work, I can get someone else to help me." Gigi folded her arms over her chest.

I pulled her arms apart. "Don't threaten me, Gigi."

"Then you'll be honest with me?"

"As much as I can."

"Fine. I'll let you think about my proposal. I don't want to go home just yet."

I sighed, grasped her hand, and led her out of the barn.

She looked deep in thought, staring at the landscape, as we drove down the road. "I care for you, Axel."

I glanced at her before turning at the curve in the road.

"If I invited you to dinner, would you go?"

I chuckled at the question.

"What's funny?" She turned to face me in her seat.

"I know how to ask a woman out."

"Then ask me." Her eyes sparkled at the curl of my top lip.

I looked at her and licked my lips, then lifted her hand and kissed the back of her palm. "Dinner between friends."

"For now." She turned to face forward, and I thought about what I just agreed to do with no hesitation.

Laurent might have thought I stepped over the line with his daughter today. I couldn't help but feel regret if she ended up hurt by my actions. A fake marriage could complicate her life more than she knew. "Dinner is the only thing I can offer."

I hadn't dated since I turned eighteen and before my parents' death. When I became locked in with the cartel, the only thing I had time for with women was sex, and often with two or three women at a time. Many times, they bored me easily and didn't understand we weren't in a relationship, so I cut them off and found a replacement until even that didn't fill the loneliness. To this day, I could recall only a few specific women who'd satisfied me enough to get through the night. If Gigi went with Dario, at least she'd know the traditional route of marriage when the husband had a mistress.

She sat back, typing on her phone as I drove, turning on the radio. Today came as a surprise in a good way; the car ride and being alone with her put me at peace. I might sleep through the night without an issue for once.

Chapter 11

Rosa

"**W**here the hell have you been?" Dario snapped as soon as I answered his call.

I took it off speakerphone and glanced over my shoulder to make sure no one was eavesdropping on the call. "Lower your tone," I hissed.

"That bitch made me look like a fool!" Dario shouted.

When I got the paperwork about the family business being taken over, I knew it would cause problems. "I know." I stood from the bed, walked into the adjoining room of the hotel, and paced.

"I'm trying to give you time, but my patience has run out."

"She knows nothing about running a gun and drug cartel," I insisted.

Dario was pissed. "Then you need to force her to marry me."

I gripped the phone tighter. "If you give me time, I can be convincing."

His voice held disdain. "Seems like you're more

concerned with the trust fund and keeping the details of Laurent's death to yourself."

I froze at the statement. "Are you threatening me?"

"Figure it out. It's too late to change the wedding plans. The deal will be off and your shit will unravel."

Men often thought I was some idiot they could manipulate, but underneath the beauty was brains and anyone could be taken for a ride and set up. Dario was foolish if he thought I'd drop to my knees and do his bidding without a backup plan.

"Then let me figure it out. This is your mess," I argued.

"You better fix it. She's your daughter, and you ensured we'd have no problems."

"Gigi is different. You knew this."

"I promise you. If I go down, you're going down with me."

I winced at his words, then remembered who I was. His lack of manhood was showing. "Fuck you, Dario. You don't get to tell me what to do or threaten me."

"It's your fault that the little witch is running the business."

I paced back and forth in front of the TV. Gigi would never disobey me. "She still has to marry you."

"Have you not been listening to me?" Dario demanded.

"What are you talking about?" A headache formed, and I rubbed my temple.

"She's fucking marrying Axel."

I gasped. "What the hell do you mean she's marrying Axel?"

"She came to the meeting, told everyone she was running the show, and that she was marrying Axel."

There was no way Gigi and Axel were a couple. I shook my head. "Dario, I think you misunderstood."

"She called off our wedding. Do you know how much time I have put in with her? And he waltzes in and takes what's mine."

"Calm down. I need to think. She's my daughter. I have to figure out what's going on."

He growled. "I'm the idiot who listened to you and my parents."

"I got a message from Cyrus. Everything was finalized, and now you are telling me she's marrying Axel? That makes no sense. He's too old for her."

"Have you looked in the mirror? Laurent was older than you by ten or fifteen years. What the fuck does it matter?"

"It was different for me. Gigi is naïve and impressionable."

"My father will care about this. The deal will be off for Lamberto. He stuck his neck out for us and this is how you repay him. I'm supposed to be the Boss of the family."

"It doesn't matter what Gigi thinks. I'm still in control of her trust. I'll get her back on board. Your wedding will go ahead."

"My trust is very thin in your hands."

"Let me do things my way. I understand her. She is my child, after all. I gave birth to her. I know how she thinks."

"We're past that."

"She wants someone to listen to her and go along with her ideas. I can get her back on board. This could still work. I didn't set all this up to have her destroy everything."

"All our plans will be shattered because you can't control her." Dario groaned.

"Nothing has changed, just shifted, and it's all supposed to be mine."

"Then you need to get it together and figure out how to get her under control because all this does is set us back.

You're the one who wanted him gone, and now she takes over and I get nothing out of this deal."

"I'll admit I underestimated her. I shouldn't have left her alone."

"You have one day to get her back on board or we'll have bigger problems." Before I could respond, Dario ended the call.

I tapped my forehead, closed my eyes, and tried to focus on how to get things back on track. After a few relaxing breaths, I looked toward the bedroom door, then dialed Gigi's number.

"Hello," she answered.

"Where are you?"

"I'm out for dinner."

"With who?"

"Ginerva."

I knew Gigi, and she hesitated before she answered, which made me suspicious.

"What's going on?" she asked.

"Dario called and threatened not to marry you," I lied.

"The marriage to Dario was your idea. I never loved him."

"Are you calling the wedding off?"

"No, I care about someone."

Minutes passed as I tried to hold my composure. "Who?"

Gigi tried to brush me off. "We can talk when I see you at home."

"He's hurt, and you need to get him back. Dario loves you, Gigi."

"Sorry, Mom, but I don't want to marry him and you can't make me."

Cyrus fucked up all of my plans and now Gigi thought she could cut me off? She'd regret going against me. "If you want any part of your trust fund, you'll rethink your answer."

"The bank still controls my trust fund and needs both of our signatures."

I started to crumble, but held it together and counted to three. "Listen to me carefully, Gigi. I've worked hard for you, and if you back out of this marriage, I swear to God—"

"Mother, I love you, but I am no longer a child. I'm a grown woman."

Anytime she wanted to get her way, she'd throw up her age, but I didn't care. Money and power controlled this business. "The Ramini family will not be disrespected."

"I will bury the Ramini family."

"Do you hear yourself, Gigi?" I rubbed my temple.

"Who's side are you on? Your daughter's or the cartels?"

"Gigi, it's not like that." The door opened and my guest walked out with nothing but a towel around his waist. "I can't talk about this right now." If we panicked now, the plan would go up in smoke. "Who are you with? I can come to you."

"I'm heading into a meeting. I'll have to check back with you."

"You said you were at dinner with Ginerva."

"I have to go," Gigi muttered.

Everything I'd worked for was falling apart.

"Hey, why do you look annoyed?" Edmundo kissed the back of my neck, wrapping his arms around my waist.

"Gigi called off the wedding to Dario."

He froze. "Why?"

I turned in his arms, letting out a lackluster breath. Another round in bed would help, but time wasn't on my side. "She wants to be in charge of the business." I caressed his chin.

He slid his hands down to my butt, burying his face against my neck.

"Is there anything you can do with Cyrus?" Edmundo asked as he released me and sauntered to the bar, grabbing a glass and pouring a drink.

"I can try."

Bitterness spilled in his voice. "Try harder."

"At the end of the day, she's my daughter, Edmundo."

"And he's my son."

"He already threatened me. I suggest you curb your words."

He placed the glass on the table. "Come here, *mi amore*." Edmundo extended his hand.

"Where's your wife?"

"I told you about bringing her up." Edmundo grasped my hair in a tight fist.

"Ah..." I winced.

He captured my lips. "Be quiet, Rosa."

"Let me go, Edmundo," I demanded in a shrill voice.

He grinned. "You get feisty and sweet all in the same breath."

"Let me go or I'll scream."

"Get her on board." He let me go, and I stumbled back.

"I will get Gigi back on board, but you need to control Dario. Because if my daughter stays in charge, I can have her remove him and put a new underboss in his position.

He chuckled. "Carrington Cartel is not powerful right now. I would think carefully about your foolish idea."

"Then get off my case."

"You have until the end of the month."

"That's not enough time. She's planning on marrying—" I paused in fear before I spilled Axel's name. Axel was my trump card and if I spilled right now, Edmundo would take him out, removing Gigi completely. No matter how it looked, I loved my daughter.

I turned and sauntered into the bedroom, taking a moment to comprehend what had happened. I bent to retrieve my purse, jacket, and shades. Edmundo and Dario's trust was fading fast, and I needed them fully on my side.

"I need to go."

"We are not finished with this conversation."

"Didn't your wife call you an hour ago?" I cocked my head to the side.

"So you play the bitter mistress role now."

The words flowed, and power burned in my chest. "Mistress, yes. Bitter, no."

"How do you think your daughter will feel about her mother cheating and possibly setting her father up to die?" He dropped the towel and grabbed his boxers and pants.

"Go be with your wife, Edmundo. She needs you more than me."

"Jealousy looks good on you, Rosa."

I scoffed. "Dario is your problem."

"Then Gigi will be my problem if she goes through with cutting my son out."

My back was to him. "Believe me, Edmundo, you don't want to play these games with me."

"So we understand each other, *mi amore*." He grinned.

"We agree. I'll get Gigi back to the table and you'll calm Dario."

He stuck his hand out for a shake. "Not that I don't believe you, but I need this done as soon as possible."

"Clearly." We were both full of shit, but we each had information that could get the other killed. Right now, we had each to trust each other.

I looked from his hand up to his face without shaking. I

left the hotel room, furious I didn't have the upper hand. Curious about Gigi's whereabouts, I messaged Fulgenzio.

Me: *Is my daughter with you?*

Fulgenzio: *She's with Axel.*

Me: *Where are they?*

Fulgenzio: *Not sure. We met at the shooting range.*

Me: *I told you she should be protected twenty-four seven.*

Fulgenzio: *Axel stated she was fine with just him.*

Me: *If something happens to my daughter, you're dead.*

I ignored him trying to call me and threw my phone on the seat after unlocking and entering my car. I closed my eyes and tried to figure out my next steps.

* * *

"Ginerva, you're close with my daughter. I know you want what's best for her." I poured Ginerva a glass of wine.

"Yes, Mrs. Carrington."

Her usual demeanor around me was lacking. Hopefully, my smile put her at ease. "Then you must know she's been acting pretty crazy lately about the wedding."

Ginerva gulped the wine and held out her glass for another. "She hasn't talked about the wedding."

"You have to understand that as a mother and only parent, it's hard to see her go down the wrong path."

"Not sure what you're asking me, Mrs. Carrington."

I leaned across the aisle and stared into her eyes. "Her idea to drop Dario and marry someone else."

"Gigi doesn't love Dario," Ginerva announced.

I hated the word love. That would come in time. Security was more important. "Love is overrated." I waved my hand, motioning for her to continue drinking.

Ginerva looked perplexed. "But?"

"No but, Ginerva. It's time for Gigi to grow up and learn that she has to do what's best for the family."

"The family wants her to marry someone she doesn't even like," Ginerva replied.

This back-and-forth was causing me a migraine. "She knows Dario from when they were younger, so it makes sense to put them together."

"I don't know."

I covered both her hands with mine and squeezed, a loving smile on my face. "Please help me convince her she's making a mistake with Axel."

"Axel?" Her eyes grew wide in shock.

"You didn't know?"

Ginerva fumbled. "I mean..."

"Tell me, you can trust me."

"She's always had a crush on him."

That revelation surprised me. "Really?" Men weren't allowed near Gigi or me unless it was a guard and they'd been with us for years.

"Maybe I shouldn't be talking about this with you, Mrs. Carrington."

"Ginerva, stop stressing. I'm her mother, the only person you should talk to about her feelings."

"He likes her. Well, I think he does."

My plan might crumble if their feelings were mutual. "Interesting."

My phone startled us and I raised my finger for her to hold on.

I put on my best smile. "Well, isn't this lovely to hear from you?"

"Sorry, I've been busy," Lamberto responded dryly.

Ginerva focused on her phone, and I turned my back to her. "Where are you?"

Lamberto answered, "At the farm."

I glanced over my shoulder at Ginerva, and she smiled as she finished her wine. I picked up the bottle and poured more into her glass. "Ginerva, I need to take this. Give me a second." I walked out of the kitchen.

"Dario and Edmundo have called me," Lamberto expressed.

"What did they say?"

"Not good things, I'm afraid."

"You're not listening, are you?"

"Rosa, you've always been a good talker."

"Good at a lot of things." I turned to look in the kitchen.

Lamberto sighed over the phone. "Gigi is not stable."

"I heard." Our butler walked past me, holding a few items in his hand, and I gestured for him to leave me alone.

"Then get her to put Dario in charge."

I harshly whispered, "Won't be easy. Apparently, she's in love with Axel."

"Who told you that?"

I looked out of the window near my front door, responding hurriedly, "Dario. And Ginerva just confirmed."

"Axel's working with Gigi?"

"Not sure, but we need to keep an eye on him." Axel could be a problem, and that made my skin crawl.

"What if he knows?"

I shook my head. "All of our bases are covered."

"This can get messy."

"I made the call and I regret nothing."

"You say that now, but when she gets deeper into the business and finds missing money and decisions that aren't approved by Laurent—"

"Keep your voice down." I covered the phone with my hand.

"Alvar is dead, and Orson wants answers," Lamberto explained.

Another headache started. All I craved was a harder drink from the wet bar tucked into the alcove. I could take away my home from me because of all this bullshit. The original works of art Laurent purchased for me, the custom banisters and Italian floor tiles that cost a hundred thousand to be installed. "Then handle it. It's not my problem."

Lamberto ignored my comment. "Obviously Axel is behind his death."

"Do you have proof?"

"He was to meet Alvar during the night of the shooting."

Ginerva walked into the hallway.

"Are you leaving, Ginerva? I planned to cook dinner and we could talk more."

"Unfortunately, my parents want to meet up for dinner," Ginerva responded.

"Tell them we should get together for dinner one day soon." I hugged her goodbye.

I watched her leave and close the door behind her.

"Handle Orson and I'll figure out Gigi." I clicked the end button and sauntered back into the kitchen. I prepared some noodles for a stir-fry and mixed them with chicken and veggies.

. Gigi impressed me today and showed she wasn't as naïve as I thought.

"Axel might be a problem." I sank down on top of the stools and ate my dinner. Families would fall if my dreams didn't happen, and I'd have no problem pulling strings within my family in America if it brought Gigi back to my side. Might be time for a reunion. I'd keep that in my back pocket in case Axel tried to come for me.

Chapter 12

Gigi

Axel allowed me to enter first, and I scanned the living room, marveling at the artwork on his walls. His place was decorated in warm colors, and had an enormous fireplace, a black leather couch, and pictures of his family on the mantel.

Axel grinned. "You can have a seat on the couch."

"What are you going to order?"

"I can order or I can cook."

I rested on his couch. "You cook?"

"Yes, I can cook, Gigi." He removed his jacket and placed it in the closet.

Axel's place was cute, with wooden floors, brick walls, high ceilings and bookcases. "I want a tour of your place."

He rolled up his sleeves, extended his hand, and escorted me down the hallway, where I noticed more artwork on the walls.

"You love art," I observed

"Yeah, something I picked up from my father."

"Surprised you like something other than being an enforcer."

He chortled, releasing my hand when we made it into the kitchen. "First, you help me cook."

"If this is a date, shouldn't I be on the receiving end?"

He paused with a wide grin.

"Not that type of receiving. Well, not yet anyway," I kidded.

He opened the fridge and grabbed spinach, tomatoes, and frozen fish. The minute I told Ginerva about my date, she'd be asking if I slept with him.

"Do you want something to drink?"

"Wine, if you have it." The view of him from the back elicited sinful thoughts.

"Wine for the Mafia Boss." He placed the glass in front of me and studied the amber liquid in his glass.

"Have you at least thought about what I said?"

"Tonight, no business talk."

I took a large swig of my wine. "Marriage is a big deal."

"Which is why I said in the first place not to go down this path with Dario or me."

I removed my jacket and picked up the knife to slice the tomatoes. "Truth or Dare?"

He drained his drink, then poured another. "What?"

"Truth or Dare. It's a game."

"Too old to play games, Gigi."

I put the knife down, turning to face him. "If you tell me the truth, I'll drop the fake marriage idea. If you take the dare, you have to take it seriously."

He shook his head as he refilled my wine glass. "You never learn."

"Pick one."

"Truth."

"How did I know you'd choose the truth?" I laughed, took the glass out of his hand, and sipped it all down.

"Do you think with your parents' death, and my father's recent death, that you're afraid to give yourself room to love someone fully?"

Axel stood with a stern look on his face. Finally, he moved to the stove, turned it on, and poured his ingredients together. "My parents are off-limits."

I slammed my glass down. "But mine aren't?"

He looked at me. "We're not doing this, Gigi."

"Why? Give me a good reason. All those nights of you coming to sit with me at the gazebo. Was that just 'babysitting?'" I emphasized with air quotes.

"Enough!"

"You want me and you're scared."

"Childish." He turned his back to me.

I grabbed his arm and turned him to face me. "I might be twenty-two, but you're the one acting like a child."

He glared.

"Dario might be an asshole, but at least he doesn't pretend and hide his feelings." I knew my words would sting.

"He's probably better for you," he murmured.

"If you truly believe that, then I should go and prepare for my wedding."

We had a standoff as he towered over me, but I wasn't intimidated by him anymore.

He clenched his fists. "What do you want me to say?"

"Anything. Hell, you were there when I got my car, and taught me how to drive. You were there when I found out about Dario and me, and every time I sneaked out because of a fight with my parents. You always talk to me like a real person." I teared up.

"It will get messy."

"Feelings are messy." I slid closer to him. "I have feelings for you, Axel, and no matter how much you try to push me away, you're in here." I lifted his hand and placed it over my heart.

Axel released a breath, ran his hand up to my neck, and gently gripped it from behind. His other moved to my waist as our lips crashed together in an intense kiss.

"The minute someone hurts you, I'll kill them," he stated, rubbing his thumb across my lips.

"Is that your way of confirming that you like me a lot?"

The fire alarm went off, and we pulled away to maneuver the burnt food into the sink.

"Guess we're ordering out now," I teased.

* * *

I finished my third glass of wine, dropped the pizza crust, and wiped my hands.

As soon as we cleaned up the mess from the burned food, Axel went out to grab a pizza. I suggested we get it delivered, but he explained he didn't want people to know where he lived. It was easy for me to relate to his line of thinking, so I stayed behind and roamed around his place.

"Exhausted." I collapsed under the blanket.

Axel massaged my feet as he sat at the other end of the couch. "It's late."

"What time is it?"

He glanced at his watch. "Almost one a.m. You can sleep in the guest room."

"Thanks. I have a meeting after class tomorrow."

"How are you going to run a gun business and college?"

"Always get myself into situations."

"Then Laurent bails you out." He chuckled.

"Either my father or you. I guess I am spoiled." He released my feet, and I climbed over his lap.

"What are you doing?"

"Just talking." I unbuttoned his shirt slowly.

"Not happening, angel." He grabbed me around the waist, lifted me up, and walked us to the guest room, where he placed me on top of the bed.

"Wait. Can you stay with me until I fall asleep?" When I reached for his hand, he lay down behind me, his arms around my waist.

"I refuse to spoil you." He kissed the back of my neck.

I turned and outlined his tattoo on his chest with my fingers. "Tell me about this tattoo."

"It's my parents."

"When's the last time you went to their grave?"

His gaze was fixed on the ceiling. "Recently."

"I think about my dad every day."

"Still fresh for you, the way he died."

"Deep in my soul, I know something is fishy with Dario."

"If that's true, let me handle him."

"When's the last time you brought a woman home?"

"I told you I've never brought anyone here."

"Never?"

"You are the first."

I observed him. "The first girl to be in your guest room."

"You think I'm some man whore?"

"Yes."

It was wonderful to see his guard come down with me when he laughed. "I've devoted all of my time to work."

"Have you ever thought about retiring?"

"This is my life, angel."

"What about kids?"

"No one should want me as a father."

"Why? You've shown me how loyal and special you are."

He climbed off the bed. "Go to sleep." He kissed me on the forehead.

I pouted. "Good night, Axel."

He paused at the door. "Good night, angel."

* * *

Two years ago.

I wrapped the towel around my waist and stepped out of the bathroom, accidentally bumping into Axel. My hands fell to his arms, while he caught me around the wrist before the towel and I fell to the floor.

"Sorry," he replied gruffly.

"What are you doing here so late?"

"Business."

"Is my dad still in his office?" I looked over my shoulder.

"Yeah." His eyes trailed down my body.

"I guess I should get dressed." As I walked around him and brushed against his shoulder, I ran my hand through my wet hair.

"You should."

"Morning." I stretched and sat up in the bed in only my panties and the shirt he gave me to sleep in for the night.

"I need to get you home," he said.

"What time is it?"

"Early."

"Thank you for last night."

He stared as I rose out of bed, picking up my dress and heels.

"You're welcome." He pushed my hair behind my ear.

An hour later, I stepped out of his car and bent, looking at him with his shades on, and smiled. "You still owe me that Truth or Dare."

"Get to class, angel."

"I like it when you call me angel." Turning, I sauntered into the house and shut the door behind me. I leaned against it, sighing dreamily.

"Someone looks like they had a good time last night." Mother stood with a cup of coffee in her hand.

"Mother, good morning." I stepped away from the door and headed toward the stairs.

"I hope you used protection," she remarked.

I paused at her comment, whirling around. "All we did was talk."

"You expect me to believe that, little girl?"

"If I want to sleep with him, it's my choice."

"So you'll whore yourself out! I'm so glad your father isn't here. He'd be ashamed."

"Funny, that's how you got that ring on your finger."

My head whipped back as she slapped me. "Understand something, little girl. I am the parent. I could take all of this away like *that*." She snapped her fingers.

"Then do it! I refuse to live my life in a bubble for you and cartel rules." I threw my hands in the air.

"That marriage is not happening. Over my dead body will I allow Axel to become your husband."

"Not up to you."

"We'll see about that." She sipped on her coffee and stared at me.

I left her alone and went to get ready for my day. I only had one class and then I'd work with Lamberto to get all the files on running the business.

Chapter 13

Axel

Gigi had plans to go to the office later, and I had Turin set up recording a few days after the initial meeting to announce her. I knew we had a snake in the family, but I couldn't pinpoint if it was one or two people working together.

"For now, I'll pretend." I removed my jacket and laid it on the chair as my phone rang

"Who's that?" Turin stood next to me in the slaughterhouse.

Our little problem squirmed in the seat, his mouth muffled.

"Gigi." I padded to the back room with the two-way mirror. "Hello."

"I thought I told you about swarming all these guards at my school."

"What are you talking about?"

"My professor is going to kill me with all these guys around me."

"I can talk to him."

"No, sir. I'd rather not have that happen, and he ends up missing."

"Did you talk with them about moving to online classes?"

She sighed. "I did and they're not happy, but I want to try."

Turin talked to Lazaro, tying the problem's hands to the chair.

"Are you listening to me, Axel?"

"Yes, you want to handle the meeting later today."

"Will that be a problem?"

"Should it become a problem, I will let you know."

"I can tell you're distracted."

"Turin and I are dealing with a problem."

"Why didn't you tell me?"

"Because it's my job to get rid of problems before they come to you."

"Only way they will respect me, Axel, is because of you."

How did this become my fault?

"Never mind. I'll talk to you later."

"Gigi, did you get the notes from today?" A deep voice on the other end of the line asked.

"Who is that?"

Gigi ignored me. "Hey, Jacque. Can I finish this call first?"

"Sure, sorry about that," Jacque replied.

"Sorry, what did you say?" Gigi responded to me.

"Tell Jacque to take his own notes," I grumbled.

Gigi giggled. "Never knew you would be jealous."

"I've never lied about being possessive over what's mine."

"When did I become yours?"

I chuckled at her question. "Not having this conversation with you."

"Fine, act like an asshole." Gigi ended the end call.

The door opened, and Turin popped his head in to check. "We need to hurry."

I marched out behind him and tossed the phone on the table. "Open your eyes," I demanded, smacking him across the face.

He screamed and tried to pull himself off the chair.

"We know you were in on Laurent's death."

He shook his head.

"Tell me the truth and I might let you live."

"I promise you, Axel, I don't know anything."

"That's too bad. You want to die at my hands?"

"Lazaro, please..." he begged.

I cut my eyes at him. "Lazaro can't help you, Franco."

He cried as snot and blood spilled down his cheeks.

Turin put in the work of getting the video footage and found Franco was the driver of the car that night. Lazaro and he went way back to childhood, and he thought I would spare him.

I squatted in front of him with the pliers and cut off two of his toes.

"Please! Argh... Ugh." He started to pass out.

"Give me the hammer."

"We need some information," Lazaro commented.

I shook my head. "He's not going to talk."

I hit both of his knees and his eyes rolled in the back of his head, his bloody mouth causing him to choke.

I shot him in the head and chest.

"What now?" Lazaro inquired.

"Keep looking."

*　*　*

"I'll call you about the tutoring thing," a guy I assumed was the one from earlier remarked and I watched him hug her, then walk toward his car.

I left Turin with Lazaro to clean up the mess and went to Gigi's school to surprise her with a ride home. I watched Gigi get in the car with Fulgenzio and drive off. Placing the cigar in the tray, I opened the door and jogged over to her little friend. Before he could slam the door shut, I yanked it wide open and snatched him out.

"Hey, man!" he shouted.

"Shut the fuck up."

"Who are you?"

I pulled the gun from behind my back.

He held hands in prayer. "Wait... Wait!"

"What's your name?"

"Huh?"

"Name!" I yelled.

"J-Jacque," he stuttered.

I smirked. "Stay away from Gigi."

"She's just a friend."

"She doesn't have friends," I drawled arrogantly.

"Okay, sorry."

"Next time she tries to talk to you, ignore her."

"But—"

I slammed the gun across his face.

"Sorry. I promise to stay away."

"Good. As her husband, I'd hate to kill you," I lied.

His eyes widened in shock.

After handling that issue, I jumped back in the car and drove to the office. Gigi was addressing the men for the second time in her capacity as Boss, and I wouldn't wait to fuck somebody up if they tried her again.

I talked to security as I passed through the double doors of the office building and onto the elevator. "Is she here?"

The doors opened to reveal Turin with a scowl on his face. "She is, but you need to see something."

"Can it wait?"

"Has to do with the cameras," Turin whispered.

I glanced at him with a hiked brow. We stepped into an office and shut the door behind us.

Turin handed me his phone. "Watch."

"She's fucking playing us. I know this marriage is bull- shit," Dario said.

"What do you want me to do about it? I'm not in control," Lamberto replied.

"We need to get evidence and push it off on him. Maybe if she sees he's behind Laurent's killing, she will come crawling back to me," Dario answered.

"When this first came up, I thought it would be easy to get rid of Laurent."

"I didn't realize he would change his will on us," Dario mentioned.

"The plan was properly set to make everything easier on us. This is beyond what we need to do. Laurent should have been an easy target. You become the Boss and I get half of the business," Lamberto admitted.

"Gigi is too stupid to be the Boss. Maybe go after Casella. We set it up where Casella is behind now," Dario announced.

"Gigi wants to meet and go over shipments. If she notices numbers moved around, I'm beyond fucked, which is why we need to figure out how we can get rid of Axel."

"I'm better for her. We shouldn't be seen together for a little while."

"What are you saying?" Lamberto asked.

"I'm saying that it's too hot right now. Let her think she's

in charge, and if she fucks up, it's on her. Then we vote her out," Dario answered.

"I need to talk with Orson," Lamberto said.

"Fine. Get what you can out of him. We're back in charge again."

"Gigi and Axel really a couple?"

"I don't know. I hate his smug look. Gigi was a virgin. I don't care if she let him fuck her. The little bitch was only going to be allowed to have my babies. Entire marriage would be for show and I have my women on the side."

"Women like her are pure. You have to mold them to be the perfect wife and put them in their place if they step out of line," Lamberto suggested.

Their conversation disgusted me and I wanted to kill them both where they stood. Gigi had no clue about the deception wrapped around her life.

Turin took the phone out of my hands and I sat back in my seat to think.

"He's going to make a move on her," Turin said grimly.

"I think she's right."

"About what?"

"Us getting married."

Turin nodded. "That puts more legit backing of her within the family if she has a husband."

"Dario has to be taken out."

"Too powerful. His family would join forces with Casella if we did."

My mind raced with how I would kill them all. "We have a tail on them both, correct?" I headed out the door and down the hallway to the conference room.

"I'll beef it up."

I made it to the door and stood outside, staring at Gigi

while she talked at the head of the table. "Keep them on watch while I figure out the play."

The door opened, and one of the guys came out. I headed inside and went to stand in the back of the room to face Dario and Lamberto.

"As I said, I saw the layout of the farm and started looking at our numbers," Gigi continued.

"Laurent trusted me to handle the orders, Gigi." Lamberto said, sipping on his water.

"He's no longer here, Lamberto, and we were all still grieving, but I want to spread in another direction."

Lamberto and Dario glanced at each other.

"Spread?" Lamberto repeated.

"The De Luca and Fuertes Cartels are friendly. We've done business in the past."

"The Casella family won't like this, let alone my family," Dario argued.

"Casella has been taking advantage for a long time. We need to find new sources."

A whispered conversation ensued.

"Gentleman, I can triple our income with this move," Gigi insisted, clasping her hands in front of her.

"No," Dario answered swiftly.

"Your permission is not needed. I'm only bringing this up as a courtesy."

When she was in her hoss mode, I wanted to grab her and suck on her full lips.

"Gigi, I have to agree with Dario about moving away from Casella Cartel," Lamberto said.

"You said it yourself, Casella doesn't like us. If we go in a different direction, they'll have to reassess their prices because we'll find someone to outbid them," Gigi explained.

"The three families have worked together for years. You

can't come in and change things up like you're changing your fucking panties," Dario joked.

Everyone laughed.

I surged to my feet and Gigi motioned for me to stop.

"Dario, what you and everyone else fails to understand is that I make the calls."

"You'll start a war," Dario seethed through his teeth.

Gigi leaned her elbows on the table. "War is what I'm after."

I took Gigi to pick up her clothes from her place two hours after the meeting, and she insisted we go out together. Initially, I said no because I disliked being around people, but she said she'd stop talking to me if I didn't go. When I asked Gigi if that was what her mother and father did on a daily basis, she replied that her mother was worse because she talked more and wrecked the entire house if no one listened.

"You look like a killer." Gigi placed the menu on the table.

The men had checked the place out before we came inside, and I ensured the server put us in the back corner with my back to the wall so I could see when someone came through the door.

"I am a killer."

"Tonight, can you just be my date?"

"Gigi, I'm here."

"Yes, but you don't seem to be in the mood."

She was right. I didn't know how to tell her I had evidence and was ready to kill two people in the organization —one being her ex-fiancé.

"I'll always give you my attention."

"Thank you, but I wanted to talk to you about something."

"Go ahead."

"Hello, can I get you two anything?" The server arrived at our table.

Gigi ordered for both of us and the server left to get our drinks after placing water on the table.

"What did you think of my ideas today?"

"I understand you need to do what Laurent would want to continue his legacy."

"That's why I'm worried I might have made a mistake." She cupped her chin, leaning on the table.

"You're brilliant, Gigi. Never let anyone get in your head."

Her lips curled into a smile. "I want to travel to America. Can you set up a meeting with Antonio De Luca and Joaquin? I know you're close with them."

"That won't be a problem."

Our drinks were planted in front of us and silence filled the air between us for a minute.

"Who's Jacque?"

"Jacque?"

"Is he a problem?"

She leaned back in the chair with a cocky smile. "He's in my class."

Our server returned with the food.

"He sounded familiar with you," I said once she was gone.

"Are you jealous?"

"It would get messy between Dario and now me."

Her grin fell from her face. "Are you calling me a slut?"

"No. I need to make sure I only have one person I might need to kill."

Gigi blew out a long-held breath. "No killing unless it's mafia-related."

"That I can't promise."

"Please," she begged.

"Don't beg for him."

"Axel, it's not that serious."

"Everything with you is serious," I commented.

"I'll stay away from him."

"Good, but I already talked to him."

Her eyes widened. "Please tell me you didn't threaten him?"

"If you sit in front of me and beg for his life, we're going to have a problem."

"I'm ready to go."

"Eat." I grabbed my napkin and fork.

"No longer hungry."

I groaned and pulled out my wallet, waving for the server to put our food in bags to go. I walked Gigi to my car, dropped the food in the back seat, and drove back to her place.

Her mouth opened and closed. "Why are we here?"

"I have work to do."

She turned in her seat. "You're lying."

"Gigi, I told you, I will not play games."

"I know, but Jacque is harmless."

"To you, but I know what he's trying to do."

"I want to go back to your place."

"No."

She reached for me and I moved out of her hold.

"Axel, please." She leaned over and kissed the side of my neck, sucking on my ear.

I grabbed her thigh and gripped her head, pulling her lips to my mouth.

"Mmmmm," she moaned.

I bit her bottom lip, pulled away, and started the car, heading for my place. A part of me knew the next step I was about to take would force me to put my heart in her hands and that someone, even if it was fake, had the power to undo me. The thought of being vulnerable again pissed me off, but even with Gigi being young, she'd taught me I needed to live my life.

It didn't take me long to get us home. I tossed her bag over my shoulder and dragged her upstairs to my room.

"Shit!" I pushed her against the wall and gripped her smooth brown thighs in my hands, rubbing up and down her leg before removing her heels.

"Take it all off," she whispered.

I stared at her eyes, then her lips.

"Once we do this, there's no turning back. You'll be mine, Gigi. I won't compromise."

"Same." She palmed my dick.

I gripped her dress and ripped it down the middle so her breasts popped out. "Fuck, you are beautiful."

A small breathless whisper escaped her lips.

I grabbed her hands, locking them in mine, and planted them above her head as my tongue dipped between the seam of her lips.

Chapter 14

Gigi

My dreams were about to become reality and the very thought of disappointing Axel had the hairs on the back of my neck prickling. He had way more experience than me and probably liked to be in control in the bedroom. I wanted to show him that even though I was a virgin, I could be sexy.

He trailed open-mouthed kisses along the side of my neck and my back arched off the wall as his strong hands gripped my breasts. I watched as he moved down my body until he was hovering over my pussy.

"Axel!" I gasped as his warm breath covered my sacred place.

"Keep your eyes open," he demanded. He pulled my thong aside and his tongue flicked over my heated flesh.

I propped one leg on his shoulder for deeper penetration. "Fuck!" My chest heaved rapidly.

Without thinking, I spun around to face the wall with both hands planted as he continued his meal.

"Oh!" The slap of flesh on flesh made me jump.

"That's for acting like a brat." He smacked my ass again.

He moved, pressing his large body against my back and grinding his hips against my butt. "Take me, please."

"When I'm ready." He pulled me back and grasped my neck.

"Axel!" I cried out as he tweaked my nipple.

We made it to the bed, our eyes on each other as we removed the rest of our clothes.

He shook his head as I reached for my thong. "I'll do that."

I lay back and spread my legs. Axel crawled between my thighs and lashed the tip of my nipple with his tongue. His large body covered mine, and I wrapped my legs around his waist. He looked into my eyes and smiled with a spark of eroticism. A sense of urgency drove me and I slipped a hand down his chest to grasp his thick shaft.

"You need to get on birth control," he rasped.

I nodded because kids weren't in the plan at the moment. Too much was going on and trying to manage the business and school was enough.

"This marriage might be fake, but I protect what's mine." In one fluid motion, he pushed into me.

My head flew back, and I sank my nails into his arms. The pressure was too much. He buried his head in my neck and kissed my shoulder, softly rubbing along my body to distract me from the pain. Gradually, the burning sensation gave way to pleasure. He curled into my body, slowly moving in and out of me.

"Axel!" I cried out, squirming beneath him.

I gasped when he pulled back, bent my legs wider, and picked up his strokes.

"Gigi, baby," he moaned.

His grunts of pleasure aroused me and made me feel

good. I arched off the bed, digging my heels into his back and matching his urgency. Our bodies slapped together in the quiet room, and my body soared higher and higher.

"Oh, yes."

Skin to skin, we became one.

"You ready to come, baby?"

"Yes!"

"I knew this would undo me and now I can't give you back," he muttered.

"Please! Axel! Fuck, you feel so good."

He pulled out abruptly and got behind me, holding onto my leg. "So fucking sweet and tight. Come for me, baby."

He pumped faster, rubbing my clit. I tossed my head back and moaned in ecstasy, grasping his hand when he pulled my face around to kiss me.

"Uh... I'm coming." I quivered in his arms.

* * *

My eyes popped open, inspecting the room, and saw it a little after three in the morning. I felt the urge to pee and tried to move out of Axel's tight hold, but he pulled me back.

"What are you doing?" he growled.

"I have to pee."

"Hurry back."

"I thought you would kick me out afterward." I stood in only his shirt I'd thrown on after we showered last night before falling asleep.

He grunted.

I came out of the bathroom and slid back into bed, laying my head on top of his chest.

He rubbed my back down to my butt. "Are you still sore?"

I reached beneath the sheet to caress his dick. "A little, but the bath helped."

Axel bent and kissed me on the lips. I straddled his lap, and he moved his hands under the shirt, lifting it over my head so my curls tumbled over my breasts.

His eyes burned over me. "I'm not good enough for you."

"I never needed you to be good, only to show me you care." I pressed a kiss to his lips and slid my arms around his neck, nipping his ear and rocking my hips back and forth. "What do you have to do in the morning?"

He cupped my cheeks and squeezed. "What do you have in mind?"

"Finalizing our agreement." My heart filled with anticipation of being a wife to him. Even if we didn't last long, I needed to make sure he knew I would be the best thing he'd ever have in his life once he left.

He pecked me on the lips, sliding inside me gently. He assisted me while I was on top and rubbed my nub until I shattered for him.

"Axel!" My body jerked, collapsing on top of him.

As my breathing calmed, he rubbed my back, kissing my forehead, and we drifted back to sleep.

Hours later, I reached for him and discovered an empty bed. I smiled at the soreness between my legs. Glancing around his bedroom, I noticed the large windows and a balcony beyond that I planned to explore later.

I pushed the covers to the side and climbed out of bed, sauntering to the bathroom to clean up. Forty minutes later, freshly showered, I found Axel in his office on the phone. He waved for me to enter, and I sat on his desk and crossed my legs.

Axel placed a hand on my thigh while he talked. "Set up

the flights and tell him it's an emergency." He finished his call and turned toward me.

I raised an eyebrow. "Flights? Where are you going?"

Axel leaned forward and kissed my knee. "I scheduled my jet to take us to America."

My eyes widened. "When are we going?"

"This is a work trip, Gigi. No shopping and hanging."

I pouted. "Alright, grandpa."

I jumped down off the desk and turned to leave, but he extended his arm, pulling me back into his lap.

"*Cara*, you aggravate me." He lightly bit me on the shoulder.

"I'm tired of you treating me like a child. It would be a matter of time before we went back to being distant if last night hadn't happened."

"I apologize. You're right."

"Thank you. I need to call Ginerva to see if she can meet for breakfast."

"We leave in two days."

I run a hand over his beard. "Will I see you tonight?" The look in his eyes captivated me.

"What do you think? I need you around me not only because you keep me sane, but you've given me you."

* * *

An hour later.

Ginerva scooted forward in the chair, put her phone down, and waited for me to talk. It was strange for us to go days without talking, and I missed my best friend. Before I arrived, I ordered ahead with all of our favorites.

I offered her one of my crepes. "You look pretty."

"Thanks. So what's new with you?" She slipped her

napkin on her lap and picked up her glass of water, downing it.

I forced the food down before I spoke, looking around to make sure no one was listening to our conversation. "A lot, and I apologize for being distant lately."

"Explain."

I cut into my crepes, tossing a piece into my mouth. "I slept with Axel."

Ginerva dropped her fork and choked on her food. "How was it?"

I closed my eyes and recalled our night together. "Amazing." I opened my eyes again with a smirk.

Ginerva put two fingers in the air. "Are you together now? I have so many questions. What about Dario?"

I leaned forward on the table and cupped my hands around my mouth to whisper, "Dario is not a factor in my life. Axel and I are together and getting married."

Her eyes grew bigger. "Maybe that's why your mother—" She stopped abruptly.

Her comment caught me by surprise. "My mother?"

Ginerva sighed, rubbing her temple. "I don't want to be in the middle, Gigi." She looked around nervously. She crossed her arms over her chest and lowered her head to avoid eye contact.

"You're not. You're my best friend, and I trust you."

She mumbled, "I had dinner with your mother the other night."

I frowned. "Dinner?" My mother hated having guests unless she had something to gain from it. Most times it was to get money from my father.

She nodded. "At first, I didn't think anything of it because we've done it before, but she asked me a lot of questions."

My palms became damp. "About?"

Ginerva squared her shoulders. "You and Axel."

That caused an alarm bell to go off. "Explain everything."

"Mostly about your relationship and the wedding with Dario."

"She's snooping."

Up went her eyebrows. "You need to be careful."

"She's harmless."

A worried expression marred her face. "Maybe you're right, but she seemed pissed."

"Rosa is delusional. I was blind to it at first, but now I can see she's going around trying to sabotage what my father created."

"Just be careful."

"You should listen to your friend, Gigi," Dario said, appearing from nowhere.

The last thing I needed to interrupt my day was Dario. Ginerva looked between us as he slid a chair up to the table.

"Ginerva, do you mind if I speak with Gigi for a second?"

I grabbed her wrist as she stood. "No, we have nothing to talk about." My brow puckered threateningly.

Dario picked up the butter knife and cut into my food. "Gigi, we have plenty to talk about. I suggest Ginerva leaves if she wants to make it home safely." He tossed the food in his mouth and smirked.

Whenever I talked back, his first course of action was to threaten me.

"Gigi, it's fine. We can catch up later." Ginerva grabbed her bag and left the restaurant.

I watched her walk out to her car, then narrowed my eyes on Dario as I sat back in my seat.

"This idea to push Casella out will not work," Dario muttered.

"Okay." I pressed my fingers together on the table.

Disapproval gleamed in Dario's eyes. "Are you listening? I'm the only one keeping the men from revolting against you."

"Okay." Each nonchalant answer pushed his buttons.

Dario's icy gaze ran over my body. "Something is different about you."

I reached for my bag and coat. "What do you want, Dario? I'll never be with you."

"While you've continued to act like a bitch, I've secured the men's trust and if they believe you're taking them in the wrong direction... It won't be good for you."

"Of course, because you believe you have all the answers." I snorted.

"I know I do."

I pushed the chair back, sliding my arms into my coat. "Casella is behind my father's murder, and you want to keep working with him?"

"There's no evidence of that."

"Because of you!" I yelled, and the other guests glanced in our direction.

He grasped my hand as I spun to leave.

"Don't do anything stupid," he warned.

I yanked away and marched out of the restaurant. Fulgenzio held the car door open, and I climbed in, waiting as he jogged around to the driver's side.

Me: Ginerva, I promise to explain everything soon.

Ginerva: Are you all right?

Me: Axel and I are flying to America. When I get back, we can talk.

Ginerva: Please be safe.

Me: You too, and stay away from my mother.

I closed out of that message thread and went to text Axel when Dario's name popped up.

Dario: *War with Casella will break Carrington Cartel.*

Me: *I see your threats continue.*

Dario: *I can forget everything if you come back and we get married.*

I smirked at his response.

Me: *I have a real man now.*

Dario: *Fuck you and Axel.*

Me: *He did, and I liked it.*

I blocked him and scrolled to Axel's name.

Me: *Hey, Dario crashed my date with Ginerva.*

Axel: *Did he touch you?*

I nibbled on my bottom lip nervously, wondering if I should answer that question. Axel was possessive as my bodyguard. Now we'd stepped over that line, he could kill Dario before we found out the truth.

Me: *No, just threatened me.*

Axel: *Don't lie to me.*

Me: *He didn't. He brought up the Casella deal.*

Axel: *Stay home until I get you.*

Me: *Okay.*

Chapter 15

Axel

New York, two days later.

I slipped a tip to room service and pushed the cart of food to the table, setting everything up. After we'd flown in, we came straight to the hotel, unpacked, and slept for hours. Gigi had plans to check out the property her father had set aside for her.

The door to the bathroom opened, and she emerged with a towel wrapped around her hair. "I didn't hear room service knock."

"The door was already open when I stepped out for the paper."

She sat down and grabbed the orange juice. "What's on the agenda for today?"

"I set up a meeting with Joaquin and Antonio. Tomorrow we can do whatever you want."

A grin curved her lips. "Maybe a show or something."

Second thoughts poked in my head with her vision of why we were here. "This isn't a vacation, baby."

I didn't miss the glare flash across her face.

Silence sprinkled the room. "Never said it was."

"Good, Antonio might want us to show favor."

She tipped her head. "Show favor how?"

"A few guns for free."

Gigi popped a strawberry in her mouth. "Is that what has happened in the past?"

"A few times."

"Then I'm fine with that arrangement."

I admired her awareness of the cartel business and was pleased she took her position seriously. "All right." I picked up my phone and sent a message.

"What time do we have to be at the meeting?"

"This afternoon."

A grin creased her face. "Can you go with me to see the house?"

"I need to get the shipment arranged."

"How about Lazaro or Turin handle the drop?"

Her prompt negotiation had me smiling. "You have something else on your mind?"

Gigi drummed her fingers on the table. "I know it's a fake marriage, but can we get a ring?"

"Already have the papers drafted and signed, Gigi."

"I know, but I'd like to get a ring. To make it official."

Her eagerness was cute, but something behind her eyes told a different story.

I stood and walked over to my briefcase and grabbed the paperwork stating we were husband and wife.

"Mr. Bresciani, I have the papers you ordered." Cyrus handed me a white envelope.

I flipped it over and removed the documents with a certificate of marriage on top. "No one knows you have these, correct?"

His breath quickened. "Only you and me."

"And after a year, she can take over her trust fund?"

"She could, unless someone has it reversed."

I tensed. "Do you think Rosa would protest?"

He lowered his eyes. "Mrs. Carrington approached me about changing it to Gigi's thirtieth birthday, but I refused."

"From now on, anything dealing with Gigi, you call me first."

"You sure it's fake between you two?"

"Yes. Remember to call me if anyone attempts anything else."

That night, I'd planned on talking to Gigi, but work had us both preoccupied, followed by a flight on top of Dario showing his ass.

"Axel. Axel!"

"Huh?"

Frustration bubbled in her face. "Where did you drift off to?"

I tapped my foot. "Thinking."

"About?"

"You."

She smiled. "What about me?"

"I had Cyrus draw up the marriage license."

"Did you sign it?" Heat flushed her cheeks.

Air stalled in my lungs. "I did."

Gigi held her hand out. "Let me see."

I slid it over.

Gigi searched through the papers. "Everything looks fine."

"We're married on paper, but not legally." My eyes roamed over her intently.

She shifted in her seat. "It says my trust fund can be released if I stay married for one year."

"Yeah, it's a loophole Cyrus never explained at the reading."

Her face showed softness. "Oh."

My eyes sharpened at her quietness.

"Dario and my mother can't know about this at all, or I'll be sitting in a dark room until the wedding day."

I reached over and lifted her face to look at me. "Cyrus said she tried to change it after we left."

Gigi's mouth tightened. "There's something evil about a mother who refuses at every turn to love a child."

"Underneath the hate, she loves you."

Gigi went back to eating her food. "Doubt we're talking about the same Rosa Carrington."

"Anyway, you can get your ring now," I teased.

She dropped the papers on the table. "Well, I kind of had a thought now."

"No more ideas." I rose from the chair.

She grabbed my hand and pulled me back down to the chair. "Wait! Hear me out."

"Go ahead." I shoved my hands in my pockets.

"Why do we have to fake it, when we can do a year and I can get my inheritance?"

"Gigi, you're not thinking clearly." I shook my head.

"More clearly than you. The other night, you told me I belonged to you. Unless that was a lie." Gigi leaned over the table with her lips a few inches from mine.

My nostrils flared. The glow of her skin entranced me. "Angel, you're mine, from your pink toes to your plump lips, curly hair and soft thighs. I can't sleep without you."

"So I propose we get married for real, and stay married for a year and I'll get my trust fund and give you—"

"I don't want your money."

She stepped back. "So, what do you want?"

"You think I'm doing all this for money?"

Gigi drew back and moved from the table. "If it's not

money, then what? To clear your conscience over my father's death?"

"Angel, I'm going to pretend you didn't say that." I stopped and inhaled a deep breath before we got into a full-blown argument.

"Think about what I said. I need to change." She turned and went to the bedroom.

I huffed. A real marriage. The thought of her with someone else filled me with anger to the point of wanting to kill anyone that looked her way. Her on top of an empire and me behind her to watch her back and protect against any enemy.

The bedroom door opened again, and she strutted out in a gray pantsuit. Her makeup was subtle and her hair cascaded down to her back. "Are you ready? I already called the realtor."

"Give me a minute." I hopped up and went to change.

* * *

Dullness shrouded the room. When I made the call to come here, I'd provided little detail on the nature of the visit or who I would bring with me.

Both gentlemen sat silent and waited for me to begin, avoiding Gigi's glare. When they found out about Laurent, everything was halted on their end until a leader was appointed they could trust. Since Gigi came aboard, there was still hesitation on their part.

"Miss Carrington, my wife, Sofia, and I would like to extend our condolences on your loss." Joaquín said.

Antonio did what he does best and stayed silent.

"Thank you. I appreciated the flowers at the funeral," Gigi answered.

"Axel, it's been a minute since we've talked," Joaquín said.

"Work, plus changes in the family."

"Axel informed us you're the new cartel leader, Gigi," Antonio challenged.

"That's true."

"Tell us why you've come here."

I began to speak when Gigi remained silent.

Antonio held up a hand to stop me. "We want to hear from her."

"Mr. De Luca, you've known me as Laurent's daughter, a kid in your eyes, but tragically, things change."

"I agree," Antonio replied.

"Axel told me you are loyal to my father and have a long-standing business relationship."

"He's made us very rich," Joaquin answered.

"And I want to continue what he started."

"Women aren't usually in charge."

"I've learned, which is why I came to you both, because I need your backing and trust."

Antonio raised an eyebrow. "With whom?"

"My family and associates."

"Casella and Ramini family," I added.

"Explain," Joaquin probed.

"I believe they're behind my father's death and if they want me out, I'll be next. When I said I wanted to do business with you, it became apparent I would be on my own."

"You think it's an inside job?" Antonio asked.

"I have evidence."

Gigi whipped her head toward me. "What evidence?"

"Recording. I wanted to wait before I showed you."

"How long have you known?" she questioned.

"A few days."

"One thing I can tell you, Gigi, is that the men you love in this business make decisions that are best for you in their minds. Don't take it personally," Antonio explained.

"I know that now."

I reached in my pocket, removed the phone, and played the voice recording.

"That's Dario," Gigi said.

"Turin set up devices in the office."

"Wow," she responded.

"What do you need from us?" Joaquin queried.

"Come on board and we'll give you ten crates as a favor."

"That can lead to war. Orson Casella isn't my favorite, but we've been cordial," Antonio said.

"Understood, but Dario and Lamberto are trying to take over and push Gigi out." At this point, we need to call in all our favors.

Joaquin looked from me to Gigi.

"The fake marriage... is that true?" Joaquin asked.

"Yes, my mother and father arranged for me to be with Dario, but he's never been someone I wanted."

"How does Axel fit into your plans?" Antonio challenged.

I didn't like to put her on the spot, but we had to show our cards in order to get support.

"I love Axel, but my mother hates him. When Cyrus told me it didn't matter who I married, I talked with Axel and he felt the same."

"I'd like for you to come to dinner with my wife," Antonio said.

Gigi glanced at me, and I nodded.

She nodded. "We can arrange that while we're here in town."

"Twenty crates, plus kilos," Joaquin stated.

Gigi eyed him. "I can agree to those terms. You've given your full support to handling Ramini and Orson."

"Whatever you need," Antonio replied.

Gigi smiled in answer.

***

Once we finished our meeting, the realtor sent the address of where to meet her. Fulgenzio came with us, along with a few more men for protection, who drove behind us to the location. Gigi had an idea to go to the jewelry store before dinner with Antonio and his wife. I didn't need a ring, but she explained women can get catty about those things and she hated to look like an embarrassment on her first trip.

"That's her." Gigi pointed at the brunette standing on the porch after the gate closed behind us.

The property was miles out of the city in Upstate New York and sat on forty acres of land. After parking, I came around to help Gigi out.

"Ms. Carrington, so happy to finally meet you," the realtor said.

Gigi extended a hand. "You too, Lois. Please call me Gigi."

"Gigi it is, and this must be your husband." Lois reached her hand out for a shake.

"Axel," I responded.

"Welcome home to you both. Your father and his lawyer talked about you fondly."

Lois held up a phone to the door, and it unlocked automatically. We stepped inside and I heard doors close behind me.

"Check the perimeter, and see what we need to do for security," I instructed Fulgenzio. "I know Laurent bought the place a while ago, but in case we're not here all the time, I want eyes on the place."

The front entrance felt like a museum. It was white with a winding staircase and art on the walls. Gigi talked with Lois as they toured the living room. I went in the opposite direction, down the hall to the other rooms, finding a door at the end of the hall with a light on. I pushed forward and saw it was a bedroom with a few pictures on the wall.

"Hey." Gigi touched my shoulder.

"Yeah."

She leaned toward me. "Do you like the place?"

I spread my hands around her waist. "It's fine."

"Just fine?"

"What do you want me to say?" I pulled her into my chest.

"Anything besides fine."

Reluctantly, I let her go. "How about this place is amazing and I can't wait to eat your pussy in every room?"

"Is that all you think about? Sex?"

"Possibly."

She stretched her arms around my neck. I ran my hands down to her ass and cupped both cheeks.

"Mmmmm," Gigi moaned into my mouth.

I pulled her into the bedroom and shut the door behind us, nudging her to the bed on her back. The memory of her smell incited me into an animalistic lust. I quickly stripped her of her clothes, kissed up her thighs, and nuzzled my nose against her smooth silky, brown skin. She never denied me on our first night, and I hoped she wouldn't now since we weren't at my place.

I trailed a hand across her stomach, taking in the sight of her plump breasts. I dipped my head and devoured her caramel toned nipples, and she arched off the bed.

"Axel. Oh, baby," she groaned, rubbing a hand across my head.

I let her control the flow as she kissed me, sucking on my tongue. Slipping a finger in her panties, I circled in and out as she writhed beneath me.

"Did you lock the door?" she whispered.

I looked at her seductively. "No."

"Axel!" Her eyes popped open.

"Shush." My gaze was bold on her body.

"But what if—"

I covered her mouth with mine to shut her up. Unbuckling my belt, I lined myself up and slid inside her, caressing her cheek. We stared at each other for a moment, enjoying our connection.

"Damn, Gigi," I groaned when she met my strokes.

"Oh, God! Right there." Her eyes rolled and her face filled with lust, her voice almost unrecognizable.

I spread her wider, speeding up my strokes before we had guests interrupt.

"God, you're everything." I never spoke during sex, but Gigi wasn't like most women. She had no idea of the hold she had on me. She didn't know a year of marriage was all I could give her.

Gigi turned us over so she was on top. She braced her hands on my chest and bounced up and down. "Make me come, baby."

There was a maddening hint of torture when I was inside of her I couldn't describe. "Fuck, you're the best of me."

"Tell me again."

I knew it was wrong because she was emotionally invested. "I can't imagine a world without you."

"Shit!" she gasped. "I can't hold it any longer."

I pumped harder and faster.

Then came a knock on the door.

"Go away!" I yelled.

Gigi laughed. "Be nice."

Aching for another round, I plunged back into her sweet entrance and circled my hips slowly. I buried my face in her neck. I never wanted to let her go.

Chapter 16

Gigi

I slid my bottom lip between my teeth as Axel pressed a thumb against my opening. I cleared my throat, flushed from our earlier lovemaking. Antonio had a car pick us up to bring us to his home for dinner with his wife, Sabrina. We'd met before briefly at a party, and now we would be doing business, we could get to know each other better.

"Gigi, you're in school, correct?" Sabrina asked.

I cleared my throat and nudged Axel's hand away. "Uh... huh."

"Newlyweds," Sabrina teased.

Axel chuckled at my embarrassment.

"Nothing to be ashamed of. Antonio never lets me go a day without touching me." Sabrina placed her hand over his, and he lifted it to his lips.

I changed the subject. "How did you and Antonio meet?"

They looked at each other. "His club."

"Was it love at first sight?"

"Yes," Antonio said as Sabrina responded simultaneously with, "No."

Axel chortled.

"We tell this story all the time, but he's going to make it seem like love at first sight," Sabrina replied.

"The moment she came into my orbit, she became mine," Antonio stated.

"I know you have kids now, but was it hard in the beginning juggling work and married life?" They seemed like a replica of Axel and me in that I wanted him from the first time I saw him, and he kept me at arm's length.

Sabrina looked at Antonio for a moment. "At first I played hard to get. He made it very clear I was his woman even before we even went out on a date."

Sabrina laughed, and Antonio winked at her.

"Reminds me of someone." I poked Axel in the shoulder.

"Love is a complicated thing, but I don't regret the struggles we had because he was everything I needed," Sabrina explained.

"Marriage is the number one priority, business second," Antonio expressed.

"How long are you two here in town?" Sabrina asked.

"Until tomorrow," I answered.

"You should come to lunch with Janice and me," Sabrina suggested.

"I haven't seen her since the party."

Sabrina chuckled. "She would love to get away from the kids."

"Axel, do you mind?"

"No, have fun."

"Great. You men can do business tomorrow, while we have lunch and maybe some shopping," Sabrina tittered.

"Pops, where's the other control?" Their eldest son came into the room. He was the spitting image of his dad.

"AJ, how many times have I told you to keep your games together?" Sabrina fussed.

"Sorry, Mom," he murmured. He seemed like a sweet boy.

"Where's your brothers and sisters?" Antonio questioned.

AJ shrugged.

"I'd advise you to wait on children, so you're not dealing with these types of nonverbal answers," Sabrina hissed.

"Look in the toy room," Antonio replied.

"Are you going to speak to our guests, AJ?" Sabrina challenged.

"Hi." Their son darted out of the room and we burst into laughter.

"That's your son," Sabrina sighed.

Antonio reached for her, pulling her out of her seat and into his lap. "She's grumpy because she might be pregnant." Antonio ran a hand over her cheek.

Sabrina slapped him on the arm. "Stop telling people that. Not pregnant," Sabrina argued.

"Spoiled."

"Because of you."

They fussed back and forth.

* * *

Sabrina invited me out to her family's restaurant for lunch with her friend, Janice. Their other friend, Liz, was out of town with her husband, Bruno. They explained about the weekly hangout the girls organized without the husbands and kids.

Food filled the entire table, and we had a massive choice. Antonio told his staff to give us anything we wanted and was even going to close the place down for us, but Sabrina told

183

him not to stress everybody. Still, the guards assigned to us remained laser-locked on our table.

As soon as we clinked glasses, I drank the entire wine. I looked at Sabrina and Janice as mentors because they were older and for their work as a boss.

"I remember meeting you at the party, Gigi," Janice remarked. "How is everything going?"

"Life has been crazy," I replied, refilling my glass.

"Sabrina told me about your father's death. We all live this life, but it hurts when someone close to you is taken away," Janice said softly.

"I've had so many condolences, I almost feel numb," I said sadly.

"We understand. You're young to be dealing with so much," Sabrina expressed.

I drained my drink. "Axel has been a great help."

"He's not bad to look at either." Janice hiked a brow.

I covered my face in embarrassment.

"You two have good taste. Antonio and Carlo are nice to look at."

"Momma always said if you open your legs, make sure it's something to brag about," Janice joked. "Those eyes captured me. One thing led to another, and I ended up having all his babies."

"Not babies anymore." Sabrina laughed.

"That's true. I remember a time when I only had to worry about changing a diaper. Now it's girlfriends and boyfriends calling." Janice gulped her champagne.

"Antonio never told me if you liked the guy who was arranged to be your husband," Sabrina said, turning her gaze on me.

"He and I grew up around each other, but I never liked him in that way. He's always been a jerk."

"Probably the playboy type," Janice commented.

I nodded. "He's an asshole who wants me to be the little wife at home and give him sex. I know he wants my money."

"So he doesn't love you?" Sabrina queried.

"No. He told me it's all about him being in charge of the business. I refuse to give up my family's business and my body to him," I snarled.

"Good. You did the right thing," Janice replied.

"I'm not sure what I mean to Axel. I don't know if we'd be here if my father was still alive."

"Are you having a big wedding?" Janice asked.

"No. We're already married on paper, but I need to get my ring."

"Why not go to the courthouse before you head back and we'll have a little party before you fly home," Sabrina suggested.

"I can't. Axel's not the party type."

"On paper, without people you know as witnesses of your love, doesn't seem like something your father would want," Janice remarked.

"A dream wedding would be somewhere like Greece, but I have to get back to running a business."

"Maybe we could do a little something at Sabrina's house." Janice volunteered her best friend's home.

Sabrina spat out her drink. "How are you giving up my place for a wedding?"

"Oh, please. You love to throw parties," Janice teased.

"Shut up, Janice. But if you want a small, intimate ceremony, Gigi, I'm sure we can pull something off," Sabrina announced.

"Thank you. Let me talk to Axel first."

* * *

Later that evening.

"We are gathered here to entwine two souls as one," the pastor announced.

I smiled at Axel before scanning the room. Sabrina, Janice and their husbands and kids were all witnessing as we tied the knot. My dream wedding would have been with my father walking me down the aisle in a church surrounded by family and friends who loved me.

I clasped Axel's hand and thought back to all those times he let me talk his ear off about my fucked-up life and the decisions that were placed upon me because I was the daughter of the most ruthless Mob Boss in Italy. This time, I had the choice and did what was best for me.

I repeated the words from the pastor. "I do."

"Axel Bresciani, do you take Gigi Carrington to be your wife, to have and to hold, in sickness and health?"

"I do." He pulled me into his chest as the pastor pronounced us husband and wife.

The room erupted in cheers and claps.

"Really mine."

I looked into his eyes. "All yours for real."

Love shined bright in his eyes.

"Time to really party," Janice joked.

We laughed.

"She'll party for anything, a wedding, a promotion. Hell, a new car," Carlo quipped.

Janice slapped him on the arm and everyone laughed at the two of them as they went back and forth.

I wrapped my arms around Axel's neck and leaned into his chest, cupping his chin.

"Husband."

"Wife." He rubbed my cheek.

"Before you two party, let's go into my office," Antonio interrupted.

Sabrina pursed her lips at his request. "Business was taken care of yesterday, Antonio. We only have them for a small amount of time."

"*Bella*, let me finish up, and I'll get them back to you in a minute." Antonio kissed the tip of her nose, and she puckered up for another kiss.

"Here they go." Janice chortled.

I giggled and strode through the hallway into Antonio's office with Axel, while the rest went to gather around the dining room for dinner. Axel closed the door behind us. Antonio sat on the edge of his desk, shifting to pick up an envelope, and holding it out to me.

"Here's the agreement we spoke about, plus a few names of my best assets in Italy who can help on your return journey."

I removed the paperwork, skimming over it before handing it to Axel.

"I'm familiar with these names. Joaquin is fine with giving a portion of his percentage to cut ties with Casella?" Axel probed.

"Joaquin, more than anything, is about loyalty, and if Orson betrayed Laurent, it's only a matter of time before Fuertes would get stiffed," Antonio implied.

"Are you letting us handle it our way?" I needed to know before any decisions were made without my input. Men instantly tried to protect women—it was a natural state. But I was in power and wanted to make the moves that would have an impact.

"To an extent. I need assurance my name won't be implicated. As you know, I've cleared my name in high-profile issues, but any type of rumblings of war business—"

"Could hurt the De Luca Cartel. We understand."

"You know, you remind me of someone," Antonio mentioned.

"Who?"

"A former foe, Queen. Like you, she was dealt a blow with her father's death," Antonio remarked.

"I believe my father might have talked about her a time or two."

"She was impressive. A boss in her own right."

"But?"

"She became too invested in trying to kill me."

"What happened to her?" I questioned.

Antonio paused in thought. "Same thing that will happen to Dario."

I understood clearly what I had to do—kill Dario before he tried to kill me. I glanced at Axel. "We'll fly out and get to work."

"Tonight, we strategize, and when we get back, it's time to put our moves in place," Axel announced.

"All roads lead to the Carrington Cartel," I resolved, letting out a deep sigh.

Hours after a lively celebration, we went back to the hotel, showered, and lounged on the balcony.

Axel held me against his chest. "Did you enjoy the trip?"

My chest felt as if it would burst. "I have. I could stay here forever."

The tense lines on his face relaxed. "Is that right?"

"Anywhere with you is my home, but I'd like a fresh start."

"Have you made arrangements for school?"

I went silent.

"Gigi." He nudged me.

"No. I'm stuck on learning the business." I became

uneasy at the thought of my path now that I didn't have my father—or my mother—in my corner.

"You know I can't live here forever with you."

I pulled away. "What do you mean?"

"Gigi, my life is in Italy."

That set alarm bells ringing. I cleared my throat. "Business will be wherever I want it to be."

He stared at me. "Not how it works with me."

My guard went up. "Explain."

"I travel, in and out, no matter the time."

"So if we had children, I'd basically be raising them alone."

His face showed confusion. "Children?"

"Tell me you want children, Axel?" My misgivings increased by the minute.

He gave me a narrowed glance. "I don't argue."

"Who says we're arguing?" I raised my voice.

"Your parents might have had a relationship like that, but I'll never raise my voice to you, and I expect the same in return." He clipped my chin, rose from the chair, and headed back into the suite.

I stayed out and gazed at the night sky. His demeanor had completely changed, and I wasn't sure if I should continue with the conversation while we're both upset or let things calm down and try to talk tomorrow. I would love children in the future, but not while I was in school. Sabrina and Janice were prime examples of married women with kids who handled their responsibilities.

For Axel to blow me off like I was crazy to want kids was stupid. We hadn't talked about the big stuff, but I knew we loved each other. He'd see that being an enforcer for the rest of his life and having nothing to show for it beyond money couldn't bring happiness.

I got up, stepped into the suite and found him lying in bed watching American football. I climbed over his lap and placed a hand on his naked chest. "I don't want to fight."

"I don't either."

I chose my words carefully. "Can we call a truce for now?"

He turned to face me. "Laurent put me in a position to be who I wanted to be. Nothing will change that. My conscience is clear and I stand behind my decision to stay in the cartel."

"I get that."

"Then I will never have this conversation again. You may have the Carrington last name, but it means nothing to me as your husband. You might be the Boss of the cartel, but not me."

My only response to his words was a nod of agreement. He kissed me and shifted his attention back to the game. I climbed under the covers and dozed off with a lot on my mind to take back with me to Italy. We had plenty of opportunities to create whatever we wanted together. Children weren't an immediate priority, but I couldn't deny I wanted Axel's babies at some future point. I wanted children to love, especially with the way I grew up. I didn't want to continue the negative cycle and pressure placed upon me.

Chapter 17

Axel

Silence spread as soon as the metal door closed. Gigi's boots clanked against the floor. We'd been back from Italy for a week and stayed low, only coming out briefly to handle business at the farm.

I'd helped to assemble Gigi's resources for battle with Lamberto and Dario, but it was up to Gigi to command the room and get all the guys to respect her as the Don of the family.

My eyes raked over each man as they studied her. The only thing they wanted was to know she wouldn't lead them into something without a plan. There were two types of Bosses—those who led without crumbling and those who did. Dario left crumbs that would lead to his own demise.

Today, Antonio had arranged for us to meet with the team for backup to deal with Dario and Casella.

"Gael, pleasure to meet you." Gigi extended a hand.

"Nice to see you both," Gael responded.

"What did Joaquin have to promise you to assist?" I asked.

He chortled. "More than you can imagine. I had to leave my wife and kid, so it cost you a lot."

"I'll be more than happy to repay," Gigi replied.

Gael glanced at Axel. "You know he owes me."

"Your husband owes me for saving his life, plus he can afford it," Gael remarked.

Gigi frowned. "I don't understand."

"Axel isn't broke. I hope you don't think he's only operating off his money from the mafia," Gael said to annoy me. We'd bantered back and forth like brothers for years.

"She knows enough," I countered.

My heart raced as Gigi stared at me suspiciously.

"Investments and money from my parents," I said, easing her mind.

"Oh," Gigi responded.

"Tell me what this is all about and why I needed to be here," Gael grumbled.

Gigi leveled her gaze on every person in the room. "I requested for you all to be here today. This is life or death, but I would not ask for something I wasn't prepared to sacrifice myself for."

"Casella has hands in everything. What are you proposing?" a guy in the corner of the room asked.

"Orson Casella is behind my father's murder."

The room fell silent.

"What proof do you have?" another soldier demanded.

"Dario Ramini and Lamberto, my underboss, set it in motion," I responded.

There were grumblings and whispers.

"To state something like that without proof could mean death for us all," one blurted out, brows knitted together.

"We have proof," I answered, dragging my eyes away.

Gael's gaze darkened.

"Axel and I are married. Dario is hell-bent on destroying my life because I chose someone else," Gigi explained.

"Antonio and Joaquin okayed this union?" Gael wondered.

I opened my mouth to reply when the windows shattered with the staccato of gunfire. I lunged for Gigi and pulled her down, covering her with my body.

"Stay down!" I patted along her arms and legs to check for any wounds.

"Are you hit?" she questioned, reaching to grasp my hand.

"Fine. Stay next to me." Pulling the weapon attached to my ankle, I handed it to her before pulling my gun.

Gunfire exploded around us as I lifted Gigi into my arms and backed out of the room toward the exit stairs.

Gigi screamed, and I tightened my grip on her, running and aiming my gun, when the door behind us burst open.

"It's me!" Gael yelled.

A few men entered behind him as bullets hit the walls. Sirens blared close by, and I spotted the door leading to the alley just as someone yanked it open.

I raised my gun and returned fire. The other person dropped to the ground.

"Shit!" Gigi's voice trembled as I lowered her to her feet.

"You're fine. We're almost out of here."

We stepped over the body, and I peeked into the hallway. "This way." I kept her behind me, with Gael at her back.

"How did they know we'd be here?" Gigi whispered.

I didn't reply, but my gut told me Dario was behind this.

A quick glance through the office windows showed nobody there. "Fulgenzio is probably in the back if he heard the gunshots," I muttered.

"Take the stairs. The elevator is sitting ducks," Gael spoke.

I ran a hand over my head and glanced out of the window to the streets, now slammed with police and ambulances.

"Fuck. We have to go through the back before the cops come."

"Follow me." Gael was loyal, and I knew he wouldn't sabotage or jeopardize our friendship.

We ran through the exit to the back alley. I was relieved when I saw Fulgenzio with the car, waving for us to climb inside. I got Gigi in safely and slammed the door behind Gael and me, punching the window in frustration.

"Calm down. We're okay," Gigi said, her eyes filling with tears.

"Fulgenzio, take the alley onto the freeway. We need to stay off the radar," I commanded. I pulled Gigi to me and pressed a kiss on her forehead.

Gael pulled his phone out and sent a text as Fulgenzio swerved onto the main road.

* * *

Hours later, we ended up at the farm. Gigi showered in the bathroom with the door open while I contemplated my next moves.

"Is she alright?" Turin asked at the end of the phone.

I watched her warily when her head fell into her hands. "No, she's shaken up."

"Do you need me to come out there?"

I chewed on my lower lip. "No. Find Dario and Lamberto."

"Did you lock down the farm?"

"Yeah." I rubbed my eyes.

"Whenever you give one-word answers, I know you're ready to kill someone."

I huff in amusement. "He made a bad choice today."

"Dario and Lamberto often do, but that doesn't mean you retaliate out of frustration without thought."

Turin was always giving me a reason to pause before reacting, but no one would be able to stop me once I got my hands on them. Not even God.

"Gael is here," I muttered.

"He's a good pick. Listen to him."

"Any news on Orson?"

Turin sighed. "Not yet, and it's pissing me off. Usual hangouts are dry."

"Make sure we get word soon. Be ready to kill everybody if no one comes clean."

His voice faded in and out. "Lamberto won't let you kill Dario."

"He'll have no choice once I kill his family."

"Think before you act."

The shower turned off. Gigi stepped out and wrapped herself in a large towel.

The nagging in the back of my mind refused to let me think straight. "Keep me updated."

"I pray you remember you have a soul," Turin said.

"My soul died with my parents." I clicked end and dropped the phone on the counter.

Gigi approached, and I pushed a few wet strands of hair out of her face.

She exhaled a heavy breath. "How are you feeling?"

"Worried about you," I answered.

Gigi stepped into my arms, and I buried my face in her neck, caressing her back as I held her close.

"I was proud of you today."

A sense of inadequacy swept over me. "Me? Why?"

Slowly, she picked up the dry towel on the counter and wiped the excess water off her

chest. "You protected me like you promised."

That surprised me. "I'll always protect you."

Looking away, she muttered, "Yes, but to see it in action made me love you more."

"We should eat."

She shook her head and stifled a smile. "There you go, changing the subject, when feelings are involved."

I took a seat on the couch near the window, watching Gigi continue to dry off and change into fresh clothes. Trucks arrived on schedule to take the next load out for a gun sale with the Irish Mob. I drew my fist up in frustration at the thought of all of my enemies being able to get that close.

"My father built up an incredible reputation. To see his life cut short isn't fair," Gigi murmured.

"Too bad he won't see how far you've come."

She slipped onto my lap. "Is that a bad or good thing?"

I kneaded her thigh gently. "You're a good thing, Gigi." I pointed to her heart. "Never think otherwise."

"Honestly, I felt like you thought I was a selfish, spoiled, naive girl."

I nipped her chin. "You were."

She gasped and slapped me on the chest. "I knew I shouldn't have married you. Maybe I can find someone to take your place."

I held her down as she started to get off my lap. "What I mean is that you showed growth and maturity, but I liked when you were selfish and spoiled because at least you owned who you were. Not like most women."

"We've never talked about your past girlfriends."

I measured how to answer her question. "Girlfriends don't work in my world."

Her eyes narrowed at my answer. "Ugh, you are an asshole."

"Yeah, but I'm your asshole." I smirked, kissing her lightly. "We need to go talk to Gael about our next moves."

My phone rang in the bedroom, and I extricated myself from Gigi to answer it.

"Where is she?" Dario demanded.

"In front of me. Why?" I asked as Gigi joined me.

"I heard what happened."

My lip curled. "How did you hear?"

"Some of my men called me. Plus, my father."

"Tell everyone she's fine with her husband."

He laughed. "You think that fake marriage means anything to me?"

"You can believe whatever you want. The marriage license proves we're married."

"Cyrus was paid off. That won't hold up in court."

"That's the excuse you're going to use? Just admit she wants nothing to do with you beyond work." If I let on that I knew he was behind everything, we'd spook him and Orson.

"The moment she sees you for the crazed animal you are, she'll crawl back to me."

"There's always a risk of that."

"Are you making moves outside of the cartel?" Dario asked, indicating he knew about New York.

My forehead creased in irritation. "Why do you ask?"

"Any time my family is in jeopardy, I need to know."

"The Ramini family has no sway with me."

"Carry on, Axel, and find yourself on an island alone." Dario's anger was punctuated by the dial tone.

I could only wonder what his next move would be.

Gigi took one look at me and anger lit her eyes. "Dario threatened me again?"

"Leave the worrying to me."

She cuddled up to me. "Our life will never be normal."

I kissed the top of her head. "Only we can make it normal."

She sighed. "I need to talk to my mom and check in on her."

"Make sure to leave out the shooting."

Gigi nodded, picked up my phone, and dialed her number. I climbed off the bed and went to check in with Gael and Fulgenzio, who were outside by the barn.

"That was a close call today." Gael stood with his arms crossed.

I kicked the rocks into the grass. "You're here for a short time, and I appreciate the backup. If you need to get back to your family, I understand."

"Never ran away from a fight."

"She's all I care about." I pointed at Gigi as she stood in the window on the phone.

"Wouldn't doubt that. My family comes first for me."

"A battle with three other families won't turn out well," I said as more trucks drove away without supplies of guns.

"Joaquin and Antonio knew what they were doing when they requested I come here to help," Gael reminded me.

"Liaise with my right hand, Turin, to catch you up on everything."

"Send me his number."

"Fulgenzio is going into town and can drop you off."

"If we strike now, they'll be caught off guard. Set up an exit plan," Gael suggested.

"I never run from a fight," I said, repeating his earlier words.

"Only cowards run. But we may need to lie low after the smoke clears. Bloodshed tends to reach the political spectrum in Italy."

"Gigi's talked about moving permanently to America."

"An option you should keep in your back pocket."

"Weakest move he made was killing Laurent."

"Men like him only think in the moment," Gael pointed out. "Laurent probably got close to the truth."

"I tested him earlier about how he heard what happened."

Gael smirked. "Dario deserves credit for being so bold."

"When I wrap my hands around his throat, I'll give him all the credit he deserves."

Chapter 18

Axel

A turbulent passion swirled around Gigi; it was like she held my heart in her palm. To please was my mission and goal tonight.

She stepped off the bed and sauntered toward me in only her lingerie. When I tried to speak, she covered my mouth with her finger. "Let me take your jacket." She slid her hand under my jacket and threw it on top of the dresser.

Gigi held her breath as my fingers teased the soft skin of her inner thigh. I tugged at her nipple and moved my free hand between her thighs.

"One thing you haven't let me explore is how to please you," she murmured, unbuckling my pants as she walked us back to the bed. She cupped my erection in her hand and stroked.

Sitting on the edge of the bed, Gigi kissed the head of my dick. She looked up at me, her eyes burning with desire and the need to please me.

"Fuck, you're beautiful like this." I snatched off my shirt

and kicked off my shoes. "Just take it easy, and don't use your teeth."

The flush of her cheeks showed she was inexperienced, but I loved to see her become more confident in the bedroom. A shiver ran up my spine when her warm mouth engulfed my dick, then suddenly eased back.

"Am I doing it right?"

"Yeah. Shit," I grunted

Gigi went further until she gagged and her lips swelled. A low groan left my lips when a few tears appeared in her eyes. Ready to be inside her, I grabbed the back of her head and gently pulled myself out of her mouth before claiming her swollen lips in a heated kiss. Hungry moans escaped her mouth as I nudged her back on the bed. I skimmed over her hips, pressing a kiss to both and nibbling her stomach.

"You smell so fucking good." I dipped a finger into her wetness, slowly flicking it across her nub.

"Baby," she choked.

I nipped at her soft skin. "Am I pleasing you right?"

"Yes. Oh, God." Gigi whimpered under my hold.

I pushed her thong down and slowly unrolled her stockings, planting kisses up each leg. Her stomach flexed with each touch as I tasted her. My tongue slowly circled her naval before I licked a trail to her breasts and gently bit each covered nipple.

I slid each bra strap from her shoulder, unhooked it, and tossed it aside. Picking up her wrist, I checked her pulse and smiled.

I kissed her deeply, leaving her weak and confused. "Just breathe, baby."

"Axel!" She gasped as I inserted a finger in her wet heat.

Moving down her body, I tossed her legs over my shoulder, keeping eye contact with the slow penetration of my tongue.

"Fuck," Gigi whispered as I snaked a hand up to tweak her nipple.

She jerked and tried to clap her legs around my head, the first hint of her orgasm coiling. I smacked her thigh, pushed her legs to her chest, and stuck my tongue in her asshole.

"Yes!" she cried as slick wetness coated her thighs.

Desperate to be inside her, I removed my pants, lined up my dick, and pushed forward, savoring the tightness of her pussy.

I let out a raw groan, pulling out and pushing back in three more times. My mouth grazed her earlobe before I kissed her on the lips. "Pretty pink pussy."

She smiled as she squeezed her inner muscles. I growled and interlocked our hands, hovering over her chest and drove harder and faster into her slick folds.

Releasing one hand, I caressed her sensitive, swollen nipples. "Goddamn," I grunted.

Her pussy throbbed around me. "Ah! Keep going."

"You sure, baby? You like this?" I shivered at the delight of her touch.

She nodded.

"No! Tell me with your words," I demanded, searching her eyes for understanding.

Her mouth dropped open, then closed.

"If you don't speak, I'm going to stop." I ran a thumb along her delicious wetness.

Her eyes popped open wide. "Yes, that's all I want."

"Let me hear you."

"All I want is you."

The shapely beauty of her naked body taunted me for more. "Every day I see you, I think of how good you feel."

"Uh, uh, shit," she whimpered

"I would drown with you." I told her my deepest thoughts. Sweat dripped down my body as I lowered to whisper in her ear. "I love you."

Tears pooled in her eyes, and I kissed each one away as we both came together. My dick twitched again. I closed my lips around hers, snaking my tongue inside her mouth to tangle with hers. Gigi wrapped her arms around my shoulders and we fell into a long make-out session, slowly rocking back and forth.

"I love you too," she purred.

* * *

"Any word yet?" I stood in the bathroom as I talked to Turin.

"We got something better."

My head pounded with anxiousness. "What?"

"Edmundo."

I looked over my shoulder to make sure Gigi was still asleep.

"We take a hit on him. That puts a bug in his ear."

Anticipation buzzed through my body. "Where is he?"

"I got him at a hotel."

A tense silence enveloped me. "Where are you?"

"Outside your house."

I grinned. "Keep the car running."

I marched back to the bedroom and checked the time. 3 a.m. I pulled on jeans and a black shirt and snatched up my jacket, wallet, and gun, then jogged out of the house to Turin's car. Fulgenzio was on high alert, and I lifted my chin in acknowledgment that I was leaving.

I climbed in the car. "How long has he been there?"

Turin glanced at me. "Four hours, maybe longer."

I checked the chamber on my gun. "Is someone sitting on him now?"

Turin held his phone out to show a photo of Edmundo going into a hotel room.

"He seemed like the type to be faithful."

"Men like him are only faithful to power. The minute his son was ready to take over as Boss, Edmundo set himself to get millions off these deals."

"Can't blame him."

"Are we going after Lamberto as well?"

I shook my head. "Not tonight. Depends on the conversation with Edmundo."

Turin inquired, "Did you tell Gigi?"

"No."

"Keeping things from her won't end well."

"Focus on the road."

It took an hour to reach the hotel where Turin had tracked Edmundo. Obtaining the room number, we stepped into the elevator. I watched the floors go up and breathed deeply to compose myself.

We stepped off the elevator and I followed Turin to a door, where he slipped a key into the lock quietly. We eased into the dark presidential suite with our guns drawn. The front room was empty, the TV off, and the blinds closed.

I opened the closet door and noticed a suitcase. I held it up, saw it was locked, and placed it back down. Wandering into the bedroom, I pressed my ear to the door. Turin made a motion with his hand and gun out, ready to go.

I slowly unlatched the door and opened it to see Edmundo in bed asleep with someone next to him. At Turin's nod, I moved to one side of the best while Turin moved to the other, his gun aimed at the sleeping man. I tapped Edmundo on the nose with the butt of the gun, and his eyes blinked open slowly.

"Huh... What the...?"

I place a finger to my lips to be quiet. Edmundo's eyes widened as they focused on me. He turned his head to see Turin.

"Axel," Turin whispered.

I watched as he drew back the covers from the other person to reveal Rosa Carrington.

"It's not what you think," Edmundo said, trying to get out of bed.

I gripped him by the shoulder and dragged him out.

"Edmundo, what is going on?" Rosa screamed.

"Keep quiet, Mrs. Carrington," Turin barked.

"Turin, have you lost your mind?" Rosa spat.

"How long has this been going on?" I queried.

Rosa pulled the covers up to her neck. "Edmundo, keep your mouth shut."

I nudged the gun to the side of his head. "Answer me."

"We've been having an affair for a while," Edmundo muttered under his breath.

"I told you to shut up. He's lying!" Rosa shrieked.

"Rosa!" Edmundo spat.

"Did Laurent know?" I rasped.

Rosa was clearly annoyed at us finding out. "What I do in my marriage is none of your business."

"Get dressed," I ordered, storming out of the room.

"No. You get out of here," Rosa replied.

I turned to face them. "Does Gigi know about your little affair?"

Rosa paled but ignored my question. "Why are you here?"

"Get dressed."

I marched into the living room, pacing back and forth. Minutes rolled by before they emerged from the bedroom with Turin.

"Sit." I gestured to the couch.

Rosa sat on the couch. "What we do as adults is none of your business."

"Where's Dario?" Turin questioned.

Edmundo hunched his shoulders.

I hit him across the face with the butt of my gun.

Edmundo yelped and covered his cheek.

"Have you lost your mind?" Rosa shrieked, standing in front of Edmundo.

"Laurent is dead because of his family and Casella."

Her eyes narrowed. "Nothing could be further from the truth. Laurent was friends with Edmundo and Orson."

"Then he'll tell me where Dario is hiding."

"My son is not hiding, and you're making a grave mistake." Edmundo grunted.

"Did Lamberto put you up to this?" Rosa demanded.

"Lamberto has no clue."

"So you follow your own rules like always." Rosa shifted and reached for the phone, putting it on speaker.

"Rosa, it's almost four in the morning," Lamberto grumbled.

"Axel has Edmundo at gunpoint," Rosa explained.

"Huh?" Lamberto mumbled.

"The real question is why are you here in a hotel room with Edmundo, a married man, and the Boss of another cartel?" I said coldly.

She shifted from one foot to the other. "Laurent and I had an understanding," Rosa revealed.

"Axel, what you are doing can't be undone," Lamberto stated.

"Then meet me at the office. We have a lot to discuss."

"Including you faking a marriage with my child," Rosa hissed.

"Gigi and I are married in every sense of the word."

"Under duress. I will have her committed to get her away from you."

"Rosa," Edmundo whispered.

"No, Edmundo. I'm sick and tired of her doing things behind my back."

"She's an adult. You haven't complained about the money in her trust fund," I pointed out.

"Another thing you have no clue about."

"Rosa, shut up!" Lamberto yelled.

I squatted down in front of Edmundo. "I'll ask you again. Where is Dario?"

"You don't have to answer that," Lamberto replied.

"If he wants to live—"

"Dario isn't responsible for your parents' deaths," Rosa snapped.

I froze. "Leave my parents out of this."

"You think avenging my husband will ease your guilt over not being able to save your parents," Rosa continued, undaunted.

"Rosa, leave it alone," Lamberto warned.

"He needs to know."

"Know what?" My voice was deadly calm.

"Your father was disloyal," Rosa stated.

Shock flew through me. "Liar!"

"It's not a lie, and you poisoning my daughter about Dario will only end in her leaving you," she seethed.

Ignoring her, I returned my attention to Edmundo. "I won't ask again."

"Axel!" Lamberto shouted.

Frustrated, I fired a warning shot.

Rosa screamed.

"Shit," Turin groaned.

I wrapped a hand around Edmundo's neck and squeezed. "Tell me what you know."

Edmundo looked from me to Rosa.

"Shut up, Edmundo," she said coldly.

"Why look at her? Rosa, is there something I should know?"

Her mouth tightened. "I can help you if you want answers about your parents."

"You're trying to save yourself."

"At this point, I would be a fool to not give you the truth."

"Go ahead."

"Laurent had your parents killed," Rosa confessed.

Edmundo's eyes ballooned in surprise.

I got in her face. "You're lying."

Rosa backed up. "Axel, I would never lie about something like that."

"Laurent and my father got along great, like brothers."

"Edmundo can explain, but he was stealing from my husband."

Edmundo lowered his head, covering his eyes in frustration.

"Keep going."

She darted her eyes around the room. "Only if you remove the gun."

"Not happening."

"He stole two million dollars. I overheard him in conversation with Lamberto and Edmundo," Rosa whispered.

"Shut the fuck up, Rosa," Edmundo barked.

Amusement glinted in her eyes. "You loved your father, but he was disloyal to the family."

"Stop with the lies. Rosa. You're just trying to cover for your affair."

"How do you think you got the money from the insurance policy? Laurent felt terrible about everything and gave you a job."

"Then who set the bomb?"

Rosa was momentarily speechless. "That I don't know."

"Dario isn't off the hook."

Tongue-tied, she sat in shock. "You need to keep this under wraps."

"Gigi has to deal with her parents' betrayals the same as I have." I turned and walked away.

Rosa wasn't off the hook, and Edmundo was worthless, like his son, allowing others to handle his business decisions. Even if their affair was based on love, the cartel wouldn't allow it to go on once everything was out in the open. It would look bad on all fronts.

Chapter 19

Gigi

Dario was off the radar, and that pissed me off and stressed me out. Axel hadn't come back to the farm, so I had Fulgenzio drive me back to his condo, ready to confront my husband for skipping out on me during the night.

Before I could insert the key, the door was yanked open. "Turin!"

"Hi, Gigi. He's in there, but he's in a mood," he replied in a low, husky tone.

"What do you mean?"

"He can explain everything, but it has to do with his parents and your mother."

My brows dipped low in confusion as I stepped through the door and removed my coat. "Okay. Are you going to the office?"

He checked his watch. "For a little bit. We have to run the surveillance from the shooting."

"Please make sure I have the information by the end of the day."

"Sure thing." Turin hugged me.

I sauntered into the living room and laid my coat on the couch, smelling cigar smoke through the air. I approached the kitchen and saw Axel with a glass in his hand and a cigar.

"Either you killed someone, or someone pissed you off," I joked, but he didn't laugh. I closed the space between us. "Hey, you all right?"

He blew out smoke. "Have you spoken with your mother?"

"No. I came back from the farm because you left in the middle of the night."

He grunted, drank the rest of his vodka, and poured another one.

I pointed at the glass. "How much have you had to drink?"

"Not enough."

"Seems like something is bothering you," I said in a soft voice, letting him know I wasn't the enemy.

"Something or someone." He gazed at me.

I planted a hand on his chest. "Did I do something to hurt you?"

"No."

"What's with the attitude and the distance?"

His laugh was harsh. "I can't have space?"

My mouth dropped open. "In what world does a married couple need space?" Maybe I was naïve, but we couldn't go to sleep angry at each other, not after the last few days of us getting closer.

"Gigi, I need a break."

"A break?" I scoffed.

He rubbed his forehead. "A few minutes to think."

"About what? Talk to me and I may be able to help."

"Rosa said your father killed my parents." His voice broke.

My heart beat faster. "And you believed her?"

"Who else can I trust to tell me the truth?"

"Me! Your wife."

"If you knew the things I've seen over the years, you would understand."

There was truth in his statement. I'd never be able to understand his life, but I would always listen and remind him of the great man he'd become. "Then talk to me about them."

"She said he stole two million dollars and your father found out."

I cupped his face. "He loved your father."

"I guess not enough."

"Rosa is a liar. You can't trust her."

"I caught—" He stopped abruptly.

"Caught what?"

"Nothing." He relaxed and put the glass on the table.

"Trust works both ways and I've given you my trust in this marriage, from my heart, body, mind, and soul. Let me help you."

"You know Dario and Lamberto are working together."

I nodded. "Yes, I saw the evidence."

"Last night, Turin called me to meet him."

"Okay, did you find Dario or Orson?"

He shook his head. "No, but it was still a surprise."

"Feels like you're keeping something from me. Same as my parents."

He regarded me with impassive coldness. "Never compare me to them."

Only a few hours ago, we'd given each other undeniable respect and admiration. "Speak then."

"Rosa was in bed with Edmundo."

I stared at him. "Edmundo Ramini?"

"Yes."

I laughed. "Axel, I think you've had too many glasses of vodka."

"It's true, Gigi."

I shook my head. "My mother may be a lot of things, but she isn't a cheater."

"Ask Turin."

"I can ask my mother. She wouldn't lie about something that big."

"I'm starting to think you only hear what you want rather than the truth, Gigi."

"Rosa is a bitch. I know her better than you, but she would never betray my father like that."

"I saw it with my own eyes! Edmundo and Rosa in bed at a hotel."

I dug into my pocket and removed my phone and sent a message to Turin.

Me: *Send me the picture of Edmundo.*

"Who are you texting?" His brows knitted together.

"Turin."

His eyes darkened dangerously. "Are you saying you don't trust me?"

I cocked my head to the side. "Even you have to know it would never happen. It's gossip, and my family doesn't need to be hounded."

"No, I'm trying to get you to understand. As the Don of the cartel, you can't leave room to fuck up, even if it's your family," he remarked.

My heart raced. Maybe I was in denial because why would she do something like this and trample over the family name? Dad hadn't even been gone six months, and she'd already found someone who was not only married, but his son was supposed to be my husband.

Turin: *She's back home now.*

Me: *Thank you.*

I stared at the photo, and sure enough, she was in a shirt in a hotel room with Edmundo on the couch. My throat tightened with emotion. "Wow."

Axel pulled me closer and kissed my forehead. "I know you're pissed, but you need to wait before you confront her."

"She's disloyal. How can you say I should ignore what's in front of me?"

"Because Edmundo will lead us to Dario, and if Rosa can control Edmundo..."

I hated that Axel was right.

"My instinct is always to protect you, even from yourself."

"I can't believe my father would kill your parents," I whispered.

He paused, dropping his hands to the side. "The truth will come out."

"What does that mean for us?"

"As of right now, you trust me, and I trust you."

* * *

The moment I made the decision, I regretted it. It wasn't right, but I needed answers, and he was the only one who could give them to me. Axel and I had been distant the last few days after his huge bombshell. I was disgusted that my mom would lie on her back for someone else.

"Stay in the car, Fulgenzio." I reached for the door handle, pushing it open. Fulgenzio hadn't been happy when I demanded to be taken to a potential enemy's home.

"He's going to kill me if I don't go inside with you."

"Who's going to tell him?"

His mouth tightened and he shook his head.

"Besides, they won't do anything in broad daylight with cameras everywhere." I stepped out and shut the door, sauntering up to the front door and ringing the bell.

"Miss Carrington, we've missed you around here," the Ramini's housekeeper said.

"It's Mrs. Bresciani now, Celestina." I held up my left hand.

"You got married." Her eyebrows stretched high.

"I did. Is Mr. Ramini here?"

"Yes, in the backyard. Follow me." She stepped aside and closed the door behind me.

I hadn't been back to their home in months, possibly a year. Nothing had changed. Mrs. Ramini was a stickler for ensuring the place looked like a show home.

I thanked Celestina as she opened the back door. Edmundo was pacing back and forth while on the phone. I removed my purse and placed it on the table before taking a seat.

"Gigi, what a surprise." He finished the call and motioned for Celestina to leave us alone.

"Is it?" I clasped my hands together, crossed my legs and made direct eye contact.

He took a seat across from me. "Not an unpleasant surprise, but to what do we owe this visit?"

"Come on, Edmundo. Let's not kid ourselves."

His eyes narrowed. "Edmundo?"

"That's your name."

"A few weeks ago, I was going to be your father-in-law. Have you forgotten I'm cartel hierarchy?"

I lifted my shoulders. "Is that supposed to mean some-thing? I'm the Don of the family and I go by Gigi."

He gritted his teeth. "Watch it."

"Or what? Tell me exactly how you will disrespect me? Because you've betrayed my father by sleeping with his wife," I hissed.

His eyes shifted as he gulped. "I don't know where you heard that ridiculous allegation, but it's not true."

"Were you talking to my mother before I interrupted?" I propped my arm on the back of the chair.

"Rosa and I are friends."

"I would respect you more if you were honest with me."

"He lied. We were only talking."

"Oh, talking? And who is he?"

"Listen to me. Dario is not happy about your broken engagement. There's still time to get back together and move forward as a united family."

"Unlike you, Edmundo, I respect my marriage."

He chuckled, and his eyes darkened. "You little bitch. You have no idea what to do with the power you have."

I was finally seeing the real Edmundo. "Tell me what to do with it then?"

He pressed his finger on the table. "I should have trusted my instincts and told Dario to drop the idea of you and him."

"Something we can agree on."

"Yes, I slept with your mother and will continue to sleep with her."

The casual way he spoke about their affair disgusted me.

"Nothing to say? I guess the cat's got your tongue now. What can I say? Your mother's an attractive woman and she needed comfort. She felt abandoned by your father."

"Son of a bitch!" I slammed my hand on the table.

"Little princess can't handle the truth about her father."

"My father got you in the position you're in today and this is how you repay him?"

"Laurent was a bastard. He wanted to control everything and cut my family out."

"That's not true."

"If you take the blinders off, Gigi, you'll find your parents aren't perfect."

"Sounds like I should be saying this to Dario."

"Get out of my house. We have nothing else to discuss."

"We have plenty to discuss, considering someone tried to kill me."

"Not my burden."

"Where's your son?"

"Dario is out of town."

"Why are you lying for him?"

"He's preparing deals for the cartel."

"Without consulting me first?"

"Lamberto should have communicated. He's the underboss."

"I know you're behind the lie that my father killed Axel's parents."

Edmundo grinned.

Our stare-off continued until the door slid open.

"Gigi, I heard from Celestina you were here." Mrs. Ramini held her arms out for a hug.

I embraced her out of obligation, but nothing between us felt like genuine love anymore. "I came to talk with your husband."

"I'd love for you to stay for lunch."

"Sorry, I have another engagement."

"Gigi, we aren't mad that you and Dario can't work out your differences," Mrs. Ramini stated.

"Thank you."

She glanced at me, then at her husband. "I guess you two have something important to talk about. We can chat some other time."

"Yes, another time."

"Oh, tell your mother I said hello and not to forget our shopping trip," Mrs. Ramini remarked.

"She will love that, won't she, Edmundo?" A solid look of guilt appeared on his face.

Mrs. Ramini smiled and walked away.

Edmundo jumped out of his seat and charged at me.

I reached into my purse to grab my gun, and he gripped my arm. "Try anything and I'll scream," I seethed.

"Get the fuck out of my house. If you want to continue to have my support, you'll ignore what you've heard."

I dropped the frown and smirked, snatching my arm away.

"Fuck your support." I strode into the house and out the front to my awaiting car.

"Everything worked out?" Fulgenzio pushed the gas and drove out of the area.

"It will in time."

My phone rang and I pulled it out of my purse to see Axel's name. I looked at Fulgenzio. "Did you tell him?"

"Who?"

"Fulgenzio, you're my guard. I have to trust you."

His eyes cast down. "I'm sorry, Mrs. Bresciani. He's my boss."

"No, I'm your boss and friend. I can handle myself. Axel will freak out for no reason."

"Yes, ma'am."

I tossed the phone back in my purse and threw it on the seat.

Later that evening, I visited the farm to inspect how

things were going and found Turin in the office. I walked in and shut the door behind me, scanning the office holding records of my father's business.

Turin studied my face. "Gigi, what are you doing here so late?"

"Axel doesn't know I'm here." I dropped my coat on the chair.

Turin looked behind me and saw Fulgenzio at the door for protection. The scowl on his face reminded me of Axel. "Where is he?"

"Working."

His expression stilled and grew serious. "Sit, please."

"Thank you." We'd never had a conversation without other people around, and I wanted to pick his brain. Not only about my father's business, but as a longtime friend of Axel.

"Running through the numbers."

"How are they looking?"

He scratched the back of his head. "Not great."

"Tell me the truth, Turin. Seems like everybody wants to control me."

"You know how this business runs. Laurent would tell you to focus on what you can see in front of you."

"He would want me to be two steps ahead and not foolish."

Turin sat back in his seat, lacing his hands behind his head. "What do you know so far?"

A faint smirk spread across my face in disgust at my comment. "Edmundo and my mother are having an affair."

He waited before he spoke. "Did you talk to her yet?"

I sat back in the chair in a huff. "No, but I plan on it."

Turin ran down the details. "Okay, well, you know Dario and Lamberto are working together."

"Yes. How do all the pieces come together?"

"That's the mystery. Orson is working with Edmundo somehow."

"But Ramini and Carrington have a long-standing deal. Casella is not to have more than what they negotiated in the truce."

Turin flipped the papers in his hands. "Money is being taken monthly."

I sat forward. "Where does it go?"

"Million-dollar question."

"I know Dario is behind the shooting and he's supposedly out of the country."

He lifted a folder and placed it in the drawer. "Did Edmundo tell you that?"

"Yeah, and something tells me he's lying."

Turin clasped his hands together. "Protecting his money."

"They've never had a loving father-and-son relationship beyond Dario wanting to be in his shadow."

"We'll catch Dario, but Lamberto needs to be handled."

"Trying to take him out too early would put me in a bad spot."

"All the families will have to agree on his removal."

I spread my hands wide. "Do you think... never mind."

"Tell me." Turin leaned back on his elbows.

"Do you think all the families gave permission to kill my father?"

The door slammed open and I swung around to see an angry Axel.

"Turin, give me the room," Axel said quietly.

"Axel, I can—"

He lifted a hand to cut me off.

Turin stood and approached Axel, whispering something in his ear before leaving the office.

Axel rolled up his sleeves and glared at me.

I stood slowly, my throat tight with nerves.

"What did you accomplish?" he asked in his thick accent.

I paused. "Accomplish?"

"Please don't repeat. You heard me."

His dominating attitude and boldness to challenge me proved I wouldn't run over him like I did with everybody else. I shouldn't be turned on, but it was kind of hot.

"Edmundo only confirmed the affair."

"Anything else?" He stalked toward me.

"Dario is out of town working on a deal." I mumbled the last part.

"Out of town. Right."

"Where were you?" I changed the subject.

"Busy." With long, purposeful steps, he moved in front of me.

I licked my lips, awaiting his next move. "With what?"

"I had to oversee a drop-off at the dock."

"Is that why you're mean and aggravated right now? Did something happen?"

His hand dragged over my cheek. "Everything is fine."

"Did Orson get a clue that we are moving away from them?"

"He didn't. I'll let him know, though."

I ran my hands over his shoulders and up his neck, standing on tiptoes to press my forehead against his. "I want to be there."

"No."

I poked him in the chest.

He looked down at my finger. "You went to see Edmundo and came here without telling me. You need to lie low."

"I'm not running."

"One thing Laurent always told me is to never get

comfortable." His words were etched in my mind, and I knew what my next decisions would mean for me. I couldn't attempt a big shot at anyone without having a backup plan. None of those men took me seriously as a mob boss. I needed to stand firm in what I wanted, with or without Axel's approval.

"Edmundo is spooked now, so we need to be careful," he muttered.

"Are you still upset about my father?"

He released a breath. "I don't want to believe he's behind my pain, especially when he brought me into the fold. At some point, he probably figured I would find out."

"Do you believe Edmundo and my mom? Because it could've been an excuse to throw you off."

"Maybe, but I'll find out."

"Let's go home."

He kissed the top of my head. "No more going rogue."

"Can't promise you anything."

I repeated his words from the fake marriage. Our noses nuzzled, and I sank into his chest, closing my eyes. Our relationship would be different from my parents' and I wouldn't let anyone determine how it should be. Turin made some valid points, and I wanted to ensure my decisions were clear to the family. Rosa made it her mission to hurt me no matter what, but she wouldn't win at taking Axel away from me.

Chapter 20

Axel

I dried off, dropped the towel on the counter, and brushed my teeth. Earlier this morning, Turin called and said he wanted to meet and it was important for me to come alone. I'd crawled out of my warm bed with Gigi still asleep to get prepared for more bullshit.

"Morning, are you hungry?" Gigi wrapped her arms around me from behind.

I looked down at her hands. "I'll get some on the way."

Gigi released me, and I turned to face her. She lifted a hand to smooth my hair. "Who are you meeting?"

"Turin."

"Should I be there?" Gigi took my hand and interlocked our fingers.

I pulled back to watch her. "No."

"Axel, are you keeping something from me?"

I ignored her question and leaned down to kiss her.

"Where is your head at after the news of your mother?" I had issues I wanted to escape from, but I wanted to make sure she was handling the situation with her mother.

She placed her hands on my chest. "Trying to decide if I want to confront her."

My hands slipped down to her hips. "That's a decision you have to make alone."

She raised her lips for another kiss. "What if I want your opinion?"

"My feelings about your mother wouldn't be helpful." I patted her on the butt. "Talk to her."

"She betrayed me."

"She betrayed your father, not you."

Gigi's face dropped and she stepped back, walking out of the room.

I stopped her before she left. "What did I say wrong?"

"Nothing, Axel."

"You say it like you're pissed at me."

She paused, dropping her shoulders. "Wouldn't matter."

"I'm confused. Explain."

"You have no feelings, so you don't care."

Her words pissed me off, but now wasn't the time for me to get upset. "My feelings are you should do what you want."

I walked into the closet and picked out a suit and shirt for the day. I placed them on the bed and started to get dressed.

"Why can't you give me an inch of sensitivity and listen?"

"I've given you more than any other woman."

Her eyes grew into slits. She marched out of the bedroom and I finished getting dressed. Ten minutes later, I entered the living room of an empty condo.

"Gigi!"

Silence.

"She's pissing me off," I mumbled and walked down the hall to the guest bedroom. Wrapping a hand around the knob, I found it locked.

"Unlock the door."

Silence.

I hated to be ignored. "Gigi, unlock this door right now."

Silence.

"If I shoot it open, I'll have a lot of people scared."

Silence.

I grinned at her avoiding me. "I guess this is what I have to expect whenever we disagree."

Silence.

My phone rang. I figured it was Turin letting me know he was here. I grabbed my wallet, keys, and gun, and left the apartment.

* * *

Turin pulled up in front of the local bar he owned and put the car in park. "He's in there."

"How many people are with him?"

"About three guards."

"What else do you know?"

"I did some digging about the day Laurent was killed."

My head spun toward him.

Turin handed me his phone. "I should have told you the same night, but I wanted to triple-check."

"These are text messages." I glanced at him.

"Rosa and Dario."

That caught my attention.

"She made the call," Turin announced.

My eyebrows slumped in disgust. "Rosa planned it all."

Rosa: *I'm giving you the chance to own the world.*

Dario: *How do I know this isn't a setup?*

Rosa: *No reason to lie to you.*

Dario: *Gigi will hate you.*

Rosa: *Edmundo and Lamberto got onboard.*

Dario: *I want Don's position.*
Rosa: *Then kill Laurent.*
Dario: *If I made it, what insurance do I have that I won't get caught?*
Rosa: *Boss moves come with Boss decisions.*

"Shit." I continued to scroll through Rosa's messages from Lamberto and Edmundo. Rosa even talked with Orson a few times.

"No one is trustworthy," Turin explained.

"Fuck!" Air stalled in my lungs. I couldn't breathe. Turin was right, I needed to have control and moving too fast would disrupt things.

"See now why I wanted to wait?"

It made my skin crawl that Rosa had more hands involved. "If this gets out, Rosa's not the only one who gets hurt."

"Gigi will be devastated."

It felt like the walls were closing in. I absentmindedly cracked my knuckles. "Fuck. Fuck!"

"It's your call." Turin waited for my answer.

"I need to think." Fear was something I'd never dealt with, and now it assailed me. It made me second guess all my choices with Gigi. I'd never had to worry about keeping promises until I agreed to us going into marriage.

"First, we handle Orson. Then I need to talk to Rosa."

Turin cocked his head to the side. "Is that wise?"

"She's my wife's mother."

He smirked. "Your wife."

"Fuck you."

"Time to get to Orson."

I thought of how crushed Gigi would be by Rosa's involvement with Laurent's death. It could send her to a place I wouldn't be able to reach.

Turin removed his gun, checked it, and climbed out of the car. A few men came from the alley and I moved around to the back to enter through the exit. Loud cheers rained over the room. I slipped up to the side of the bar and looked around the crowd, spotting a few people sitting in a corner booth. Orson kissed one girl, while another poured him a drink. Orson laughed with one of his guys, then picked up the glass of bourbon and forced the rest into his girl's mouth.

"Have someone bring him to the bathroom," I demanded, then turned and went to the men's bathroom, waiting in a stall.

A few guys walked by as I waited. I heard a loud laugh and knew it was Orson. I pushed the stall open and heard Orson grumble as he took a piss with his head down. Slipping on my black gloves, I stalked up to him, gripped the back of his head, and slammed it down on the top of the stall.

He shrieked in pain and swung his head to look up at me. "Shush..."

Orson tried to get up, and I knocked him back down. "A-Axel."

"You forced my hand, Orson."

His shoulders slumped. "I didn't do anything."

My mouth twisted in a threat. "I want the truth."

"Please, it wasn't me."

I slammed him into the stall again. Orson had fucked us over by deciding to not follow the rules Laurent had put in place. "What do you know about Rosa and Dario?"

Blood dripped down his face. "Rosa?"

"Rosa Carrington."

"We never talk."

"I know Rosa is behind Laurent's death."

Orson stiffened. "Laurent and I weren't friends, but we had an understanding."

I removed my gun and pushed it against his cheek. "What do you know?"

He raised his hands in the air. He was fucking disgusting.

I got a whiff of piss and became even more aggravated. "Tell me!"

"Rosa made a deal with Lamberto and Edmundo!" he shouted.

There's more to the story. "What did you get out of it?"

"If Laurent was taken out, Dario stepped in to broker a Casella and Ramini Cartel alliance."

"Who would control the zones?"

"If the plan goes through, Edmundo and Dario," Orson croaked out.

Carrington owned all the borders of Italy. We allowed Casella to get a portion through a truce, but they must have found a way to get rid of Laurent, and Edmundo had talked his son into running a bigger deal.

"Once again, Orson, you've disappointed me." I removed the safety and shoved it in his face.

"Please, Axel. We can help each other."

"Where's Dario?"

He stuttered. "I-I don't know."

"Wrong answer."

I pulled the trigger and Orson's dead body slid to the floor. I wiped the blood off my gloves and walked to the door, letting Turin inside.

"Cleanup crew is on the way," he said.

My hands itched to shoot him again. "He told me Rosa and Lamberto were on board with controlling all the borders."

"That would leave Gigi with nothing."

"They're trying to take over."

As we left the bathroom, the cleanup crew came in with their supplies to get rid of Orson's body.

"Time to deal with Edmundo."

"If we tip him off, that's a red flag and he might come after you," Turin pointed out.

After climbing into the car, I took my phone out and dialed Gigi's number. There was still tension between us from our argument earlier in the morning. Turin hit the gas and sped into oncoming traffic.

"She's not answering."

"Do you think she's still at the condo?"

"Let me check my cameras." I logged into the camera feed of my condo and watched each room; Gigi was not around. "She's not there."

"Check in with Fulgenzio."

Ending the feed, I dialed Fulgenzio.

"Sir, I'm with Mrs. Bresciani. Do you need to speak with her?"

I let out a relieved breath. "Where are you?"

Gigi knew I'd be irate if something happened to her, so skipping to hangout beyond school was an issue.

"At her usual lunch place with her friend," Fulgenzio answered.

"Keep her there. I'm on my way."

* * *

Turin kept the car running, and I hopped out and marched into the restaurant. Fulgenzio stood a few tables away. I glanced around him and saw Gigi, Ginerva, and two other people sitting at their table. Usually jealousy never peeked into my mind, but seeing my wife laughing with another man pissed me off.

I cleared my throat, cupped the back of Gigi's head, and bent down to kiss her on the lips. At first, she resisted and tried to move back, but I held her fast until she fully opened her mouth to my tongue.

"Why are you here?" Gigi quizzed.

"Who are your friends?" I pointed at the girl and the guy.

"These are classmates."

New people I never wanted to be around. "Come with me."

She halted my steps. "I'm in the middle of lunch."

"It won't take long."

"Axel," she sighed.

"Either we talk in private, or I can empty the entire restaurant." I held out my hand for her to take and pulled her into the hallway.

"You want to tell me why you interrupted my friends and me?"

I kissed her on the forehead and she flinched. "Get rid of your friend."

"Huh?"

I smiled at her discomfort. "The guy."

"Axel, you can't be serious."

"Have I ever joked?"

Alarm crept into her expression. "He's harmless."

"I told you already. I'm not in a playing mood. I know Ginerva and her family, but the new people will need to be vetted. And no guys."

"Jealousy. That's what this is right now."

"You ignored my call."

"It was on silent."

"Never have your phone on silent."

"Why are there so many rules? I want a normal life." Gigi threw her hands up.

A rebellious streak blazed inside me. "Too late for that. You're one of the most important people in Italy, even presidents and prime ministers."

She blew out a breath. "I needed to think after our fight."

"It was a disagreement, not a fight."

Gigi glared at me. "You always come back with semantics."

This was the complexity of being with me I wanted to avoid, no matter who I had in my bed—let alone as a husband. "How much longer are you going to be here?"

"Why?"

"We need some alone time."

"Is something wrong?"

"When we get home, I can explain."

"That sounds like more trouble," she huffed.

"I made a move and we need to discuss the consequences."

She looked apprehensive. "What move?"

"Say goodbye to your friends and meet me at the house."

"Wait! Tell me what you found out."

I started to walk off. "Not here."

"Okay, let me wrap up with Ginerva and my friends."

"I'll come with you so I can meet your little friend." I thought about all the ways I could alter her new friend's face.

"Please don't embarrass me," she pleaded.

"He should be embarrassed to be out in public looking for a death wish." I palmed her ass.

"Guys, sorry, I have a family emergency. I need to leave," Gigi explained, and they all stood to give her a hug.

"You can sit." I pointed at the guy.

His brows scrunched in confusion. "Excuse me?"

"Axel, please." Gigi grabbed my hand to calm me down.

"What's your name?" I was still high on adrenaline after

taking care of Orson, and anyone could be the cause of their own death if they pissed me off.

"Don't answer that," Gigi told her friend.

"He can speak for himself. From the way he laughed at your joke, he's comfortable in your presence," I snipped.

"Turin, can you help?" Gigi pleaded.

Turin stood off to the side with a hard expression.

"Turin can't save your little friend."

"Maybe you should go." Gigi tried to get the guy to leave.

I placed my gun on the table. Everyone jumped back.

"Axel!" Gigi hissed.

"Hey, I only take a class with her," the guy stuttered.

"As of today, you'll transfer to another class. Better yet, another school," I demanded.

All eyes widened in shock.

"Are you insane? I'm sorry, everyone. Talk later." Gigi shifted around me and walked out the door.

I removed money from my wallet to place on the table and picked up my gun. "By the end of today, I expect you to no longer be in her school."

He agreed with a nod.

Turin and Fulgenzio were outside as Gigi sat in the back seat with the door open.

"That was embarrassing," Gigi snapped.

I leaned down, poking my head inside. "Go home. We'll talk."

"I'm not in the mood to talk."

"Then we can find something else to do."

I straightened and shut the door, waiting for Fulgenzio to start the ignition and pull off before stalking toward Turin's car.

Turin raised an eyebrow. "That could have been handled differently."

"When have I ever handled anything easy?"

He chuckled.

Gigi would learn soon enough. There were too many people out to end her, and the smallest slip up could be fatal if she let her guard down.

Chapter 21

Gigi

I used the tip of my tongue, making circular motions up and down his length as he jerked out the last of his cum. I was giddy. I was still new at giving him oral pleasure and he allowed me to take my time. A tremor heated my thighs and pussy. He helped me stand in the shower and turned me to face the wall. One hand rested on my hip and the other on my shoulder.

I planted my hands on the wall as he thrust forward. "Oh, God."

"Shit." He licked my neck and sucked on my ear.

His touch was divine ecstasy. A deep feeling of peace entered my being every time I was with him.

My head dropped forward. I closed my eyes, biting my lip as I stretched my legs out further. He leaned over my back and grasped my breasts, stroking me harder.

"My God. Don't stop, Axel."

"Good girl," he groaned when I rubbed his balls.

"Go faster, please." The quivering of my limbs weakened my knees.

He slapped my ass. "I give the orders," he growled, smacking my ass again.

I trembled under his grip. Axel pulled out and cut the water off. He picked me up and carried me to the bedroom, putting me on top of the dresser. He kissed a path down my stomach, spread my legs, and gently sank his tongue into my warm center.

"I want you forever, baby," he panted.

"Show me how much," I challenged.

My words spurred him on and something dark came over his eyes. He hooked my leg over his shoulder, slipping a hand under my ass to stroke his finger close to my asshole.

"Oh... yes. Oh... keep going," I panted as his warm fingers closed around me.

"Take it, baby. Take what you own."

"God, Axel. I... too much!" My body exploded with heat and I quivered with pleasure.

Axel dipped his head and sucked on my nipple. "You had enough?"

I wanted to say yes, but he'd win, so I shook my head.

Suddenly, he lifted me off the dresser. I yelped. "Don't drop me!"

He cupped my head and kissed me deeply. "Hold on."

I thought we'd move to the bed, but nope, he flipped me upside down and held onto my waist.

I clung to his legs as he entered me again. "Sir, please."

My heart rushed faster, and noises of our skin smacking together made him more determined to push me to the edge.

Axel lifted me up from my waist and I reached my arm around to grip his neck. Before I could say another word, we landed on the bed. His manly scent covered me while his thrusts excited me, causing ripple effects.

"Are you ready to come now, angel?"

"Yes," I whimpered.

"Then come for me, angel."

All I could feel then was his tongue on my pussy as I came. He covered me on the bed, caressing my body as I quivered from my orgasm. I slowly opened my eyes as Axel rose to see him grabbing a cloth from the bathroom. He cleaned me up, and gently pulled the covers around us as I drifted into a deep sleep. I had no man to compare him to, but he made me feel like I was the only woman for him.

* * *

Rosa still continued to play the naïve role and pretended she was innocent of the issues within our family. My heart broke when she didn't own up to the bullshit involving Dario. I had thoughts of her lying in the ground instead of my dad. Maybe then it would make sense why she went behind my back.

Fulgenzio opened the door of the slaughterhouse.

I strolled in and saw a few of Dario's men tied up on the ground. "What did you find out?"

Turin, Axel, and his men stood around.

"Lamberto and Edmundo are hiding Dario."

I arched my brow. "Hiding?"

"After the confrontation with Lamberto, Edmundo set it up for him to escape," Turin said.

"Where are they?"

"That's what they're here for." Turin indicated the bound men.

I removed my shades and moved closer to look at the four men on the ground.

"Keep your distance," Axel warned.

I nodded in agreement. "Gentleman, do you know why you're here?"

They stared at me without speaking.

"Remove his gag." I pointed at the blond, lean-built soldier with blood running down his eye. "What's your name?"

He didn't respond.

I cracked my neck. "I can do this all day if you want?" I snapped my fingers and he turned to face me. "Is Dario your boss?"

"Fuck you." He spat on the floor.

I smiled. "Is that supposed to scare me?" I squatted down in front of him. "I'm Gigi." Making them feel comfortable was something I'd learned from my father and mother.

He grunted and looked away.

"Today is your last day to hurt, my friend. Men like you worship your boss and somehow become delusional enough to die for them. I can help you." It would be naïve to think them scared by my words alone. I had to show them I called the shots and held their lives in my hand. They would tell me the truth, but they wouldn't be leaving this room alive.

"You're Laurent's bitch daughter."

Axel approached, but I lifted my hand as I stood. "I can handle him."

He grinned.

"Handle me then, bitch," he hissed, trying to lunge at me.

I kicked him in the head. "Tell my men where Dario is hiding!"

He scrambled to sit up. "Dario isn't hiding."

"Then where is he?"

"Where you least expect him to be." His statement gave me no clues, and I was tired of dealing with people who tried to mess with my head. "So you're ready to die for him?"

His eyes jolted up as Axel passed me the gun. I cocked it while he stood behind me with his hand on my hip.

"Aim for the head," he whispered.

I pulled the trigger, turned the gun toward the other men, and shot each one.

"Hey." Axel took the gun and cupped my face.

"I'm fine."

He kissed me on the forehead. "I'll clean this up."

"I need to run by the house."

Axel stood with me. "Okay. Take Fulgenzio."

"All right." I brushed a kiss against his lips and marched out to the awaiting car. The door shut, and Fulgenzio accelerated out of the area. I lay against the seat with my head down in thought.

I looked down at my phone as it buzzed.

Rosa: *Sweetheart, can we talk?*

I blew out a breath.

Me: *Yeah, call me.*

Rosa: *In person, Gigi.*

She always needed things her way.

Rosa: *Please.*

Me: *Okay. On my way.*

"Fulgenzio, can you go by my parents' home?"

"Yes, Mrs. Bresciani."

"Thanks. We won't be long. My mother needs to talk to me."

The distance would help to clear my mind. I sat back, crossing my arms over my chest.

Axel texted to check up on me.

Husband: *Are you good?*

Me: *I will be soon.*

Husband: *What does that mean?*

Me: *About to have that conversation I've been avoiding.*

Husband: *What are you talking about?*

Me: *We can talk later.*

Husband: *I don't like you being vague with me.*

Me: *I promise I'm fine.*

I set my phone on vibrate and waited to arrive.

Once at my parents, I got Fulgenzio to give me a few minutes alone.

"I'll scream if I need your help," I told him.

I shoved my key in the lock when it swung open.

"Finally. I was worried you'd forgotten," Mother said, reaching out for a hug.

I followed her to the kitchen and saw she had lunch prepared for us. "Is Aurora here?" I removed my jacket, putting it on the back of the chair.

"No, I sent her to the store. I wanted alone time with you."

"Alone time? Since when?" I picked up the fork and took a mouthful of the scallops.

"Stop playing, Gigi. You've always been my priority," Mother responded.

"How many drinks have you had?"

She dropped her fork. "I am the mother, Gigi, and you are the child. Please stop trying to control my decisions."

That was the opening I needed. "Control *your* decisions? That's funny, because I've heard a lot about you lately."

"From whom? That husband of yours? Please, don't become one of those wives who turns her back on her family for a man," she scoffed.

"Family? You've done nothing but sabotage this family."

"How dare you speak to me that way!"

"Mother, please, come down off your high horse and be honest with me."

"Shut up!"

My brow hiked at her balled fists by her side. To get this

upset meant some truth was in the air. If she thought I would let this go, she was mistaken.

"No, I won't shut up, Mother. I can't believe you had an affair with Edmundo Ramini."

She moved quickly, getting in my face. "That's a lie."

My muscles tensed. "Is it? Be honest."

"Baby, I love your father. We had many wonderful years." A change came across her face as she went into nurturing mode. Rosa couldn't fool me. I knew all sides of her personality.

I tried to calm my tone. "But you cheated."

She shook her head. "No, I've never cheated on him."

"I've tried so hard to gain your love."

"You have my love, but liking you lately is questionable by the company you keep." The real Rosa was back.

"Edmundo? Dario? Any of those names ring a bell?"

Her shoulders bunched up. "Both families are in business, so it's inevitable that people will see us out together."

"Turin and Axel found you in a hotel room with Edmundo."

She pointed her finger in my face. "That is disgusting! How dare you come in here and accuse me? You will regret how you've treated me," she growled.

"Why am I even here, Mother?"

"I wanted to clear the air between us and come to some sort of compromise. I'd like to build our relationship back to how it was before your father's death."

"You broke that trust."

"Everything I've done is for you."

I clapped my hands to emphasize my words. "Then. Tell. Me. The. Truth."

"Yes! I slept with Edmundo and I'll continue to see him."

"Make me sick to my stomach."

"Get over it and pray Dario takes you back. You're damaged goods now, but maybe we can convince him you were manipulated by Axel."

"I wanted Axel and pursued him. Dario and I will never be together."

"Axel is dangerous. You should want someone better for yourself."

"I want a mother who loves me."

She waved off my comment. If we would have had this conversation years ago, maybe we could have avoided this trauma.

Mother pointed the fork at my plate. "Eat your food."

"There's something else I need to speak to you about." I sat up straight.

"All these questions. My God, Gigi. Grow up."

"Did you work with Dario to take over the Carrington Cartel with Casella?"

Offended, she covered her chest with a hand. "I've never interfered in your father's business."

"I have it on tape." The idea of bribery stirred up in me.

My statement caught her off guard. "I... That can be doctored."

"At what point will you act your age and come clean?"

Her face twisted in anger. "You want the real truth?"

"For once, please."

"Axel is only using you for money."

"He has his own money," I corrected.

"From your father, of course, but he's after your trust fund."

"Then I gladly give it to him."

"Over my dead body."

"Well, hopefully you have protection because it's not looking good for you, Mother."

"What are you saying?" She blinked repeatedly; it finally seemed like I had her attention.

"I've tried to protect you, but Axel is on to you."

"On to me?"

"He told me you slept with Edmundo and worked with him to get Casella on board."

Mother grasped my chin. "Because he's trying to drive a wedge between us. Open your eyes!"

I removed her hand and put distance between us. "He loves me."

"The money is what he loves."

"Is it true Daddy killed his father?"

She shrugged.

"I need to know."

"If I told you, what would I get out of things?"

"That's all you care about? Money?"

"Yes."

"Wow."

She pressed her lips together, lifting her chin. "In time, you'll understand my choices."

I shook my head, annoyed by her response. "You're such a liar."

"I learned from your father. You think he was a saint? You're in for a rude awakening."

"He loved you."

"That man wasn't God, Gigi. Sorry I wasn't the perfect mother you wanted and needed, but I had to make adjustments and I'm owed for the time I put in with him."

"By trying to marry your daughter to a killer."

"You married Axel."

"Dario is behind Daddy's death."

She shook her head dramatically. "Dario would never hurt your father."

"Edmundo used you, and Dario is behind his death."

Rosa rolled her eyes and pushed her nose in the air. "That can't be any worse than the man you married."

"When you come to grips with who I love and where I am in life, I hope we can get back to a healthy relationship."

"You'll be waiting a long time." Rosa turned her back to me.

"Goodbye, Mother."

* * *

As soon as I got home, I stripped out of my clothes and threw up. If only my father was still here, he could tell me what to do.

I soaked in the tub with a glass of wine, candles, and the TV playing in the background. The disaster at lunch with my mother replayed over and over in my head as I tried to comprehend her actions. It was like she was a different person and not the mother I'd known all my life. How did you create a marriage, a life together, then have a child just to throw it all away for meaningless sex or money?

"So tired." I rested my head back.

The door squeaked open. "Fulgenzio told me you went to see your mother."

"Yeah." I took a deep breath, staring as he came closer.

"Anything you want to talk about?" He sat on the edge of the tub, caressing my cheek.

I rubbed my forehead. "So much. My head is spinning."

He shifted his weight. "We can talk, or if you need space, I can leave."

I grabbed his hand to stop him. "No, you're fine. I'm still in shock."

"Did she admit to anything?"

I released a long breath. "Sleeping with Edmundo. And she basically confirmed she worked with Dario to get Orson to cut a deal."

"Orson is conniving, but he's not a liar."

"I know."

"How long have you been in this tub?" Axel stuck his hand in the water; it was mildly hot.

He slid his hand across my shoulder, up to my neck. He titled my head back and leaned in to kiss me.

I moaned as his tongue swiped across my lips. "About an hour. As soon as I came back from her house."

Axel held my favorite soap sponge in his hand. He looked worn out. "I won't make excuses for her."

"She didn't make excuses beyond you being after my money, and I should go back to Dario."

Axel remarked, "That's never going to happen."

"I know. You've never asked me for money."

"Money never crossed my mind, but going back to Dario will never happen because he's going to be dead."

I smirked. "How was your day?" I put the wine glass on the floor, laying my head on his lap to face him.

He pinched my nose. "Worked some contacts to find Dario."

My hand slid up his chest. "What about Edmundo and Lamberto?"

"Lamberto isn't foolish like Dario. He knows hiding would make him look guilty."

I interlocked our hands, bringing them to my stomach. "Should I confront him?"

"Not yet. We got Orson, so they're scrambling. We can get him anytime." Axel leaned over to rub his nose against mine. His fingers lingered on my arm, and his breathing calmed.

"Wish I could go back."

"Life," he murmured.

"Harder than I thought."

We released each other and smiled.

"Maybe a little getaway will help you," Axel commented.

"The two of us."

Axel lifted my chin, eyeing me. "And a few men for protection."

"I'd love to hang with Sabrina and Janice again."

His hand caressed my breast. "In America." He reached for the sponge, dipped it in the water, and ran it across my chest to my stomach.

"Your hands feel so good."

"What about this?" He sucked on my bottom lip.

"More." I grinned, trying to pull him in for a deeper kiss. The tub was big enough for us both to continue an evening of bliss after the craziness of the day.

Axel stood. "Finish your bath and come eat. I'm in for the night."

I stuck my hand out for a shake. "Promise."

He chortled and lifted it up, kissing my hand. "Yes, angel."

He tempted me with another kiss, which spurred me to want sex. Axel pulled back, and I groaned in aggravation.

"Temptress," he joked.

I finished up and brushed my teeth. I came out of the bathroom and marched into the kitchen to dinner on the table and candles lit.

My mood was peaceful. "Axel, I wasn't expecting all this."

He pulled out my chair. "You know I don't do feelings or emotions well, but I see you're hurt."

"You're hurting too. If my father really is behind your parents' death, what will happen to us?"

"We can talk about that another time."

"Are you avoiding the topic?"

"No, I want a quiet dinner with my wife."

His words warmed me. "Okay."

He poured us a glass of champagne. "To us."

I smiled. "To us."

Chapter 22

Gigi

I was on the phone with Ginerva, walking to my next class, when a guy bumped into me and I dropped it on the ground.

"Sorry!" He hurried off into the library behind me.

"Jackass!" I yelled back and bent down to pick it up.

Large hands with a familiar tattoo appeared in my line of vision. "Don't scream, or I'll kill Fulgenzio where he sits."

"Dario, what are you doing?" I hissed, looking up to see his signature smirk.

"Turn around and pretend you forgot something."

"No." I swallowed hard, challenging his order.

A gun appeared in his hand. "Turn around."

"Axel will kill you." I slowed my steps to halt his kidnapping attempt.

"He won't catch me."

"You don't know my husband."

Dario yanked the library door open, shoving me down the hallway and to the closet in the corner. "You think you've won?" he growled.

"I know your father is going to have a closed casket for you," I taunted.

I gasped as his palm connected with my cheek.

Dario's eyes narrowed. "Talk to me like that again and see what happens."

I pushed him back. "Get the fuck off me!"

"Axel's gotten in your head, but I'm running things now, sweetheart," Dario said without remorse.

"Ramini's family is washed up. I no longer care what happens to your family."

His lip curled with contempt. "My family goes down, so will yours."

I was tired of being underestimated. "Try it and see."

Dario removed his phone and clicked on a video of my mother on the ground. She was dead.

I covered my mouth in horror. "You killed her! Mother-fucking bastard!"

"She owed me, same as your father," he seethed.

"Where is she?" I snatched the phone out of his hand to make sure I wasn't caught in some nightmare.

Dario's eyes glittered with satisfaction. "Dead in her home."

I shook my head in disbelief. "What about...?"

"Everyone is gone. The only way you survive is by committing to me. We stick to the original agreement and get married."

Savage anger burned in my chest. "That will never happen."

"Then you'll die like her."

"I'll never be with you."

"The Carrington name is no longer valuable, little one. I made sure of that."

"I'll die before I agree to marry you."

"Axel can't save you. Look at you. A pathetic and stupid little whore!" he snarled.

The door opened, and a professor stood there, his eyes flicking between us. Dario smirked and sauntered out of the closet.

I grabbed my things and ran for the car. "Get to my mother's house. Now!"

I yanked off my jacket and held a hand to my stomach, willing myself to breathe.

"What's the matter?" Fulgenzio asked urgently.

My hands shook as I dropped everything on the seat to look for my phone. "Oh, God, please be all right."

"Mrs. Bresciani, talk to me."

"Dario was here."

Fulgenzio looked around. "Where?"

I wiped the tears off my face. "He just—"

"Gigi, calm down and tell me what happened."

"He killed my mother." I burst into tears.

My phone rang. Finally locating it, I saw Ginerva's name scrolling across the screen. "Ginerva? God, I'm so glad—"

A sinister laugh cut me off.

"Who is this?" I whispered.

"Since we got interrupted, I didn't get a chance to tell you that Ginerva won't be available to take your calls."

"Dario, what have you done?"

"Taken everything from you."

My stomach lurched. "Ginerva has nothing to do with this."

Dario chuckled. "Really? Because from her screams, I think she wanted you to leave me."

I forced myself to speak calmly. "Think about what you're doing."

Dario paused as if weighing his options. "If I can't have

you, then everyone in your world is going to die." He ended the call.

I dialed the number again, but it went to voicemail.

"Call Axel," Fulgenzio barked.

"Fuck! I can't believe him."

"Gigi, call Axel," Fulgenzio repeated.

We reached the open gate of my mother's house. That was a sign that something was wrong. Fulgenzio swerved around to the entrance and I hopped out without waiting.

"Gigi, stop!" he yelled.

The door was open, and I slowly creeped. A blood trail led to our house manager, who was face down on the floor.

"Oh my God!" I froze, whirling around the room in shock, hands shaking, heart pounding.

I ran into the kitchen and tripped over a body. "Aurora, no!"

I crawled to check her pulse. Her eyes were closed and blood leaked from her stomach and neck.

Fulgenzio appeared at the entryway, "Damn! Gigi, we can't stay here."

Tears poured down my cheeks. "I... I... can't leave her alone."

Fulgenzio tried to pull me away. "Axel is on his way."

"No! He needs to find Dario." I stood up and looked around the kitchen. Everything was a disaster.

I ran out of the kitchen and up the stairs to my parents' bedroom. My eyes fell to her body on the floor.

"Mommy?" I dropped to my knees next to her. "Wake up, please."

I hated what she'd done. I said I'd never forgive her. Words that would haunt me for the rest of my life. She told me I was too weak for this world. She was right because this pain was unbearable.

"The neighbors called the police," Fulgenzio said from behind me.

"I want him dead," I said through numb lips.

"We have to go."

I paused for a moment and prayed for my family. I kissed my mother's forehead, and Fulgenzio helped me to stand, supporting my weight as we left the house.

"Get the jet ready," I instructed. "I need to rethink some things."

"Where are you planning to go?"

"America."

"*Breaking news. Prominent families are grieving tonight at the news of Rosa Carrington's death, along with her house staff, who were all found murdered. Many are speculating about a mob hit...*" the newscaster read off the report.

The man I was supposed to marry had wiped out my entire family.

Fulgenzio rushed me to the airport. Axel met and hadn't left my side since we'd boarded the plane.

"You need to eat, Gigi." Axel ran a hand up my leg.

"I'm not hungry."

"I understand. But you have to keep your strength up."

Food was the last thing on my mind, but I told the flight attendant to keep the drinks coming throughout the flight. There was still no word from Ginerva. I wanted to check before we left, but Axel put a stop to that. He thought it best we recoup and let Dario think we'd given up before we struck back.

The tears stopped flowing after a while. I was numb to the pain and finally understood the place Axel was living in after the death of his parents.

I stared at the screen and watched the news report my mother's death over and over. I had no one now.

My gaze moved to our security team; Lazaro and Sandro whispered in a corner, and Fulgenzio and Turin were on their phones.

"Any update on Ginerva?"

Axel wrapped his arm around my shoulder and tugged me close.

"Turin is still checking."

I grew up in the church, but I stopped going when I turned sixteen. My decision caused a huge fight with my parents, but being Italian and not living by my religious standards felt like a hypocrisy. Still, I'd always believed in a higher being and right now, I needed my prayers answered.

Axel rubbed my leg. "Do you want to lie down in the bed?"

Fulgenzio sat in the corner of the plane with some of Axel's crew.

"No."

"Dario will be found."

I frowned. "How did he get through the gate?"

"What?"

"Dario. How did he get through the gate?"

"He has resources," Axel reminded me.

"Yeah."

I pulled the blanket up to my chin and laid my head on Axel's his shoulder. "How long long have you known Lazaro?" I whispered under the covers. "No, keep your eyes on me," I added when he glanced at him.

Axel examined me. "What are you saying?"

I tapped my foot restlessly. "It's probably nothing."

* * *

The plane landed hours later, and Antonio provided a security detail to escort us to our home. Our reach went up high, but most of our team were in Italy. In New York, we needed more support.

Lazaro sat up front, and I watched him out of the corner of my eye. He was behaving as if nothing had happened today. Maybe I was paranoid. Maybe Dario was working alone, but only a select few had the code to my parents' gate.

The doors shut, drawing my attention to Axel standing with Joaquin at the front steps. I opened my door and waved off the help.

"How is she holding up?" I heard Joaquin inquire.

"Not good," I answered.

"If you need anything, let me know," Joaquin responded.

"Thank you."

"Any leads?" Joaquin asked.

I glanced over my shoulder at Lazaro texting on his phone. "No."

"Talk inside," Axel said.

I held the phone up to the lock screen on the door and we headed inside, sitting in the living room.

"Antonio offered his condolences and talked to the police in Italy to keep the details under wraps."

"Thank you, Joaquin," I responded, sauntering around the home I would live in for the next few months while we regrouped.

"The girls texted and wanted to know if you're up for a visit," Joaquin expressed.

"Um, maybe in a few days. I need to get things squared away here."

"Understandable," Joaquin replied.

I looked at Axel. "Did you tell him my suspicions?"

"What suspicions?" Joaquin asked.

"Let's take it to the office," Axel commanded.

We went to his office on the first floor and I sat in the chair near the bookcase. "Everyone is going to think I'm crazy." I rubbed my hands.

"Tell him," Axel pushed.

"No one had complete access to my family's property except a few people we trusted."

"You think it was an inside job," Joaquin pried.

"At first, I thought it could be Fulgenzio, but he's way too loyal to Axel to betray him or me."

"Then who?" Joaquin asked softly.

I looked from Joaquin to Axel. "Lazaro. One of our foot soldiers. He's come to my family's home with Axel a few times."

"Dario has access, and she thinks they worked together," Axel explained.

Joaquin's eyes narrowed. "He's here with you now, right?"

I discreetly motioned toward Lazaro with my eyes. "Unfortunately, yes. And that scares me."

"We can't tip him off if he is working with Dario. It's our only way to find him," Axel reminded me.

Joaquin clasped his hands together. "You know I like to torture and kill to get information, but if you want to take things slow..."

"Normally, I would let you, and be the first one in line to shoot, but it's Gigi's theory and I want her to have a say in what's going to happen." Axel showed me a long time ago how much he cared and listened when we talked. He was letting the world know I was capable of running a cartel like my father.

"Lazaro texted with someone in the car. We need to get his phone," I suggested.

"He won't give it up without a fight."

Axel smiled. "If he lost it?"

Joaquin answered with a mischievous grin. "Lost and found."

Axel cupped my face. "Right now, you need to act normally."

"Maybe I should hang out with the girls, then." I glanced at them both.

Joaquin encouraged, "Shopping and drinks at Ryde."

"Guards in and outside of the club," Axel demanded.

"Never worry. We always protect our women," Joaquin replied.

Sabrina rode with Janice to meet me at the mall, and the first stop was at a lingerie store to pick up some items Janice had on hold.

"Carlo is going to rip that off of you," Sabrina joked.

"Always the plan." Janice giggled.

"Gigi, you'd look gorgeous in this light-blue lace number." Sabrina pushed the garments into my hands.

"Axel would kill me for even thinking of buying something this risqué."

"He'll be grateful. Crotchless panties. Carlo almost had a heart attack after he ate me out." Janice laughed and high-fived Sabrina.

"Oh, Lord, you have to forgive Janice. The girl has no filter," Sabrina remarked.

"If you're hanging with us, Gigi, I suggest you get used to my mouth now, because I'll never change." She poked her lip out.

"Carlo knows that already," Sabrina jested.

"Don't let Sabrina fool you. She's crazy like me, but tries to hide her wickedness," Janice stated.

Sabrina chortled. "Here she goes."

"You two are hilarious."

Janice jested, "Do you and your best friend act the same way?"

"A little, but minus the mafia part."

"We traded our roles for being wives and mothers. That world will drive you crazy, but if my man needs me to ride shotgun, he knows I'm right there with my gun," Janice explained.

"Yep. Antonio is the same way with me. He hates knowing I'm capable of taking that risk, but I love my husband." Sabrina picked up two red gowns.

"Axel and I are still fresh and new in the love department and working together. Hard to separate the two."

Sabrina wanted our pick of which was cuter, and I pointed at the deep plunging gown. "Marriage is hard, but you have the double-edged sword since you're the boss and he's under you."

Axel's perception meant the world to me. "I know."

Janice looked at the price and put it back on the rack. "Has he ever tried to get you to step down?"

"Not really," I lied.

Janice tried on a long robe, standing in front of the mirror. "Lie to everybody else, but you can't lie to Sabrina and me. We've been in your shoes."

"Axel is great, but sometimes the age difference makes me wonder if he'll love me beyond what people think about us."

"Everything will work out how it should." Sabrina showed me a silk leopard-print bra set.

"Tonight we're going to Ryde nightclub." Janice took the robe off.

The distraction would be good. "My first time going."

Sabrina said, "It's mostly young people. You'll like it."

Janice pressed her lips together. "I'm still young."

"Girl," Sabrina cackled.

"Sabrina wants to play like she's an innocent do-gooder. When we get a chance, I'll tell you about the time she almost killed a woman over Antonio," Janice whispered.

"Leave my business alone," Sabrina muttered, grabbing a few thongs and walking to the register.

"Anytime you want to shut her up, say that." Janice and I burst into laughter.

They continued to banter back and forth, reminding me of Ginerva, so I picked up my phone and dialed her number. "Shit."

"What?" Janice queried.

They both stared at me. "Nothing."

The thought of Ginerva being in danger hurt my heart. We still hadn't heard any news.

"Tell us. Maybe we can help," Janice suggested. She grabbed her purchases and interlocked our arms, strutting out of the store and around the corner.

It felt like Dario was punishing me for going against him. "I still can't get in touch with my best friend."

"Did you talk to her parents?"

"No. It's like they dropped off the face of the earth."

Janice said, "Maybe a vacation."

"No. I called her number and my ex picked up." I felt a tightness in my chest.

"Did you put a tracker on her parents' car?" Janice investigated.

A tracker should have been the first thing I figured out, but everything happened so fast. "No, but maybe I can get Axel to have our men in Italy do a search. Since we found out about my family, we flew out of the country quickly."

Sabrina proclaimed, "It will work out in due time."

"Don't stress yourself out," Janice implored.

The girls tried to encourage me, but I felt as time went by, things would only get worse. My nerves rattled more with no any updates. "It's hard with everything going on."

Janice laid her head on my shoulder as we walked. "As long as you have Antonio, Carlo, and Joaquin, you'll be fine. Just stay focused on the goals."

"Thanks, Janice. I appreciate you."

"You're welcome."

Sabrina walked onto the escalator and turned to face us. "It's time we head back to your place and get dressed for the night."

"Have you arranged the funerals for your family?"

"A family friend handled it for us."

Cyrus stepped up to the plate with his wife and made all the arrangements. Also, it released my trust fund to me. Now I was the sole surviving child of the Carrington name, everything from houses, cars, property, and accounts belonged to me. Money wouldn't bring them back, but I made donations to the families of our staff.

"I'm still grieving my father's death. And now my mother and all the people who worked with us were murdered. So it's still embedded in my mind when I walk through the house."

"Give yourself time to grieve. It's gonna all work itself out." Sabrina comforted me.

Janice pulled me into a hug. "In the meantime, we'll distract you."

I checked my phone for messages from Axel. "Where are we hanging out?"

"My husband's nightclub," Sabrina answered.

"Can I ask one more question?"

"Go ahead," Sabrina replied.

Fulgenzio took my bags, and we went to the car.

"How naïve were you to this life?"

Sabrina popped a piece of gum in her mouth, offering us one. "Extremely."

I motioned I was fine and Janice took a piece. "Both of us were, but that will go away soon."

Sabrina remarked, "And remember, keep friends close, but enemies next door."

"*Enemies next door*," I mumbled to myself.

Our car drove out of the parking structure toward the main road. I turned to see extra security behind us. Janice sat forward to get Fulgenzio to turn the radio on and Sabrina chuckled at her friend negotiating which channel to play.

Two hours passed in a flurry of makeup, dresses, and hair styling

Fulgenzio escorted us inside the Ryde nightclub, along with Lazaro and a couple of other guards. Axel was off working on Dario's whereabouts. He told me they captured Edmundo to figure out where his son was, but he hadn't talked yet.

All three of us stared up at the cocktail server.

"What do you want to drink?" Janice asked me.

"Whatever you're having."

"We will take two Aces of Spades bottles, Don Julio, Circo and Long Island Iced Teas. Just keep the bar open for us." Janice laughed.

Loud bass from the DJ booth reached all around us. The decor was modern and expensive, from the long drapes and each booth with its private bar.

I wasn't in the party mood, but I agreed to come to get out of the house. Every time I closed my eyes, I could see my mother and Aurora on the floor, covered in blood. I had to figure out what my life would be like without them. How could I be who I needed to be and remain true to the person I was inside?

Sabrina fiddled with her dress. "Do you want to dance?"

"No, I think I'm just gonna sit and watch people." I scanned the crowds; most of the women flirted with the men for drinks. I didn't miss those days of being single.

Janice clapped her hands in excitement. "We can start slow. All the kids are asleep and our men are working."

"Do you have babysitters?" I asked.

"Longtime babysitter," Sabrina replied.

"Took me a while. I never trusted anyone with my babies."

Sabrina clapped her hands when our drinks came to our table. "Janice said she's gonna be in a mood all night. So be prepared to drink and have fun."

"Thank you," I told our server.

All three of us toasted and took sips. Janice twisted in her chair in excitement and we laughed. My attention went around the room, seeing the men and women flirting and make out. I remembered those days of wanting to be accepted by someone. I rubbed my wedding ring. I was almost empty inside without Axel next to me.

Our guards surrounded our table, and I figured no guy would press us for our number. Even the backup protection made me feel a little insecure.

I removed my phone, seeing it was almost dead. I rose out of my seat, and Janice reached over to grab my wrist.

"Where are you going?"

I pointed to the hallway. "I'm gonna go and call Axel. Check in real quick."

Janice and Sabrina stood . "We'll go with you."

"Oh, no. You guys sit. I'll be fine. I promise I'll be right back."

I grabbed my purse and sauntered down the hallway until I saw the bathroom and an office next to it. I stepped in a corner and started to dial Axel's number when a familiar voice reached my ears.

"What do you mean, after everything I've done? I want my money," Lazaro muttered.

"Be patient," Dario responded.

I gasped, covering my mouth, and put my ear closer to the door.

Lazaro growled, "I put my life on the line for this."

I heard a scuffle.

"That's fucking bullshit. You knew the risks."

"Listen to me. I will give you up if you don't give me my money," Lazaro spat.

Dario cackled. "They'll kill you before you even get a chance to come find me."

"Fuck you, Dario."

"Where is she?"

It sounded like Lazaro choked on a cough. "Out front. Why?"

"Keep a close eye on her until I make a move."

Lazaro barked, "And my money?"

"You'll get the fucking money after I get her. She owes me for fucking up the plan."

Chapter 23

Axel

Fulgenzio sat in the car while I talked to Gigi, trying to get her calmed down. Janice and Sabrina were in the car with Carlo and Joaquin. Antonio was out of town, so we called for backup. When Gigi ran out of the club, Turin and I were twenty minutes away.

Gigi continued to take deep breaths while I rubbed her back.

"He can't hurt you," I promised.

Gigi muttered, "He's inside with Lazaro. They're still back there." She turned in her seat to look at the car behind her. "He doesn't know we left the table?"

I spun around to watch the door. "No."

Gigi cocked her chin up to face me. "Should I go back inside?"

I bent down to press a kiss on her lips. "I'm going in to grab him."

Gigi begged in a whisper, "Please be careful."

I pressed my forehead to hers and caressed her cheek. "Never worry about me."

Turin spoke. "Dario could have set a trap."

Gigi reluctantly released her hold on my hand. "It won't matter. Edmundo is gone and now his son will follow him."

I stood tall, shutting the car door behind me. "You see him?"

Turin nodded. "Lazaro's in the bathroom."

"Grab him, and we will take them both."

Antonio's guards allowed us entry. I heard the doors shut behind me. Carlo and Joaquin jogged to catch up. Music blasted as Carlo walked ahead to show us where the offices were. I kept a hand on my gun and walked through the dark hall. A few girls came out of a bathroom and waved at Carlo.

The door opened on our right, and Lazaro stepped back in shock. "Boss, I had to use the restroom."

"Where's Gigi?" I already knew where she was, but for him to leave her alone for so long would put a red flag in his mind.

Lazaro gulped. "At the table with the girls." He tried to step around me, and I cut him off.

"Anything you want to mention to me?"

He looked between from me to Turin and Carlo. "Tonight went fine."

"Lazaro, I thought we had an understanding."

He slid a hand to his hip. "Boss?"

All three of us moved in closer. "You know I don't like excuses."

Lazaro held a hand up, pleading, "I can explain."

"Why would you need to explain? Did something happen?"

Lazaro glanced around for help. The bathroom door opened again and a few drunk guys stepped out. Lazaro pushed them toward us and ran to the front.

"Hey, man!" one of the drunk patrons yelled as I shoved him to the floor.

I chased after Lazaro and saw him run through the crowd of dancers. Turin motioned to the right, and I went left.

"Watch the entrance!" I shouted to Carlo.

"Stop pushing." One girl turned to smack Lazaro across the face.

He knocked her down and ran through the side employee curtains. I charged across the dance floor after him. I jumped and grabbed the back of his shirt as he reached the exit doors.

"I'm sorry! Please!" Lazaro panicked, trying to twist out of my headlock.

"Shut the fuck up," I seethed.

"Dario's not here."

"Where is he?" I barked.

Lazaro fell to the floor. "I don't know."

"Get up."

Turin pointed his gun at him and I reinstated a headlock until I could remove my gun and point at his back.

"Walk normally or you die."

He nodded, visibly shaken.

Carlo talked to his guards and passed me a pair of the zip ties they used on anybody rowdy.

I escorted Lazaro to the gray van we used for work and pushed him in the back, then slid the door closed. "Take him."

"If we kill him, we might lose sight of Dario," Turin remarked.

I watched people go up and down the streets. It wasn't a crowded night in New York; most of the traffic was a few blocks over. Glancing down the street, something told me a busted Honda with expired tags was misplaced in this area. I moved toward it when it pulled off with a tall figure inside. Our eyes briefly held, and I caught the arrogant smirk on his face.

Soon after, we rushed Lazaro back to the destination we purchased to get answers—painfully.

"No, please. I didn't have a choice!" Lazaro screamed in pain.

I twisted the knife in his leg. "He promised you how much?"

His head hung low. "A million."

"What was that?" I gripped his hair and pulled his head forward, ensuring he stayed awake.

"A million."

My lips twisted with disgust. "You betrayed my trust and family for a million dollars?"

Snot ran down his chin. "I can make it up to you."

"A promise he didn't even keep. He wanted to give you the money at the end, right?"

He glared at me.

I chuckled.

His frown lines deepened. "Fuck you."

"I hope you're happy with your life." I raised the sledge hammer and brought it down on his stomach and he convulsed in pain. "Bring me the needle."

The two guards stood beside him to make sure he didn't squirm around too much. I took the needle out of Turin's hand.

"No, listen, we're family," Lazaro begged.

"Family! Motherfucker, you helped the people who hurt my wife and killed one of my mentors. You will die." The syringe would numb him as I used the chainsaw to cut him up and drop him off at the bottom of the ocean.

I positioned the chainsaw over his foot, then knees. "Dario won't need to worry about that million now." I smiled in appreciation at being one step closer to ending Dario's life.

An hour went by until we boarded the boat and drove out through the river and finished out the night. The Meat Factory had a shower for us to change, then I jumped in the car while Turin drove.

Turin drove through the gate of Gigi's home, up to the side of the garage.

I opened the glove compartment and grabbed some wipes to clean my hand. "I think Dario saw me outside."

"He has too many resources. It's pissing me off."

"Now Lazaro is done, he's going to be even more frightened."

"I have to fly back to Italy and check on the farm," Turin reminded me.

"Hold off on that. I need someone I can trust here with me."

"How is Gigi?"

"A little shaken, but she'll be fine."

"Make sure you stick around here for the next day or two."

I turned my back to the door. "Are you an expert in relationships now?"

"Get out of my car, and act like you have some sense," he growled.

I stepped out of the car and stalked through the side garage door into the house. I placed my wallet and keys on the counter, reached in the fridge for a bottle of water, and climbed the stairs to our bedroom. The door opened to an empty bedroom, and I was immediately concerned about Gigi's whereabouts. I headed back downstairs to the man cave I had built, and found her lying on the couch with a blanket covering her lower half, watching a movie. I stood in the entryway and watched her for a few minutes.

"How long are you going to stare?"

I dug my hands in my pockets. "Long as I want."

Gigi lifted her hand for me to come forward. I came off the wall, approaching her on the couch and lay down behind her, wrapping my arms around her waist.

She rubbed circles on my arm. "Tell me what happened. And before you deny it, I can handle it if you killed him."

"Dario escaped."

Gigi tensed. "How?"

"I don't know for sure, but I think we saw each other."

She sat up, and I pushed her back down. "Meaning?"

I rubbed up and down her back. "Stop and relax."

"A crazy stalker has killed everyone in my life."

"Baby, relax for me." I cupped her cheek, pressing a kiss on her mouth.

Tears fell, but I kissed them away. Even though she was here in my arms, I knew her mind was a thousand miles away. To have so much taken away from her and the person still not caught would eat away at anybody.

"Dario wants the one thing he will never have."

"What?"

"You. Which means he's not that stupid to hurt you," I reasoned.

"He never loved me. He only wanted power."

"People get desperate when they have nothing to lose, but I will lay my life on the line before he ever hurts you."

"The regret I have sometimes is that my family would be alive if I'd given him what he wanted," she whispered.

The look in her eyes caused my heart to ache. She

thought she should've given in to her mother's demands, but I needed her to understand her choices were up to her.

I breathed in her sweet floral perfume, caressing her hair. Being with her brought out the boyish affection I'd closed off at a young age.

Tonight, she felt powerless. Dario stole something from her a long time ago and I needed to show her that she held all the power and no man, not even me, could cause her to break.

I captured her lips in a gentle kiss, moving down her cheek and shoulder. I lifted my head and found her studying me and pleading for the warmth our bodies created together.

While the movie continued to play, I removed the top of her dress, kissing each of her breasts while she watched me. Her delicate breath caught in her throat when I slid my hand in between her thighs.

"So wet, baby."

Her eyes glowed with excitement as she brushed a thumb over my lips. I kissed the back of her palm, allowing her to push my shirt and jacket off.

Gigi kissed me with burning desire. My mouth sealed over hers. I deepened the kiss as our tongues moved in sync.

I eased the strapless bra down, then tugged on her thong to move it down to her feet, and she kicked it off. Her tongue made a path down my chest and stomach. With her teeth, she tugged on my belt buckle. Everything she did turned me on, even when we fought.

My hands slid over her back to her breast, and I flicked my thumb over her nipple. Deliciously, her warmth got wetter, and I eased a finger in and out before pushing it into her mouth to taste herself.

"Mmmm," she moaned.

The beauty of her like this made me even harder. Her moans prickled my ears. "Fucking goddess, angel."

I pulled her chest to chest, wrapped a hand around her waist, and pushed another finger inside from the back while she moaned into my mouth.

"Baby, that feels so good," she purred, grinding back and forth as I pressed my hand against her pussy.

I discarded my pants and boxers, and Gigi rubbed up and down on my shaft while I continued to please her.

Finally, she lifted her leg, easing down on my dick, and we both groaned in pleasure. She lifted her neck and pushed her breast forward so I sucked on her sensitive nipples. Locking eyes with my beauty, I focused on her tantalizing moans in my ear.

"Y-y-yes," she stuttered, shivering against me.

I moved in and out of my wife's sweet essence with purpose. Over time, I'd seen her become more comfortable with herself and demand how she wanted to be fucked. I gently stroked her neck, nipped around her ear, and added a little pressure.

Gigi closed her eyes. "Oh, shit, baby."

Her voice made me want to stay inside her forever.

She clawed at my chest, and the sting pumped me up more. With her eyes closed, she bit her bottom lip before her mouth dropped agape. "Baby, right there."

I made her feel this way, and she would own my heart even after I died. "No one can compare. You're the one for me."

The blanket beneath us was saturated with our juices.

My heart beat faster. I wanted to take her away and erase every negative thought in her mind.

"Ah, fuck." I grunted when she bent backward out of my grip and exposed more of our connected bodies, spreading her legs and grinding faster as I played with her pussy.

I thrust harder, and we had an unspoken competition of

who would make who come first. She moved my hands away and turned around. Pushing herself back down, she tossed her hair back and rode me.

"Beautiful as fuck."

I could feel her ready to come. I surged up and grasped her hair with one hand, the other on her shoulder. My head lowered, and I licked and nibbled up to her ear. "Feel so good. Ready to come, baby?"

She nodded.

"Let me hear you."

Gigi gasped when my thumb slipped into her asshole. "Axel, please," she begged.

"Come for me, angel."

That was all I needed to say, and she came in a low moan, her juices dripping down her thighs to wet our couch. I held her as I stroked into her for a few minutes until I released fell back on the couch with her in my arms.

Her hair fell on the side of my face and I rubbed her stomach and thighs as her skin glowed with sweat. Silence drifted over us until Gigi turned around to face me, thighs parted to accommodate my length.

I closed my eyes and felt the comfort of her warm breath against my ear, and I knew all was right in our world.

* * *

My father sat with me while I watched TV. "Being in this world isn't about who has the biggest balls or guns."

I glanced up and ignored my toys. "What do you mean?"

He patted me on the head. "I know you understand what I do, son."

I kept my head down.

Father wasn't the typical father who had a lot of rules for me, especially being the only child.

"Look at me, son."

"Yes, Poppa."

"Everyone isn't your friend in my world."

His statement gave me pause. Something in me stirred with alarm. "What are you talking about?"

"While I do work for Laurent, we are friendly. Not everything is clear to be seen right away."

Even as a kid, I needed to figure out if something was wrong. "I don't understand."

"My job is to protect his business. Some people don't like that."

My brows bunched in frustration. "Who?"

He chuckled when I balled up my fist. "Calm down, Axel."

I was ready to go to war for my father. "Are you in trouble?"

"No, nothing for you to worry about."

"Well—"

"What I meant is that Laurent has enemies and friends around him at all times. My job is to protect his business from both. He's done a lot for our family, but people will try to cast doubt on me."

"To make you an enemy?" A frown covered my face.

"Enemy or friend to Laurent would be a terrible thing, but one thing I can say is he would never make a move without knowing the full truth."

We never finished the conversation when my mother came from the kitchen to make us come eat.

. . .

Those words from my father replayed in my mind. Casella made it known he was after Gigi. Dario and Lamberto partnered up to hurt her. So many enemies, and then we found out her mother was involved in her father's death.

After my parents' funeral, I had some of his work packed up. I dug through everything and saw Lamberto's signature on a few accounts. Laurent seemed to put a lot of trust in Lamberto, and I wondered if Rosa had influenced that decision.

"Life insurance policy," I mumbled, scanning the old accounting records of his offshore accounts

Turin stepped into my office and shut the door behind him.

I waved him over to sit down. "Anything new?"

"Carlo got rid of the security cameras that night. Lazaro's family thinks he flew out of the country with a girl."

"Good, if they continue to question—"

"I know what to do."

I held the papers out to him. "Check out these accounting records."

He cradled the papers in his hand. "Where did you get these?"

"My father's records. I had them all packed away."

Turin bowed his head. "I see Laurent had a lot going on."

"True, and Lamberto made it his mission to be in control," I replied.

Turin looked at me. "Surprised?" He sat forward, grabbing more papers from the desk, along with old pictures of my father with Laurent around town.

"No, I think Rosa has worked on this plan for a long time to get rid of Laurent."

"Damn." Turin went silent.

"Makes sense, even when Cyrus put her in charge of the trust fund."

"Man, she was really in control." He rubbed his chin.

"When Gigi finds out it went this far back..." I tried to control my anger.

"Maybe you should wait until Dario is caught." Turin was always the voice of reason; bringing more problems to Gigi wouldn't help her heal.

"Probably."

Turin pushed everything back on the desk and stood. "Plan for today?"

"Stick around for Gigi. I'm not ready to leave her alone after what happened the other night."

"All right. Let me get back to work and make some calls."

"Tell Carlo and Joaquin I said thank you." Both men came through for me and I appreciated the backup on short notice.

He tapped on the doorframe. "Sure. If you need me, I have my phone on."

I rose out of my chair. "Thanks. How are the rest of the guys?"

"So far, no one has asked about Lazaro."

"Good. We keep this to ourselves."

"Yeah. If more snakes are in the garden, I'll find out."

I walked Turin out of the office and to the front door, shaking hands with him before letting him out. I pushed my hands in my pockets and looked around the kitchen, then the living room for Gigi, but didn't find her. I heard talking from outside as I stalked through the house and into the backyard, and saw her talking with Quinn.

"Thank you, Quinn." Gigi pushed her shades over her eyes.

I watched Quinn grab the empty plate and head back

into the house. I greeted her before moving out of the way and approached Gigi laid out under the cabana.

"Are you done with work?"

I sat on the edge, picked up her legs, and placed them in my lap. "For now."

Gigi's hand caressed my arm. "Is Turin gone?"

"Yes. How long have you been out here?"

"Not long. I did a little work and came out here for some sun."

"How are you feeling?"

She gave me a soft smile. "You don't have to keep checking on me."

"My job is to make sure."

"I know. You've explained multiple times over the past few years. Thank you for last night." Gigi grinned, leaning forward for a peck on the lips.

My fingers fluttered to her neck. "Never thank me for loving you."

She lifted her arms around my neck. "Loving you is the one thing I've gotten right in my life."

Since being with her, I'd felt more open to having conversations about my family. "I had the time to look over some of my father's old files."

Gigi withdrew her kisses. "What did you find?"

"I don't think your father had anything to do with my parents' deaths."

I registered a change in her mood. "Are you sure?"

"Never a hundred percent, but my gut is telling me to look in a different direction."

She sighed. "Imagine that's how I felt when I found out about my mother's affair."

I wrapped my arm around her waist. "Stop beating yourself up."

"Hard to do when she plagues my mind."

"We'll get clarity in time."

For the rest of the day, we talked and reminisced about the old days when I was younger and growing up. Turin hadn't reported back any updates, so I took that as a chance to enjoy my wife and spoil her with food, movies, and shopping for her favorite things.

Chapter 24

Gigi

A month later.

"**Y**ou continue to play up the role of devoted soldier to Axel, and let me handle everything else."

"They have your father."

"I know. I'm working with Lamberto to figure out how to get them out. My mother is pissed off," Dario hissed.

"The hit on her mom was too much. It put a bigger target on your back," Lazaro confirmed.

"Just wait. She won't know what hit her."

I stepped back, covering my face, the call to Axel forgotten.

I sprinted down the hallway back to our section. "We have to go."

"Why?" Sabrina perked up.

"We have to go. He's here."

"Who's here?" Sabrina looked around the club.

"Dario," I whispered.

Janice scanned the crowd. "He's in here right now?"

I planted a hand on her shoulder. "Yes, and I don't want more people to get killed. We need to go."

She reached out and clamped a hand on top of mine. "Okay, just stay calm,"

"Let's walk out calmly so they don't suspect anything."

"Do you know who he's with?" Sabrina quizzed.

An air of dread came over me. "Yeah. One of my guards. I overhead them talking to Dario."

We sauntered out of the club.

"Fuck," Janice said, sliding into the passenger side of the limo.

"We need to call the guys," Sabrina suggested.

My heart beat fast. "Wait. Maybe we could follow him."

"No," Janice argued.

Noises from downstairs broke through my memory. I continued to be plagued with the events of the other night at the club. I shook it off and opened my eyes, turning to see the empty spot on Axel's side of the bed.

I was becoming more paranoid, even though Lazaro was gone. Dario was still missing, and Lamberto, last we heard, had killed himself. I should be happy and ready to live life, but I felt another problem would drop into my lap and interrupt our happiness.

I tossed the covers back, climbed out of bed. Grabbing my robe, I removed my hair wrap and combed through my hair with my fingers. Entering the bathroom, I brushed my teeth and did my morning routine to get ready for the day. It usually took Axel about forty minutes, but I needed an hour or more. It was why we had separate bathrooms and closets because he complained about me taking too long.

I finished up and went downstairs to a full kitchen of staff cooking and cleaning.

"Morning, Mrs. Bresciani." Quinn was all smooth skin and slim figured.

"Morning, Quinn. Have you seen Axel?"

Quinn answered, "No, ma'am. His car was gone when I got here this morning." She strode to the table and poured my coffee.

I had our dining room decorated in my parents' favorite colors and photos filled our home of my family and Axel's.

"Maybe he's working." I yawned, scraping jam on my toast.

"Do you need me to gather anything else for you?"

"That won't be necessary. I can handle it from here."

Quinn's oval face rose in a smile. "Sure, Mrs. Bresciani. I have a few errands to run."

"Thank you, Quinn. I left a list of items we need from the store."

"Yes, the first thing I picked up from your desk."

Quinn was referred by Janice, and she was fluent in Italian. She took care of her mother and wanted to pick up extra money since she couldn't be away from her for long hours. Axel did his usual background check, and we brought her on.

Our daily lives in America had come a long way over the past weeks. I'd gotten things off the ground for the business, and Antonio helped with locations to handle drop-offs and access to the ports. Today, I had a meeting scheduled with a new client who wanted to use our services. Axel hated when I suggested branching out from our normal operations, but things needed to expand.

The doorbell chimed and I tossed the napkin on the table, scurrying to the door.

"What are you two doing here?"

"Wanted to see how you're doing?" Janice and Sabrina hugged me, passing me a cup of coffee.

"Come in. Quinn has breakfast laid out if you're hungry."

Quinn stood behind me, ready to go to the store. "Don't forget to stay with your guards, Quinn."

"Yes ma'am."

Quinn climbed into the second jeep we'd purchased specifically for her use.

"Where's Axel?" Sabrina asked.

Still pissed he left, I waved it off. "Working. I woke up to an empty bed."

Janice rolled her eyes. "Husbands! How did you sleep?"

"I tossed and turned all night."

They followed me into the dining room.

"We wanted to take you out," Sabrina said.

I gestured for them to sit down. "I have a meeting."

Sabrina frowned. "How long will it take?"

"Maybe a few hours. It's been on my calendar for a while."

"Then call us, and we can get together for a spa day later." Janice took a sip of the orange juice.

For the next hour, I listened to them talk about their children, and how they had started to get disrespectful as they grew up.

Dressed in my best suit and heels, I checked my lipstick and came out of the house armed with my purse, gun, and phone. I hopped in my chauffeured car and saw a text message from one of our crew members at the Meat Factory.

Jesus: *Mrs. Bresciani, the packages arrived.*

Me: *Everything good?*

Jesus: *On the scale, it was short.*

Me: *How many pounds?*

We talked in code.

Jesus: *At least fifteen pounds.*

Me: *Make sure you let Axel know and tell them know we want full payment for wasting our time.*

Jesus: *Yes, Boss.*

Fulgenzio whipped around the traffic, parking out front

of the mutual location we agreed to meet at for protection on both sides.

"Keep the car running."

He planted his hand on the steering wheel. "You have your gun?"

I smirked. "Fulgenzio, you don't have to check up on me."

He smiled. "Mrs. Bresciani, I will always check up on you."

We both burst into laughter.

"Fine. I should only be an hour."

He pulled out his phone. "All set."

The Meat Factory housed meat, but underneath, it was loaded with cocaine, while the guns were kept in another location. Axel set it in motion to fly under the radar with local politicians, and the businesses we set up in America came in handy to fund their lifestyles.

I shoved the door open, sauntering toward the closed furniture store that looked outdated. Both parties didn't trust each other, even though I had the upper hand. I marched in and looked around at the dingy furniture.

Someone stepped out from the dark hallway into the light.

"Mrs. Bresciani, thank you for coming." Officer Ronson extended his hand.

"Mr. Ronson. When I got the call, I have to admit it surprised me."

"Sorry for the confusion and the location. Thought it was important to have discretion."

"A wise choice. Are you into decorating?" I asked as we sat at a table.

"I dabble in it from time to time," Ronson explained.

I came to meet with Ronson through mutual friends. As a cop, he would never have my full trust, but the call came the other night, and I talked with Axel, who he agreed to see what it could be about.

"Billionaire business."

"I agree. I have something for you." He reached into his pocket and held out a yellow envelope.

I stared at it. "I hope you're not setting me up on our first meeting."

"Never. I wanted to give you a peace offering as goodwill."

I flipped it open, pulled out the contents, and saw pictures. I stared at Officer Ronson, then back to the pictures. Dario and his mother were boarding a plane.

"When was this taken?"

Ronson glanced at the picture. "A day or two ago."

"So, what do you want, Officer Ronson?"

It always came down to money with these men. "As a police officer, I know how to get around red tape."

"How did you hear about me?"

"Turin." His movements were slow and steady.

I stayed focused on him without reacting. "Turin knows you're here?"

"He does," Ronson responded.

"Do you know who my husband is, Officer Ronson?"

"Axel Bresciani."

"Tell me why I should take a chance on you because my husband hates when other men are around me unless he knows them personally?"

"Strictly business. We want the same thing."

I leaned in, bracing my elbows on the table. "What is that?"

He clasped his hands together. "Not only money, but Dario Ramini dead."

I needed to test his loyalty. "Why is Dario a concern for you?"

Ronson hunched his shoulder. "He's my brother."

My eyes turned cold and I stood. "If you think you're setting me up, I suggest you never speak about this meeting again."

Ronson looked tough but easily manipulated. "Mrs. Bresciani, nothing about me is a setup. Dario is who I want to bring down."

"Edmundo is a lot of things, but he would never have a side baby."

Ronson reached out and grabbed me, and I jumped back.

"How wrong you will be, Gigi."

Dario walked inside and I turned to face him, with Officer Ronson behind me.

"Do you think I came here alone?"

"Doesn't matter. You're not leaving alive." Dario grinned snidely.

"Think again."

Gunfire exploded and I dropped to the floor. Dario ran, and I wanted to chase him, but knew it would be safe. I saw Officer Ronson take his last breath and wondered how much Dario filled him in about me.

I took the stairs and came out of the front as though nothing happened. Putting on my shades, I looked up to the top of the building across from me and saw a tall figure staring back.

My phone rang, and I dug it from my pocket. "Hello."

"You hit?"

"No." I looked from left to right as people scattered like rats to hide.

"Get in the car and go home."

I swung my head around to find him. "He wasn't hit."

"We scared him."

For Dario to get pleasure from my pain pissed me off. "I want him dead, Axel."

"Dario is dead. He just doesn't know it yet."

"Hurry home."

Police sirens and ambulances started to block off the area. People stayed on the ground to avoid any more shots.

"Don't worry. Just in the car," he directed.

"I hate leaving you here."

"Look up the block at the gray utility van."

I scanned the area and saw the van.

His tall figure mesmerized me. "Turin is driving. I have backup."

"Okay. Make sure you dump everything and I got a call about a shipment that was short."

He looked at me, then at the police and ambulance arriving. "I'll handle it later."

Suddenly, I felt the need to go to him, but he raised a hand for me to stop. "Be safe, angel."

Whenever he called me that, I knew to be strong. "I love you."

"Love you, too."

* * *

I was at the kitchen sink when strong arms engulfed me. Fulgenzio had brought me straight home, and I planned to watch a movie until Axel took care of cleaning up with his men.

"How did it go?"

"Turin is setting Officer Ronson up nicely with a background for stealing from the cases he busted."

"Good. He was ready to kill me without blinking."

"He's trained to do that."

"What are you trained for?" I turned in his arms, stretching my hand around the back of his neck.

He lifted me and placed me on the counter. "Many things, including making you happy."

I smirked. "I need to shower first."

"We'll get to that soon. I want to make sure I keep you informed." He slid his hands under my shirt.

Electricity crackled between us. "Informed, huh?"

"Dario is more dangerous than I expected. I need you to keep your eyes open."

"Yes, sir." I kissed him on the lips, rubbing the back of his head.

Axel's phone rang.

"Ugh, they can wait."

"Stop pouting." Axel reached into his pocket and pulled out his phone.

"Who's calling you at this time of night?"

Axel smirked. "Turin. What's going on?"

I watched his expression change from a smile to a frown. "You don't need to come here. I'll be there in a few minutes."

"Are you leaving?"

Axel dropped the call. "Turin has something lined up for us to inspect."

"A few more minutes before you go." I kissed him and melted into his hard body.

"Either I leave now or we don't get this deal done." Axel groaned, pulling back.

I wiped the lipstick off his mouth, and he pecked me on the cheek.

"Don't forget, we have a flight to catch tomorrow morning. Don't be late," I announced, following him to the front door.

"You take this boss role a little too far," he teased.

"Whenever the *Capo* is talking, you should listen," I teased, opening the door.

He chuckled. "I'll be back before you wake up."

"All right." I shut the door behind him and headed back into the house, laughing to myself. I paused, seeing he forgot his cell phone. Heading back to the door, I saw he had a text message.

Unknown: *My turn*

"My turn?" I muttered as I opened the door.

An explosion ricocheted around me, and a bright red fire rose in an instant. I was thrown back, hitting the ground hard, and darkness swallowed me.

* * *

I hope you enjoyed Gigi and Axel's story so far. Check the sneak peek of "**Claim**" on the next page. Follow my stand-alone, opposites attract, age gap, military romance "**Exposed**" https://books2read.com/u/bQyYZe. Are you a fan of sports romance? Then download one-night stand, billionaire romance "**Refuel**" https://books2read.com/u/boDyDA. Also, follow it up with workplace, sports romance "**Pressure**" https://books2read.com/u/3Ly1r7. If you love romantic comedy, fake relationships, enemies to lovers, find it here, "**Something Gained.**" Click the link here https://books2read.com/u/baGLYy. My stories of friends finding love started with the Heart of Stone series that includes a host of characters and family. "**Broken**" book 1 Emery and Jackson a sports, one night stand, workplace romance is here: https://books2read.com/u/3LoelX

Then you can continue with a fun side story of Emery

and Jackson with "Valentine's Day short here: https://book-s2read.com/u/4jAypY

Jordan, her best friend's story, continues here in "**Rebirth**" book 2 a single dad, widow billionaire romance here: https://books2read.com/u/ba2OMx

* * *

Please also check out a second-chance workplace romance here, "**Renew Book 4**" https://books2read.-com/u/4NXyPG with a host of characters intertwined.

Follow Desiree and Gabriel in **"Temptation"** a stand-alone contemporary, sports, curvy girl romance. Check it out here https://books2read.com/u/mle1Vv

Check out dark mafia romance here that started my journey with Antonio and Sabrina in **"Ruthless Book 1"** https://books2read.com/u/4AxKLo

The relationship continues in "**Savage**" book 2 as they get to know each other and their families: https://books2read-.com/u/bpED6g

Antonio and Sabrina have more work to do in "**Beast**" book 3 right here: https://books2read.com/links/ubl/4AxKOd

* * *

Did you know Janice and Carlo have a book? Well grab this dark mafia romance with emotional scars, and betrayal right here: https://books2read.com/u/b6je6M

Any fans of forbidden romance, political? Check out **"Mutual Agreement"** https://books2read.-

com/u/mgzzWX a steamy romance. Pre-order the full novel of "**Nasir**" here click the link here.

Have you checked out "**She's All I Need**" click here https://books2read.com/u/49lkeW a sports, opposites attract romance. What about dark romance that has everything from steamy romance, opposites attract, suspense, thriller, celebrity, and more "**Stolen Book 1**" https://books2read.com/u/mvZlgV Don't miss the follow up Joaquin and Sofia's story in book 2 "**Saved**" https://books2read.com/u/4DWwLd

The conclusion for Joaquin and Sofia comes full circle in "**Betrayed**" here: https://books2read.com/u/4A5LGp

* * *

Catch up with favorite characters in this holiday short romance which includes spoilers. "**Holiday collection**" here https://books2read.com/u/bzd59G

For small town, single mom stories check out "**Until Seren**a" https://books2read.com/u/mej8vr. Always fun when you love billionaire romances so check in with "**Cocky Catcher**" a sports romance, enemies to lovers here: https://books2read.com/u/bOxNgJ. Some familiar characters show up in "**Bossy Billionaire**" a workplace, enemies to lovers romance here: https://books2read.com/u/mvZoDq

All curvy girl, plus size romance lovers get into "**I Deserve His Love**" a standalone, second chance romance here: https://books2read.com/u/mVrGwP

The fantasy romance readers look no further than a "Red Light District" a curvy girl, fling romance here: https://books s2read.com/u/m2RQ6G

Reader Questions

1. Do you think Dario was wrong for going behind Gigi's back to work with her mother?
2. Do you think Gigi will survive as the mafia boss?
3. Should Axel have walked away from Gigi instead of going along with the plan of a fake marriage?
4. Will the other mafia families want revenge?
5. Do you think Gigi should forgive her parents?

Claim

A Protector Vengeance Dark Mafia
Romance

Disclaimer

This work of fiction contains strong language and explicit sexual content and is only intended for mature readers. This story may contain unconventional situations, language, and sexual encounters that may offend some readers. This book is for mature readers (18+).

Notes : The Carrington Cartel

Welcome to the Carrington Cartel, a duet series that features characters from Stuck in Love, and Fuertes Cartel. Gigi, Laurent, and Axel briefly appear in the Struck in Love series as an introduction. You do not have to read the entire series, but spoilers are included in this new series. If you want the entire reading order of Struck in Love Universe, check the next page.

Struck In Love Universe

https://books2read.com/u/49Zjnw

Ruthless Struck in Love Book 1

https://books2read.com/u/4AxKLo

Savage Struck in Love Book 2

https://books2read.com/u/bpED6g

Beast Struck in Love Book 3

https://books2read.com/u/3LpgdJ

Janice and Carlo Captivated by His Love

https://books2read.com/u/b6je6M

Brutal Struck in Love Book 4

https://books2read.com/u/4NQyE9

Stolen-The Fuertes Cartel Book 1
https://books2read.com/u/mvZlgV
Saved-The Fuertes Cartel Book 2
https://books2read.com/u/4DWwLd
Redemption Struck in Love Book 5
https://books2read.com/u/b5kZ8O
Betrayed-The Fuertes Cartel Book 3
https://books2read.com/u/4A5LGp
Torn: The Carrington Cartel Book 1
https://books2read.com/u/mqXare
Claim: The Carrington Cartel Book 2
https://books2read.com/u/bwyjPY

Synopsis:

They might have won the first battle, but the war is about to start.

When Gigi and Axel unexpectedly fell in love, the events that followed were expected yet terrible. Turning away from the match her father secured for her to strengthen the cartel left Axel fighting for his life.

Balancing her new role as Boss becomes more complicated than Gigi ever anticipated. But stepping down isn't an option.

Secrets from the past linger in the shadows, and if they come to light, they will destroy everything.

Gigi has always been underestimated, and it's time to show her true wrath and take revenge on her enemies.

Gigi wants blood to pay for what she lost.

Chapter 1

Gigi

Seven months later.

I tossed and turned all night, trying to get a good night's sleep, but nightmares continued to cloud my dreams. The rain descended for the third day in a row, pounding on the roof. Usually, I could sleep if I had Axel next to me, but now it was different.

I felt a kick in my stomach. "Shush," I muttered tiredly. "You decided to keep me company again, huh?"

I turned over, sat up, and stretched my arms over my head. My stomach calmed down a little while I checked the time on my phone. It rang, startling me.

"Yes?" I answered, rubbing my stomach.

"We're outside?" Turin said.

I stood and walked to the window, seeing a few of my men lined up. "All right. I'm on my way down. Give me a few minutes."

Turin blew out a breath. "Boss?"

"Yes, Turin."

"Are you sure you want to do this?"

My eyes stung with tears. "Positive. Please don't question me again."

"Have to look out for you, since he's not here."

My voice was calm. "He would want me to handle business."

"You're right," he responded, amused.

"I'll be down soon."

"No heels this time," he muttered.

I giggled and looked down at my swollen feet. "Let it go, Turin."

"No, because you need someone to watch over you."

"They're only three inches," I teased.

He'd become more of a big brother over the past few months. Our back-and-forth banter was the highlight of my days.

Turin grumbled. "You're determined to drive me crazy."

"As my friend, you should be used to it by now."

"Get dressed." He ended the call.

I shook my head, stood, and walked into the bathroom to shower and dress for another late-night meet-up. The local meat factory had become the destination in order for me to not travel too far during my pregnancy.

Forty minutes later, Turin parked the car in the usual spot and turned toward me.

I frowned. "What?"

He grasped my hand. "The moment I think it's too much, you're leaving."

"Who put you in charge of babysitting me?"

"I put myself in charge. What are the rules again?"

"Turin, I'm fine. Rules are for kids."

The look on his face had me laughing. Most people would think I was crazy pushing a mafia guy around.

"You're pregnant and running a cartel. You need someone to tell you no."

I twisted the ring on my finger and stared off into the night. "That someone isn't here."

"Let's go, so we can get you back home." Turin pushed the door open and rounded the car to help me out.

I stepped out in my long black stretch dress with the split up the right side and three-inch heels. My belly made an appearance before my face. "Is he conscious?"

The guard on duty opened the door to the basement.

Turin held his hand out for me, so I didn't miss a step. "Yeah. I told them to leave you enough to finish him off."

"Thank you."

I scanned the room and took in my surrounding crew as they waited for my orders. I'd reconstructed the Carrington Cartel after what happened with my family and Axel.

"Please, I don't know anything," Sandro pleaded.

I rubbed my belly to calm my baby. "Sandro, I thought we could trust you."

Blood trickled down his face as he lifted his head. Seems they did more than enough damage before I arrived. His clothes were torn, and his wounds were fresh.

"Gigi, I swear Lazaro acted alone!"

My brows pinched together. "Did he?"

"Yes! I can help you, Gigi. Whatever you need."

My frown set into a dark mask. "Dario is missing, and I want his head."

I knew Sandro was lying. I wanted to cut him up into pieces, but we didn't have enough time.

"He's never contacted me," Sandro stated.

"Really? Because I have a phone record that says differently."

Sandro bowed his head.

"Dario is my enemy, and you're going to tell me what you know."

Turin grabbed my arm as I moved in closer.

"Turin, let me go." I stuck my hand in my purse to pull out my gun.

"Gigi, I swear," Sandro whimpered.

"It's Boss to you, Sandro, and I'm afraid you're no longer worth my time."

I pulled the trigger and watched his lifeless body slump. My baby boy kicked up a storm as Turin and I walked out, and our soldiers cleaned up.

I dozed as the music played on the radio and we headed home.

Turin's phone rang, and he pulled it from his pocket. "It's for you."

"Who is this?" I demanded, rubbing my stomach.

"Angel."

I dropped the phone in shock.

"Gigi!" Turin nudged my arm. "You're dreaming again."

I was startled awake as Turin pulled up outside the house. I released a shaky breath and lifted my head toward him. "When is he going to wake up?"

Turin leaned his head on the headrest. "He's fighting for you and the little one in your stomach."

"I keep hoping this is all a dream and the bombing never happened."

Turin's brow creased with worry as he pivoted to face me. "Maybe you should take some time off. Step away from the business, at least until the baby is born."

"No."

His jaw clenched, and his eyes narrowed. "Gigi, I know you want to prove yourself, but it's getting dangerous."

"Until Dario is found and killed, I won't rest." I reached for the door handle.

Turin's firm hand stopped me. "You know I'm not letting you walk in alone."

"Turin, you worry too much."

"That's my job until my brother comes back."

Turin climbed out of the car and jogged around to my side to help me out. He took the key from my hand and unlocked the door.

I hung my coat on the rack before removing my heels. "You want a drink?"

"No. I need to get some sleep."

"You can sleep in the guestroom. It's late to be driving."

Turin checked the living room and then into the kitchen. This was his routine, and now he had my other guards doing the same thing. When my family was killed in our home in Italy, my protection increased. Turin had become the friend I needed in Axel's absence. Since moving to New York, I'd mostly stayed home unless the girls came and wanted to hang out or I had a business meeting.

I grabbed a bottle of water from the fridge and took a sip as I leaned against the counter. "What?" I asked Turin as he glared at me.

"Put a hold on your plans," he pleaded.

I slowly placed the water bottle on the counter and winced as the baby kicked. "Calm down. Uncle Turin is here," I soothed, rubbing my stomach. I looked at Turin. "I promise I'll think about it."

He placed a hand on my shoulder. "Do more than think, Gigi. Axel wouldn't want you meeting with his enemies while you're pregnant."

"How will he know?" I asked as I turned and left the kitchen.

Turin shrugged as I reached the stairs. "Because when he wakes up, I'll be the first to tell him."

I laughed. "Snitch."

Turin smirked. "Take it with pride."

I punched him lightly on the shoulder before continuing up the stairs to my bedroom. "You need to find yourself a girl-friend," I yelled and closed my bedroom door.

I heard Turin chuckle as he went to the guest room.

* * *

The next day.

I smiled in the clinical room as the monitor echoed my baby's heartbeat. My days had moved more slowly without Axel in my life, and knowing our baby was growing inside me was the only thing keeping me going.

"Everything is right on track. Have you decided if you want a natural birth without medicine? We're not that far off at eight months," Dr. Noella said, turning off the monitor and cleaning the gel from my stomach.

I sat up and straightened my clothing. "Part of me is scared to go through this for the first time without my parents. I'm eight months along and about to be someone's mom."

Dr. Noella rested a hand on my shoulder. "Did you take my advice and schedule an appointment with a therapist?"

I appreciated Dr. Noella's help, but my problems couldn't be solved with therapy. The only things that would help were my husband waking up from his coma and finding the person who tried to kill him.

* * *

A few minutes later, I left Dr. Noella's private facility after scheduling my next appointment and slipped into the back seat of the waiting car.

"Where to, ma'am?" Ralfie, my driver, asked.

Usually, I would head to the office to look over the books, but my gut told me I needed to see Axel today. "The hospital."

As Ralfie pulled out of the parking lot and made a left down Forty-Eighth Street, nightmarish memories played on repeat in my head. Fulgenzio being blown apart as he started the car, and Axel being thrown back by the blast...

"Ma'am, do you know where you are?"

My eyes felt heavy and my chest was tight. I could barely breathe. "Axel," I whimpered, looking at the stranger. I pushed his hand away as he tried to put an oxygen mask over my face.

"We'll be at the hospital soon. I need you to calm down."

I coughed and tried to sit up, but the EMTs placed me on a stretcher and moved me to an ambulance. Chaos unfolded in front of my home, with the fire department and police surrounding us.

"Where's Axel?" I cried, trying to get out of the ambulance.

"Please try to calm down. Your heart rate is through the roof."

I didn't care about myself. I wanted my husband. "I need Axel."

I glimpsed Axel's lifeless form as they moved him to another ambulance. I reached for him, but darkness dragged me under.

* * *

I blinked my eyes open to a sterile room. Tubes ran from my arm and oxygen hissed at my nose. Janice and Sabrina stood in the corner, talking to a nurse. I glanced toward the window and saw Turin. My throat was dry. I tried to clear it but only made it worse.

"Axel," I whispered.

Everybody scrambled to my side.

Sabrina gripped my hand, and Janice smoothed my hair off my face.

"Where's Axel?" I croaked.

Janice and Sabrina shared a look.

"Turin, where is Axel?" I demanded, my voice stronger.

Turin rubbed the back of his neck, dipping his head to avoid my glare.

"Gigi, you need to relax," Janice said calmly.

Something was wrong. They were trying not to upset me. I snatched the wires out of my arm and the nurse hit a button to call for the doctor.

"Mrs. Carrington, I need you to relax and take deep breaths," she encouraged.

I didn't care what she needed because I needed my husband. "Is he dead, Turin? Tell me, please!" A tear tracked down my cheek. I'd lost so much already and to have the best thing that had ever happened to me taken away would undo me forever.

Turin lifted my chin and looked into my eyes. "He's alive."

"Thank god!"

"But he's in a coma," he continued. "And they're not sure if he'll ever wake up."

I gasped and my chest tightened. "I can't breathe."

"I told you we should've waited." Janice focused on me as more nurses and doctors burst through the door.

"Clear the room!" the doctor shouted as my eyes rolled to the back of my head.

The next day, I found out I was pregnant.

* * *

Once we arrived at the hospital and parked in the visitor's section, it didn't take long to get checked in. Ralfie let the other guests step off of the elevator and motioned that it was safe. I slipped off my shades as we rode the elevator to Axel's private room. The blinds were open. I figured the nurses must have changed his sheets and left them open for him. He looked like he was sleeping peacefully and could wake up at any moment.

I placed my purse and glasses on the chair, removed my coat, and leaned forward to kiss his forehead and then lips. I caressed his cheek. "Time to wake up, baby."

Axel was the one who reassured me, and I felt confident and safe in his world. It was my turn to reassure him and show that I could protect our family now that he was the one who was hurt.

I rubbed his arm. "Turin and I are close to finding him."

The monitors beeped.

I ran a hand across his chest and up to his full beard. His brows were bushy and thick. "Soon as you get out of here, we'll get you a fresh cut and trim your beard. You know it itches when you kiss me." I laughed softly, and the monitor beeped faster. The doctors had told me that people in comas could hear you and feel your presence.

"We know nothing in life is easy, but I could use your love right now. That was always easy." Remembering the warmth of his smile made me feel like his arms were around me.

The door opened and Trina, one of the nurses, came in. She was in her late forties and had come recommended by Janice. She knew how to be discreet.

"Any changes?" I asked as she wrote on the whiteboard.

"Not yet, honey, but the more you visit and talk, the more it helps," Nurse Trina explained with a smile.

"Hope so."

Her smile grew. "How are you feeling? You're going to be a mommy soon."

The monitors went crazy.

"What's happening?" I panicked and reached out to rub Axel's forehead.

Trina gripped my shoulders. "Gigi, step outside for me."

"No! Tell me what's going on?"

Trina lowered Axel's bed as more nurses and doctors came into the room. "Get her out of here!" she yelled.

Nausea clawed up my throat. He wasn't going to make it, and we'd be all alone in this world. More staff piled in as I was led from the room. I held a hand over my heart and mumbled a prayer to God to keep Axel safe. My life had just started to make sense with him. My confidence in his recovery was fading.

Chapter 2

Gigi

The doctors later explained that Axel was going to be fine and for me to get some rest, but I refused to leave his side. Hours rolled by, so I lay on the couch to grab some sleep.

"Gigi! Gigi!"

Someone nudged me, and I woke with a jump. My gaze flew to Axel, and I sighed in relief to see him still in bed.

"When was the last time you ate?" Turin demanded.

His chiding tone made me angry. "What are you doing here?"

He shook his head. "Don't deflect the question."

I sucked in a breath and rolled my eyes. "Probably this morning."

"Probably? Gigi, you know Axel would be livid that you're not taking care of yourself."

"Who told you I was here?" I asked, ignoring his statement.

Turin looked at Axel. "Ralfie called me once the nurses got things under control with Axel."

"Remind me to fire him," I sassed as I stood and stretched.

"We got a possible hit on Dario," Turin stated.

I spun to face him. "Why didn't you say that first?"

"You've been through a lot, Gigi. I know you feel like everything is on your shoulders, but let me help," Turin pleaded.

He was right. I held a lot of things close to my chest because my trust was shot after what Dario and Lazaro had done. "What do you have?"

He stroked his chin. "It's in Chicago."

I watched him intensely. "Chicago."

Turin stepped to Axel's bed and stared at his best friend. "A few contacts told me that Igor Mendoza might be doing business with the Ramini family." His lips pressed into a disapproving line.

My ears perked up. "Since when?"

The Mendoza Cartel had a long-standing deal with our family, plus the De Lucas made it clear they wouldn't work with anyone who supported Dario or his family.

"Dario shouldn't be underestimated. We made that mistake before. He had to have made contingency plans." I slid my feet into my heels. "Get the jet ready to leave first thing tomorrow."

Turin grimaced. "I can handle Igor alone."

"Turin, we've had this conversation too many times."

He motioned to my stomach. "That was before you were eight months pregnant."

"You'll be with me, and so will Ralfie. Igor would be stupid to do anything to a pregnant woman."

"Sometimes that naivety won't work."

"That's what I'm counting on."

He sighed. "Shouldn't you be resting and preparing for the baby?"

I ignored Turin's comment and scooped up my things. I kissed Axel goodbye and left the hospital with Turin and Ralfie.

* * *

Turin was right. I should take more time to enjoy my pregnancy. I decided to call the girls over that night before we headed to Chicago to handle Igor. Even though I couldn't drink, I made sure they had more than enough alcohol to enjoy themselves, plus food.

The doorbell rang as I popped a strawberry into my mouth. I slid off the bar stool and sauntered to the door while the chef continued to set up the food. Lately, the business took a front-row seat, and my self-care was lacking, even though I stayed on top of my doctor's visits. Knowing Dario was still out there made it difficult for me to fully embrace my pregnancy because all I wanted was revenge.

I opened the door, and Janice held up two bottles of champagne. I stepped aside to allow her and Sabrina to enter, shaking my head at her goofiness.

"You know I can't drink." I pouted as I grabbed one of the bottles and checked the label.

"Apple cider. We can fake it until you drop," Janice joked.

I chuckled, waving them into the kitchen. "Chef Ebony, you remember my friends, Janice and Sabrina, from the funeral?"

Months ago, after the incident, I had a small gathering to honor Fulgenzio. Chef Ebony took care of the entire meal without complaints and even handled the cleanup.

"Nice to meet you ladies again, and please call me Ebony," she said with a smile.

Janice picked up a plate and filled it with pancakes, French toast, casserole, fruit, scrambled eggs, and grits. Another thing I'd learned with my new life in America was not to worry about my size. It was freeing because my mother had always tried to make me skinny like a model to attract a husband. Trying different foods and having a chef was fun because I could have whatever I wanted—a blessing considering the cravings that came with being pregnant. No longer did I have to be picky, but I made sure to balance healthy days with splurge days, especially now I was eating for two.

"Come on and eat in the dining room." I grabbed hot tea and my food.

Janice sat across from me, and Sabrina sat beside me at the head of the table.

Sabrina poured a glass of juice. "Antonio told us you and Turin might be close to finding Dario."

Any mention of Dario made me anxious and caused my blood pressure to rise. I took a sip of my drink. "Yes. I have to fly to Chicago tomorrow."

Sabrina and Janice looked at each other, then eyed me. In two seconds, the questions would start.

Janice dabbed her mouth with her napkin and cleared her throat. "Chicago? For what?"

I placed my fork on the table. "A potential lead on Dario."

"Have you thought about leaving this alone? Or at least wait until the baby is born and Axel wakes up."

I huffed. Janice and Sabrina had taken things into their own hands several times. "No, he has to pay now."

"What about Axel's condition?" Sabrina inquired.

My chest throbbed with pain. "Axel would want me to do this for him."

"Not true, Gigi. Axel made it his business to keep you out of trouble," Janice pointed out.

She was right, to some extent. At the beginning of our relationship, Axel didn't like me being in the cartel, but when I became the Boss, he supported my decisions. "You had family and your husband's backing. I'm alone."

Sabrina jumped up and wrapped her arms around me. "You will never be alone, Gigi. I promise. We're here for you." She wiped the tears from my eyes with her napkin.

I fanned myself to calm the flow of tears. "Did Carlo and Antonio do a good job of keeping you two out of trouble?"

Sabrina nodded as she sat down.

"I need you to support my decisions," I stated, looking between them.

"Whatever you need, we'll help," Janice said, placing her hand on top of mine.

I smiled and squeezed her hand. "Thank you."

"So, tell us about Chicago. Who are you meeting?" Sabrina asked.

"Have you heard of the Mendoza Cartel?"

Janice gave me a knowing look. "Carlo has talked about them before."

"I need to make a good impression."

Janice grinned. "I think meeting a very pregnant Boss will make an impression."

I smiled and rubbed my stomach. "My secret weapon."

Janice and Sabrina looked perplexed but didn't say anything.

We finished eating and watched a movie in the theater before it got too late, and they headed home to their families.

Tonight had helped to clear my mind and feel normal, if only for a little while.

* * *

After a good sleep, I showered and listened to old-school love songs, thinking of Axel as I got ready for the day.

The plane journey passed quickly, and before I knew it, we were landing in Chicago. My driver was waiting with a fur coat which I wrapped around my shoulders to keep the winter chill at bay. I wasn't sure why we needed to meet with the Mendoza Cartel on such short notice, but I figured it was a test to see if they could trust me.

The strip club doors opened, and the guard reached for me to check for weapons.

I stepped back in annoyance. "I don't think so."

He sneered at me. "It's the rules."

"Tell your boss I don't follow the rules."

I heard a chuckle as men approached us in the hallway. "Gigi Carrington." Igor Mendoza extended a hand.

I needed to put on a brave face and not show any sign of weakness. "Tell your men to back off."

Igor regarded me cooly. "No offense, but everybody gets checked in my presence."

"Offense taken. I came to talk business. I have no reason to carry a gun and am no threat to you."

He stared at me for a long moment before nodding for me to pass. I smirked at his bodyguard and followed Igor with my guard behind me. My heels clicked against the floor as we approached a tall steel door.

Igor opened it and indicated I should precede him, but he stopped my guard at the door. His gaze moved to me. "Only you."

"Are you scared, Igor?" I challenged him.

He grunted and shut the door behind him.

I took a seat and crossed my legs as I watched him pace around the table. "You're making me nervous, Igor."

"I got a call to meet with the daughter of Laurent Carrington, and she came. Would make any man nervous." Igor sat on the edge of the table in front of me. He reached out and gently caressed my cheek.

I slapped his hand away. "Don't touch me."

"Aren't you scared I'll do something to you?"

I grinned and leaned forward so our lips were an inch apart. Slipping my hand beneath my dress, I pulled out my small pistol.

The smile dropped from his face.

"Here's the problem, Igor. All men are the same, and you've proven how stupid you are to fall for a pretty face."

"You won't get away with this," he sneered.

I chuckled. "I'm not killing you. Today, Igor, you will do what I want."

His brow hiked. "And if I don't?"

"While you were allowing me to come in without getting a pat down, my men were surrounding the building. Every dancer, bouncer, and customer will die, and the blame lies with the Mendoza Mafia family. What do you think the news will say about you?"

He clenched his teeth. "What do you want?"

I smiled and gently tapped him on the cheek with the gun. "You work for me now."

"Bullshit!" A belligerent and inflamed curse escaped his lips.

"Oh, is the big bad bully mad?" I stood and gripped his chin.

The Mendoza Cartel had run Chicago for years, so to

have me come in and take over was crippling to his ego. My plan to dominate and weed out the snakes started now, and Igor would help me.

"Either you realize I have you by the balls, or the police would love to investigate how an entire strip club blew up with the owner inside over a drug deal that ended badly," I explained. I placed the gun back under my dress and headed for the door.

"How much?"

I looked back at him. "Your percentage would be fifteen. I'm feeling generous."

His anger became a scalding fury. "Bitch! My men would look at me like a fool for fifteen percent."

"I'm willing to negotiate, but since you want to call me a bitch... Five percent sounds good to me." I pulled the door open and motioned to my men for us to leave as Igor yelled and cursed.

"How did it work out?" Ralfie asked.

"Keep walking," I muttered, wanting to get out of the building as quickly as possible.

Igor didn't need to know that I'd lied about having explosives set up. I could almost hear Axel now, pissed that I'd taken a chance with another powerful family by blackmailing them to get what I wanted.

We finally made it back to the hotel I'd reserved for the two-day trip. I told my guards we'd leave tomorrow and to make sure the pilot was ready to take off on time. My priority was checking in on Axel at the hospital.

My phone rang and Turin's name flashed on the screen. I grabbed a bottle of water from the fridge as I answered. "Yes, Turin."

"You think it was a wise move to threaten Mendoza?"

"He's on board, isn't he?"

"Gigi, that's not how things work," he hissed.

"In my world, they do," I responded sharply.

"All you did was buy him time to come up with another alternative."

I sauntered into the bathroom and turned on the shower, scanning my face in the mirror. The bags under my eyes were becoming more prominent.

"Turin, what's done is done. Either you're on board or you're not, but wasting time arguing won't change my answer."

Silence greeted me on the other end.

"Hello?"

"I went to see Axel today."

I closed my eyes. "Did he wake up?"

Turin's voice was low. "No."

Steam fogged the bathroom. "I'll call you tomorrow on the flight back."

Before he could respond, I ended the call. I dropped the phone on the counter and gripped the edge, taking deep breaths. My little guy could feel the tension and knew my energy was off.

"It's okay, Peanut. Mommy's fine."

I released another breath before undressing and stepping into the shower. Twenty minutes later, clean and refreshed, I ordered food from room service and climbed into bed to watch a movie.

* * *

I woke to a presence around me, like someone watching me when a familiar gritty voice caused my heart to race.

"I was going to give you another two minutes before I woke you up."

I reached over and turned on the lamp. Igor was sitting in the chair beside the bed. "How did you get in here?"

Igor ignored my question. "Nice trick you pulled earlier?"

"How did you get into my hotel room?" I demanded in a shrill voice.

Igor boasted. "Someone owed me a favor. This is my town, Princess."

I reached under the pillow and cursed under my breath.

Igor held up my pistol. "Is this what you're looking for?"

I leaned against the headboard, feigning a calmness I didn't feel. "What do you want, Igor?"

"You played me earlier today, Princess." His voice was bitter.

I tilted my head. "It was business."

Igor caressed the gun between his fingers.

"Don't even think about killing me. I can assure you the second you walk out, you're dead."

His eyes pierced the distance between us. "Dario told me how feisty are."

My mouth was set in a stubborn line. "Did he also tell you how easily I could have you killed?"

His mouth twisted wryly. "That doesn't scare me, Princess."

"Stop calling me that!"

He laughed, and I wanted to wring his neck. Axel taught me to not lose my composure, but Igor had me in a vulnerable situation.

"The proposal is, how do you Americans say? Null and void."

"Like hell it is!"

He rose from his seat. "New terms for you."

"And if I don't agree?"

He pointed a finger at my stomach.

"Igor, you're swimming in dangerous waters, my friend."

Igor smirked and stepped toward the bed. I kicked out and reached for the phone, but he smacked it off the night-stand and gripped the back of my head. "Bitch! I'm the Boss of this city!"

I tried to keep my body covered while yanking his fingers from my hair. Suddenly, the door flew open, and Igor's eyes widened as Turin burst in with two of my men, their guns drawn.

Igor tried to pull me in front of him as leverage, but I punched him in the balls and crawled across the bed.

"Fuck!" he roared, just as Turin fired a shot into his leg.

I grabbed my robe and tightened it around my body to cover my nightgown.

"Are you hurt?" Turin asked.

I waved him off. "I'm fine. Give me the gun."

"Gigi—"

"Now!" I was tired of people telling me what to do and how to behave.

Turin handed me the gun, and I walked around the bed. Igor was squirming on the floor, clutching his leg. I raised the gun to his face.

"Kill me and you'll never find Dario," he seethed.

"That's a risk I'm willing to take."

"My family will seek revenge."

"The Mendoza Cartel is more than welcome to come see me. I'm not running, motherfucker." I pulled the trigger.

Turin took the gun from me. "We need to get out of here." He moved to the window to check the area.

"Let me get--" I paused and bent over the bed when I felt a sharp pain.

"What's wrong? Gigi, is it the baby?"

I winced. "I'm fine."

Turin ran off orders to the other men. "Clean this up and pay off the hotel staff. Get the security footage from the past three days."

Finally, the sharp pains stopped, and I headed to the bathroom to get dressed.

"I'm taking you to the hospital." Turin said as we piled into the car five minutes later.

"Turin, please. It's been a long day."

"You're the Boss of them, not me," Turin said, motioning to my men. "If Axel were here, he'd be pissed."

"But he's not!" I yelled, angry that I let my guard down.

I knew Turin was right, but everything had happened so fast. I just wanted to be with Axel like it was in the beginning.

"You need to be hundred percent when he wakes up. Focus on you and the baby. Dario isn't going anywhere."

I turned to stare out the window as we headed for the hospital.

An hour later, I was resting in a hospital bed while my and the baby's vitals were monitored. Turin stood in the corner talking with Ralfie.

The door opened, and a doctor arrived with a nurse.

"Is everything okay with my baby?" I asked immediately.

"Everything is fine, Mrs. Carrington," the doctor replied, looking at the folder in his hand.

"Then I can leave?"

The doctor looked at his nurse, then back at me with a serious expression. "I'd advise you to stay here for the next few days as a precaution so we can monitor you and the baby."

"But I thought you said the baby is fine."

"He's perfectly healthy, but based on you traveling on such short notice and having pains…"

I glared at Turin for revealing my personal business. Returning my gaze to the doctor, I asked, "Can I fly back home, yes or no?"

"I talked with your doctor and she said you can fly home, but you'll be on bed rest if anything else comes up."

"Great. Please send me the discharge papers."

"Sure, but first, let the nurse check your vitals one more time."

I thanked the doctor as he left the room, along with Turin and Ralfie. I allowed the nurse to look me over and then relaxed in the bed in deep thought once she left me alone.

"Mommy will protect you, Peanut." I leaned my head back on the pillow and forced myself to eat the hospital food.

* * *

As the plane lifted off for New York, all I had to show from our time in Chicago was a dead body. Dario was still on the run, and I was probably going to be put on bed rest if I didn't slow down on my manhunt. Turin, Janice, Sabrina, and Dr. Noella were pushing me to focus on my health.

"Mrs. Carrington, would you like something to drink?" the flight attendant asked with a tray full of my favorites.

"No, thank you. I'm going to take a nap in the bedroom," I replied with a smile. I turned to Turin. "Wake me when we land."

Turin nodded and continued to work on his computer. Ralfie was asleep in the chair. I locked the door behind me and slid under the covers, dozing off to my favorite dream of Axel and me with our son.

When the plane landed, we climbed into the bulletproof

cars and left the airstrip. As usual, Turin and Ralfie checked the house on our return. I left them to do any check-in with security and climbed into bed in one of Axel's shirts. If he were here, he'd have an arm wrapped around me and his face buried in my neck, whispering how much he loved me. That always put a smile on my face when going to sleep.

Chapter 3

Axel

A month later.

"So how many kids do you want?" Gigi asked.

"None," I replied.

"You can't be serious, Axel." Her hands landed on her hips.

"I'm very serious, Gigi. I told you, I'm not your friend."

"How many times are you going to pretend you don't like me?"

I'd let my guard down a few times with her, and tonight she'd skipped out on her parents' party to hide at the lake. Laurent threw lavish parties all the time to close deals. Tonight, some of his most trusted associates would be there and, I figured, a few enemies.

Gigi stuck her feet in the water. Her metallic-gold dress clung to her curves. "My personal life has nothing to do with you." She turned to look at me with a grin. "Axel, are you scared of my questions or your attraction to me?"

I stood my ground. "None of the above."

"Then why are you out here?"

"Because I was asked to keep an eye on you."

Gigi flicked the water with her feet and giggled. "No one is going to bother me in my parents' home."

"Sounds like a spoiled princess."

Gigi inclined her head back. "Excuse me, I work very hard."

"Sure you do."

She faced me and planted her hands on her hips.

I knew what she was about to do would piss me off. "If you even try it..." I threatened.

"What are you going to do?" Gigi raised her leg high and before she could send a splash of water, I stepped back a few feet.

"Gigi!" her mother called, heading toward us.

"What?" Gigi shouted.

"Have you lost the small amount of dignity we instilled in you?" Her mother marched to the edge of the water.

Gigi always looked vulnerable when her mother was around. "I needed a break."

"Break's over. Come back inside," Rosa demanded.

"Why?" Gigi whined.

"Because Dario is looking for you."

"Fuck Dario," she mumbled.

Rosa's voice rose an octave. "What did you say?"

"Nothing, Mother." Gigi strolled out of the water in a huff as her mother whirled and stalked back to the house.

Gigi turned to me. "Your first child will be a boy."

I followed a few feet behind her as she walked back to the house. "What makes you say that?"

She stopped walking and stared at me. "Because you seem like the type who would be a Girl Dad, and I want to be the only woman you spoil."

The long-forgotten memory replayed in my head and tugged at my heart. I flinched at the pain in my chest. The door opened, and I glanced at the short woman who entered the room.

Her eyes widened as she approached the bed. "Mr. Bresciani! You've finally come back to us. We were worried you'd never wake up."

I tried to lift my hand, but it wouldn't move.

"Just relax. I'm going to call the doctor." She pressed the call button and checked my chart.

I opened my mouth to speak, but something obstructed my throat. I reached for the tube in my mouth.

"I'll take it out soon as the doctor arrives," the nurse assured me.

A few moments later, the doctor came in with another nurse. I was used to being in control, but I was currently at the mercy of others. I'd promised myself I'd never depend on anybody after my parents' death.

I scanned the name on the doctor's white coat as he directed the nurse with the red-haired to check my feet and legs.

He wasn't more than five-seven, with glasses and gray streaks in his hair. "Mr. Bresciani, welcome back. I'm Doctor Nathaniel."

I pointed again at the tube in my throat, and he checked my pulse before removing it. The minute it was gone, I felt relief. I tried to speak, but my voice was raspy and hollow.

"Here, drink some water. It'll help," the nurse explained.

I took a sip. "When did I get here?"

"Sir, you've been here for several months," Dr. Nathaniel informed me.

"What happened?"

"A car explosion from what the police said. They've been waiting for you to wake up to talk with you and your wife."

My wife.

"Do you know where you are?"

"New York."

Dr. Nathaniel nodded. "Good. And your wife's name?"

My voice was raspy and my throat was dry. "Gigi."

"Excellent. We'll contact her as soon as we run more tests."

Every muscle went rigid. "Is she all right?"

"Do you remember what happened to you that night?" Dr. Nathaniel folded his hands in front of him.

"I remember leaving my house after talking to my wife. I was with Fulgenzio."

Dr. Nathaniel exchanged a somber look with the nurse. "Unfortunately, your friend didn't make it."

"Fulgenzio is dead?" I whispered.

Dr. Nathaniel nodded. "I'm sorry. As soon as we run some more tests, we'll call your wife."

Fulgenzio was young, with a long life ahead of him. There was a new pain in my heart that my wife wasn't here with me. I had so many dreams of us together and happy. "But is she okay?"

"Your wife is fine, sir. You'll see her soon."

Evidently, there was more to the situation, but they avoided my questions. I frowned when the door opened again, and in walked my best friend and a man I considered a brother.

Turin's face was marked with new lines. "Axel, you're awake! I just came to check in on you."

I didn't wait for the nurse to change the bandage on my stomach. "Where's Gigi?"

"Is he alright, Doc?" Turin avoided my question.

"Tell me, Turin." I needed to get out of here. Something was going on with Gigi, and everybody knew except me. I turned to the doctor. "Discharge me."

"Sir, you've just woken from a coma," Dr. Nathaniel reminded me.

I pushed the covers back and tried to get out of bed, but exhaustion engulfed me. I needed my wife.

The nurse tugged on my arm to keep me in bed. "Sir, you can't leave yet."

"Discharge me or I'm leaving anyway," I growled as beads of sweat trickled down my face.

"Axel, she's in labor. I just got the call," Turin finally answered my question.

I tried to lunge at him for betraying me, but he was too strong and pressed me back on the bed.

"Calm the fuck down. It's me, your best friend."

"She's pregnant," I grumbled. I felt empty and nauseated.

He gripped my arms. "It's your baby, you stupid mother-fucker. Relax and let the doctors finish, and I'll wheel you up there."

"Get the fuck off me!" I shouted.

He backed up.

Did I believe he betrayed me? No. But I'd had enough lies and betrayal over the past few years not to trust even my closest people.

Doctor Nathaniel continued with his exam and checked my eyes, ears, and legs. He decided I would be okay to go to Gigi's room, but he wanted me back in bed soon.

Turin pushed me in the wheelchair up to the labor and

delivery area. He explained that Gigi had a private floor, considering our enemies were still lingering. I was grateful to him for being here to help her in my absence.

We arrived at her door, where two guards were stationed. They straightened when they saw me, and their eyes widened as if they'd seen a ghost.

"Run down everything that happened," I demanded.

"We can talk about it afterward."

"Turin, I need answers." The ache in my chest almost exploded with panic.

He rocked on his feet and ran a hand down his face. "You remember me coming to get you that night we had a hit on Dario?"

"It was late. I told Gigi I wouldn't be out long, and I kissed her goodnight."

"It happened before I got there, but Gigi said you were caught in the explosion."

"Was she hurt?"

"No, but she was shaken up. Remember, she'll be all over the place. She's in labor."

"I'm a father."

"Yeah, so stay calm."

"What do you mean?"

"There are things we can discuss when you leave here."

I swallowed the lump in my throat. I'd left Gigi for so long to deal with so much stress.

Turin opened the door and wheeled me inside. We both froze.

Janice and Sabrina stood at the side of the bed as Gigi slept. A gasp left Janice's mouth.

"We thought you were still in a coma," Sabrina said, her eyes wide.

My mouth was dry and my stomach was tight. "I woke a little while ago. Is that—"

Janice came around the bed with the baby in her arms and held him out to me.

I shook my head. "Not yet."

"Axel, it's your son," Janice said softly.

I cleared my throat. "Afraid I might drop him."

Janice raised her eyebrows and handed him to me. She helped me to support his head properly and rolled my wheelchair next to Gigi's bed.

"She's been sleeping for a while," Sabrina added from where she sat on the couch near the window.

I brushed a finger across my son's cheek. "Can you give us a few minutes?"

Janice, Sabrina, and Turin all looked at each other.

"Okay, we'll be right outside if you need anything or the baby gets fussy," Janice said.

My gaze dropped to my son. His eyes were closed. Never did I imagine being a husband, let alone a father. Everything I thought made me weak or broken disappeared the second I looked at him. Gigi and my son made me stronger and wiser. Dario might have lit the match, but I controlled the flames.

A small voice whispered. "Axel?"

Gigi extended her hand to me. I took it, kissing her palm before holding it to my cheek and then my heart.

My eyes darted toward our son. "You scared me."

Gigi winced when she tried to sit up. "That makes two of us."

Slowly, I lifted him up to her. "He looks just like you."

She yawned. "Wish you were with me."

"I can't apologize enough for missing our son's birth."

She reached over and tilted my chin up. "Never blame yourself."

"What's his name?"

"I wanted to wait for you, but Sabrina and Janice thought it would be a good idea to give him an identity before we left the hospital if you didn't wake up."

"They're right."

For the rest of my life, I would show my son how much I loved him and his mom. I wanted another child already, though I knew it was bad timing to bring it up. "He's going to need a sister or brother soon."

Gigi chuckled and shook her head.

My attention went to my son as he started to feed. Something so simple yet so beautiful.

Gigi smiled down at him. "Axel, meet your son, Gaspare Laurent Bresciani."

"You named him after my father."

Gigi rocked him back and forth. "Thought it would honor both our fathers. Is that too much?"

Her words tugged at my heart. Nobody imagined Gigi and me together. Our personalities were so different, and she was young when we met.

Now I'm her husband.

Now we have a son.

And I'll do whatever it takes to protect my family.

* * *

After spending time with Gigi and my son, the nurse wanted to take him to get cleaned up, and Gigi needed her rest. Turin wheeled me back to my room to pack up my things. I'd decided to go home, even without the doctor's permission, to recover in my own space.

Doctor Nathaniel tried to persuade me to stay in the hospital a little longer, but I ignored his requests and set

Turin in charge of putting what I needed in my home for me to get better. I felt too vulnerable at the hospital, knowing that Dario could get to my family. Whoever was helping Dario would do anything to get to us, and I wasn't strong enough to fight anyone—yet.

I sat in the chair beside the bed and looked at Turin. "I've been here for months. What happened with Dario?"

"I wanted to wait until you both came out of the hospital."

"Turin, I can take it, whatever you have to say."

"For at least seven months, I've tried to keep Gigi clear-headed, but she's taken things too far."

My eyebrows knitted together. "How?"

"The Mendoza Cartel."

The Mendozas weren't necessarily our enemies, but they were closer to the Ramini family than us, even though we'd done business together. "What happened?"

"We may have bigger problems besides Dario."

I sat up straight. "As in Hugo?"

"We killed Igor Mendoza."

My brow hiked. "We?"

"A tip came through that Dario made it here from Italy because of Igor Mendoza. I checked it out, and it's true based on the flight schedule." Turin pulled up his phone and explained how our tech team tracked phone records of Dario and Casella's men who worked with the Mendoza Cartel. The flight manifest of a private jet showed one person on board fitting Dario's description.

I was sure Gigi's actions were warranted, but killing Igor Mendoza would cause a bigger fight that we weren't fully prepared to handle. "How did you let this happen?"

"You know better than me how stubborn Gigi is when her mind is made up."

"She was pregnant!" I bellowed. "You should have controlled the situation."

"Each step she took became more complicated and sometimes she went alone."

That's why Gigi needed to step down and put Turin or someone else in charge while we both recovered. The thought of Gigi and our unborn child in danger pissed me off, and she knew I would be infuriated at her for trying to chase Dario down.

"Something else you should know."

"What?"

Turin grabbed the rest of my things and dropped them in the bag. "Gigi's mother is behind your parents' death. She had help from Edmundo."

My jaw clenched. "She's lucky she's dead."

My son, with his dark brown eyes, short curly hair, and golden-brown skin, was the only thing keeping me sane. He and his mother.

* * *

Turin brought the car around while the nurse pushed the wheelchair to the SUV and helped me climb in.

Janice stood by with her arms crossed and a scowl on her face, pissed that I'd decided to check myself out against the doctor's orders. "Gigi is going to be pissed when she finds out."

"She'll be fine. I'll call and check up on her in a few hours."

"Axel, are you sure about leaving?" Sabrina asked.

"I need to be home to work on getting better. Being here keeps me paranoid."

"Antonio will want to hear from you." Sabrina studied my face in the light.

"I'll call him when I make it home."

Turin shut the door and hurried around to the driver's side. As we left the parking structure of the hospital, he passed me a new phone and gun. I had to get back in shape as soon as possible because Dario partnering with Mendoza would impact my family's safety.

Chapter 4

Gigi

A few hours earlier.

"I want the baby's toys in that closet over there," I directed my staff while Janice and Sabrina helped me carry in the shopping bags.

Since returning from Chicago, I'd listened to my body and relaxed my efforts to find Dario until after the baby was born. Turin ignored me on the plane, all the while making sure he paid off the right people to get the security footage removed. Killing Igor was a mistake, but not something I regretted because it was him or me.

I separated the baby clothes into different piles and made sure I checked off my list of last-minute items I'd need for a newborn.

"Gigi?" Janice called.

I left the bedroom and walked to the hallway to peer over the balcony. "Please tell me you finished bringing in the bags."

Janice crossed her arms over her chest. "Come down here."

"Why?"

"The police would like to ask a few questions."

"Police?"

Sabrina stepped out of the bedroom with her phone in her hand. "I'm going to call Antonio."

Shit. "Call Turin first."

The police coming to my house could only spell trouble. The officer's nasally voice made me cringe as I got closer. "I'm Gigi Bresciani."

The officer lifted his badge in front of my face. "Detective Soren, and this is Raymond."

I placed a hand on my stomach. "Yes, detectives. How can I help you?"

"Do you know Igor Mendoza?"

Sabrina snapped. "Don't answer that."

I raised an eyebrow. "Why are you at my home?"

"We have a few questions about the death of Igor Mendoza."

"Not sure how I can help you."

Detective Soren glanced around my home. "Nothing to be alarmed about unless you're hiding something."

Someone had betrayed me if the detectives were at my home investigating Igor's death.

"Do you know Hugo Mendoza?"

"I'd suggest you speak with my attorney for further questions—" My words were cut short as I bent over in pain. "Oh god."

"Gigi! Are you all right?" Sabrina rushed to my side, coaching me to take deep breaths. "I think the baby is coming."

"I'll have to ask you to leave," Janice told the detectives firmly.

Sabrina helped me to stand. "Hold on, Gigi. Janice, go grab her baby bag."

I watched the detectives stroll to their vehicle. "Take their license plate," I said as Sabrina helped me into the passenger seat.

Ralfie started the car as Janice jogged out of the house and slipped into the backseat with my bags.

I rubbed my stomach and continued to take deep breaths. "Ugh! The pain," I grumbled, wondering if I really could be a good mom.

* * *

Present

I smiled at my son as he cooed in Sabrina's arms.

"Are you going to tell him about the police coming by the house?" Janice asked.

Axel had checked himself out of the hospital a few hours ago, but I had one more day before we could be home together. Giving birth to my son had been the most beautiful thing in the world, and also the most painful, which had me rethinking a large family.

"Axel will want to kill them," I replied.

"Maybe he should," Janice mumbled under her breath.

Sabrina pinned her eyes on Janice. "Not funny, Janice."

"What happened with Igor Mendoza?" Sabrina laid my baby boy down.

"Nothing happened that shouldn't have."

"Should we get Carlo and Antonio to help?" Janice looked concerned.

"No, I need to handle some stuff on my own."

Janice reminded me, "Axel is going to want answers."

"When that time comes, I'll answer them. But for now, I want to enjoy my son."

I got out of bed and Sabrina helped me to the bathroom

to wash up. I felt sick to my stomach, worrying about the blowback from Igor's death. It reminded me to check with Turin to find out how it got out. After I brushed my hair, washed my face, and changed my gown, I crawled back into bed.

"We're going to head home to our babies. Keep us updated on what you need," Janice said.

"I'll be fine," I said as I hugged the two women.

Sabrina gave me a final squeeze. "We'll be here tomorrow to help you leave."

The girls checked on my son one more time and waved goodbye.

I picked up my phone and saw a message from Axel.

Axel: *I made it home. Are you and my son okay?*

Me: *Yes, he's sleeping right now.*

Axel: *Turin will be there tomorrow to bring you home.*

Me: *Don't worry about me. Sabrina and Janice will bring me home.*

Axel: *We need to discuss some changes when you get here.*

I chose not to respond to that. Axel would do anything to protect our family, but he reminded me of Dario in some ways when it came to my being in the cartel. The culture of the cartel was that women stayed out of the men's business and tended to the home.

I logged out of the thread and went to Turin's message thread.

Me: *Call me asap.*

* * *

Finally, after two days in the hospital, I was on my way home with our son. Axel was waiting for me there with the nurse we'd hired to take care of him. Turin was busy, and I needed to schedule a meeting to discuss Igor and Hugo. The car pulled up in front of the house and Ralfie approached the passenger door to grab my bags. I steadied myself and let him pick up the car seat. Sabrina stood next to me as I slowly walked into the house.

I released a breath as I took in the peace and quiet. "Where's Axel?"

Janice took the car seat from Ralfie. "In the bedroom with the nurse."

"I'm going to check on him and then feed the baby."

I heard low voices outside the door and pushed it open to see the nurse with Axel. "How is he doing?"

"Stubborn, but fine," the nurse answered.

Axel flinched as she checked his blood pressure.

"Are you in pain?" I moved toward him and leaned in to look him in the eye.

"I'll be fine." He grabbed the back of my head and kissed me on the lips.

I wiped the lipstick from his mouth. "You're lying."

His nurse removed the stethoscope and stepped out of the room.

"Where's my son?" Axel asked.

"Janice has him." I sat on the bed.

Axel extended his palm to my stomach. "Can't believe I missed your pregnancy."

"You'll make new memories." Our hands interlocked.

Axel rested his head on the headboard. "Not the same. Dario took you away from me."

"Dario will answer for that." My heart skittered when his hand went to my thigh. I craved every inch of him.

"Not soon enough."

I trailed my fingers along his cheek. "The only thing you need to focus on is your health, Axel."

He closed his eyes. "Turin filled me in on a few details."

"All of that can be discussed later."

"Avoiding it won't help."

I frowned. "Who says I'm avoiding anything?"

"I know the truth, Gigi."

My mind stilled at the thought of him being angry with me about killing Igor. I tried to climb off the bed. "Axel," I complained as he grabbed my arm and pulled me down on top of him. "You'll hurt yourself. I'm too heavy."

His hands moved to my butt and down to my thighs. "Turin told me that Rosa, Lamberto, and Edmundo all worked together to plan my parents' death and frame Laurent."

"Yes," I whispered. Rosa had resented me for being headstrong and wanting a different life than the one she'd planned. But to kill innocent people to get her way? That was cold.

Axel looked me in the eye. "I want you to step down."

I tried to move, and he tightened his grip. "Let me go." I pushed my hand flat on his chest.

"Gigi, let me explain." His face was hard, his voice commanding.

"Not right now. I need to feed the baby."

His eyes searched my face. "He's fine."

"Axel, I'm not talking about this right now."

He drew me closer, and his breath stirred my hair. "Dario will be found and killed."

"I know he will because I'm going to be the one to do it."

He brushed his hand down my arm as I stood. "I feel like you're keeping something from me."

I looked over my shoulder at him as I strolled to the door. "Turin should keep his opinions about my business to himself."

"Gigi—"

"I'll have Ebony bring you something to eat."

"Gigi!" Axel yelled.

I wanted to tell him the truth but now wasn't the time with him still in pain. He was in a different headspace right now, and I didn't need judgment from my husband about how I handled people.

Janice passed me a plate of food. I sat next to Gaspare and smiled as I tugged on his tiny foot.

I had the house reconstructed after the bombing. Some people said I should have moved, but my father bought this place for me to start fresh.

"You seem pissed." Janice sat down next to me and grabbed a glass of iced tea.

I smiled at my son as I pushed the food around on my plate. "Ebony, can you send food up to my husband, please?"

"Yes, Mrs. Bresciani." Ebony reached for a tray and set up a plate for Axel.

I waited for her to finish and leave the kitchen to talk. "Axel wants me to step down."

Janice sighed. "You can't be surprised."

"Sabrina?" I wanted her opinion.

"He's seen a lot before you and knows how ugly it can get."

"Everybody acts like I'm some delicate flower. I know what I'm doing."

Janice tapped me on the shoulder. "We're on your side."

Gaspare started to cry, so I reached over to pick him up, unhooking my nursing bra to feed him. That put him in a better mood, and I patted his butt and rubbed his back.

Janice picked up her wineglass. "Only advice we can give you is to trust your husband. Dario will win if you shut Axel out."

"I'll tell him when the time is right," I said as Gaspare finished eating. I leaned him against my shoulder and burped him before putting him back in his seat to rest. "Did Axel eat?" I asked Ebony as she returned.

Ebony chuckled. "He said to make him a steak, rice, and potatoes."

I rolled my eyes. Axel had to go against the doctor's orders of eating healthy and building strength. "Thanks, Ebony."

I wiped Gaspare's face and finished my food while the girls continued to talk.

* * *

Later that night, I stood beneath the shower in our bathroom and let the hot water soothe my aches. I looked down at my stomach—it felt empty since the birth of my baby. Gaspare had experienced every emotion these past few months as I tried to keep him safe, and it was odd to be so alone in my body again.

I jumped as the shower door opened and strong arms wrapped around my waist. Axel kissed the back of my neck, and I leaned my head on his shoulder. "You shouldn't be out of bed."

"I'm sorry." He cupped my chin.

I traced his mouth with my fingertips. "For what?"

"Making you think I'm like Dario or your mother by trying to control you."

His thick, long girth pressed against my ass as he

wrapped a hand around my neck. He turned my face, and his mouth locked in on mine.

Axel wasn't remotely similar to Dario. His hand slid down to my ass and I pulled back before things got out of control. "We can't. Not yet."

"I know. How long do we have to wait?"

"Six weeks." I grinned as he scowled.

Stepping out of his hold, I picked up the soapy sponge and turned to wash his chest.

Axel cupped my breast. "How the hell am I going to last six weeks?"

"You have no choice."

He grunted, kissed me again, and walked me back to the wall. Out of habit, I raised my leg around his hip and felt him growing hard. "Time to shower," I reminded him.

Axel bent to suckle my nipple and my heartbeat went crazy.

"Baby, you need to rest." I drew a shaky breath.

"I'll rest when I'm dead."

I laughed as he stepped back and finished washing. Stepping out of the shower, he picked up a large towel and dried off before leaving the bathroom. I washed and dried my hair and entered the bedroom to find Gaspare in bed with Axel.

"You didn't look like the type to bring a baby into the bedroom." I removed the towel and picked up my nightgown.

"I don't want you to wear that. I want you naked."

"Not in the mood to be naked."

Axel rose from the bed and placed Gaspare in the bassinet. He came around the bed and took my hand, pulling me in front of the mirror. A smile played on his lips. "You're beautiful."

I shook my head. "I just had a baby."

"You had *my* baby." He spoke softly.

"I don't feel beautiful." My hormones were all over the place.

"You're beautiful in here, and that's what matters," he said, touching my chest over my heart.

"Tomorrow, will you please follow the nurse's orders?"

"No." Axel moved away and climbed back into bed.

I joined him, pulling the covers over us and laying my head on his chest. "I want you to be healthy."

"I'm healthy. The doctor and nurses can work on me here at the house."

I caressed the side of his stomach. "But Axel, you just got out of a coma."

He sighed and turned off the bedroom lamp. "Go to sleep."

This conversation wasn't over. I planned to keep my eye on him and ensure he took his health seriously. Gaspare needed his dad in top shape. Maybe we could work out together; a routine to build Axel's strength and one for me to recover from childbirth.

Axel's light snores lingered in my ears as I watched him sleep. A smile curved my lips at having him back. There were so many things I wanted to tell him that he'd missed.

Chapter 5

Axel

The bedroom door squeaked open, startling me from sleep. I reached out to the empty spot where Gigi slept. I looked for the bassinet Gaspare had slept in last night, which was also gone.

"Mr. Bresciani, it's time to check your blood pressure," the nurse spoke softly as she entered.

"Where's my wife?"

"Mrs. Bresciani said she had a meeting and would check in with you later."

"Heather, right?"

"Yes."

"Just take my pressure and leave."

Heather put her bag on the floor. "Doctor Nathaniel said you shouldn't move around too much yet."

I turned my head away and ignored her comment.

Fifteen minutes later, I got up to shower and eat breakfast. Pissed that Gigi left without saying something, I grabbed my cell phone and dialed her number.

"She's pissing me off," I grumbled to myself.

The call went to voicemail. "Gigi, call me back, or I'm coming to find you!" I growled as there was a knock at the front door. I strode to answer it. "Where is she?" I asked, opening the door to Turin.

Turin pushed his phone in front of my face, showing me a picture of Hugo Mendoza and one of Casella's men. "Gigi's called the guys for an early meeting about a new order increase with the Irish."

"Is that what she told you?" I demanded as we walked through the house to my office.

"After Alvar Casella's death, his people contacted Hugo Mendoza."

"About?"

"They want protection and a new partnership," he said with a somber expression.

"You're keeping something from me."

"Gigi killed Igor Mendoza."

I paused at the office door and whirled to face him. Turin knew how I felt about being kept out of the loop. "What the fuck do you mean, she killed him?"

We entered the office, and Turin went to my computer. He slid in a flash drive and opened it to a video of Gigi in a hotel.

I sat in the chair and watched Igor step off an elevator and slip into her hotel room. My fists clenched. "When were you going to tell me?"

"I got all the footage from the hotel, but Gigi's been on another level with making decisions," he confessed.

"How did you let her-"

"Fuck you, Axel," he cut across me angrily. "You're my brother, but she's the Boss."

"You should have put a stop to her even being in the same room as Igor."

"We can't change that now, and we have bigger problems."

"Hugo Mendoza," I stated.

"Hugo wants more territory and revenge for Igor."

"By working with Dario."

Turin leaned over my desk and pointed to pictures of Dario and Hugo together. "We know he took a flight from Mendoza's people. I think Dario put the plan together for them after Casella's death."

"Gigi's going to give up her position. I'm done." I announced.

Turin folded his arms. "She won't take it that easy."

"Gigi needs to listen."

"Hugo doesn't negotiate."

That would only give me more reason to kill him. "Hugo can go to hell."

I watched the video over and over, bombarding Turin with questions. Then I went to change clothes. It was time to make my presence known at the office.

* * *

Turin thought it would be a bad idea to interrupt, but Gigi and I didn't keep secrets from each other. I walked into the conference room as she was talking.

"I want the price to increase for Chicago, Philadelphia, and New York." Gigi stood in front of a few cartel men, giving directions.

"What if they don't take to the price increase?" one man probed.

Gigi insisted. "Make them understand."

"Give us a minute," I interjected, walking toward Gigi.

"Axel, what are you doing here?" Gigi looked startled.

"I could ask you the same question. My son is at home with the nanny."

Turin cleared his throat. "Give them a second, gentleman."

He opened the door for them to leave and followed them out.

Gigi moved toward me in a figure-hugging dress that was too short to be wearing in front of her men. "Why did you come here?"

"You killed Igor Mendoza," I stated, wrapping a hand around her wrist.

Gigi tried to move in close and kiss me, but I turned my head.

"Igor was working with Dario," she justified.

"I'm back now, and you will no longer be making decisions without me."

"It doesn't work like that, Axel."

"Laurent put those kinds of decisions in my hand as the Enforcer of the family."

"Laurent is no longer in charge."

"The decisions you're making will not end well if you don't include me as the Enforcer."

"I love you, but I know what I'm doing," she said calmly.

"You only got in this position because your father was killed, and I married you." I wanted to call my words back as soon as they came out of my mouth.

Silence fell and Gigi went rigid, her eyes flashing with pain.

"Gigi, I'm sorry—"

"No, it's fine."

I pressed close to the warmth of her body. "Baby, I didn't mean it."

"Do whatever you want to do, Axel. I'll go home and be a

mother to our son." Gigi turned, snatched up her purse and left the boardroom.

"Fuck!" I slumped forward and rested my head in my hands.

Turin came back into the room. "Where is she going?"

"I said she got in this role because I married her."

Turin winced. "Damn, Axel."

"Get me Hugo's number."

"Should you be on your feet?"

"I have no choice."

"Something else I need to tell you."

"Turin, you're pissing me off."

"I heard the Irish want to move in fast. We need to let Antonio and Carlo know. If the Casellas and Mendozas come together, we're going to have even bigger problems."

"How much do the Irish want?" I inquired.

He shut the office door behind me as we left. "Enough that we'll need to agree or get rid of them before they join forces with Dario."

"I need more eyes on Dario. How the hell is he walking around free?" I demanded.

Turin and I walked off the elevator and out of the building.

"Watch it!" A guy yelled as he bumped into my shoulder.

I glared at him, feeling uneasy without my gun.

I climbed into the car and slammed the door, watching the man stop to talk to another guy on the corner.

Turin started the car and merged with the traffic. Suddenly, he yanked the wheel sharply, narrowly avoiding the vehicle that had tried to sideswipe us.

"You good?" Turin shouted.

I nodded. "Get us out of here!"

Turin put the car in drive again. "Trying. These folks are crazy, not paying attention to lights."

My head swiveled left to right. "Fuck, come on." I was agitated after the near miss.

"Chill," Turin pumped the gas and moved into the middle lane. "What's gotten into you?

"This shit has me paranoid."

"Hugo or Dario?"

I pulled out my phone and dialed Gigi's number. "Both."

"We need to get to the warehouse with the team."

"Gigi's not answering her phone."

"Give her time. You pissed her off."

Turin passed through boarded sections of Hoboken. I remembered we had a few spots holding our products close to the shipyard. Turin parked the car, and we strolled to the door. I leaned against the doorframe for a second to catch my breath.

Turin frowned. "Are you sure you're up to this meeting?"

"Yeah, I'll be fine."

"We can wait until you're fully back."

My gaze flicked to my best friend. "I can handle myself."

"Keep your attitude with Gigi, not me," Turin said, pushing the door open.

The place had electricity and an assembly line of products running in and out. Nothing like our farm in Italy but big enough to stay off the grid.

"Boss, glad to see you back." Miguel held a hand out for me to shake.

Turin folded his arms. "Miguel, what are we looking like?"

Miguel didn't show fear, and I appreciated a man who wasn't easily intimidated.

"Turin and Gigi demanded we do three ships a week. I manage all the locations, and so far, we've had no issues."

"Nothing unusual?" I challenged.

Miguel pondered my question. "A few times, I thought we may have been followed, but I couldn't be sure."

Turin's eyes narrowed as he searched Miguel's face. "You never told me."

Miguel shrugged. "I didn't think anything of it until now." He moved closer and his voice dropped low. "At the last drop off, they took the product and didn't wait for us to count the money."

My eyes narrowed on Miguel. "How many times has this happened?"

"At least twice." Miguel took his phone out to show his last few drops.

"Who was the buyer?" My head was spinning.

"Irish boys," Miguel answered, putting his phone back in his pocket.

Turin and I looked at each other. One time could be forgiven, but multiple times made me question if Dario had set this up from the beginning.

"I need names—"

I was cut off as the warehouse plunged into darkness. I had no weapon, and Turin shoved me behind him as gunfire erupted.

"We need to get to the cars!" Turin barked.

I crawled to the wall as bullets sprayed through the windows, taking down a few of our men, including Miguel.

Turin's expression was grim. "Stay close to me."

Tires squealed from the back, and Turin gestured toward the side doors he'd had installed for emergencies. The doors opened to a tunnel that led us out to the woods. I was winded from running, which only increased my frustration and anger. Sweat dripped down my face. I followed Turin, who aimed his gun high in front of us.

I removed my phone from my pocket. "We need to keep moving to get a phone signal."

Turin jerked his head in a nod. "That was a setup."

"Too easy," I mumbled.

I was livid. What if Gigi had come with us tonight? The thought of my wife being in danger made my blood burn.

We emerged from the woods and headed for a nearby gas station. Turin made a few calls while I dialed Gigi's number.

"Axel, it's late," Gigi said groggily.

"Listen to me, Gigi," I said urgently.

"What's wrong?" she asked breathlessly.

"We were ambushed," I said as Turin finished his call. I glanced back at the woods and warehouse beyond.

"Where are you?"

A car arrived, and Turin motioned for me to get in.

"On my way back to you."

"Tell me what happened, Axel."

"Someone thought we would be easy targets and tried to put a hit on us."

The urge to kill whoever was responsible was bubbling to the surface, ready to blow for threatening my family and me.

"Are you with Turin?"

"Yes. We'll be there in thirty minutes."

"Get here safe." Gigi's concern soothed my frazzled nerves.

"I will." I disconnected the call.

We were overzealous tonight and put ourselves in a vulnerable situation. The setup had Dario's stamp all over it.

All the lights were off in the house when we arrived. I ran inside and made a beeline for Gaspare's room. He was sound asleep in his crib. I pulled his cover over his little body and kissed his forehead lightly.

Slipping quietly from his room, I headed for the bedroom and saw Gigi still awake, reading a book.

"Thank God you're back. Are you okay?" she asked when she saw me, dropping her book on the bedside table.

"I'm fine, baby." I kissed her on the forehead and kicked off my shoes.

"Do you want to talk about it?"

I shook my head. "Tomorrow. For now, I just want to wash off the day and hold my wife."

If there was one thing Gigi understood, it was that sometimes you had to leave the stress at "work."

Grabbing a quick shower, I pulled on clean boxers and crawled into bed. I drew Gigi close to my chest and kissed the back of her neck. Calmed by her presence, I succumbed to sleep.

* * *

Sunlight filtered into the room, and I opened my eyes to see Gigi gazing at me. I used to wake alone, usually after carrying out a job for Laurent, but now I had a wife and child. I was a lucky fucker.

Gaspare whimpered in the room next to us, and Gigi kissed my chest before going to get him. She brought him in and sat on the loveseat in the window. Tension from our conversation in the office yesterday lingered in the air, but Gigi smiled at me.

I stretched and threw the covers back, moving to Gigi and dropping to my knees in front of her.

Gigi grinned at me. "You snored last night."

I chuckled. "I was tired."

"Must have been all that running away from bullets." Gigi grabbed my hand and intertwined our fingers. "Are you hungry?"

"Maybe later."

I stood and looked down at our son before moving to open the window. Gigi placed Gaspare in his bassinet and wrapped her arms around me from behind. The birds chirped, and the wind tossed the leaves around. Summer was coming. Soon we would be out in the pool and using the guest house.

"When I was pregnant, I craved pickles and yogurt."

I wrinkled my nose in disgust. "That's gross."

Gigi laughed. "Plus gas and the way your son sat on my bladder. I felt like he knew you weren't around."

She turned to lean against the window so she was facing me. I moved closer and braced my hands on either side of her.

"I'm here now. Do you still crave pickles with yogurt?" I would have the chef throw it away not to tempt her again.

She burst into laughter. "No."

"Good."

"Pregnancy cravings are normal."

"Yeah, but I didn't get to have you bugging me to pick something up in the middle of the night or rub your swollen feet." I pointed at her feet, and we both laughed. Moments like this felt like old times.

Gaspare fussed, and Gigi moved away to pick him up. "I don't like how we acted yesterday," she said as she sat on the edge of the bed with our son.

"I've never doubted your strength, but when it comes to Dario, I need you to step back."

"Explain last night." She rubbed Gaspare's back.

"Turin and I went to check on the product. He had a few

close contacts with a Russian deal that might hurt us if they work with Hugo Mendoza."

"Hugo wants revenge for Igor."

"Yes, and I need my wife to stay out of harm's way."

"Too late if he knows I killed his nephew."

"He knows."

Gigi bounced Gaspare on her lap. "For now, I'll cut back on my duties."

"No, I need you to step down. It's time."

"How can you ask me to go against what my father wanted?"

"Laurent wanted you safe, and Dario would've been in charge if you'd married him."

"So my mother gets her wish," she said, her voice heavy with sarcasm.

Gaspare let out a wail of hunger and she lifted her shirt, helping him to latch on.

I frowned. "Gigi, this has nothing to do with your mother."

Gigi said nothing as she nursed Gaspare. After a few minutes, he was finished, and I took him from her to burp him.

"Okay." Gigi finally responded as she fixed her shirt.

I tossed the covers back and placed our son further up on the bed near the pillows. I cupped Gigi's chin and tilted her face to look at me. "You and our son are my world. I'll move heaven and earth to keep you safe."

She wrapped hers around my neck. "I believe you."

I dropped a kiss on the tip of her nose. "Then trust me."

"I hate this. It feels like he's winning," she said unhappily.

I placed my hand over her heart. "Dario will feel the full force of my wrath."

Gigi needed to recover after giving birth, and I needed to recover from my ordeal. Dario had screwed over so many people, I half hoped he would end up dead without me even touching him. Hugo had chosen to work with the Devil.

I stared into her eyes and smiled. "How are you feeling?"

"Tired, but good."

"Did Gaspare sleep through the night?"

We glanced at him trying to fall asleep on the bed.

Gigi smiled. "He's a light sleeper, like his father."

"I want to take you both out for lunch."

"Are you sure? With everything that happened last night?"

"More guards will be assigned to you."

Gigi groaned and stood. "Axel, that's exhausting."

"For your safety and my peace of mind."

She sighed. "Okay." She walked to the closet and looked through her clothes.

My phone rang, and I grabbed it from the bedside table. "Axel."

"I wondered if you'd have the guts to pick up the phone."

"Who is this?"

"Hugo Mendoza."

"How did you get my number?" I demanded.

"Meet me in one hour."

Gigi stepped out of the closet with two dresses.

"No one summons me to a meeting. I do the calling."

Mendoza chuckled, and I balled my hand into a fist. Gigi moved to stand in front of me.

"My people will call you when I'm ready to meet," I countered.

"Your wife killed my godson," he sneered.

"Being on the wrong side of this fight to save Dario won't end well for you."

"My loyalty to the Ramini family is for life," Hugo answered.

"He's being funded by you, correct?"

Hugo chuckled again. "One hour."

The line went dead.

Gigi looked at me expectantly.

"There's something I need to take care of, baby."

"Do what needs to be done, Axel. I won't question you."

Her passive-aggressive attitude pissed me off. I didn't like being an asshole, so I let her leave the room while I contacted Turin to pick me up. A day with Gigi and my son was my priority after I discovered Hugo's intentions.

Once dressed, I got Gigi and our son settled in the limo. I kissed his head and Gigi's cheek before telling Ralfie that two cars would tail them.

"There's no need to worry," Gigi said as she shut the door.

I leaned down and spoke through the open window. "You've got two SVUs with guards following you as a precaution." I pointed behind at the two cars of soldiers ready to die for our family.

"Be safe," Gigi said.

"Make sure your phone is on," I replied and got in the car to head out first.

Chapter 6

Gigi

A few days later.

Axel and I avoided talking about Hugo. The dominant Enforcer in him was slowly seeping back into my life. Tonight, I wanted to go out and enjoy myself after the birth of my son. I was a cartel Boss and a mother, but this evening was about being Gigi. Janice had mentioned a new club called Sinful. It was in the middle of New York's Times Square with two levels, glass ceilings, neon lights, and a large dance floor. The VIP areas had one-way mirrors for privacy.

Janice waved her hands in the air as she danced. Some people would scoff at us being friends since I was so much younger, but I appreciated her and Sabrina as women in their early forties giving me wisdom about being married and being a mom in the mob.

Our bottle girl came to the table with our drinks. I slipped her two hundred dollars to keep the drinks coming, and she smiled. I pushed to my feet, grabbed my vodka and soda, and watched my girls enjoy their night out.

"We're here now, so give it up." Janice urged me to talk.

"What should I give up?" I questioned.

Janice and Sabrina laughed. Tonight was meant to be fun with no talk about our husbands.

"Lie about being pissed at Axel." Sabrina snapped her fingers, bobbing her head to the music. One of Janice's girl-friends stood, strolled down the stairs, talked to the guard, and then laughed.

"Not pissed at him." Sabrina said. "We've seen and done it all with our men, even tried to make them jealous."

Janice said, "Nothing can get past them."

"When Axel found out I'd done something that could harm us, he was upset."

"Something like what?"

"Have you ever put yourselves in harm's way by taking matters into your own hands?"

"All the time in the beginning." Janice bent forward and picked up her glass. She pushed my drink into my hand, and I gulped it down.

"He hates me because I made him marry me." My eyes raked over the crowd.

"You didn't make him marry you." Janice moved to the beat of the music.

I pressed a hand to my stomach. "Can we not talk and just enjoy the music?"

"We can, but you must come to terms with your brand-new life." Janice took the glass out of my hand and refilled it.

"My father wanted me to be strong, but I feel foolish and weak."

Sabrina touched my shoulder and smiled. "Gigi, you're still learning."

The sweat rolled off my forehead. "I feel like an idiot sometimes."

"Join the mommy club." Sabrina continued. She nudged my arm with her shoulder and gestured to the dance floor.

"As a Boss, I felt in control and powerful, like nothing could touch me." I met Sabrina's eyes.

"You craved power, and now you're a mom, you're trying to convince yourself you can have it all." Janice said, holding my gaze.

"Yes! My father handled business and took good care of me." I slammed the glass on the table and poked my lip out.

"If you think about it, was your father around for all the moments?" Sabrina asked.

I evaded her question and plastered a smile on my face, raising my glass in a toast.

"Tonight, you must shed it all, get out, and have fun," Janice stated.

We clicked glasses and drained the rest of our drinks. Janice took me by the hand and marched down the stairs into the crowd, with JayZ playing in the background. It might come as a surprise to some people, but he was extremely popular in Italy. Sabrina joined us, her guard keeping space between us and the crowd. I clapped as she whirled in a circle with her hands in the air and the rest of the girls joined us on the floor. It was refreshing to be carefree again.

* * *

Thirty minutes later, I was tired, hot, and sweaty. I was ready to see my baby and head to bed. Janice walked back to the section where we'd ordered. Sabrina grabbed my hand, and I followed her through the crowd. I was watching the other women flirting with single guys when I caught something in my peripheral vision.

"Ginerva?" I whispered.

I bumped into Sabrina as she suddenly stopped behind her guard. "Shit! Sorry," I apologized.

Sabrina put her hand on my arm. "My bad."

"I think I've had too much to drink." I blinked, wondering if I was imagining things.

"Why do you say that?" Sabrina followed my gaze.

I pointed at the couple in the corner near the edge of the bar. The guy's back was to us, but the woman looked like my old friend.

"Ginerva!" I yelled, but she didn't turn.

Janice came back down the stairs. "Time to go, ladies."

"Wait! I need to see something." I yanked my hand out of Sabrina's grip and darted through the crowd. My bodyguards would be pissed that I'd run off.

I was a short distance away when a man blocked my path. "What's your hurry, sexy?"

"Excuse me." I tried to pass him.

He stepped in front of me again. "Come on. You look like you need me in your life."

Usually I would have been happy to put him in his place, but I had bigger priorities right now. "Leave, or prepare to be questioned by my two friends," I warned, indicating my approaching bodyguards.

He smirked. "They can come with us. There's a lot of me to handle." He grabbed his crotch.

I snapped my finger, and Michael, one of the new guards, clapped his hand on the guy's shoulder. He turned him around and escorted him away. When I looked back at the corner, it was empty.

I strode closer and tapped my hand on the counter of the bar. "Hey!" I waved to grab the bartender's attention.

"What will it be?"

"Did you see where that couple went that was standing here?"

His brow rose high. "Couple?"

"The girl and guy all hugged up."

Bartender replied, "Sorry, I don't know what you're talking about."

"They were here for a few minutes making out," I countered.

The vibration of the music increased, and the crowd started screaming. It was hard to hear him.

A hand tapped on the bar top. "Mrs. Bresciani."

I looked up in surprise. "Detective Soren. You don't seem like a hookah bar type."

"Interesting to see you here tonight."

"I need to get back to my friends." I walked around him, but he grabbed my hand.

"Do you?"

"Detective, you need to let go of my hand."

"What's the hurry?" he questioned, though he released my hand.

I looked over his shoulder to see Janice heading toward me, followed by our guards.

"Are you following me, detective?" I challenged.

"I wasn't expecting to see you here." He rested his hands at his side.

"I bet."

"Gigi, time to go," Janice interrupted.

Axel could clear this place in seconds if I asked, but I wanted to have fun. "Not ready to leave."

"Axel called Carlo. He said you need to call him now." Janice held her phone up and wiggled it in front of my face.

Detective Soren smirked like he knew something.

"Detective, you might fool some people, but not me. If I

find out you're following my friends and me, I'll have my lawyer sue you."

"Mrs. Bresciani, if you change your mind, give me a call." He pulled a business card out of his pocket and held it up for me to take.

I ignored his offer and walked outside to our awaiting limo, still searching the area for that familiar woman. Janice climbed in next to Sabrina, and I slid in behind her.

Sabrina looked out of the window. "He's going to be trouble."

"Who?" I questioned.

She gestured out the window.

Detective Soren stood near the alley of the club, watching intently as our limo drove away.

I took a napkin out of my purse to wipe the sweat off my face. "I think I saw Ginerva tonight."

Janice took out her makeup case and touched up. "Your best friend, Ginerva, who was kidnapped?"

I fanned myself. "I know it sounds crazy."

"When?" Janice asked.

"Walking back to the VIP section."

"How did she get here?" Sabrina had the same thoughts as me.

I grabbed a bottle of water from the small fridge to cool down. "There's no way she's in America. I mean, we've tried everything to find her, and prayed Dario didn't kill her." I sighed and turned the air on in the car.

"Stranger things have happened," Janice muttered.

* * *

I passed Gaspare to the doctor at his follow-up visit the next day. Axel wasn't happy about me going out to the club last night. I'd told him we were having a girls' night in at Janice's.

The doctor was curious. "Gaspare looks happy and healthy. Is he sleeping through the night?"

"He wakes a few times, but for the most part, he sleeps until the morning."

"And you are breastfeeding, correct?"

I touched Gaspare's cheek. "Not the best feeling in the world, but he's latching on fine."

"Great. I like to hear that. What about you?"

"Do you think she should drink while breastfeeding?" Axel asked.

I tensed in shock. "Axel!"

"It's fine, Gigi. He can ask me anything he wants."

Emotion contracted my throat. "He's being rude."

"As long as she's taking precautions, pumping beforehand and waiting afterward, a little wine won't hurt."

"I went out the other night, Doctor, and he's pissed." I waved Axel off.

"You two have to trust each other. Gaspare can pick up on any hostility." She finished documenting his information.

I put him in his car seat, and Axel picked it up to leave the room. The doctor explained to bring him back in a few weeks for a follow up, so we made the appointment and went to the car.

"Ralfie's taking you home," Axel announced.

I noticed another car in front of my limo with our guards. "Where are you going?"

He swung around to face me. "I have business."

"So that's how we're acting, Axel?" I challenged, my frustration bubbling up.

"Gigi, you're pushing my buttons."

"I go out one time—"

"It's not just about going out." His face darkened. "Anything could have happened. I thought you were at Janice's house."

"We have triple the protection now."

He stared deeply into my eyes as he framed my face with his hands. "Dario is still out there."

I slipped my hands around his waist. "I know."

"Then act like it!" he growled.

Gaspare started to cry, and tears stung my eyes. I pulled away from him. "Take me home."

"Baby, listen." He tipped my face toward his.

My fight to make my voice heard was an issue from the past. Axel wasn't Rosa or my father. Letting my guard down with my husband showed I was open to his feelings.

"I'm afraid I'll end up like my parents," I confessed as I reached out to soothe Gaspare in his car seat.

"We're not your parents or mine," Axel reminded me.

As Gaspare cooed, I picked up the bottle I had in the fridge from pumping and placed it in his mouth. "I'm sorry about last night." I whispered, suddenly aware of what the outcome could have been.

"We need to put everything on the line." Axel scanned my face as he slipped into the car. He'd obviously decided to ride with us.

Ralfie started the car and drove out of the parking lot. Axel nipped at my neck, then nuzzled his chin over my shoulder.

"I know you're mad about last night, but something else happened."

"What happened?"

"Detective Soren was there and tried to talk to me. The same detective who came to the house."

"Came to our house when?"

I took a deep breath and exhaled. "The day I gave birth to Gaspare. They came to our house to talk about Igor Mendoza."

Axel removed his arm from around my shoulder. "They pushed you into early labor," he muttered, his mouth hardening.

"I was already overdue."

"Things could have gone wrong," he bit out.

"He has a partner, Detective Raymond."

"What else do I need to know?"

"I think I saw Ginerva."

Ralfie arrived at our home, and Axel helped me out of the car. He took Gaspare and wrapped his other hand around my waist as we walked to the front door.

"I thought you had business to handle," I said, looking up at him.

"That can wait. I want to make sure we're good." Axel smiled and kissed my cheek.

"We're always good." I cupped his face and smoothed my thumb over his beard.

I removed my jacket as Axel took Gaspare to his play pen in the living room. I could hear Ebony and Heather in the kitchen as I followed Axel to his office and closed the door.

"Dario kidnapped Ginerva," I said, picking up the conversation now we were alone. He sat at his desk and turned his computer on. "I remember."

I paced the room. "We never saw a body."

Axel rubbed his temples. "We know Igor Mendoza helped Dario to get to America through Igor's uncle Hugo."

I sat on the edge of the desk. "Then Soren and Raymond came asking questions."

Axel leaned back in his chair in thought. "Plus, the ambush at the warehouse."

An idea flickered in my mind. "You think they're connected?"

With a sour look, Axel remarked. "Yes."

I sighed. "Dario's a skilled manipulator."

"Dario is out of control."

"I want to find Ginerva."

"Ask Turin to pull the footage from the cameras at the club."

I stood to leave. "Thank you."

"Gigi?"

I turned to look at him. "Yes?"

"Never keep anything from me."

"I had my reasons."

"Doesn't matter the reasons. It could have been avoided."

"You were in a coma, Axel. I wanted you to recover." I reached the door and turned the knob to leave. "Going back and forth with you is like hitting my head against a brick wall."

"No more clubs, Gigi."

I stomped up the stairs to the bedroom, shutting the door and leaning against it. Ginerva was alive. I could feel it in my bones. If she had escaped, Dario would be looking for her. I needed to find and protect her. Bringing her here under our watch was the best thing we could do for her. Axel and I didn't agree on everything, but I knew my safety was his priority. His request for me not to get involved in cartel business was out of the question while our enemies were joining forces.

I picked up the phone to dial Sabrina's number, sitting near the window and listening to the phone ring.

"Hey, Gigi. How did Gaspare do at the doctor's office?"

she questioned immediately.

The question put a smile on my face. "He's doing good."

"Everything okay?"

"I need your help."

She probed further. "With what?"

"I want to find Ginerva."

"I thought Axel said to stay out of everything."

"Axel has enough to deal with."

Sabrina responded, "Maybe you should let him handle finding her, Gigi."

"Sabrina, if it was Janice in trouble, you'd go to the ends of the earth to find her."

Sabrina was like a big sister, wanting to protect me. "Janice and I are different."

"No different to Ginerva and me."

"Let me call Janice on three-way."

"Thanks."

A minute passes before I hear kids laughing in the background. "Sabrina, you know Carlo went to handle some business, and I'm stuck babysitting."

"Girl, those are your kids."

"I only claim them for tax time," Janice said.

I wanted to laugh so badly, but Axel walked through the door.

"Gigi is on the line," Janice added.

Axel removed his shirt, dropped his pants, kicked off his boxers, and headed to the bathroom. I admired my husband's naked body. I missed being with him in that way. Six weeks seemed like forever, and I was desperate to be intimate with him.

"Gigi wants to do what?" Janice screeched, and I hurriedly ended the call. I jumped up and sauntered to the bathroom door, watching Axel bathe.

"You going to stay and watch me?" he teased.

"No, I need to check on Gaspare." I said quickly, coming up with an excuse.

There was a teasing smile on his face. "Come here, Gigi."

I whined. "Axel, I can't."

As he pushed his hand down his chest, he licked his lips. "Why?"

"I'm too emotional right now, and we might take it there before my time is up."

He threw his head back in a laugh.

"That's not funny!" I exclaimed.

The fire in his eyes blazed down at me. "I know how to shower without having sex with you."

"No..." I hesitated, torn between what I wanted and what I worried might happen if I gave in.

He slid the door open and held out a hand out for me. Our eyes locked. I kicked off my shoes and strolled to the door, removed my clothes before stepping inside. He turned to me and dragged his hand down my cheek. I closed my eyes and took in his presence. All those months I was without him, I'd pictured us together like this.

"We're meant to be," he assured me gently.

A rush of goosebumps spread over my body. "I missed you so much."

"Nothing will keep us apart."

There was a knot in my stomach. "Don't leave me again."

He gripped my throat lightly. "Never."

"How are you feeling?"

He pulled me in close, his fingers wrapped around my waist. "I'm fine," he responded dismissively.

"You're not a doctor, Axel."

Axel pushed his fingers through my hair and kissed me, slicking his tongue against mine.

I gripped his shoulders and moaned. My body was so sensitive to his touch. I wished we'd go to bed and make love all night long. But I was still recovering from giving birth, and it would be foolish to jump back into sex too soon.

Axel dropped to his knees, threw my right leg over his shoulder, and pressed his face into my pussy.

"Axel!" I yelped and tried to step back.

He locked his arms around my thighs and gripped my hips. I almost stumbled from the intensity of his touch and grabbed his shoulders to hold myself up. My heart jolted and my pulse pounded as the water cascaded over our bodies. Our attraction had been instant from the first time we met.

Axel kneaded my ass as he buried his face in between my thighs, and a familiar ripple of excitement washed over me. My mouth dropped open as he gently dragged his tongue from my pussy up to my stomach and circled around my navel. I moved to cover myself, but he stopped me and pressed a kiss to my skin.

"You know better than to hide yourself from me."

The passion in his eyes as he looked up at me invoked an urgency to please him. Axel brushed another kiss over my stomach and stood, kissing me deeply. Reaffirming our bond, I gripped his steel rod and squeezed.

"Shit, Gigi." he groaned.

"Never hide yourself from me, either."

"I won't, baby."

I slowly dropped a kiss on his chest, on each nipple, and down his stomach before taking him in my mouth. He gripped my head, and I watched him writhe under my control. We spent a pleasurable ten minutes in the shower before we dried off. Our makeup sessions always made up for the fights.

Chapter 7

Axel

Three days earlier.

Turin drove us to the hotel where Hugo stayed while he was in New York. The bar was cleared for us to meet, and I let him do most of the talking.

Hugo smiled at the server as she sashayed away from the table. "I would have respected your wife more if she'd come to me first."

"My wife doesn't answer to you."

Hugo's brows shot up. "Aren't you the Enforcer of the Carrington Cartel?"

"Are we discussing solutions, or feeding your ego?" I asked maliciously.

"Axel," Turin warned, keeping me calm.

His grin was snakelike. "I only talk to Bosses."

"You're talking to one."

"My nephew is dead, and we're owed compensation," Hugo explained.

"Not my problem."

"I believe there's evidence of her killing him," Hugo said casually.

Turin told me that someone at the hotel had sold a copy of the video, and that's how word got back to Hugo.

I shifted in my seat, frustrated that he had an upper hand. "I want Dario Ramini."

Hugo lifted a hand and picked up his sunglasses to place on his nose. "Dario is off limits."

"Then we have nothing else to discuss."

"I'll go with the Irish, and your wife will end up in jail."

I lunged at him. Turin held me back as Hugo's men pulled out their guns.

Hugo held up a hand to stay his men. "She owes me."

"Igor's replacement is worth a million, maybe two."

He glared. "Money won't make me feel better. I want territory."

"Not giving you all of Chicago."

"You'll give me Chicago and New York."

Hugo reached in his pocket, pulled out his phone. He played a video showing Gigi at the hotel.

"Any visitors to your home lately?" he asked snidely. "Detectives Soren and Raymond."

Knowing he was behind the cops coming to our place pissed me off even more. "Tell me, Hugo, are you planning to leave here alive?"

He chortled, grabbed his scotch, and drank it before answering. "I'm in New York for a few more days. Let me know what you want to do." Hugo slid out of the booth and buttoned his jacket before leaving with his men.

Present

Gigi slept like a baby last night, after I got back from the office. She told me all the time that she couldn't sleep well without me beside her in bed. I prayed God watched over my family because the decisions I was making were meant to protect them if I was no longer around.

Gigi held Gaspare in her arms in the backyard pool. I stood at the door watching while considering how I could get to Hugo and Dario before they made a move again.

Turin stepped beside me and passed me a drink. "Does she know?"

I turned to look at him, shaking my head. "Not yet."

"If we want to avoid further bloodshed, how should we handle it??"

My hand tightened around the glass. "As far as my wife and child are concerned, it is not possible."

"I found the hotel employee who gave Hugo the video."

"Any problems with the family?"

"Burial was tasteful."

Gaspare clung to Gigi as she floated in the water.

"I want to take her to Italy and keep them safe."

"She won't go for that easily."

"Killing another cartel Don will put us on the radar of the police and FBI."

"We have a few contacts. I can see how much Detective Soren and Raymond have on Gigi."

"I need everything from blood type to their mothers' birthdays."

"Look at it from Gigi's standpoint. She was pregnant and not thinking clearly."

"What did you find on Ginerva?"

"Nothing so far. I've been looking into Hugo's contacts and the shootout at the warehouse."

"Get more people on Ginerva. Gigi's losing her mind and feeling guilty."

Turin agreed. "We'll figure it out. Oh, and you won't be

surprised to know that Hugo was behind the shooting at the warehouse."

He was right. That news was no surprise to me.

Turin stared off into space as Gaspare splashed the water. He downed his drink quickly. "Killing won't be easy like Alvar Casella, Rosa, or Edmundo."

"It's time to come up with a new plan to deal with him since he wants all of Chicago and New York. We need another meeting."

Turin grunted, knowing how hotheaded I could be. "That won't be good for any of us."

Gigi stepped out of the pool and sauntered toward us with Gaspare. I picked up the towel, wrapped it around them, and kissed her forehead.

"Turin, what are you doing here?"

Turin tickled Gaspare's feet. "I needed to talk with Axel."

Gigi bounced Gaspare in her arms. "What about?"

"Hugo."

"Has he changed his mind about Igor and revealed Dario's location?" she asked.

"Hugo's not letting Igor's death go," I replied.

Gigi snapped. "Fuck Igor." She turned her attention to my best friend. "Turin, tell Axel I was right to kill Igor."

His shoulders slumped. "Gigi, I told you not to kill him."

Gigi glared at Turin.

"Hugo wants Chicago and New York or he'll send a video to the police," I explained.

"We have people on the force, but we can't pull them in without raising suspicions of Soren and Raymond," Turin added.

"I need to change Gaspare." Gigi walked back into the house.

Turin passed me another drink. "How are you feeling after the coma? For real?"

"Sometimes, I feel fine, and other times like shit. I'm still getting my body back in shape."

"Maybe you need to wait and rest a bit more before going on this mission to get Hugo and Dario."

"I'll rest when they're dead."

* * *

Gigi and I spent the day together after Turin left and let Gaspare hang with Janice and Sabrina's kids so they could meet finally. I promised the ladies Gigi would host something at the house when I felt it was safe.

Turin picked me up, and we had two of our guns in another vehicle a few cars down for backup. Turin turned the lights off in the car and I checked my weapons, nodding that I was ready.

Hugo was here with his people at dinner, and I wanted to wait to see if he contacted Dario when he left. I sat back in the seat and watched the front door of the restaurant intently as customers came and went.

"We only watch tonight," Turin cautioned.

"Unless they try something."

"I told Gigi I'd get you back in one piece." Turin and Gigi had become good friends while I was in the coma.

I stared intensely at the restaurant door, unable to place the man standing with his friends under the light. Something felt off. Then I realized it was the same guy who'd bumped into me a few weeks ago.

"I know him from the office."

Turin surveyed them from the window. "What?"

"The guy in the front."

"What guy? There are three of them."

"The one on the left in the black leather coat and gray slacks."

"At the office when?"

"The day we got side swiped and almost killed at the warehouse."

Turin's head swiveled around fast. "You're shitting me."

"What are the odds these men are here at the same restaurant as Hugo?"

"Extremely rare."

"They set us up." I reached to open the door.

Turin grabbed my hand before I could open it. "Yeah, but we can't do anything right now."

"I'm sending a message."

Turin gripped the steering wheel. "Too many people around."

"Wait until they get to their cars."

"Shit, Axel, we might need to rethink if Hugo comes out."

"He'll get the message that I'm willing to go anywhere and do anything to protect my wife."

"Gigi's a sister to me, but we'd be killing them without cause right now."

I cocked the chamber. "Turin, drive."

He started the car, and both men looked up and down the street. If they turn out to be innocent, I'd ask for forgiveness on my deathbed, but my gut told me they were with Mendoza and Dario.

"We should take them and get some information."

"I'm done talking." I rolled the window down as he slowed and aimed the gun just as the back window of the car shattered. I fired a few shots before Turin floored the gas and took off.

"Damn it! They made us," I barked.

"I knew something was off." He shifted his gaze from the side to the rearview mirror.

Adding more bullets to my gun, I fired more shots. "Turn around."

"Axel, you have a death wish."

"Fuck!" I slammed my hand against the dashboard.

Turin made a sharp turn at the stop sign and got on the freeway.

I grumbled. "Hugo is pissing me off."

I reached in my pocket as my phone rang, seeing an unknown number.

"You were foolish tonight, boy," Hugo said.

"I won't make a mistake again."

"If you think you can get me, by all means, turn around."

I looked through the rearview mirror. "Get off the next exit," I ordered Turin.

Hugo chuckled. "I love playing games."

"All we want is Dario."

"All I want is Chicago and New York," Hugo replied.

"Greed only gets you death."

"We can have peace between our families," he suggested.

"Fuck you, Mendoza," I growled.

"The infamous Enforcer seems upset," he sneered.

"You took a shot. Now I'll take mine."

"Oh, I forgot to tell you. Dario says congrats on the new baby. He wondered if he should have gotten a DNA test, since some of his family's features could be present in Gaspare."

I gritted my teeth at the accusation. Gigi was a virgin when we got together. "Clearly, Dario wants to die slowly and painfully."

"I'm just the messenger," Hugo teased.

Thoughts of burning Dario alive assaulted me. "My wrath is not something you want to experience, Hugo."

"Then give me what I want," he demanded before hanging up.

Turin sped through the back streets to our home. He passed through the gates and stopped in front of the garage. I jumped out and rushed to the house. Running upstairs, I checked on Gaspare in his crib. The tension eased from my shoulders, and I sat in the rocking chair.

"Axel." Gigi's sweet voice came from the door, where she stood in her gown and robe.

The thought of my family being hurt was a weight on my heart. "Go back to bed."

Gigi crossed the threshold. "It's late."

Watching my son sleeping in his crib eased my anxiety. "I know. I had to take care of something."

"Something or someone? You look sweaty." Gigi strode to the crib and then turned to me.

"I made a move on Hugo."

She frowned. "Tonight?"

"Yeah."

Gigi rubbed Gaspare's stomach as he stirred. "Did they retaliate?"

My eyes dragged from her toes up to her face. She'd barely done anything, but she took my breath away like usual. "He will."

She sighed and moved to sit in my lap. I ran my hand up and down her back. "Tell me what happened?"

"I went to shoot at his people, and they made us first and shot out the window of Turin's car."

I held Gigi tightly as she went to jump out of my lap. "Is he all right?"

I nodded.

"Hugo and I should meet," Gigi stated plainly.

"Never."

"That's what he wants. To intimidate me and get you to falter."

I twirled the lace on her gown. "You will not be used as bait."

"Dario will come out of hiding if he sees I've made an agreement with Hugo," Gigi persisted.

"You're not giving Hugo anything." I cupped the back of her head.

"I've been thinking long and hard. Maybe we should let him have Chicago."

"Laurent would turn over in his grave."

Gigi stood. "It's my family's business."

I protested. "And your safety could be in jeopardy."

Gigi cupped my face. "Dario will make a stupid mistake if he sees Hugo fall in line with me."

"I hate the thought of Dario touching you."

"Baby, you're the man I want. Dario was only interested in me for selfish reasons. He backed down from his threat to harm me because of your intervention."

I grunted. "Let me think it over."

"I've decided, and it's final."

"So my opinion never mattered."

Gigi walked to the door. "I always take your opinions into consideration, but you're clearly not thinking as the Enforcer, only as my husband."

She left. I contemplated her words and realized I agreed. All my choices had been from the perspective of a husband trying to keep his wife safe. Moves needed to be made on a bigger scale and Gigi was the link to everything.

Turin came into the house, so I went downstairs and met him in the kitchen while he was on the phone.

"Tomorrow, okay." Turin opened the fridge and passed a bottle of water to me. He ended the call and turned to me. "The two guys you shot at are still alive."

I leaned back on the island. "Fuck. That's all I need."

Turin tossed the lid of his water bottle in the garbage. "We'll worry about it later."

I repeated my conversation with Gigi. "She wants to meet with Hugo."

"Good." Turin said.

"I thought you agreed she was doing too much when she was pregnant."

Turin finished his water. "She was, and Hugo is dangling evidence that can hurt her and you."

"Do you think I'm doing right by her?"

Turin went to grab another water. "Gigi knows you'll take a bullet for her."

"When I asked her to step down, I think I feared she would be killed, like my parents."

"Being a husband and Enforcer will have your emotions conflicted."

"Sometimes I wish I'd stayed the Enforcer."

"Then you wouldn't have a family to come home to protect," Turin reminded me.

"The second we get Dario, I want him brought to me."

"There's a good chance we'll find him soon."

"Not soon enough, Turin. We've never been fucked over like this."

"My hands are tied, Axel. We're not in Italy and able to control movements."

"I know."

"Carlo and Antonio could help," Turin suggested.

"Can't ask them to get involved."

"It's a thought."

"Are you sleeping here?"

"I have Ralfie taking me home. We can chat later."

"Keep me posted, no matter the time of day." I walked him out and watched as he left with the second car of guards on standby.

I made sure the alarms were set and checked with the guard at the gate before turning out the lights. I headed upstairs and hopped in the shower to wash the night from my body. After drying off, I pulled on clean boxers and slid into bed next to a sleeping Gigi. I tugged her close and kissed the top of her forehead before giving in to sleep.

Chapter 8

Dario

Days turned into weeks and months of me staying under the radar until the right moment arrived. Today I knocked on the door of the hotel and waited as my nerves flipped my stomach around. Each calculation of my movements had made me public enemy number one to a lot of people, and the only hope I had left was on the other side of this door. The door opened wide, and his guard checked my pockets. I lifted my arms to show I didn't have anything on me.

"Come in, Mr. Ramini," Hugo called from the couch in the living room of his suite.

The man had bodyguards in his room and outside the building. I didn't know how much he paid them to not cause a fuss, but he was well protected.

I shook his hand and took a seat across from him. "Thank you for assisting me, Uncle."

"Well, as my godson, I did everything for you as a little boy in Italy. Your father was like a brother to me."

"My sincere appreciation goes out to you."

"Again, I give you my condolences over your family's current fortunes." His words brought me back to Italy and how Axel and Gigi had destroyed my life.

"I plan on making the people pay."

"I trust you will because I'm here to help."

"The moment I found out the Carringtons killed Igor, I knew you'd want to get revenge."

Hugo nodded. "My nephew was a fuck up, but he was my only sister's boy and she misses him daily."

"Loss of family is hard."

"Tragic, but you're here with good news."

"I can get a meeting with the Irish cartel, the Murphys. All I want is protection and percentage."

After cutting the cigar, Hugo flicked the light at the end. "You plan on moving back to Italy?"

"I want what's rightfully mine. Ramini and Carrington joined as one."

"That will be difficult since Gigi is married to Axel."

"The minute I kill Axel and Gigi, I'm taking it back."

"Her men are loyal, aren't they?"

He offered me a cigar, but I declined. "Money and loyalty aren't the same thing to these men."

"She's a mother now. You tell me you don't care for her still?"

I shifted in my seat. "She's tainted by Axel now. I have no use for her."

"Your cousin and Raymond have been helpful."

A smirk spread across my face. "Amazing Gigi didn't look into them further or she would've discovered that he's Detective Alfeo Ramini Soren, my cousin. She fails at every step, yet still thinks she knows how to run a cartel."

"Soren dropping the Ramini name and taking his mother's last name worked for him," Hugo agreed.

"Is there anything else you need from me?" I asked.

"After Axel tried to kill my men the other night, and you got word of him following us, I was grateful."

"I only wish we'd killed him and Turin."

He put his cigar in the ashtray. "Give it time."

Hugo handed me a briefcase. "Here, take this for now, and I'll be in touch about the next meeting."

I opened it and saw hundreds of dollars wrapped for thousands. I took it from his grip and rose out of my chair. "You know where to find me."

Hugo grinned. "Tell your little friend we hope to see her one day for dinner."

I replied. "Ginerva would love that."

We shook hands, and I grinned as I left the hotel suite and took the elevator. All of my plans were slowly drawing close to the end of Gigi and Axel. The little bitch expected me to roll over and be okay with her making me look like a fool. It's why I took off the moment I got word about my father and called Igor and Hugo to get me to America to hide until I could come back full force.

The elevator stopped on the main floor, and I winked at the front clerk as I passed through the rolling doors.

I hurriedly hopped in the taxi waiting for me. "Back to the hotel you picked me up from."

"Sure thing." The driver left the meter running and moved into traffic to get back across town.

New York was a veritable melting pot to make a name for myself. I checked the time on my watch and looked out at the people who didn't have a clue about the corruption and evil that existed and controlled their lives. I popped the case open to run my hands over the money and closed it quickly as the driver stopped the car. I pulled some money from my pocket and pushed it in his hand.

* * *

I was bombarded as soon as I got through the door.

"Do you think he believed you?" Ginerva asked.

I ignored her question and went into the bedroom to transfer the money to my bag. Ginerva followed, watching as I zipped the bags and put them in the closet. She was annoyed because she'd had to stay here.

"Cheer up." I smacked her on the ass and stared while she fixed her blouse.

When Gigi heard her friend in distress months ago, I knew it would work in my favor. We'd already dealt with her family, and Gigi was worried about her best friend.

Ginerva and I had pretended to hate each other for years, all the while sleeping together. Gigi had no clue. Most times after I'd hung out with Gigi, I returned to Ginerva and we fucked the way I liked. Gigi wouldn't fuck before marriage and I had needs. None of the parents knew because took Ginerva outside the city to avoid any eyes on us.

Ginerva was ready to start a family, but I'd been putting it off until I had Gigi and Axel vanished from my life forever. After Laurent's death, my life changed dramatically. I knew I'd made mistakes that gave Gigi the opportunity to call off our engagement.

The Raminis had close ties with the Carringtons, and a family was at the least of my priorities. My father taught me that you needed money and power in the cartel world to get what you wanted. I would ensure Gigi suffered, knowing I took everything from her before I killed her.

"Can we go have lunch?" Ginerva asked.

"We can't be seen together."

She played with my tie. "We just went to the club."

"And I told you that was a one-time thing."

"Dario, why do we need to keep hiding? Gigi can't hurt us anymore," Ginerva challenged with a hiked brow.

Ginerva was clueless about me not having my full team or money besides what Hugo had given me for setting Axel up.

I clasped my hand around her throat and squeezed gently. "Gigi is slowly losing her power. Let me lead. Gigi made the same mistake, trying to dictate my moves."

Ginerva perched in my lap as I sat on the bed and wrapped her arms around my neck. "Fuck Gigi." She pushed her hand through my curly hair. I'd grown it out and had brown contacts when I first arrived in town.

"Give me a little more time."

"I miss my parents." She exhaled.

I pushed a strand of her hair away from her face. "You understand we had to leave."

Ginerva laid her head on my shoulder and grabbed my hand. She took a deep breath. "I need to tell you something, but I don't want you to get mad."

"What is it?"

"I saw Gigi at the mall." She chewed on a fingernail.

I pushed her off me and jumped up. "Repeat that again." I jammed my hands in my pockets.

"I forgot to tell you. When I went to the mall, she saw me and called my name, but I ran off."

I bent and gripped her jaw.

A sharp breath left her mouth. "Dario, you're hurting me."

"Shut the fuck up! I told you it was a bad idea to go out too early!" I shouted, releasing my hold.

"It'll be fine." Ginerva tried to grab the hem of my pants, and I shoved her away. "How do you know she didn't have anyone follow you back to the hotel?"

I stepped over her and looked out the window. We'd stayed in various hotels under different names as I wasn't ready to get an official home until I could put Axel in the ground. Gigi wouldn't be an easy kill compared to her husband. Now that she was a mother, it would be even more difficult to get her alone.

"I think she may have seen us at the bar the other night," Ginerva mumbled under her breath.

"I knew it was a mistake to go out that night."

She hung her head. "But you said all we needed to do was get Hugo on our side."

I cocked my head as I looked at her. "Hugo is only interested in what he can get out of the deal."

"He's your godfather," Ginerva argued, moving toward me.

"You're so naïve. That doesn't matter to a man like Hugo."

"I'm sorry, baby," she murmured, her eyes downcast as she leaned into me.

"I'll need to be extra cautious in the future."

"With the money Hugo gave you, we could find a place away from the city."

I took a deep breath and tried not to reveal my frustration. "That's the only good idea you've contributed so far."

Her chin rested on my chest as she purred, "Dario, I love you."

"Then start using your brain, Ginerva! One thing you have in common with Gigi is the fuck-ups."

Ginerva stamped her foot in a fit of temper. "I'm nothing like her!"

"Go order room service. I need to make a call." Moving away, I took my phone off the charger and dialed Alfeo's number.

"Fine." Ginerva pouted and stomped out of the bedroom.

"Cousin, any news?" I closed the bedroom door to talk in private.

Alfeo answered, "We installed trackers on two of her vehicles so we know where she is at all times."

"Good. I met with Hugo and he's laid out his plan."

Alfeo hissed, "You know we can't have any dealings with him and shouldn't be talking over the phone."

"I agree. Let's meet." I looked at the time on my watch.

"Same hotel?"

I gazed around the room. "Yeah, but I might be moving out of here today."

"What happened?"

"Ginerva confessed that Gigi saw her at the mall."

"How the fuck did that happen?"

From the window, I looked around the parking lot's surroundings. "A long story. We should meet now." I pulled out the bag from the closet and took a few dollars.

"Raymond's caught up with a case right now. It'll just be me."

"Fine."

"Go to the park on Flushing Meadows in Queens."

"See you soon." The call ended, and I left the room.

Ginerva appeared with the hotel phone and the room service menu. I kissed her and explained I'd be back in a little while. I placed the bag in the safe and gave her some to pay for the room. Everything was cash to be safe.

* * *

"Alfeo." I tossed my head back to signal it was me alone, with my guards near the car.

Alfeo shook my hand, and we talked while we walked while a few parents and their kids played.

"So far, I've got a few photos of Gigi going out with the wife of the De Luca Cartel and attending a few doctor appointments."

"How did she take it when you showed up at her home?" I flipped through the pictures of Gigi laughing and a few of her holding her son.

Alfeo responded, "She was pissed, as you'd expect."

"Ginerva told me she saw us at the nightclub?" Despite his shorter stature and different complexion, we had the same shaped noses and round eyes that showed the family resemblance.

"I tried to get close to her, but her friends jumped in and pulled her away.

"We made a mistake going there."

His expression grew serious. "Told you to move to another country until things cool off."

"They killed most of my family. I'm not giving them the satisfaction of running away."

He eyed me critically. "Dragging that bitch Ginerva with you will get you caught."

I glared at him. "I have love for her, and she's loyal."

"Loyal and dumb, cousin."

I waved him off.

"Listen to me, the only reason you're not dead is because of Hugo and me," he challenged.

"You're getting something out of the deal." I scanned the area to ensure nobody was watching. Reaching into my pocket, I pulled out a stack of money and passed it to him.

His brown eyes burned into mine. "I put my career on the line, so money is the least you could do. You're family, but I don't give blind loyalty."

I ignored his statement. "Anything else you've found?"

He lowered his voice. "Axel may go after Hugo following the ambush at the warehouse."

"Shit." I cursed as the walls closed in on me.

Alfeo soke harshly. "If he does, it will link to me, and I'm not going down alone."

"Will Raymond fold?" His people's loyalty was crucial to me.

"Doubt it, but you never know when life in prison or death are the only options," Alfeo replied.

"Okay, keep me updated, and I'll keep the money flowing. I want Gigi and Axel dead."

"All I can do is provide the setup. My hands are tied when it comes to pulling the trigger." Alfeo strolled away.

One day, I'd claim my rightful position as Boss of a cartel.

Chapter 9

Ginerva

inerva! Ginerva!" I'd been stuck in hotel after hotel for months, and the day I finally convince Dario to let me spend a little time at the mall, I almost get caught by Gigi. The moment I heard her voice that day, I knew it was her. But I felt if she'd caught me, it would've been the end of Dario and me. He's the only man I've ever loved, and Gigi didn't deserve him.

The engagement my parents arranged for me was the last straw, and I decided to go all in on Dario's plan to escape and start a new life together in public. But he'd forced me to stay behind these closed doors. I felt caged in and wondered what could have been if I had gone with my first choice to tell Gigi the truth about our relationship. Dario forbade me from telling Gigi the first time we had sex after one of their fights. Dario came across as tough, but he was a sweetheart to me and spoiled me with gifts and dinners, plus trips. I wanted the wedding and children, and he'd promised we would be married with our own house the minute all of this was over.

"I can have Raymond and Soren send over the photos." He was still on the phone when he walked back into the hotel again hours later. Hours that had left me bored by myself watching tv. I came in from the balcony and shut the door. Sitting on the couch, I watched him pour his second drink of the day from the bar. His constant drinking was a new thing. I'd brought it up a few times, but he only got angry and snatched it out of my hands when I tried to toss it in the sink.

He stared at me while continuing his phone conversation. "We can have dinner. I'll bring her."

I crossed my leg and waited. When Dario finished his call, he put the phone into his pocket and took a sip of his drink as he approached me.

I almost gagged when I smelled the liquor on his breath. "I missed you today."

His hand felt clammy as he touched me. "Ginerva don't start."

He removed his hand and sat beside me on the couch, picking up the remote.

The thought of him being with another woman made me jealous. "Don't you start."

"Baby, it was a long day of tying up loose ends." He stretched his arm along the back of the couch, leaning in to place a kiss behind my ear.

Persuasion was my goal. "I want to get out of this hotel." I turned my head and caught his kiss.

"The last time you almost got caught," Dario murmured through the kiss.

"It won't happen again," I promised.

"Let me think about it."

I jerked back. "No. I want my nails done. Maybe a spa day."

"They have a spa here in the hotel."

"Everything is about the damn hotel. I'm over being stuck in here, Dario!"

"Sit down," Dario demanded.

I refused, and he gripped the remote, throwing it at the wall and getting up in my face. "Bitch, sit your spoiled ass down."

I slapped his face. "Fuck you, Dario!" I was over his demands.

His hand flashed out, and he backhanded me, knocking me to the ground.

"You hit me!" I gasped in shock.

He grabbed my hair and yanked my head back. "I love you, Ginerva, but you're acting more and more like Gigi."

"That doesn't give you the right to put your hands on me."

"Baby, calm down."

"No. Let me go." I tried to remove his hand from my hair.

He kissed me on the lips, and I pushed him back. "I hate you!" I'd never had to deal with being abused by a man.

Regret crossed his face as he helped me up. "I'm sorry, Ginerva. I promise I'll never do it again. I need you to get dressed. We have dinner plans."

"Not going." My cheeks tingled with tears as I argued.

"It's important." He led me back to the couch and sat beside me.

I threw my hands in the air. "Again, all about you."

He groaned and stood. "If you come with me tonight, I'll let you pick out the house with the realtor."

I looked at him in amazement. "You found a house?"

He nodded. "That's one of the things I did today."

A part of me trusted him and I'd gone along with his excuses for the past few months. "Who's dinner with tonight?"

"Hugo Mendoza."

"Your God uncle?"

He nodded and nudged me toward the bedroom. I stood in front of my luggage and contemplated if I should continue or leave. He cupped my face, and I winced from where he'd slapped me.

"I'm sorry, baby. Please forgive me." He kissed my forehead.

I poked his chest. "If you touch me in the wrong way again, I'm leaving you, Dario."

He lifted my hand to his mouth and kissed my palm. "I hear you, baby."

* * *

"Ginerva, I hear you and my godson have been in love for years and plan to get married soon." Hugo cut into his steak.

With a gulp, I poured more wine into my empty glass. "Dario knows I want babies and marriage."

Dario stretched his arm around my shoulder at the table. The restaurant wasn't too far from the hotel. I fiddled with my plate of squash and liver.

"Hugo, thank you again for handling our little problem. I met with my cousin, and he's on board."

"Does he know what I want?" Hugo asked.

Dario rubbed his hands together. "He does, and we'll have a clear chance soon to lock you in for New York."

"Which cousin?" I asked.

Hugo raised an eyebrow. "She doesn't know everything, does she?"

"I thought it best to leave out certain details."

I frowned. "Dario, what are you hiding?"

He leaned over and kissed my cheek. "We can talk later."

I felt like a child being patted on the head. "Excuse me." I rose from the chair, dropped my napkin on the table, and picked up my purse.

"Where are you going?" Dario snarled.

"To the bathroom, if that's all right with you?" I snapped.

Dario pointed at his hired goon. "Take the guard with you."

"I'll be fine going to the bathroom." I started to walk off, but he gripped my hand.

"Take the bodyguard, honey."

I sighed. "Fine. Let's go."

He was pissing me off. I wanted to be included in all the decisions, and he was keeping me out of the loop. He didn't trust me, and that made me feel like Gigi.

I stood at the mirror in the bathroom and checked my hair and makeup. I'd applied my makeup thickly to cover the bruising on my face.

A toilet flushed and a beautiful woman stepped out of the cubicle. She smiled as she approached me. "Long night with the boyfriend?"

I chuckled. "Is it obvious?"

"I've been there before, and now he's my husband." She laughed.

"The goal is to get him to propose." I fixed my hair.

She washed her hands and grabbed paper towels to dry them.

"Give him time. Pushing will make him run off. I know from experience." She smiled and left the bathroom.

A few minutes later, I emerged to find Dario waiting outside the door.

He snatched my arm. "What the fuck did you do?"

"Dario, have you been drinking?" I threw off his hand.

"Shut up and let's go." He grabbed my arm again and pushed me to the back exit.

"What's wrong? I didn't finish my food."

Dario shoved me against the car door. "Did you tell her anything?"

"Who?"

"Dammit, this could be bad." He yanked the door open.

I snatched my arm away again. "I'm not leaving until you tell me."

"Janice Russo, the wife of Carlo Russo and best friend of Antonio De Luca."

My body tensed at the statement. "You're certain it was her?"

"In my line of work, you need to know all the players, and for the third time, you've fucked us over."

"She doesn't know me." His paranoia has returned.

"Carlo knows Hugo and me. I know them from my family's business. Get in the fucking car so we can go." His face flushed as he sneered.

He shoved me to the back door, and I climbed in with tears falling down my cheeks. I knew love took sacrifices, but we barely held a conversation.

"Do you really think she recognized me?"

His guard shut the door. "Stop talking, Ginerva."

"Dario, you can't blame me for everything that has gone wrong."

He rubbed his forehead. "Give me a minute to think."

"Where did Hugo go?"

"He took off as soon as I pointed out Carlo leaving with Janice." Dario slammed his elbow against the window.

"Maybe it was too dark, and they didn't see us."

Dario ignored me and picked up his vibrating phone, sending messages back and forth.

"We can't hide anymore," I said.

"All the pieces aren't in place for me to reveal myself," Dario argued.

"Maybe I can help," I suggested.

"How?" Dario mocked.

Maybe she would call a truce. "Let me contact Gigi."

"No." He stuffed the cell into his pocket.

"Listen, it would work because she's not expecting me to be here in America."

He paused and stared at me. Finally, he was paying attention to me without being distracted by an argument or sex.

"Gigi would be vulnerable. She'd let me come to her place. I could tell her how I escaped and used my savings to fly here to start fresh."

"No. Too dangerous," he stated as we headed down Atlantic Ave.

I extended my hand and touched his arm. "Baby, I need to help. It'll work. Let me do something."

"Let me think about it first." Dario rubbed his chin.

I kissed him on the lips and grinned.

Dario was pulling all the strings, but I had a few ideas that could work and take care of our Gigi and Axel problem much sooner. There were others who could lead cartels and be wives besides Gigi. Obviously, it would take time, but with me beside him, we'd be richer and safer.

Chapter 10

Gigi

I was hesitant to go to the main office. It sprinkled with rain this morning when Gaspare woke up around six. I fed him and spent some time with him before deciding to go into the office to check on the status of the business.

The conference room was silent, and all eyes were on me. Our top soldiers were present, along with our accountant and bodyguards. I hadn't been gone that long. Our drops were being made, and the money was rolling in.

Axel had an appointment with the doctor to check on his progress, although he'd tried to get out of it to be here. I demanded he went and told him I'd fill him in afterward.

"Thank you for coming, gentleman. I know we have a lot of work you need to oversee, so I won't keep you long."

We used Oliver's club to distribute our products since he was one of our top suppliers and the low-level Boss of the cartel. "How are we protecting our spots?"

"Hoboken is a hot spot, and our most profitable location," Oliver said.

"We will rebuild, but until then, a bigger problem has come about," I reported.

"Oliver's right, we need answers if we're going to talk to our men." Another soldier spoke, interrupting my thoughts.

"I'll fire the next person who tells me what I should be doing," I snapped. "Dario Ramini is trying to come after my business."

"Mrs. Bresciani, nice to see your entire crew here," a recognizable voice observed.

My head swiveled to see Detectives Soren and Raymond standing in the doorway. "How did you get in here?"

"Our badges mean something to security," Raymond replied.

We handled legit real estate, shipping, and importing, but a large portion of our time was spent on cartel business. "This is my office. We're a legitimate company."

Detective Soren stepped into the room, looking at the certificates of major deals hanging on the walls. "Doing what?" Soren inquired.

"Real estate, shipping, and investments."

"I highly doubt you're into investments," Detective Soren said as pulled out a chair and sat in front of me.

I raised an eyebrow at his boldness. "This is a private meeting."

"Please don't let us interrupt." Soren sat back with his hands clasped together.

"Do you have a warrant?" I reached for the phone on the desk.

"Is a warrant needed?" A smirk crossed Detective Soren's face.

I bent to look him in the eye, placing my hands on the table. "I doubt you'd be here wasting your time on a wild goose chase."

My men glared at the detectives. If I snapped my fingers, they'd make them disappear, but that would be falling into their trap.

"It's quite simple. You run a major drug and weapons cartel." Detective Raymond jumped into the conversation.

"I run an investment and real estate business," I repeated.

"Are you telling me all these men sell homes?" Soren pointed around the room at my guys.

Our cartel had a dress code that my father implemented years ago to be professional at all times, even with the legit business we handled. "Get out of my office and building." I waved for my guards to escort the cops out.

"I need you to come down to the station," Detective Soren stated.

I rose from my seat and folded my arms. "Why?"

"We'd like to ask you a few questions about the death of Igor Mendoza."

"I've answered all of your questions about Mendoza."

"Humor me." Soren stood and gestured for me to leave with him.

I stared around the room and knew it would only make me look worse if I denied his request. I nodded, grabbed my purse and jacket from my chair, and sauntered out of the conference room.

Raymond pushed the elevator button as I removed my phone to text my lawyer. It was a relief to know that Gaspare was home with the nanny and Ebony.

I shoved the phone back in my purse. "My lawyer will meet us there."

"A lawyer?" a disappointed Detective Soren asked, his mouth a tight line of disapproval.

"Yes, my lawyer. I'm not some stupid little woman you can manipulate."

He grinned as the elevator pinged.

"Unless you're feeling guilty," Detective Raymond said, holding the elevator door open for me to step out.

I raised my hand to stop the security as they approached.

"Guys, I'll be fine. Just a routine visit. Nothing to worry about."

"Mrs. Bresciani, are you sure?" one of them asked.

"Yes. Please lock the doors early today."

"Our car is right out front," Detective Raymond said.

"That won't be necessary. My driver will follow you." I pointed at Ralfie standing at my town car.

I smirked as Soren's jaw ticked with disapproval. "After you, Detective Soren." They probably thought I'd get in the car blindly and end up in some ditch, dead and beaten. Soren thought the cartel world was a new toy for me, but he'd forgotten I was Laurent Carrington's daughter.

* * *

Soren pulled the chair out. "Have a seat, Mrs. Bresciani."

"Why is my client here, detectives?" my lawyer, John Flair, demanded.

It was Detective Soren's turn to ask the question. "Mrs. Bresciani was seen at a hotel in Chicago with Igor Mendoza, a well-known mob Boss."

John flicked through pictures he'd been given from the hotel. "My client visits hotels all the time. Nothing wrong with that."

"He was seen going into her room," Detective Soren said.

"Then we should contact the hotel about him entering her room without her permission."

Soren glared at John. "Nice try, but we know Igor Mendoza and the Carrington Cartel are enemies."

"Any evidence of this?" John challenged.

Raymond and Soren exchanged a glance.

"No? Then we have no reason to be here." John closed the folder.

Soren frowned. "Igor Mendoza's death is international news. If Mrs. Bresciani wants to live a long life, she should confess to the killing and we might be able to help her."

"Are you threatening me?" I sat forward in my seat.

Soren fixed his tie. "I'm trying to help you, Gigi."

I chastised. "Mrs. Bresciani to you, Detective Soren."

His brows pulled together.

"Our only goal is to find the killer. Now would be a good time for her to tell us anything she knows." Detective Raymond pointed at me.

"Is there any evidence that shows her at the scene?" John asked.

Soren clenched his fists and watched me intently. He had to know it was me.

"She's free to go for now," Soren told us.

I stood and collected my things.

"Next time, make sure you have a warrant and concrete evidence."

"You're right about one thing," Soren said.

"What?" John asked.

"There will be a next time," Soren replied.

He made me uneasy, and I wanted to punch him in his smug face.

"Do I need to know anything, Gigi?" John asked as he pulled me away from the station.

. I shook my head. "Nothing to tell."

John faced me. "As your lawyer—'"

"Let me stop you right there, John. I didn't do anything."

"Keep your hands clean."

"If Detective Soren makes another move, I can't promise that my husband will keep *his* hands clean."

"Keep your voice down. We're still inside a police station, so making threats isn't appropriate."

"John, that wasn't a veiled threat. It was a suggestion to ensure the police stay out of my place of business."

We shook hands, and I got back in the car and headed home.

My phone rang, and I quickly grabbed it from my purse to see an unknown number.

"Hello?" I heard heavy breathing.

"Gigi?" a soft voice asked.

"Who is this?"

"Gigi, it's me."

"I think you have the wrong number." I started to hang up.

"It's Geneva."

My chest tightened. "Ginerva?"

"It's really me," she replied. "Gigi, can we meet?"

My hand flew to my mouth in shock as my phone beeped with another incoming call. "I...I... can't believe it."

"I know. I'd like to meet and talk."

"Hold on, I have another call." I pulled the phone away from my ear and clicked over in time to hear Janice shouting in the background.

"Janice, what's up?"

Janice released a breath. "Oh, thank god you answered."

"I'm leaving the police station now."

Confusion and concern from Janice. "The police station? How come?"

"A long story."

"Where's Axel?"

"He had a doctor's appointment today."

"Well, Carlo wanted me to wait for him to tell you both at the same time," Janice continued.

"Tell me what?"

"Are you almost home?" she asked, avoiding my question.

"Yeah, in about five minutes."

"I'll stop by and talk to you in person."

"Janice, you're scaring me. Ginerva is on the other line."

"The best friend who went missing?"

"Yes, and I need to call you back."

"Don't get off this phone with me," Janice pleaded urgently.

"Janice, you're not making sense."

"I know, but Carlo wants me to tell you and Axel at the same time."

"Can you give me a hint?"

"It has something to do with Dario."

"How do you know?"

She hushed her kids in the background. "Just act normal when you get back on the phone with her. I promise to explain as soon as you get home."

"I feel like you're keeping secrets from me."

"Gigi, as your friend, believe me, I will explain when you get home."

"Okay, the car is driving through the gate now."

"Give me a few minutes to get the kids settled."

"Sure. Talk later."

The car pulled into the driveway, and Ralfie opened the passenger door.

I clicked back over to Ginerva. "Hey, Minerva."

Ginerva chuckled. "Thank goodness you didn't hang up."

I removed my key from my purse and unlocked the door. "Um, how did you get to America? I mean, you are in New York, right?"

"I'll explain everything when I see you.

I smiled. "I'm a mother and wife now."

"We have a lot to catch up on."

"Where are you staying?" I removed my jacket and strode into the living room to see Axel holding Gaspare. I threw my jacket on the couch, along with my purse, and slipped my feet out of my heels.

"In the city. I'll text you the details. And Gigi?"

"Yes?"

"You're still my best friend."

My heart was filled with a familiar joy. "Me too."

Axel gave me a perplexed look. "Who was that?"

"Geneva."

"She's alive? You're positive?"

"I know! Can you believe it?" I asked in shock, tossing my phone aside.

"You okay?" Axel pulled me into his arms.

I placed a hand on Gaspare's back as he squirmed in his father's arms. "Janice called me on the way home."

"I heard about your visit to the police station from John."

The fireplace was lit and Gaspare's toys were strewn on the floor. "He knows I killed Igor."

"Soren can't prove anything," Axel reassured me.

"If one of the staff sold a copy of the video, he has me on tape."

"He won't be able to show it to anyone." Axel held me close.

The front doorbell chimed. "That's Janice."

"Turin is here. We had a meeting with Carlo and Antonio."

I smoothed my hand along his arm. "How did it go with the doctors?"

"I'm fine."

"Axel." He was as stubborn as my father when it came to his health. It was always a struggle to convince him to go to the doctor.

"Seriously, he told me to continue with what I've been doing and not overwhelm myself."

"So that means no overexertion."

Janice walked in with Turin right at the same time. "Hey, you two."

I took Gaspare from Axel and kissed his chubby cheek. "You sounded worried on the phone."

Janice put her purse down on the table and sat on the chair. "Did Carlo tell you?" She directed her question to Axel.

"Tell him what?" I asked as Janice and Axel exchanged a look.

"Gigi, I need you to listen to me and not interrupt," Janice said.

"What is this about?"

Axel placed a hand on my thigh. "Ginerva."

"Okay."

"The other night I saw Geneva with Dario," Janice said.

I blinked, not comprehending her words. "What did you say?"

"Ginerva was on a date with Dario and another guy called Hugo Mendoza."

My eyes went wide. "Ginerva would never be around Dario."

"She was," Axel answered.

"How...?"

"Carlo told me before you arrived. I waited to tell you

tonight, but Janice contacted you first. You were already on the phone with Ginerva, which confirmed what we already knew."

I shook my head in disbelief. "Are you saying Ginerva is sleeping with Dario?"

The way they looked at the table, I would say they're lovers, and have been for a while," Janice replied.

None of this made sense. "Ginerva hates Dario. I think your eyes were playing tricks on you."

"Carlo told me Hugo Mendoza and Dario were talking, and the girl got up and left for the bathroom. I met her in the bathroom when I came out."

"But-"

Janice continued to explain. "I didn't know her at first, but Carlo reminded me about your best friend."

"He must have forced her."

"Didn't look like force to me. She talked about getting a proposal from him. Even with a bruise on her right eye she tried to cover up with bad makeup," Janice said.

"He hit her!"

"Probably more, but I didn't have time to probe because Carlo noticed them and wanted to leave. I didn't want to get too involved, because she looked like a puppy in love."

"She asked to meet with me," I whispered.

"Probably to set you up," Turin announced, reminding me he was in the room.

I whispered to myself, "She would never betray me like Rosa."

"You can't meet her alone," Janice stated.

"Hugo is working with Dario and the detectives," Axel said grimly.

"We got the footage from the office today of them entering the building," Turin confirmed.

"Keep Oliver and the other guys on high alert," Axel told Turin.

"What are you going to do?" Janice asked.

As the love in my heart for my former friend faded, I let the memories fade with it. "I have to meet with Ginerva."

"I'm coming," Axel replied.

I figured. "It'll tip Dario off if you come."

"She's right," Turin agreed.

"Turin can come with me," I said.

"That's more reason Dario will stay away," Axel insisted.

"He'd probably feel secure knowing I had a guard or two with me."

"We'll talk about it later," Axel said. He stood and left the living room.

"Can you watch him? I need to talk to Axel." I handed Gaspare to Janice.

Axel was overly protective, and if anything went wrong, he'd burn the world down to find Dario. But I didn't need him doing anything that would cause Gaspare and me to lose him for good. The explosion was enough and still gave me nightmares. Going into labor without him next to me was a subject I never brought up, but I knew he had guilt. Honestly, being selfish, I wanted him to feel that guilt. Marriage wasn't rainbows and flowers. I'd had to grow up sooner than I wanted, but the person I married was the love of my life, and I had to get him to see me for who I was now. I pushed his office door open and saw him with his back to the door, staring at a picture of his parents on the wall.

"How can I make it better?" I asked, coming up behind him.

"I'm not the same person as before. They took months away from me."

"I know." I was resigned to the situation, but I wanted Axel to be at peace.

He turned around and glared. "Do you?"

I groaned. "Axel—"

He threw his hand up to stop me. "My instinct is to and kill anything that brings you pain. I'd never hesitate. Every minute, I find myself more worried about you and Gaspare's safety at."

"That's a part of being a parent."

"No, it's crippling, Gigi. Sometimes I wish I would have died."

"Axel, don't think like that."

"I lived and breathed being Enforcer for the family. Now, I second guess myself. I'm not confident that you still love me like before."

I ran into his arms. "Where is this coming from? I've never stopped loving you."

He grasped my hips. "We haven't been together as husband and wife. I missed seven months of your life. It feels like we're starting all over again."

"I had a baby, and you're still dealing with what happened. Getting back to us as a couple will come in stages. We have to be patient."

He kissed my forehead. "I'm not used to waiting. On top of my enemies being this close to us."

"I won't go to see Ginerva if you don't want me to."

He buried his face in my neck and inhaled. "I want to touch you."

"Okay."

"I want to bury my dick so far inside you, you're all I can feel."

"Yes," I moaned as he squeezed my ass.

Axel mumbled, "Shit, I want you so bad."

"My six weeks are up. But I want to check with the doctor."

"I can tell you if you're healed."

I chuckled and shook my head. "Baby, no. Let me talk to the doctor. Getting pregnant right after Gaspare is not in my plans."

"If it happens, I'll be here."

"You promise?" I brushed my tongue across his lips.

He groaned. "Fuck, yes."

"One more day. I'll make an emergency appointment."

"Gigi—"

"One more day, handsome."

Axel and I made out for the next ten minutes until Turin knocked on the door. He announced he was leaving and would be back to figure out the plan about Ginerva.

Chapter 11

Axel

My back was a little sore from working out, but I pushed through to complete the workout. I wiped my brow and sipped on the protein shake as I walked into my office for a meeting with Turin. I lifted the folder from my desk and took a seat.

Turin checked his gun. "Are you sure you're ready for today?"

I closed the folder. "I'm ready. I just need to shower."

Turin nodded. "As your brother, I have to check."

"Did you get Onyx for today?"

"He's here."

I placed the folder on the desk and headed for the shower.

Some of our soldiers were hand-picked to be on point when Gigi went to meet with Ginerva. They were the best trained assassins the cartel had.

The folder Turin obtained from surveillance showed Ginerva was in the club with Dario. On a couple of occasions, she'd also been there alone with a guard. She'd been here for months and had lied to Gigi. It would take more than killing her and Dario to make me feel whole again. I wanted to wipe out her entire bloodline in Italy.

Hugo had scheduled a meeting with the Irish today. I planned on crashing it to reinforce that the Carringtons owned the territory Hugo was trying to take. The Irish were only loyal to themselves, and Hugo would learn not to cross my wife or me again.

Once I was showered and dressed, I headed back to my office and grabbed two guns and some money from the safe. Gigi had an appointment with her doctor for an update and even if she wasn't at the six-week mark, it was time to be with my wife.

Turin was waiting outside with the car.

"Hugo is to be left alive," I stated.

"What if Dario is there?" Onyx asked.

"He won't step foot near the deal," Turin explained.

Onyx frowned. "How can you be sure?"

"Ginerva," I replied.

"He's banking on Gigi seeing Ginerva, so he'll lie low," Turin explained.

"You two take the rear. Turin and I will be up front," I instructed.

"I'll drive," Turin announced.

"What if the Irish get involved?" Onyx asked.

I shrugged. "Kill them."

I walked to the Jeep and climbed in. Arriving in a limo would draw too much attention, and the Jeep had better maneuverability to get us out of a situation unharmed. It was bulletproof, so no more ambushes unless we were the ones doing them.

Turin drove for fifteen minutes in silence. The guys checked and rechecked their guns, and I blocked out everyone except Hugo's face as my target. Finally, we approached the restaurant where Hugo was planning to meet with the Russians, and we climbed out and walked to the back door. It was opened by one of the servers Turin had paid off to get us inside.

"They just got here," he said.

Turin handed him a thousand dollars. "You never saw us."

"Saw who?" He grinned and ran out the door.

No one was back here, so we had a clear path of the hallway to the bathrooms. Onyx checked them, but they were empty. Turin followed behind him.

I waited before moving forward. "You on the right. I'll take the left," I whispered to Turin.

"Gotcha—"

Bullets came flying in our direction before we could move. We took cover and backed up out of the building in a rush.

"Fuck!"

I fired off two shots, but only saw a server down on the ground.

"Time to go. They made us!" Turin yelled.

I refused to leave. "No."

Gunfire exploded, and Turin pushed me out of the way, taking the bullet meant for me.

"Turin!"

"Shit! We need to get him to a doctor!" Onyx shouted.

We hauled Turin to his feet between us.

"I'm good. Shit... my shoulder," Turin groaned.

"Start the car, Onyx." I shoved the keys into his hand.

I helped Turin into the backseat while our other men watched our backs, providing cover from the gunfire.

"Let's get the fuck out of here!" Onyx ripped the door

open, slid into the driver's seat, and started the engine as Mendoza's men emerged from the building. I pulled my cell from my pocket and dialed Gigi's number.

No answer.

I redialed her number.

"Take the smaller streets..." Turin's head fell on my shoulder.

I dropped my phone and tapped him on the cheek to stay awake. "Turin, hold on. We're almost there."

"We can't go to the hospital. Too many questions!" Onyx swerved in and out of traffic.

"Get to my house. I'll take care of everything," I ordered.

Onyx sped up, ignoring the red light and cutting off a cab.

"Stay awake," I told Turin.

"Fuck, I'm good. Just a flesh wound," Turin replied.

Neither of us were doctors, but it looked worse than a flesh wound.

Onyx made it to the house. The guards opened the door and helped Turin out while I dialed Gigi again.

"Put him in the guest house," I barked as the nurse, Heather, stepped out of the house.

"Mr. Bresciani, we had a scheduled appointment today."

"I need your help."

"Missing appointments won't help your recovery."

"Come with me." I grabbed her hand and led her to the guesthouse.

"Wait a minute! What's going on?"

"No time to explain. I need you to help my friend."

"But—"

"We can't take him to the hospital. Too many questions."

"Sir, I'm not a doctor."

"Then do what you can to keep him alive."

"How bad is it?"

"He's lost a lot of blood." I opened the door to reveal Turin lying on the couch, holding his arm.

Heather ran over and lifted his shirt to reveal another bullet wound on his right side. "He needs a hospital."

"Do what you can to keep him alive. I have someone who might be able to help."

"I need my bag."

I motioned for one of my guards to go to the main house and grab her things. Stepping outside, I ran my hand through my hair and released a shaky breath.

"He's going to make it." Onyx came to stand next to me.

"Hugo's going to pay."

"He's gotten the jump on us twice."

"Won't be a third." I stalked to the garage, opened the door, and stood back in thought.

"What are you doing?" Onyx squinted at me.

"Checking the cars."

"For what?" Onyx wondered.

"A tracker."

I went to the Mercedes, limo, and Lamborghini and found the same small black box underneath the wheel well. I stomped on each one and threw them in the trash.

Onyx rushed toward the other two-door garage. "You won't believe what the fuck I found."

He removed a device from the front wheel of the BMW that Gigi drove and held up the same black tracker.

* * *

Once we'd swept the cars clean, I had Onyx take me to my doctor. We needed discretion, and the only person I could think of was Dr. Nathaniel.

"Mr. Bresciani, I'm a doctor. I can't be involved with this," he said anxiously as we sat in his office.

"Is this your family?" I indicated the picture frame on his desk.

"Yes, my wife and daughter."

"You love your family?"

"What kind of question is that?"

"Just answer the question."

"I do."

"Turin is my brother. One of only two people I trust in this world."

"I understand your friend is hurt."

I raised my gun and pointed it at his face. "Come with me willingly or forcefully."

"I could lose my license."

"No one will know. It's a house call."

He dropped his head in defeat.

"All right, Doc. We only have a few minutes to get Turin some help," Onyx added.

"You will be compensated," I added.

"I don't want your money."

"Even better." I stood and tucked my gun away.

"Fine. Let me tell my staff."

"No. Give me your phone."

"What? I need to be able to contact my staff and family."

"Soon as Turin is stable, you'll get your phone back." I wiggled my fingers for him to pass it to me.

The doctor lifted his medical bag and jacket, then reached into his pocket and took out his cell.

"The pager as well," I said.

"What makes you think I won't talk after I help your friend?"

"Because your family will be under surveillance for the

rest of your lives. If I get one inkling of police at my door, you can kiss your wife goodbye."

We made it back to the house as Heather stepped out of the guesthouse, wiping her hands clean of blood. "Doctor Nathaniel?"

"You've been pulled into this mess, too?" Nathaniel asked.

I pushed him toward the guest house. "Another time, Doc."

"What is he doing here?" Heather demanded.

"Work. Go assist him and keep your mouth shut about what you've seen here."

"This isn't the way." Heather rolled her eyes.

"I learned a long time ago that life doesn't play fair."

They worked on Turin for hours. I stood watch as they removed the bullets and cleaned the wounds. I marched out of the guest house, leaving Onyx to guard them, and went into the main house to find Gigi asleep in bed. I kissed her on the forehead and went into the bathroom to shower and change.

Forty minutes into my sleep, I felt kisses on my neck and chest as Gigi pressed her body against mine.

"Gigi," I whispered. She was my calm, the cure I needed when my head was clouded. "I missed you all day."

I pulled her leg over my thigh as my dick probed at her opening and brushed my thumb over the soft pillow of her bottom lip.

"Axel, we shouldn't," Gigi moaned.

"Why not?" I wound a lock of her hair around my finger.

"What if I get pregnant again before I fully heal?"

"I'll pull out." I rocked her back and forth slowly.

Gigi leaned forward and kissed me on the lips. "I missed us together."

My fingers slowly pushed forward into her pussy, and she dug her nails into my shoulder. "I had a rough day and I need you," I groaned.

"Yes, right there." She lifted her hips in invitation.

I captured her lips and held her there as I devoured her tongue, then pushed into her warm, tight pussy.

"Axel," she breathed, tossing her head back.

"I'll go slow, baby."

She dipped her head, avoiding eye contact while I did all the work to make us both comfortable. She wasn't the only one who was nervous. This was our first time since the car bomb. My heart beat faster and sweat dripped down my forehead. I moved my hands over her back and smacked her ass before flipping her onto her back.

Gigi cried out. "Axel, I missed you."

"Tell me again."

Gigi laid her palm on my chest. "I missed you. You feel so good."

I cupped her stomach. "I missed your first appointment with the doctor when you were growing our baby."

"It's okay." Gigi covered my hand with hers.

I shook my head. "It will never be okay. You're mine to care for and protect."

Heat spread to her cheeks at my words. I smoothed my hands up her arms, bringing her closer and locking her into my embrace. My mouth covered hers hungrily. I fondled her plump breast and tasted her sweet nipple while I stroked slowly inside her. The pleasure was pure, out of this world.

"I'll always be yours," she panted.

I covered her mouth with mine to capture her screams as she flew over the edge. I stroked into her twice more before I released and fell on top of her. I knew she'd be pissed about me not pulling out, but I couldn't move.

Gigi's arms locked around me and she whimpered, "I love you."

Her words gave me hope we would be okay once our enemies were dead.

I started to thrust again. "Fuck those six weeks."

She bit my shoulder as I sucked on her nipple, and we lost ourselves in each other.

* * *

Days passed. I was running on adrenaline and focused on ending anyone who came after my family. In the mornings, I had breakfast with Gigi and Gaspare and after a few days of hanging around the house, I made plans to meet Antonio at his club, Ryde.

The liquor cabinet was the first place he went as we sat in his nightclub while Carlo stood at the door.

Antonio had his back to me. Carlo told the staff they'd be unavailable for a few hours while we met. I rubbed the back of my neck, still sore as I'd pushed myself hard in physical therapy.

Antonio said, "I don't like what I'm seeing in my city."

"What have you heard?" I asked.

Antonio sat at his desk and pushed a glass in front of me. "Hugo Mendoza is trying to take over."

My throat burned with panic. De Luca starting a war with Mendoza when we already had the Irish trying to gain footing would cut into our profits. Gigi had done well to manage and expand the business because of the friendship we had with Antonio and Carlo.

"It's true." I informed him.

Antonio tapped his finger against his glass. "He's gotten too close."

"A plan is in the works to get him," I said.

"What about the Irish?" Carlo asked.

"Unless they can get Hugo, they'll probably want a lower price," I responded.

"Is there anything we can help you with?" Antonio asked. "My money shouldn't be held up by someone snooping around my place."

"Our goal is to get rid of the problems. Gigi and I are working on it," I explained.

Antonio checked up. "How are you doing outside of the issues at hand?"

"Taking it one day at a time."

"They tell you marriage and cartel life don't mix. My wife and I have been through everything you could think of. The most critical thing is to make sure your wife is your partner, first and foremost," Antonio said.

I stood, and I extended a hand to Antonio.

He shook it. "We'll be in touch."

"Sabrina and Janice will have extra security until things die down," Carlo said.

"I wouldn't expect anything less. I'll tell my men," I replied.

Chapter 12

Gigi

"Mrs. Bresciani."

I turned to see Ralfie holding a phone.

I panicked. "What's wrong? Is it Axel? My son?"

Ralfie held out the phone to me. "It's Oliver, ma'am."

I took the phone. "Hello?"

Oliver grumbled, "We have a problem."

My senses went on alert and I slipped into mob Boss mode. "Where?"

"My club."

"I'm on my way." I ended the call.

"Do you need me to call Mr. Bresciani?" Ralfie asked.

My nostrils twitched. "No. He has enough to deal with handling Turin's recovery."

Ralfie escorted me back to the limo, and we headed into the city. I nibbled on my nails to control my nerves. Hugo had our cars tracked, and that's how we'd gotten hit on so many times. Oliver was one of our top men in our organization. He was arrogant and hated to lose money, so had no choice but to see him.

"You two stay behind me," I told my other soldiers as Ralfie opened my door.

The club was quiet as they prepared for opening time later tonight. I knocked on Oliver's door and it was yanked open by an angry-looking girl who bumped into me on her way out.

"I was standing here," I remarked.

She poked her chest out like she was ready to fight. "Please. He'll sleep with you and leave you like he does all the girls."

"I don't work here, sweetheart."

"You're not his type, anyway," she huffed.

"Tiffany, get back to the bar," Oliver barked.

I watched her stomp off before entering the office and closing the door. "I told you about sleeping with the women here."

He hunched his shoulders. "Habit I can't break."

"What did you call me about?"

"This." He clicked the remote in his hand and the TV showed Dario and Ginerva sitting in a booth.

I stumbled back. "They're bold."

"Extremely. My product was taken last night."

I looked at Oliver. "How did they get in here?"

"Killed a few of my men and left through the side exit." Oliver pointed at the screen.

"How much was taken?"

"At least two bags."

I rubbed my forehead. "Shit."

"The guns were stripped of their serial numbers."

"That was a sale we'd planned to go down at the end of the month with the Irish mafia."

"The Irish aren't happy. They want their product now."

I paced in front of his desk. "We need to buy some time."

Oliver sighed. "I've put them off for now, but I don't like losing money, Gigi."

I whipped around to look at him. "You won't."

"Axel needs to know."

"He will."

Oliver motioned at the screen. "And them?"

"I plan on making contact soon."

"I heard Mendoza's with them."

"He wants our territory."

"I have too much tied in with the Carrington's. I don't plan on Hugo taking a cut of my percentage."

"He'll be dead soon."

"And the Irish boys? What do I do about holding them off?"

I opened the door to leave. "Give me some time to think, but for now, we move some things around and take from the warehouse in Queens."

* * *

When I got home, Axel surprised me with a date. I wore my best dress, curled my hair, and put on some light makeup. Axel was so taken with my look, he was ready to get me undressed again.

"What did you do to the doctor?" Turin's getting shot had scared me, and I was glad he was on the mend.

"I paid Dr. Nathaniel and Heather to keep quiet," Axel responded, knocking back the rest of his vodka.

He looked more like his old self tonight in a black suit, with his shirt partially open, showing his muscular chest. The restaurant outside the city was heavily guarded, inside and out.

I took a sip from my water glass. "Any idea if he'll talk?"

Axel reached across the table for my hand. "He's not stupid. Neither is the nurse."

"Oliver called me earlier today."

Axel motioned for the server to refill his glass. "How did you handle it?"

"Ginerva and Dario stole two bags of guns that were reserved for the Irish."

"Do you need me to handle anything?" He caressed my palm.

"Not yet. How is Turin doing?"

"He's up on his feet. I told him to stay with us for a few more days."

"What did Antonio talk with you about?"

"Hugo tried to contact him to make a deal without us."

"Antonio doesn't like people who come in from the outside."

Axel reached in his pocket and pulled out his wallet, putting cash on top of the check. "Hugo tried to play it off like we agreed to give up some areas."

I put my dessert in the to-go box. "I think it's time I contacted Ginerva, then you get the Irish to show up."

Axel opened the back door for me, escorting me out of the restaurant. I pressed my hand on his chest and kissed him on the lips. When we reached the limo, he held the door then climbed in after me.

Ralfie started the engine and pulled away from the restaurant into traffic. I grabbed Axel's hand and leaned my head against his shoulder. His hand traveled to the top of my knee, and I listened to his heartbeat.

My phone rang, and I grabbed it from my purse.

"Mrs. Carrington, I see why all the men in your life grovel at your feet."

"Hugo...Hugo Mendoza?" My gaze flew to Axel.

"I know we got off on the wrong foot, but I think we can establish a friendship."

"You tried to have my husband and me killed."

"Igor was my favorite nephew."

"Igor tried to kill me."

"A little mistake."

"My husband is going to kill you."

"Dario said you were fiery. I like that in a woman."

"Never use Dario's and my name in the same sentence."

"I believe he killed your mother and father, correct?"

"I want my guns back."

"I want Chicago and New York."

"Return my property, and I'll think about letting you live."

He laughed. "Threats. My, my. Dario was right. I may have to taste you before I kill you."

Axel snatched the phone out of my hand. "Mendoza, you're messing with the wrong person."

"Axel, I suggest you buckle up tight. A bigger explosion could always happen." Hugo dropped the call.

Axel handed me my phone as we arrived home. We stepped into the house to find Turin sitting at the kitchen island talking with Ebony, while the nanny held Gaspare.

"Take him upstairs," Axel demanded.

"Axel, calm down."

"Gigi, not now." Axel paced back and forth.

"What's going on?" Turin asked.

Axel smacked his hand against the wall, and Gaspare started to cry.

"You're scaring him." I picked up my son and kissed him on the cheek.

"Hugo sent a message," Axel growled.

I glared at Axel. "Can you put him to bed?" I asked the nanny.

"Yes, of course," she answered.

"Ebony, you can go for the night," I informed her with a smile, watching as she removed her apron and left the kitchen.

"No more bullshitting. We need to find them now," Axel muttered.

I followed behind him to his office with Turin. "I can contact Ginerva tomorrow."

Axel opened his door and reached for the telephone. "I'll be ready," Turin responded.

"I have an idea, but you won't like it," I said.

"Then it's a no." Axel took a seat in his chair.

"Axel, hear me out." I took the phone out of his hand and hung it up.

Turin agreed with me. "She can get to Ginerva, which will lead us to Dario."

I bit my lip. "Antonio will back us up, so... what if I confess to Igor's death?"

Axel jumped out of his seat. *"What?"*

I pushed him down and sat in his lap, caressing his cheek. "I'll confess to Raymond and Soren."

"No." Axel was resolute.

"Gigi, that only creates more problems," Turin pointed out.

"What if we ensure Ginerva *and* Hugo attend?" I suggested.

Axel murmured. "You mean, kidnap Ginerva?"

"With Ginerva gone, Dario will have no choice but to raise his head," I reasoned.

"Could work," Turin agreed.

I had another idea as backup. "I could pretend I want Dario back."

"Dario won't fall for that," Axel snapped.

"He will if I confess to Igor's death and make Hugo a deal. Soren wants money. We fake it and have each of them turn on the other."

"It won't work."

"Axel, you said to think more like an Enforcer instead of a husband. This is the perfect opportunity. We're doing it my way."

I knew once Turin left and Gaspare was asleep, Axel would punish me for my direct challenge.

* * *

The bedroom door slammed. I stood in place, not reacting. His breath tickled the back of my neck as he wrapped his hand around my hair and yanked. I gasped as his chest met my back.

"Put your palms out." Slowly, his hands moved downward, skimming either side of my body to my thighs.

"Axel."

"Now!" He caressed the skin of my thigh, and the gentle massage sent currents of desire through my body.

"Yes, sir."

Axel's fingers burned into my tingling skin as I placed my palms on top of the dresser. He kicked my legs apart and pressed his lips to my shoulder before tracing the curve of my neck. "Do you know who the fuck I am?"

I heard the clink of his belt buckle. He slipped a hand to

the front of my dress and yanked the straps down to expose my breasts. He gripped them and flicked my nipples.

"You're m-my husband," I moaned as I pushed my ass into him.

Axel turned and lifted me onto the dresser. He dipped his head and sucked on my neck while he pinched my nipple.

I tossed my head back and gripped the back of his head, pushing my chest forward. "Yes, please."

His eyes were fathomless, an abyss of pleasure. "If you ever talk to me like that again—"

I pushed him off me and jumped down. "What are you going to do, Axel?"

His frown cleared at my challenge, and he pushed me up against the wall. I wrapped my legs around his waist, and we moaned as he slid his hard length inside me.

"God! I can't go without you again," he groaned.

"Baby!"

His hand circled my throat. "I can't live without you, Gigi."

"Fuck me harder." I pleaded.

Axel brushed his lips against mine. "God, I love this tight pussy. Fucking kills me every time."

I swallowed my cry and gripped his shoulders as he rutted me further up the wall. "Axel, oh God. You can't hold me... like... fuck!" I cried out as he pulled out and spun to face the wall. He thrust back inside me, pumping in and out. "Oh, God. Don't stop!"

"Shush," he grunted. "You'll wake Gaspare."

I smacked my hand on the wall. "I can't help...Axel!"

Axel took my mouth with a savage intensity. I breathed in a deep. Soul-yearning tremor when his hardness stroked against my spot and my thighs flooded with my arousal.

He pulled out, and I glared at him over my shoulder.

"Kneel on the floor."

"Are you sure you can handle me?" I wrapped my hand around his dick.

He bent down and pressed a kiss on my lips. "More than capable of handling you."

Hypnotized by the sexiness of his girth, I took him in my mouth and fixed my eyes on his. I breathed through my nose and rubbed his balls as he whispered encouragement in a low, silky voice. I extended my tongue and relaxed my throat as he guided me up and down on his dick.

"Suck it just like that, baby," he grunted.

I bobbed my head up and down until his hand grew tight around my hair and I knew he was about to explode.

I pulled back and spat on his tip, twisting my hand up and down and watching his head fall back.

He slowly fucked my face, and I took him all the way down to his pubic bone.

"Fuck! Gigi."

I pushed a finger into my pussy as he released in my mouth. I closed my eyes as I thought of his dick pounding me and came in a rush.

Afterward, we showered and curled up in bed.

In the middle of the night, Gaspare cried, and I left the bed with a little fight from Axel. I slipped on my robe, went to his room, and lifted him from his crib.

"You couldn't sleep?" I walked around the room cradled him in my arms.

He yawned and smiled.

"My biggest blessing."

Gaspare reached for my hand and tried to put it in his mouth.

"Such a good boy."

Axel stood at the door. "He's going to get spoiled."

"Like his daddy."

Axel took Gaspare and rubbed his back. "Buddy, you need to sleep, so Mommy can get what she needs."

I stood and watched him put Gaspare back in his crib. "What do I need?" I gnawed on my top lip.

Axel hooked an arm around my waist. "Sleep, so you're ready to take on the Mendoza Cartel."

"Is this you finally understanding I need an Enforcer *and* a husband?"

"Yes." Axel kissed me. "Forgive me."

I nodded. "Always."

Chapter 13

Axel

The hot water from the shower pelted me, easing muscles that were numb from working out. I'd been avoiding extra appointments with a physical therapist and doing my own thing, keeping Gigi out of the loop. I'd always been the one to handle the storm when anything came our way, but now I needed to rely more and more on her. Seemed the only way to get my body back to a hundred percent was to follow doctor's orders and stick to my routine.

Sleep was the only time I had bursts of memory of the explosion. Otherwise, it didn't cross my mind because Gaspare and Gigi kept me busy throughout the day.

I turned off the shower, picked up the towel, and wrapped it around my waist. Drying my hair with another one, I left the bathroom and got dressed to prepare for my doctor's visit. Downstairs, Gigi was feeding Gaspare on the sofa with a cartoon of a pig on in the background.

She smiled as she saw me. "Where are you off to so early?"

"To meet with Oliver," I lied.

"Why didn't you tell me last night?"

I bent and kissed her on the lips before kissing Gaspare's forehead. "Forgot. I won't be gone long."

"Hey." Gigi grabbed my wrist as I turned to leave. "Is everything okay with us?"

"Yeah."

She smiled and released my wrist.

* * *

Ralfie pulled up to the hospital and since it would be a brief visit, I asked him to wait outside. Soon as I checked in, the nurse took me Doctor Nathaniel's office. He was on the phone as I entered and obviously harbored anxiety from my previous visit as he stiffened in his chair. He told whoever he was talking to on the phone to call back.

"What are you doing here?"

I held up my hands. "I come in peace. I need to get a checkup."

"Checkup?"

"For me."

"But—"

I waved my hand in his face. "Only you can do it, so cancel whatever appointments you have for the next hour or two."

"Mr. Bresciani, it doesn't work like that at this hospital."

"As far as what works, we had a talk about what's in store for your family, and you're the only one who knows my lifestyle."

"Not by choice."

"You're being paid handsomely."

"Money isn't the reason."

"The nurse comes by, but I wanted to get your opinion."

"On what?"

"If I'm ever going to be me again."

"I'm not a therapist."

"And I don't need you to be, but sometimes I feel like I lost my body in the coma."

"Unfortunately, that's normal. Give yourself time to heal."

"My work lacks vacation time."

He stood and grabbed his equipment. "Come with me and I'll do some follow-up testing if that will make you feel better."

"It will."

* * *

I listened to Gigi talk about her day and plans for Gaspare.

"I'll call you later. Be safe." I ended our call.

"She good?" Turin asked.

I told Turin to stay home, but he was stubborn, like me. "No."

"What happened?"

"She's stressed because we didn't wait the full six weeks."

"Damn. Did the doctor say something?"

I rubbed a hand over my face. "She's worried if we don't use protection, she'll end up pregnant again."

"Man, you sure didn't wait," Turin joked.

"I could never do that with her." I grinned.

"Keep your focus." Turin lifted his gun.

I tapped on the window as I strolled to the shipyard to meet Hugo. A few cars arrived with backup from Antonio, and I lifted my chin in recognition. Onyx led the way through the door, where Hugo was sitting at a table surrounded by his men.

He clasped his hands together and stared at me, his face emotionless. I clenched my jaw. I couldn't kill until we had what we needed.

"My deal is final, no negotiations," Hugo stated.

"Deal with Dario or the Irish mafia?" I asked.

"All of the above. You decided your terms, and I have mine." He reached into his pocket and grabbed a cigarette and lighter.

"The terms my wife gave Igor in Chicago are still on the table, as is letting you live."

Anger heated his face. "Threats only get you more pain, and I would say you've been through enough."

"Hugo, we've made it clear that if you go against us, you become the bigger threat we have to eliminate."

Hugo pulled on the cigarette and put it out on the table. "The Irish received a package from Dario. You will have no choice but to send your pretty little wife to prison unless I receive the money as compensation for her killing my nephew."

I reached for my gun and every soldier in the room raised their weapons.

Hugo frowned and stood. "You're not the only one prepared to die."

"Keep my wife out of this."

The door opened and heels clicked against the floor. I knew only one person who discover something I wanted to keep secret.

Gigi stood next to me and dropped her purse on the table. "Hugo, I suggest you move that gun away from my husband's face."

"Is this bad cop, good cop?"

I scoffed and rose from the chair.

Gigi placed a hand on my shoulder to stop me. "Hugo, I killed your nephew, and I don't regret it, so I suggest you listen carefully."

"Bitch!" he snarled and lunged at her.

I pushed her behind me and charged at him, but Ralfie and his guard got between us.

"Axel, I'm fine," Gigi said.

"Detective Soren will hear about this," Hugo threatened.

"You can get whoever you want. We will never give you territory," Gigi said calmly.

"The Irish deal will give me more power. I can take New York. Fuck the De Lucas," Hugo spat, jerking out of Onyx's hold.

"I won't forget the ambush you set up," I warned him.

Hugo ignored me and walked out of the room.

Gigi whipped to face me with a glare. She planted on her hips on her hips and tapped her foot.

"Leave us," I instructed our men.

"You lied to me," she accused as soon as we were alone.

"It was easier to make you believe I came to visit Oliver."

"So you met with Hugo behind my back?"

"I did."

"And the doctor's visit?"

"How did you—"

"The nurse called and said your tests came back clear."

I didn't want her thinking I was trying to hinder her from being the person she was born to be. "I apologize."

Gigi walked up to me and looped her arms around my neck. "I forgive you, but we don't keep secrets. Ever."

I raised her chin. "That means we're locked in for life."

"Locked in for life, and I want you to be honest about

everything you're dealing with when it comes to your health. I'm still pissed that we didn't wait my six weeks."

I grinned, and she smacked me on the chest.

Gigi and I looked toward the door as Turin honked the car horn, his signal that he was ready to go. I reached for her hand and we walked out to a surprise appearance from Detectives Soren and Raymond.

"Mr. and Mrs. Bresciani! Is there a reason you're at an abandoned shipyard?" Soren asked.

I opened the car door and helped Gigi get in before sliding in next to her. "It's a free country, Detective."

Detective Soren kept his hand on his phone as Raymond glanced around the building.

"Anything else?" I asked politely.

"We'll be seeing you very soon."

"Unless we see you first, Detective."

* * *

I filled Gigi in on the plan to get Ginerva, and the location of the motel.

"Are you sure you want to go through with this?" I asked her.

"Yes," Gigi immediately replied.

"There's no turning back after this," I said, searching her eyes.

Gigi confirmed, "I have no remorse."

"Okay, here are the schematics for the location where we believe she's staying with Dario."

"Are you going in with them?" Gigi asked.

"Yeah, and if Dario is there, we take him."

"I know you want his blood, but don't kill him."

"I promised I would keep him for you."

"I wish you didn't have to go." She rubbed her palm over my chest.

I leaned in and pecked her on the lips.

Gigi shoved the pictures of Dario away and picked up the picture of Ginerva eating lunch alone.

"Better to make sure they pick up the right girl. It's a motel, so anything could go wrong."

Gigi begged, "Just come home safe."

"My only thought is you and our son." I rubbed her stomach.

Gigi moved my hand off her stomach. "No more of that, either."

"Why? We've already made the leap."

"Leap? That's what you call us having sex?"

I held in my laugh and kissed the back of her hand before moving off the bed. I grabbed my holster, gun, jacket, and the knife I liked to use when I chased someone down. "We can talk about that when I get back."

Gigi followed me downstairs and watched me from the front door of the house as Turin started the car and I climbed into the passenger seat.

Turin announced. "Ready?"

"For kidnapping? Always."

Turin followed behind Onyx, and we headed for the motel. The ride passed quickly, and it was just past 9 PM when we pulled up outside. Turin looked left and right as we approached the building, to ensure no one saw us while walked ahead of us.

We took the elevator to the fifth floor. As we stopped out, a gunshot rang out, and a bullet whizzed past us.

"Shit!"

I raised my gun as her motel door opened, and Ginerva poked her head out.

"Get down!" Her guard yelled as I sent shots back at him and took cover around the corner. Turin was on the opposite side with Onyx.

"What is going on?" Ginerva screamed.

"Dario's not here. We need to run!" the guard shouted.

Ginerva panicked. "I don't have my things."

"Leave them!" he yelled.

I peeked from behind the wall as he grabbed and started for the exit.

"Don't move!" I yelled, levelling my weapon at the guard.

He raised his gun, and I fired off two shots. Ginerva screamed and dropped to the floor as his body fell in the exit door. I jogged over and kicked the gun away from him before checking for a pulse.

"Get her and check the room," I instructed Onyx.

"No! Help me!"

Onyx covered her mouth, carrying her down the stairs and through the back exit to the alley. Turin entered the room with me while Ralfie got rid of the guard's body.

I scanned the room. Clothes, shoes and newspapers were strewn around, along with empty takeout cartons. Dario must have felt closed in for him to put her up in such a dingy place.

Turin picked up her purse, removed her phone, and scrolled through the unknown numbers. He dialed the one number that appeared repeatedly.

"Ginerva, what the fuck you doing calling me?"

Turin put the phone on speaker. "This isn't Ginerva."

Dario chuckled. "I guess it was time you found her."

I said, "Maybe you should come and meet us."

"She won't talk."

"Are you sure about that?"

"Does Gigi miss me? It's been a while since we've talked."

"She's busy being a wife and mother."

The phone went silent.

"You picked up my seconds. I might take her back once I kill you," Dario taunted me.

I took the phone out of Turin's hand. "You fucked up. You should've made sure I died in the explosion."

"Next time, I'll do it myself."

"Hugo can't save you."

"I have other resources. Don't underestimate me," he growled.

"I'd suggest you get your will in order because it's time to end this."

"Make sure you're ready because I don't plan on going down easy," he snapped, then hung up.

We stepped out of the room as Ralfie approached. "From the motel security," he said, holding up the tapes.

"Did you have problems getting them?"

He grinned. "Security's asleep."

I took the tapes, and we drove to the warehouse to destroy them and my clothes. Ginerva tried to bite Ralfie and Onyx as they took her to a secure room and tied her to a chair. I gave orders to the team to keep her locked without water and food until I said so.

"Dario's going to kill you!" she screamed.

I shut the warehouse door behind me and went to the car to wait for Turin.

A few minutes passed before Turin slid into the passenger seat. "She's asleep."

"What did you give her?"

"Something to keep her knocked out for a few hours."

"Good. I want Gigi to be here when we get answers. She needs this closure."

We backed out of the dirt road and headed to my place to regroup. I needed to shower and climb into bed with my wife.

I gripped the steering wheel in anticipation. Dario was the reason my parents weren't here anymore. Death would be too easy for him, so I intended to make it painful.

"What are you thinking about?"

"How much I'll enjoy ending everybody who has destroyed something in my life."

The thought of Gigi never feeling safe would end soon, our dark place wouldn't last much longer. Ginerva would talk or not, but she'd sealed her fate with her betrayal.

Chapter 14

Axel

The smell of piss and acid filled the air from the awful cologne Connor Murphy continued to drown himself in every time we met. He was one of those guys who thought people fell at their feet.

I'd avoided most of the meetings with the Murphy Cartel and let Turin handle them back in Italy. Hugo trying to partner with the Irish and putting the police on our tails made me more testy than usual.

Gigi stood beside me. I hadn't wanted her here, but with everything going on, I preferred to keep her close.

"Axel, the last time we met, you had a gun in my face," Connor said with a smirk.

I let him have his little remark. I knew it was a jab to get me riled up. I tipped my head at him. "Connor."

He grinned. "I hear my guns are gone."

"And I hear you're trying to set a deal up with Hugo Mendoza."

He shrugged. "Business."

"Mr. Murphy, I'm Gigi Bresciani, the Boss of Carrington Cartel and Axel's wife." She extended her hand to him.

I pulled it back, and Connor chuckled.

"I see you don't let stray animals go to waste by choosing Axel of all people," Connor remarked.

I drew Gigi close. "I'm the lucky one."

"We're here because you went behind our backs to deal with the Mendoza Cartel. Are you aware that Hugo Mendoza and Dario Ramini are trying to cut us out on the sale?" Gigi asked.

"At the moment, all I care about are my guns. We've been in business for years, but we want to make New York one of our bigger distribution hubs," Connor explained.

"That can't happen, Mr. Murphy, because De Luca and I have this territory, and we're not selling." Gigi glared at him.

He didn't seem happy at her statement. "Mendoza gave me better numbers. Dario brought the opportunity to me, and I agreed."

"He stole your guns," I said.

"To sell back to you at a higher rate," Gigi added.

Connor whispered to his partners, Cillian and Fionn, and they all nodded. "How will you make this worth our time if we don't go with Hugo?"

Gigi and I made eye contact. "We are willing to give you a lower rate on future sales and cut ties with any other Ireland deals. We'll only deal with you from now on."

Connor didn't wait to confirm with his men before he held his hand out. "I like the sound of that. You know we want you gone from our territory as soon as possible."

Laurent had land in Ireland and years of deals set in place. It would take a little time to get everything transferred over while we handled Hugo and Dario.

"We need a little time. The Carringtons have a long history in Ireland," I answered.

"You have one week," Connor countered and left with his men.

Oliver jumped up in irritation. "What the fuck just happened?"

"Business, Oliver," Gigi responded.

"That leaves us out of pocket. No offense, Axel, but leaving Ireland deals off the table will cost us."

"Oliver, we know what we're doing," Gigi replied.

"Losing Ireland will cost us, but we need to eliminate Hugo and Dario for good," I explained.

Not in the mood for more questions, I grabbed Gigi's hand and escorted her from the building. I helped Gigi into the car, and as I was about to climb in, my skin prickled with a premonition. Tires screeched as a car roared past, a gun leveled at us through the passenger window.

I pulled my weapon and fired at the gunman. The rest of our men returned fire, and the car screeched off with the shooter slumped in the seat, riddled with bullets. I yanked the car door open and released a breath when I saw Gigi had taken cover. I pulled her to me and checked her over for any wounds.

"Hey, you're safe. I'm here," I whispered in her ear, kissing her forehead and cheek.

Gigi tugged my head down and her lips crashed into mine.

My gun automatically went up as Turin climbed in the car.

He grinned and raised his hands in the air when he saw my weapon. "It's just me. You good, Gigi?"

"I'm fine, Turin. Anyone hit?"

"They're fine. The shooter was focused on you."

I climbed out of the car and helped Gigi to stand. "Did anybody get their license?"

The block was empty considering it was afternoon in the New York business district. Someone knew we had a meeting today.

"No, but what are the odds Connor and Hugo are behind an ambush?"

I rubbed my chin in thought. "Connor's not dumb. We just handed him at least a hundred million by pulling out of Ireland. He won't shed blood."

"Then it's Dario and Hugo."

"I agree with Turin. Any news on Dario?" Gigi questioned.

"We got Ginerva," Turin said.

"What?"

"I wanted to wait and tell you, but I got home late," I explained.

"You had her and didn't tell me?"

"Now's not the time to argue. We can talk when we get home."

Another car arrived, and I helped Gigi inside. I sat beside her as Ralfie removed our things from the limo.

"I'll meet you later," Turin said, and went to speak with Onyx.

We hurried to leave the scene before the police arrived. Gigi ignored me and stared out of the window. I hadn't deliberately held anything back from her; it was just late when I made it home and my only thought had been of being with her and my son. Her mood would improve once I got her alone.

"I want to take you somewhere," I murmured.

"We can't."

"We haven't had a proper honeymoon or been alone together."

"Right now is not the time, Axel."

"Gigi, I didn't keep the news about Ginerva from you on purpose."

She turned to face me. "I believe you."

I rubbed her thigh. "The Connor deal was a good decision."

"Oliver thinks it was stupid."

"Oliver's opinion doesn't matter. He'll never understand how you run the cartel."

"He's in a position where we need his support."

"His support, but not his opinions."

Gigi's eyes met mine. "I've been thinking of stepping back and focusing on our son more."

"You worked hard as the Don of the cartel."

She rubbed my knuckles. "Did Ginerva say anything?"

"Not yet. I wanted to keep her under wraps until you could get to her."

She smiled. "You're always thinking about me."

"You're my wife."

Gigi reached for the partition button and rolled it up as she ran her fingers through my hair. "I want to do something for you."

"What do you have in mind?"

"Something that will make us both very happy," she said, grinding against my hard length.

"So you're no longer worried about me using protection and getting pregnant?"

"Still worried, but maybe you could—"

I slowly drew my tongue across her bottom lip, keeping my eyes on hers as I sucked it into my mouth. "No pulling out."

She nibbled on my neck, and I moaned when she reached down to grab my stiff dick. Cool air hit me as she lowered my zipper, and I closed my eyes as she ran the tip of her tongue over my crown. My hips jerked, and I grabbed the back of her head in a haze. The way she moved her mouth up and down should be against the law. I knew when we first got together that she was inexperienced, but time and practice had made her a pro at pleasing me. My wife knew how to get me to the brink and keep me satisfied, over and over again. She was the only woman who could turn me on and piss me off in equal measure, and I wanted to fuck her until we passed out.

The second the car pulled up at the house, I pulled her out and carried her up the stairs to our bedroom. I stripped us of our clothes, and Gigi dropped to her knees before I could even give her sweet pussy a kiss.

"Damn it, Gigi." My head fell back, and I pictured our first time making love.

My desire for my wife echoed in my mind all day, every day, and seeing her body after giving birth to our baby only made me hotter for her.

Her eyes closed, and she rubbed across my stomach. A wave of emotions swept over me when she touched me. I needed to be buried deep inside her to get my thoughts together. During these vulnerable moments, my Italian blood came to the forefront.

"*Amore mio*! Get up here."

Gigi released me with a pop and stroked me with her hand before straddling me. With her eyes fixed on mine, she lined me up with her core and slowly took me inside her tight heat.

"I...oh, God," she cooed.

"Feels like heaven."

I didn't want to end our play too early, so I pulled out of

her and switched position, delving my tongue into her sweet honey. Her juices created a wet spot on the bed and drove me crazy every time.

I eased a finger inside her, watching as she wriggled under my hold. Her movements anticipated mine, and she gripped my shoulders as my tongue moved in and out. Her back arched off the bed, and I planted my hand on her stomach to keep her down while I feasted on her. I kissed her inner thigh, biting and nibbling as I moved my tongue down her leg and kissed her toes.

Our problems melted away as we connected on a deeper level.

A bite to her inner thigh caused her to shiver under my grip and caused one of my favorite things to happen.

I growled as she squirted in my face, and I crawled up the bed like a lion. I hovered over her body and thrust back into her core, planted my hands on either side of her as I drove deep and circled my hips.

"Shit! I'm going to come," she gasped.

"Fuck! Look at me, baby. You take my dick so well. All I want is you."

"Oh...yes! Yes!"

I nutted as soon as she came and fell on top of her, out of breath. I pulled Gigi into my arms and kissed her on the forehead and lips.

Gigi purred. "That was unexpected."

Taking a piece of her hair, I twisted it. "It was necessary to release the stress."

She looked up at me and pushed her leg over my hip. "Everything good with you ?" she asked, caressing my cheek.

"Never been more focused than now." I was ready to go out on a killing spree, but I needed to make sure my family was happy and safe.

I went to get out of bed, but she climbed on top of me. The covers fell down, and my eyes went to her full breasts. I took one in my mouth and she moaned.

She gently cupped the back of my head. "We need to eat and see Gaspare first."

I released her breast and nodded. "I missed him."

Gigi rose from the bed and grabbed her robe. "Me, too. Ebony probably has lunch ready."

I watched her go into the drawer and grab fresh panties and a bra.

"Come shower with me."

"You go ahead. I need to check on things."

"Don't be too long." Gigi winked and headed for the bathroom, leaving the door open as she showered.

I scrolled to Turin's message thread to see if there were any updates on Ginerva.

Me: *How is she?*

Turin: *She woke up, and we offered her food, but she refused to eat.*

Me: *She probably thinks Dario will save her.*

Turin: *I had her put back to sleep.*

Me: *Good. We'll keep her on ice for another day to see if he makes contact.*

I tossed the phone on the bed and strolled into the bathroom. I stood at the counter and watched Gigi in the shower as she hummed while washing her hair. Laurent put me in this life. All I'd cared about was revenge and making Laurent and my parents proud. To have Gigi and my son was a blessing I never thought possible. No woman would ever compare to her.

I pushed off the counter and nudged the door open.

She looked over her shoulder and smiled. "Everything okay?"

"Everything is fine." I stepped inside and picked up the sponge and bodywash to wash her shoulders and back. I kissed her neck, and she reached behind her to pull me close.

"I love you, Axel, and I know you're doing what's best for our family."

"I love you more, Gigi."

Much later, we left the bathroom to find our son.

Gaspare sat in the nanny's arms playing with his toy bear, but as soon as Gigi and I came into the room and he saw us, he smiled and clapped his hands for us to pick him up. Gigi took him and kissed all over his face. I sat down, smiling as I watched them interact. He slobbered all over her face as she nuzzled their noses together.

"You want to see Daddy?" Gigi asked, smiling as he replied in his own baby talk.

"Baby, you spoil him."

"You spoiled me." She passed him to me and I kissed his cheek and smelled his hair.

"Nothing about him looks like me," Gigi complained.

Gigi was right. He looked just like me as a baby. "The next one will come out looking more like you." I winked at her.

Her lips twitched. "Next one? I think that's a no-go, buddy."

The nanny laughed and stood to leave the room as I sat back on the couch.

"One, maybe two more," Gigi conceded. "In a few years."

Gaspare played in my arms while she explained how we needed to wait before we had another baby.

"When are we going to see Ginerva?" she suddenly asked.

"Tomorrow. She refused to talk, so we need to let her sit."

"I want to talk to her."

"You will. Give her time to realize that Dario can't save her."

"How did she seem when you caught her?"

"He'd put her up in a shabby motel on the outskirts of Queens."

"Dario's running scared." Gigi picked up Gaspare's baby bib and wiped the slobber off his lips and chin. She grabbed the bottle off the floor and handed it to me to feed him.

At moments like this, I realized how my son would have me at his beck and call for the rest of his life. "He doesn't seem to care that we took her. All he talked about was you."

She jerked back at my words. "Me? He's lost his mind."

"Once Connor lets Hugo know the deal, Dario will try to run. So be ready."

"He can't hurt me anymore."

I reached around and pulled her to my side. She picked up the remote and turned on the TV. We watched a movie for the rest of the day and had dinner as a family. It was just the three of us, and I preferred it that way.

Chapter 15

Gigi

After sleeping in, I took Gaspare for a check-up.

"Baby Gaspare is gaining weight nicely," the doctor said.

I smiled. "He's such a happy baby. I want him to stay like this forever."

She laughed. "And how is mom doing?"

I leaned against the table. "Good. Busy."

"Remember, you need to take care of yourself, too."

"Sometimes it feels like there aren't enough hours in the day."

"As a mother, I understand, but Gaspare needs you rested and healthy."

"Thanks. I promise, Doctor."

"He's all set."

I put Gaspare back in his car seat and grabbed his baby bag. I thanked the doctor again and headed to the front desk to make a follow-up appointment. Ralfie and Onyx were waiting at the car when I emerged from the building.

When Gaspare was of age, he'd have guards for the rest

of his life. Growing up in a cartel family wasn't ideal for any child, and I knew how it hurt me when I wanted to be free and explore at a young age. My mother and father had forbidden me from doing anything. Now I was a parent, I understood the stress and constant worry that someone might try to hurt my child to get back at me.

"Ralfie, take me to the mall first. I need to grab a few things for Gaspare."

"Ma'am, Mr. Bresciani wanted me to drop you right off."

"It won't take long."

Ralfie looked at Onyx. They seemed scared to defy my husband's orders.

"I will take the blame, gentleman. One hour, tops."

Ralfie drove to the mall closest to our house, which was a compromise I could handle. The drive was peaceful and didn't take more than ten minutes as Gaspare slept in the car seat. Onyx grabbed the stroller, and I took Gaspare out and picked up my purse, then walked with them behind me.

"One hour," Ralfie confirmed.

I lifted my pinky finger. "One hour, Scouts honor."

The Baby's Emperor was my favorite store to shop for my baby boy, and they had new items every week. I had some things put on hold and wanted to grab a few new trinkets. But as we made it to the entrance, I smelled a familiar cologne and wrinkled my nose in disgust.

Detectives Soren and Raymond blocked me from entering the store. "I knew we'd see each other soon."

"What can I do for you, Detective Soren?"

"How's Connor Murphy?"

"Who?"

He chuckled and his partner glared at me. "Keep up the fakeness. I like to play dumb, too."

"I have no idea what you're talking about."

"Connor Murphy is in town."

"Okay."

Detective Soren tilted his head. "An Irish cartel is in my city and you have no idea why?"

"Nope."

"Don't play games!" he hissed, gripping my arm.

Ralfie pushed him back. He stumbled and would have fallen if Raymond hadn't caught him.

"Don't touch her," Ralfie growled.

"It's fine, Ralfie," I reassured him. "Detective Soren's not crazy enough to do anything to me in public."

"I can have you arrested for assaulting an officer," he hissed, poking a finger at Ralfie's chest.

"You approached me and harassed my guards." I pointed out.

"Fuck you and your guards. I know you met with Connor Murphy."

"How many times are you going to throw accusations at me?" I sighed and shook my head. "Connor. Mendoza. Please find a hobby and leave me alone."

He tried to lunge at me, but Raymond held him back.

"You should leave, Detective. You're only making things worse for yourself."

"We'll meet again," he threatened.

"Clearly you have a vendetta against me."

"Nothing would give me more pleasure than to see you behind bars."

"How much do you make, Detective?"

"Are you bribing me? That's against the law."

I raised my hands. "Not bribing, just curious if you make a decent living. Every time I turn around, I see your face, so that tells me being a cop pays very little. Maybe I could put in a few referrals with your superiors to get you a raise." I patted him on the arm and walked around him into the store.

Ralfie called Axel while I shopped. Axel demanded I go home when he found out about Detective Soren approached us. Being out of the house was nice, and I was not ready to go home, so the compromise was having me on FaceTime while I shopped.

The detectives followed us out of the mall, but we ditched them on the way home when we stopped to get groceries.

After I got Gaspare down with the nanny, I went out again, this time to the club to meet Connor. Oliver handled sales at his club, but I promised to personally handle the transaction so no other mistakes occurred. Oliver glared while Connor spoke with his men while, not happy we were making a deal that would cost us money.

"Mr. Murphy, we have ten crates ready. You can check them now."

Connor stopped talking and scanned the shipment in the corner. "What if we want more?"

My brow went up. "More?"

"You think we shouldn't do business with him, but Mendoza had a great offer."

"Sorry you think you have a choice in the matter, but the deal is non-negotiable."

He balled his hands into fists. "Anything can be bought." He licked his lips and leered at me.

"Take what you came for and leave, motherfucker," Oliver barked.

"Oliver, our past business is a fond memory, but you know disrespect is not tolerated," Connor warned, stepping in his face.

"Connor, step back. Oliver is right. You agreed to this deal, and you'll get your money and guns."

"Mendoza promised us New York and the distribution of guns."

"He can't promise something he doesn't even have."

"Not our problem," Cillian, Connor's brother, argued.

I blew out a breath and closed my eyes. I counted to three and opened them again. Something had changed with Connor over the past few days, and he thought he could renege on the deal. But I knew a selfish spoiled brat when I saw one because that used to be me.

I clenched my teeth. "What did he promise you?"

Connor frowned. "Who?"

"Detective Soren." Connor was far too comfortable with Hugo and Dario's deal, which meant he was in the bed with the cops as well.

"Detective Soren?" Oliver looked from me to Connor.

I raised my hand as Connor approached me. "That's what your little show is about, right?"

"I'm not an actor, sweetheart," Connor said smugly.

"Only an actor or a liar would try to swindle me and my family."

"Deals can be broken."

I got in his face. "Not without repercussions."

Connor glanced at Cillian as I moved away.

After a moment, Oliver approached me. "What are you thinking?"

I grimace. "He's playing us, and I'm pissed he thought I would let him."

"I knew we shouldn't have given him what he wanted."

"Oliver, relax. He won't be able to get far or live to tell anyone about this deal."

"He's the head of the Murphy crime family," Oliver muttered.

I knew exactly who and what Connor Murphy was and the people behind him.

Connor stood over the crates of guns. He bent to pick one up, and Oliver reached for his weapon.

I motioned for him to wait. "Connor, I don't have all day."

He dropped the gun back in the crate and turned to face me.

"If we take the deal, we want exclusive sale on drugs into Spain and Italy."

"Are you crazy or high?"

"Plus the crate, and you out of Ireland. I thought you understood this business. Usually, men make concessions in these types of situations."

"I have a better offer. You can leave."

"Leave?"

"Yes. Leave with nothing." I waved a hand in the air.

Oliver looked shocked at my words.

Connor's eyes narrowed. "We aren't leaving without our merchandise."

"The deal is no longer yours to take. As of one minute ago, I refused to pull out of Ireland or give you the order of guns. The money will be returned to you in one hour. Have a nice flight back to Ireland, gentleman."

"Bitch! You can't cut us out!" Connor snarled. "Mendoza was right about you."

"Good! Because I can be a lot of things, but a whining bitch is not one of them. I gave you the opportunity, and you dismissed it, so now I'm done playing nice with you assholes."

Connor reached for his gun. Ralfie and Oliver pulled their weapons.

"Neither of you will walk out of here alive," I announced.

"Fuck you!" Cillian barked.

"Detective Soren must have given you a deal to come here and betray us. Cillian, are you ready to die or go to jail for Connor?" I asked.

I knew Cillian would be loyal to his brother, but even he knew Connor was being stupid by not taking my warning.

"Shut up!" Connor shouted.

"Leave while you still can, and I'll consider not having your heads blown off on the way home."

Connor tried to negotiate. "I want what we came for."

"Sorry, the deal is off the table."

He glanced at Oliver for help.

"Oliver doesn't make deals. I run this family."

Connor lowered his gun. He could see I wouldn't bulge and left while he still could. My shoulders slumped in relief that no blood had been shed. His ego had taken a blow at the expense of a woman.

* * *

We finished at the club with Oliver and added extra security as a precaution. Then I had Ralfie take me to Axel at the warehouse. Hugo was more pissed off than usual as he paced in front of his car on the phone.

I approached Axel and kissed him on the lips. "Are you good?"

"You pulled the deal with Connor," he stated.

"He tried to play us. I think Soren was behind it."

Axel grinned. "Nice move."

"You think I did the right thing?"

"I would have done the same. He's too eager. He became unhinged when his father put him in charge."

"I'm glad."

"Did anyone follow you?"

"No. Ralfie took the side streets."

"Hugo looks unhappy."

"How long have you been here?"

"About thirty minutes."

"Is Ginerva awake?"

"I tried to get her to eat, but she refused again."

"I'm going to go see her."

"Take someone with you."

"I will." I stood on my tiptoes and kissed him on the lips.

I walked through the warehouse and down the hall to the room where they were keeping Ginerva. Ralfie opened the door and scanned the room before I stepped around him and saw a thinner Ginerva lying on the bed in the fetal position.

"Ginerva."

She didn't move.

"Ginerva." I kicked the bed.

She mumbled under her breath and slowly turned over, blinking from the small light in the room. She still wore the cami shorts and top from the night they took her. I barely recognized my friend with her hair matted and her arms chained to the bed.

"Ginerva, we need to talk."

"Gigi."

"Wake up."

Her eyes fully aligned with mine and she snarled, "Let me out of here!"

She tried to get loose, and I stood back and watched her.

I'd been looking for her for months. I'd dropped everything and pooled my resources into finding her. To discover that she'd been playing me all along broke my heart. I'd fooled myself into believing that Dario had threatened her, but now I knew that wasn't true. I was her enemy. She hated me and wanted me dead. Our friendship was built on lies. All the times we'd stayed talking on the phone and sharing our secrets meant nothing.

"I thought it was a dream when I saw you that day in the mall," I said softly.

"Let me out of here."

"I called your name."

"Are you going to let me go?"

"Why did you run?"

"Dario is looking for me."

"Dario?"

"He's going to find me and kill all of you."

"What happened to you, Ginerva? I don't get it."

"Kidnapping me? Dario is right about you."

"Do you hear yourself?"

"Dario loves me!"

"He's brainwashed you."

"He loves me, and you're jealous."

"I'm married. You were supposed to be married. We planned play dates with our kids."

Her laugh was evil. "Dario never wanted you. He belonged to me and only me."

"What about your parents and family?"

Remorse flickered across her face. "My family has nothing to do with Dario and me."

"I'm sorry, Ginerva. There's no coming back from what you've done."

"He's not the only one who hates you!"

I turned my back on her and walked out. Too much anger lived in her heart, and it made me question our entire lives together. My mind raced at how Dario had manipulated everyone around him to do his bidding.

I reached the front of the warehouse and saw one of our guards holding a gun to Hugo's head. His men had their weapons raised, ready for a shootout. The rooms had no sound because of what went on here and I hadn't heard a peep from Ralfie that anything went down.

I rushed to Axel and hugged him tight. "What happened?"

Axel placed a hand around my waist. "Hugo thought he could call for backup."

"I still have the evidence on your wife," Hugo shouted, banging his palm on the table.

I moved toward him, but Axel held me back. "Evidence or not, you will never walk out of here alive."

"My team is aware I'm here," he said smugly.

"He's right, Axel."

Hugo chuckled. "Listen to your wife like a good little boy."

Axel fired a shot into his leg, and he screamed in pain. His men tried to run to him, but Axel raised his gun.

One way or another, this bullshit ended now. "Take out your phone," I demanded.

"No," he gritted as his wound poured with blood.

"He may have put Soren onto us. He followed me into the mall earlier," I told Axel, trying to get him to calm down and think rationally. Killing Hugo was not beneficial when too many pieces were missing from the puzzle.

"My wife just saved your life, but let me be clear. You're going to die." Axel struck Hugo across the face with the gun. "Now get out."

"This isn't over," Hugo seethed as blood dripped down his chin.

His men helped him out of the chair and escorted him from the warehouse.

I turned to face Axel and took the gun from him. "Big move, baby."

"Only move we needed to take. Put them all on notice. No more hiding." He pressed a kiss on my cheek and ran his hand down my back.

"He and Connor might become best friends over the idea of killing us."

Axel squeezed my ass. "Let them. Turin put a tracker on his car and now we have the upper hand."

Our men cleaned up the area as we left the warehouse headed to our car. We headed home to relax and wait for Hugo to make his next move.

* * *

When we got home, Axel disappeared into his office and I went to shower the day off without him trying to join me and distract me with sex. I was still sore from our last session and I just wanted to cuddle tonight in bed. The doctor had finally scheduled my appointment for birth control and I couldn't wait to get on the pill again. I didn't want to get pregnant before we'd handled Dario.

I dried off, wrapped my hair in a tight bun, and pulled on shorts and a t-shirt for the rest of the evening.

My phone rang, and I grabbed it from my purse. Heavy breathing came over the line.

"He can't save you."

"Dario?"

"Too many got in the way of what we had."

"We never had anything."

"Shut the fuck up!"

I ended the call, but it rang again immediately.

I took a moment to gather my thoughts before answering. "Hello."

"Where's my money?"

"Do you miss your little girlfriend, Dario?"

"My money, Gigi."

"I'll give you credit, Dario. You had people fooled, but I saw the real devil living inside you."

"Where's your little boy, Gigi?"

I dropped the phone and ran from the bedroom to his room. His crib was empty.

"Gaspare!" I screamed his name and sprinted down the stairs to the playroom. I burst through the door to see him in the swing with the nanny, who was reading him a book.

"Is everything all right, Mrs. Bresciani?" she questioned.

Gaspare burst into tears, and I felt bad for disturbing his peace. I couldn't shake the feeling that Dario had done something.

I took him from the nanny and kissed his warm cheeks, wiping away his tears. I rocked him to calm him. "I'm sorry, baby bear. Mommy's sorry."

Axel ran into the room with his gun raised. "What's wrong? Did something happen?" He holstered his gun and charged toward, taking Gaspare from my arms to check him over.

"He's fine. I had a nightmare," I lied, my nerves raw.

"Can you give us a minute?" he asked the nanny.

She nodded and left the room. I sat on the couch to catch my breath. My hands shook and my heart raced. I closed my eyes and took some deep breaths.

"Dario called, and he asked about Gaspare. I got scared that he'd done something, so I ran to find him," I explained.

Axel pulled me off the couch to stand and rubbed my

back. "Dario's time is up. I promise. He's playing mind games."

"It's working."

Axel looked at our son. "Gaspare is ready for a nap, and I'm ready to spend time with my wife."

Chapter 16

Gigi

Axel stuck to his promise and let me handle how I would approach the final moments with Ginerva. The day dawned like any other. The sun was shining, and a light breeze stirred the air, but I couldn't enjoy it. My heart was breaking and my hands were sweaty with the knowledge of what was to come.

Will I regret taking a life that meant so much to me growing up?

The warehouse was on lockdown, with only a handful of trusted soldiers on duty. I knew they were waiting for me to make a move, but I needed answers before I made the call.

Looking at Ginerva now, I could see that she lacked any remorse. I'd spent months trying to help her family find her, only to discover she was living with Dario.

Ginerva raised her chin, her eyes flashing fire. "He loves me."

Dario had her believing everything that came out of his mouth. She'd allowed his lies to cripple our relationship.

Ginerva had let him destroy my family, and for that, she would have to pay.

"We had everyone looking for you," I told her.

She pressed her lips together.

"We did everything together, and you were sleeping with Dario Ramini behind my back." I laughed without humor.

"He wanted me first!" she yelled.

I ignored her outburst. "How do you expect me to forgive you?"

"You never loved Dario. Your engagement was a business arrangement."

"It was, but you know what our relationship was, and I hate to think about the lies you've told me."

She cackled and tugged at the ropes binding her wrists.

"All the times you were out with him but told me it was your fiancé." I tilted my head and glared at her.

"Dario said you never had sex with him. A man like him has needs."

I moved closer and cupped her chin, lifting her face to mine. "Janice told me about a bruise on your face."

Ginerva yanked her head away. "He never hit me."

"Do you think he's going to come and rescue you?"

"We could have been married."

I laughed. "I bet you would've slept with him even after we married."

"Dario is going to kill you and become the Boss. Then, he'll marry me."

"Marry you? How naïve are you, Ginerva?"

"He brought you along for the sex. Nothing about you will fulfil him."

"Dario told me that Axel's abusive."

"Please tell me when Axel was abusive."

"Let me go!"

"No."

"I covered so much for you with your parents. You owe me," she seethed.

"My parents have nothing to do with us."

"Please. You've always been dramatic and spoiled. Your parents gave you everything you wanted."

Her head snapped back from the force of my hand as I slapped her face. "The man killed my fucking family! He had my father killed and almost kill my husband and me. He's threatened my son!"

"Once Dario gets the Irish and Mendoza on his side, you'll beg for my help," she spat.

"You think I'm just gonna let you run off and be happy? You're delusional, Ginerva."

"Where is he?" Axel demanded.

"I don't know."

"He left you to die alone." Axel reminded her.

I threw my hands in the air. "He's gonna leave you to take your last breath alone, Ginerva."

"Gigi, don't, please. What about my family?" Ginerva begged.

"What about them? You weren't thinking about them before." I gestured to Onyx to remove her from the chair and put her on the table.

"Hold up! Wait!" She tried to fight, and he smacked her across the face.

I shook my head. "You decided to work with Dario."

"Okay! Okay!"

"Too late."

"Please, give me one more chance!" Ginerva begged.

I stood back and watched Axel pick up a saw and move toward her, while Onyx tied her to the table.

I turned my head to avoid her sorrowful look.

"Stop! No! My leg!" she screamed and suddenly went silent.

I turned to see she'd passed out.

"Wake her up," I commanded.

"Can you handle this, Gigi?" Axel asked, studying my face.

Nothing would distract me from what needed to be done. "Cut her arms next."

Ginerva woke groggily.

I marched to the table. "Where is Dario?"

"I... I... do-"

"I treated you like a sister."

She shivered. "I hate you."

I caressed her hair. "Neither hate nor love live in my heart anymore for you."

"He booked a flight to get out of town," she mumbled weakly.

I kissed her forehead.

"Kill her."

* * *

Onyx, Axel, and I jumped in the car to make in it time before Dario flew out of town. Traffic was busy during this time of day. Axel was on the phone to his soldiers, telling them to get to the private airport we knew Dario would use. I held onto the door handle as Onyx cut off cars and hopped on the freeway.

Axel handed me a gun. "In case you need to protect yourself."

I leaned forward and kissed him. "Be careful."

He winked at me.

Thirty minutes went by before Onyx sped through the

security gate. My heart was resolute at the thought of Dario taking his last breath. All the lies, the manipulation of my father, the arranged marriage deal that was sealed years ago would end today. He wouldn't haunt my dreams anymore.

Axel pointed up ahead. Here was my chance to show Dario, my father, and Axel that I'd completed my mission of vengeance. I was married and a new mother, but I could handle the business of the Carrington Cartel. Dario hadn't defeated me.

The car whizzed down the road, and Onyx swerved around to the back of the airstrip.

"Send men on the other side, and we'll take the front," Axel stated.

"I want Dario taken alive," I reminded them.

"You ready?" Axel cocked his gun.

We ducked as gunfire exploded and Dario's guys shot at our cars.

"Stay down!" Axel yelled.

"Hold on!" Onyx reversed while Axel fired toward Dario.

I got on the other side and did the same.

Onyx turned the car to block the plane from leaving the runway. Axel and Onyx jumped out while I covered the rear. Axel walked alongside the plane, and I shot another solider when she tried to run up on Axel from behind.

"Watch out, Axel!" I picked up the dead soldier's AK 47 and shot the windows and tires of the plane.

Axel grabbed me and looked into my eyes. "You good?" he asked, out of breath.

"Great. Let's go." I crushed my lips to his.

Onyx shot the guard at the plane door. Axel yanked the door open and Onyx went first and shot the flight attendant.

Onyx checked his watch. "We've got a few minutes

before we need to get out of here and employees come looking."

Axel pointed the gun at Dario and he threw his hands up in the air.

"Dario, why did you use Ginerva?"

"She was easy." He smirked, showing no remorse.

The Casella family and Mendoza probably had him set to fly to Chicago or Italy if we hadn't stopped him today. All the deaths that followed him would see him in hell when we were finished with him. But first, I needed answers about Detective Soren and the Casella Cartel's role in all this.

Axel motioned for Dario to stand and dragged him off the plane. More bullets flew past us. Mendoza had Dario more protected than his nephew. I directed my soldiers to split up while we got him loaded in the car.

Dario's man was injured, and Onyx shot him in the head as he fell to the ground. I climbed in the back of the car and Ralfie headed away from the airstrip. Axel pulled out his phone and started texting. I stared out of the window as we drove out of the area before the cops arrived.

* * *

Axel nudged his phone in my face with a text from Antonio.

Antonio: *Clear.*

Axel: *Pulling up now.*

I nodded, relieved to finally finish what we'd started. We came around back, and I waited in the car while the men pulled Dario out in handcuffs with a bag over his head. Axel talked with Carlo at the door and waved for me to get out of the car.

Ralfie held it open and Axel's hand grasped my neck. "You up for what's going to happen?"

"Very much ready to end him."

Carlo and Axel escorted me inside and walked to the bar. Carlo motioned for his bartender to pour a drink. Carlo and Axel ordered food, but I was on pins and needles.

An hour passed with Dario loc up in Ryde nightclub's basement. Antonio said we needed discretion, since Detective Soren had already sniffed around our warehouses. I couldn't wait to hear what Dario had to say to explain his choices.

The door to Antonio's office closed and Axel kissed my head.

"Any word yet?"

"No. Mendoza hasn't called, or Soren."

"Then we can handle him now?"

Axel calmly lifted me from the seat and pulled me to the couch with me on his lap. "Soon as the club shuts down."

"That's a few hours from now."

"I know, but the staff is still lingering."

I was impatient and ready to get things over with. I leaned my head on his shoulder. "Soren will go nuts."

"He's the least of my worries."

The door flew open to Onyx and Ralfie with glares on their faces.

"What's wrong?" I asked.

Onyx said, "He's not talking."

Axel snaked his arm around my waist.

Onyx held up his phone. "Dario's people made some threats."

I saw a text from someone unknown discussing Dario missing. "Casella's men and Mendoza have no idea we have him."

"Unless Soren made him aware."

"You want to wait or kill him now?" I asked Axel.

"Let's do it." Axel grabbed my hand, and we took the elevator to the underground basement.

The door opened and Axel stepped into the room.

Ralfie looked down at his phone and scowled. "He's outside."

"Who?" Axel grew agitated.

"Detective Soren," he answered.

"We need to go see what he wants before Antonio shuts the place down with blood and we have more police in our business."

As we took the elevator to the main floor, I had a gut feeling Soren was trying to buy time for Dario. If he only knew it would lead to his own demise. As we got to the front, we saw it was surrounded by police and in the middle of them was Soren.

"I know he's here," Soren declared.

"Who?" I asked.

He crossed his arms over his chest. "A call came in of shots at a private airport and it seems the passenger was one Dario Ramini."

I shrugged. "What does that have to do with us?"

Detective Soren got in my face, but Axel pulled me behind him.

"If you have questions, take them up with our lawyer," Axel snapped at the detective.

"We have a search warrant."

"Go ahead. You won't find anything," Carlo announced.

The elevator was behind a wall that looked like a janitorial closet. No one expected there would be a secret trap in a club.

"You two need to come down to the station to answer some questions."

I narrowed my eyes. "What are we being charged with?"

"Conspiracy to commit murder, RICO charges, and drug trafficking."

I burst into laughter. "Where's the evidence, Detective? Or are you going by a 'he said' type of thing?" I mocked him.

"Take them in and search the place." Soren ignored my question and motioned for us to be handcuffed.

"If we're not being charged, we can drive ourselves," I countered.

Soren went to grab me, but Axel charged and punched him in the face.

"Fuck! Grab him," Detective Soren shouted. Two officers pulled Axel off him.

"Get the fuck away from my wife!" Axel grunted.

I stared into his eyes to get him to calm down. I knew Soren would use the punch as ammunition to get us locked up.

"Baby, I'm fine. I promise."

The look in his eyes was that of a man sick of people trying to keep us apart and destroy our lives.

Carlo and Ralfie talked him down and helped us out of the club with no further incidents. I took my phone and called our lawyer to meet us at the station. Two police officers escorted us into the station before Detective Soren and Raymond came to the door and watched me.

I lingered in the room alone while they held Axel in another area. We hadn't been charged or finger printed. No water or food was offered, and I knew they wanted to keep us in suspense. Finally, they seemed to have enough of me pacing, and Soren and Raymond came in and shut the door while a guard stood in the corner.

"You think as a mafia Boss you can get away with killing people at an airstrip and no one notices?" Soren demanded.

"I'm not talking to anyone until I speak with my lawyer and my husband."

"He's busy."

"Where is Axel?"

"Tied up," Soren muttered with a satisfied look.

"If anything happens to him—"

"Are you threatening an officer?"

"Sounds like she's putting a hit out on you," Raymond responded.

I scoffed at the feeble attempt to trap me.

"Where is Dario Ramini?" Soren questioned.

"Hopefully in hell."

"You think this is fun and games?"

"What I know and think are two different things, Detective."

"Women like you make me sick."

"So you have mommy issues. A woman broke your heart. Your parents didn't love you enough." I ran off scenarios and his nostrils flared.

"Dario was an informant for the police," Raymond explained.

"Why are you telling me?"

"If something happens to him and we find out it was you..." Raymond let his words trail off ominously.

"Nothing for me to say. I haven't talked to Dario in months."

"He goes missing right when a flight is supposed to take off?"

"Again, I have no clue."

"She's lying." Soren slammed his hand on the table.

"How would you know unless you've been following me, Detective? Stalking and harassment is against the law."

Soren stood, threw the chair into the corner, and charged at me. Raymond blocked him before he could touch me.

"Bitch. You're not innocent," Soren growled.

I smiled. "Dario had the same expression the last time I talked to him."

The room went still as the door flew open to my lawyer and Axel. Raymond pushed Soren back and Axel marched toward me. He smoothed his hands up and down my arms, checking my face for any bruises.

Soren said, "Dead bodies were found at the airstrip."

"Tragic," I replied.

"No witnesses. We received a call from an employee. We discover it's connected to a mob cartel, and you want me to let her go?" Soren muttered to my lawyer.

"There is no evidence linking my client to any of this," John challenged.

I stood. "Can we go? I need to get home to my son."

"This isn't over," Raymond hissed.

Axel kept his eyes on Soren and Raymond as I walked out of the interrogation room and down the corridor.

"Keep walking," John said, leading us outside.

"Soren is like a bomb ready to explode at any moment," Axel muttered.

"How did you get us out?" I asked.

"I have evidence that you guys were traveling to take a flight and came upon a situation." John grinned.

Axel shook hands with him before helping me into the waiting town car. I clung to Axel's side as he slid in beside me.

"Are you all right? Are you hurt?" he asked.

"No, I'm fine. We need to get to Dario and finish him."

"I agree. Let's go." He nodded at Ralfie to drive.

Everybody piled in their cars and drove back to Antonio's club to finish putting out the trash.

The forty-minute drive gave me time to decide how I'd like to spread out Dario's torture and pain, but another part of me wanted to put a bullet straight through his brain. After all, he didn't show my family mercy.

* * *

Seconds after we made it back to the club, John gave us the rundown on keeping things clean so Soren wouldn't return to harass us. Axel shook his hand, and I waved goodbye before we walked back into the club.

The bartender chucked his chin at us, and we stepped into the elevator to head down to the basement. My stomach was queasy at the thought of killing the person who had torched my life.

Ralfie stepped aside when the elevator doors opened and let us approach first. I heard screams. The door was open, and Dario and Mendoza's men were on the floor with their hands tied behind their back. I looked into Dario's empty eyes and wondered if he had any regrets. The little girl in me who grew up with Dario felt bad, but she needed to stay locked away because at one time I did care for him as a family friend.

Turin whistled, and the guards stepped away from Dario. I moved closer to see the bruises they'd put on his face. I'd demanded they leave his death to me.

Chapter 17

Axel

She held her head high, her entire body stoic and commanding. I knew I couldn't take this moment away from her. Gigi needed this closure in order for us to move on and be a family, to not have enemies who wanted us dead. As her husband, I watched and gave her what she needed—control of Dario's last breath.

I stood back and watched as she sauntered toward him. She clipped his chin and peeped into his eyes, and I wanted to pull them out of his head. After everything he'd done, he deserved it. But I couldn't get too overwhelmed. Today was Gigi's closure.

"You think she's going to be okay?" Onyx asked.

"After we finish everything, I do."

"Soren and Mendoza?"

My top lip twitched. "Both need to die for threatening my family."

Onyx said, "He never talked."

"We're trained not to talk."

"Soren didn't find anything when they searched," Turin said.

"Did Antonio come down?" I asked.

Turin shook his head. "No. Carlo let him know we handled Soren. Is retirement still a go?"

"After this, I think she will. But it's her choice. Gigi was controlled by her parents. I don't want to be that way with her." I was pretty close to losing her at the airstrip, then with Soren arresting us.

The conversation in the room brought me back to the issue at hand.

"Tell me the truth, Dario," Gigi demanded.

"Everything you have was meant for me. You are too stupid, too naïve, and too precious as Laurent's daughter to see the bigger picture," Dario taunted, looking from Gigi to me.

I clenched my jaw, ready to punch his teeth out.

"You killed my mother and father. For money and power. It's all about power." Gigi balled up her fists.

Dario threw his head back dramatically. "God, stop being naïve. You're doing the same thing."

"I didn't kill to get there," Gigi hissed.

He licked his lips and blew a kiss. "Ginerva understands the legacy of the cartel. She gave me what I wanted."

"You used her to get to me. For power you didn't have, so you could kill my father."

"Laurent wouldn't have let me lead the way I wanted to. He wouldn't let go. He wanted control even when he retired. I had other plans."

"Well, lucky you. I have other plans, too."

She picked up the knife and plunged it into his stomach.

Dario cried out and tried to move away. Gigi pulled the knife out and plunged it into his shoulder. She dropped the knife on the ground, reached for the gun, and moved back a few steps.

Gigi shot him twice in the knee caps.

"Bitch!" he screamed.

"Power will always be up for grabs when it comes to the cartel. You only achieve loyalty and power from the people who believe in your shared goals. I led my cartel with loyalty, and they devoted their lives to me. Tell Rosa she didn't win."

Gigi pushed the button, and a small steel door opened to a fire Antonio used to destroy any evidence when doing business around the building.

Dario tried to wiggle away, but our men ensured he was strapped tight when they laid him on top of the table and watched him burn alive. One after the other, we took care of each goon, listening to their screams as they died.

When Gigi was ready to leave, Turin stayed to clean up and ensure there were no traces of us ever being there.

* * *

I slipped the key in the door soon as we got out of the car and made it home. Gigi rolled her neck, and I drew her in close, kissing her head.

"Let me check on Gaspare." Gigi yawned.

I smoothed my hands along her back. "I'll run a bath for you."

Gigi nodded and walked off. I set the alarm and headed to the bar. Grabbing the bottle of cognac, I poured a glass and went upstairs. I unbuttoned my shirt on the way to the bathroom and turned the light on. Placing the glass on the counter, I kicked off my shoes and turned the faucet on to fill the jacuzzi tub. I poured Gigi's favorite lavender and vanilla bubble bath soap into the water.

Gigi appeared as I lit the last candle and I helped her undress and climb into the water to relax and let the day go.

"Detective Soren," she murmured.

I kissed her forehead. "Shush... relax for me."

She gazed into my eyes. "Are you heading back out tonight?"

"No, I'm here for the night. Turin can handle the cleanup."

"I feel a weight lifted off our shoulders."

"He can't hurt you anymore."

"He had no remorse."

"People like him never do."

"Get in the water with me."

I bent over the tub and nibbled on her bottom lip. "If I get in the water, more than relaxing is going to happen."

"A little relaxation in the form of you inside me could help."

"I love you," I growled.

"Hearing you say and prove your love is all I ever need in life."

Her words caused warmth to spread in my chest and my dick to twitch. Hurriedly, I removed my clothes and stepped into the large jacuzzi tub, helping Gigi climb on top of my lap. Slowly, she reached in between us and placed my rod at her entrance. We felt the contact immediately, and needed a moment before we could move. With her full breasts and doe-eyes filled with lust, I couldn't help but want to dominate her tonight.

She leaned forward and kissed me on the lips once, twice, until I caught her tongue. I gripped her ass cheeks and rocked her slowly back and forth.

"Feel our connection," Gigi whispered, nuzzling her face along my shoulder and neck.

"Ah, fuck."

"Oh, god, baby," she moaned.

Our bodies formed a rhythm and slapped against the water as our sighs filled the room. I gathered her hair in my hand and tugged her head back, sucking, licking, and nibbling my way down to her breasts.

Gigi cried out, "Fuck! I feel you, baby."

Ready to take her to bed, I removed the plug from the tub. Lifting her in my arms, I carefully stepped out of the tub and walked to the bedroom. We were still soaking wet as I planted her on the bed. I sucked her nipple as I grasped her leg and slid back into her warm, tight hole.

"Like it was the first time," I muttered, picking up my thrusts.

I scanned down our bodies, watching her sex contort as I pushed her legs back to her chest and pumped in and out.

"Yes, Axel! Keep going."

"I swear to love you forever, baby. Fuck! I'm gonna come."

"Come inside me, please," she begged as her soft hands rubbed up and down my back.

I squeezed my eyes shut and released inside her pussy as we kissed. Soon after, she straddled me and put her feet flat on the bed, moving herself up and down.

I smacked her ass and pushed her breasts together and she came with a long moan. She fell forward and pressed her lips to mine as her movements slowed.

We made love for the rest of the night.

* * *

The next morning, I had Turin meet me at the office to go over the plan for dealing with Detectives Soren and

Raymond. All the information had finally come in, and we knew he was Dario's cousin. It was why he'd been stalking my family. The contact Laurent used in the past was sent to me to do his job. The chief of police tried to avoid us, but Antonio let him know what needed to be done or he would be handled directly. We'd have more eyes on us when they went missing, but we'd paid enough people to look the other way.

"You've never had a problem with handling a coverup," Antonio told the chief as we sat in my office.

The chief fidgeted in his seat. "That was before more bodies went missing at the hands of the Carrington Cartel."

"Either you get rid of him or we will."

The chief grumbled, "It's not easy removing two detectives."

"Perhaps you could send them on an assignment that goes tragically wrong."

"Your family made a bigger problem when you landed here. I'll do what I can, but it's going to take time." He blew out a breath.

"We don't have time." I slammed my hand on the desk.

"Soren won't be a problem for much longer." The chief held up his hands.

I pointed at his face. "He's trying to make a name for himself. Being related to Dario should help speed up the process of his cases being looked at for bias."

The chief ran a hand down the back of his neck. "Give me a few days."

"You have twenty-fours."

"Either your family or Detective Soren," I stated.

"He's too high-profile right now," the chief argued.

"All the more reason to take him out." I gritted my teeth.

The chief nodded, picked up the file, and turned to leave

the office. I kept my eyes on him when Gigi passed him in the hallway.

"You think he's going to do his job?" Turin inquired.

"No reason not to believe him."

Gigi pushed the door open with a look of gloom on her face. "What was the Chief doing here?"

"Taking care of a rat," I replied.

"Oh, well, I wanted to tell you I need to run out for a moment before my meeting."

"Is everything good?"

Turin stepped out of the room and gave us some privacy.

Gigi looked everywhere but at me.

"If something is bothering you, I need to know."

"Stop worrying. Can you pick up Gaspare from the park? The nanny has to take her mom to the doctor," Gigi informed me.

I nodded and as soon as she left, I met Turin outside in the car and headed to the park. My phone vibrated, and I pulled it from my pocket.

Mendoza: *Two down. You'll still end up losing.*

Me: *You're on borrowed time.*

Mendoza: *Fuck you.*

Me: *I only do that with my wife.*

Mendoza: *Casella may have left, but I'll get what's mine.*

Me: *Try me.*

"That look on your face says you're ready to kill," Turin remarked.

"Mendoza pisses me off." I sent a message to our tech to pinpoint his location.

"He's back in Chicago," Turin added.

"How do you know?"

Turin shrugged. "I've been keeping an eye on him."

"So he ran off after finding out Dario was dead?"

"Probably, plus Casella's people decided to make other arrangements."

"We need to make plans to visit the Windy City."

"Already went to the windy city with your wife."

"And we all know how that turned out."

"She killed the nephew, and you kill the uncle. Can't take either of you anywhere."

I chuckled. "They say a couple acts alike after a while."

We reached the park, and I opened the door to meet our nanny halfway with Gaspare. Turin popped the trunk and grabbed his baby bags.

"He ate an hour ago," the nanny said.

I rocked him in my arms and he smiled at me. "Great, I'll let his mom know and you can take the rest of the day off."

"Thank you, sir."

I nodded and watched her get in her car.

"Where now?" Turin asked.

"Home. I need to make sure the chief does what he promised."

"He's not stupid."

"All of them are at some point."

Mendoza thought I was letting our dealings go without payback because we hadn't immediately gone after him. I liked to keep people waiting until they got comfortable before I helped them to leave the earth.

Once I got Gaspare settled, I called to check on Gigi, but the phone went straight to voicemail. I hung up and dialed again from my office phone.

"*I can't come to the phone right now. Please leave a message.*"

I pulled up the location from the app we shared on my

phone and saw she was at Janice's home. I'd give her a few minutes before I jumped in my car to bring her back.

My phone rang, and I recognized the chief's number. "Is it done?"

"In all my years of being a police officer, I can count on one hand how many times I've had to eliminate a fellow officer."

"Don't feel bad. It was him or you."

"That's not funny," the chief argued.

"Not meant to be."

"He's going to turn up in a motel dead from an overdose."

"Send me the location and who called it in?"

"A few junkies." The chief rambled off the location.

I typed it in my cell, grabbed my jacket, and left the house manager to keep an eye on Gaspare. Turin wouldn't be needed while I made a run to check on Detective Soren's final resting place. I sped down the freeway for an hour toward Brooklyn and was greeted by police cars and ambulances out front. I parked and jumped out, closing in on the reporters and nosy neighbors speculating about what had happened.

"What happened here?"

An older woman in a postal uniform eyed me before she answered. "Some police officer was found dead."

"Alone?"

"Probably a drug bust gone wrong. This neighborhood has so much going on. I'm not surprised."

"Tough times."

I turned to go back to my car, tipping my head to the chief standing in the corner with fellow officers. The body was rolled out of the motel in a body bag.

My phone rang, and I snapped it to my ear. "You home?"

"Yes, and you're not here," Gigi said softly.

"Had to handle something."

"Should I be worried?"

"No, all our problems are being solved."

"Well not all."

I climbed into the car and slid the key into the ignition.

I startled as someone banged on the window. I looked to see Raymond trying to open my door.

"What the fuck?"

"Axel? What's that noise?"

"I'll call you back."

"No! Stay on the phone with me."

I pushed the door open and tossed the phone aside. "The fuck is your problem?" I shouted, shoving him in the chest.

"I know you killed him," Raymond snarled.

"Raymond, calm down." The chief marched over to us.

"Listen to your boss."

"Fuck you. He told me you'd be responsible if anything happened to him," Raymond hissed.

"Throwing around accusations like that could get you in trouble, Detective."

"Chief, arrest him!"

"Raymond, you need to calm down and go sit in the car," the chief demanded.

"He needs to be off the streets. Dario Ramini goes missing, and Soren is dead."

"Maybe they're together." I grinned.

Raymond didn't like my snarky reply and lunged at me. I stepped aside, and he collided with my car.

"You've been drinking, Detective," the chief said and motioned for his men to take Raymond away.

I waited for him to leave and glared at the chief. "I told you to take care of them both."

"He was held up," the chief mumbled.

I poked him in the chest. "Fix it, or you'll be next on the news."

"Give me a few days. It'll look weird if both detectives end up dead," the chief grumbled.

I saw his point, but the last thing on my mind was how the optics looked. His job was to take care of our problems. The cartel made him a lot of money and put him in places he wouldn't be otherwise, socializing with political leaders.

I nodded. "One more day."

Chapter 18

Gigi

I lay on the cold bed and waited for the doctor to return with my blood test results. I hadn't felt good for a while, and I knew why, but I was in denial. Axel and I hadn't been careful at all and ignored my six weeks. The idea of being pregnant again was nerve-racking. No matter what, I would love my child, but two babies close together was stressful. Plus, starting a new business was on my list of things I wanted to do. The thought of having two kids to run behind, all while tending to a husband and my personal needs, made me anxious.

"Well, you were right to come in for a checkup," the doctor said as she entered the room.

I blew out a shaky breath. "Tell me."

"Congratulations. You're pregnant."

I removed my feet from the stirrups and groaned. I was more scared of being pregnant than murdering someone. "Oh god. I knew it."

"Young couples tend to ignore the six weeks."

"My husband for sure didn't care."

She laughed, and I joined in. I knew Axel would love this news.

"You're a great mom, so this one will be blessed."

"Thank you, Doctor. I'm just stressed because Gaspare is so young."

"Try not to worry, and maybe take a vacation."

"I'll think about that."

"Make another appointment in a few weeks."

She left, and I climbed off the table and dressed. I grabbed my phone, debating whether to tell Axel now or wait and surprise him.

My phone vibrated in my hand and I saw Axel's name. Speak of the devil.

"Hello."

"You on your way home?"

"About to leave the doctor's office now."

"Gaspare misses you."

I smile. "Just Gaspare?"

"Come find out." Axel suggested.

I nodded at Ralfie and climbed in the back. He shut the door, climbed behind the wheel, and started the car.

"What did the doc say?" Axel asked.

"I'm fine."

"Good."

I released my breath. "I'm pregnant."

The phone grew quiet. "Pregnant?"

"Yes. How do you feel?"

"I expect you're not too happy, but I'm overjoyed." Axel said quietly.

I groaned and threw my head back. "You couldn't wait and now we'll have two kids under the age of two."

He chuckled. "We can handle it."

"Not funny, Axel."

"Life is funny like that, baby."

"Well, you should have kept your hands to yourself."

He chuckled again. "Get home safe."

"You, too."

"I need to get Gaspare home before he cries my ears off."

"Okay. I'll probably call the girls over to hangout."

"That's fine. See you later."

"See you later. Be safe."

"You too, *mi amore*."

Ralfie whisked us back to the house while I thought about what our next child would look like. I'd fallen instantly in love with Gaspare, and I wondered if my love would grow to include another child. Would I be able to balance everything with two?

Ralfie parked the car and opened my door. I thanked him entered the house to find Janice and Sabrina already there.

"What in the world are you two doing here?" I hugged both ladies.

"Axel told us you had a doctor's appointment today and wanted us to be here when you made it home," Janice said.

"I just got off the phone with him and said I would call you two."

"He figured, so we decided to surprise you instead." Sabrina grinned.

"I'm pregnant."

Janice smirked and sipped on her glass of mimosa. "You won't be drinking with us then."

"He's to blame." I pouted and followed them into the kitchen where Ebony had food displayed across the island.

"Blame him all you want, but your legs stayed open twenty-four-seven for that man," Janice joked.

I flipped her off. "Coming from you, that means a lot,"

I laughed at her sly expression. Carlo would have a fleet

of kids if Janice allowed it, but she had plans to enjoy her life once all the kids moved out.

"Sabrina, you're laughing a little too hard for my liking, ma'am." Janice poked her lip out and Sabrina cackled. She and Antonio had five kids.

Sabrina hunched her shoulders and picked up a plate of waffles and fruit. "You'll have two babies while you're still young. I know it can be scary, but we're here to help."

"Thanks. Remember I told you I wanted to start my charity work?"

"Yes. Did you get the paperwork started?" Janice queried.

"My lawyer is sending everything over for me after he files."

Sabrina nodded. "Axel's fine with you working?"

"Charity work is better than me sticking with cartel life."

"True, and we work normal jobs. Never missed being in the men's business once we left," Janice said.

"Dario and Ginerva are dealt with now," I confirmed.

Sabrina shook her head. "Hard to believe she'd been holding on to so much hate for you."

No more pretending she cared about our friendship. "Yeah. I'm glad I'll never see the look of disgust in her eyes again."

The memory of Ginerva's hate for me would probably haunt me for a while, but the realization that I needed to protect myself and family came first. I was right about leaving the cartel behind.

"Have you picked out a location?" Janice asked.

I cut into my pancakes and took a bite. "A place that's at least two stories, maybe three. And not too far from home, so the travel isn't rough with me being home on time for Gaspare."

"We can talk to our realtor and look at commercial property," Sabrina suggested.

"Wonderful. I appreciate the help."

"If you need donations, please hit me up. I'd love to run Carlo's pockets." Janice smirked.

"Carlo is going to put you on an allowance," I chuckled.

She lifted her glass and refilled it for a second round of mimosa. "Carlo will never put me on an allowance if he wants to sleep with both eyes closed."

"You threaten that man so much," I quipped.

Janice brushed us off. "He likes it. It's my love language."

Sabrina choked on her drink, and Janice and I burst into laughter. You never knew what would come out of her mouth.

Janice tapped on her phone while Sabrina and I talked about the realtor she could put me in touch with to look at spaces. A few moments later, the door opened and Axel and Turin walked in.

"Ladies," Axel greeted, bending to kiss my cheek.

"Axel, tell your friend, Carlo, he'd better answer my phone calls," Janice said, hopping off the stool with her phone to her ear as she waited for him to answer. Those two went back and forth all the time.

Axel took a bite of my food and caressed my cheek. "How's my baby doing?"

"I'm a few seconds pregnant," I dryly answered.

He smirked, and I rolled my eyes.

"Reminds me of when Antonio got me pregnant back-to-back." Sabrina sighed.

"He knew what he was doing." I gulped my orange juice.

"I'm taking Gigi to look at property if you can spare her for a few hours?" Sabrina put her plate in the sink and I followed. Our housekeeper would take care of the dishes once everyone was cleared out.

"Do you mind if I step out? I could wait and go tomorrow, but I need to keep my mind distracted."

"No, go ahead. Keep the guards with you. Still have to be careful."

He interlocked our hands and kissed me twice before he smacked me on the butt and let me go.

* * *

A week later, I stood around the table with our men and waited for them to quiet before we discussed the news.

"Casella is back in Italy."

"What about Mendoza?" one of my men asked.

All eyes focused on Axel and me.

"He's in Chicago, still trying to get support to take us out," Axel replied.

"And you are not willing to deal with him?"

I cleared my throat. "Pointless, but that's not the only thing we need to talk about."

"Anything to do with cops looking for Dario Ramini?" another of my men questioned.

"Dario is no longer a concern, but I'm pregnant."

The room went silent.

"What does this mean?" The man's eyes narrowed.

We made them a lot of money and gave them a generous percentage when doing business. I figured they were nervous that if I left the business, the new Boss would cut them out of deals. I lifted my eyes to Axel. I didn't need his permission. But I liked to get his thoughts and opinions. Like me, he hated to be questioned about how we ran our business.

"I'm stepping down."

"Who will run the Carrington Cartel?"

"Me," Axel answered.

"As the enforcer of the cartel, shouldn't you stick to that role?" our talkative friend asked.

"Axel is more than capable of handling the role of leader—"

Axel raised his hand to cut me off. "The business will remain true to what Laurent put in place. But let me be very clear; loyalty is to this family."

Axel made eye contact with everyone in the room. Tension was high, but no one replied and all nodded in agreement.

We left together, and I expressed my gratitude for his support in the limo. We pulled up at the building I wanted to get his opinion on before I made the big purchase.

We got out of the limo and Axel scanned the area. "The outside looks good, and it's not a high traffic area."

"I asked the realtor to make sure the place wasn't in a bad area for my first building."

I'd decided to open a child center. I was blessed growing up with a staff of people surrounding me, and Gaspare would have the same. The idea was to spread care and love to other families with a top-of-the-line facility where money wouldn't be a problem. The place would have every item a kid would love when not at home. The staff and parents would be comfortable and know we took pride in wanting the kids to be safe and loved like they were our own.

Axel walked around the front and noticed the open space and large windows.

I stood in the back and watched him look around the room. "Too much?"

"No. If you like it, get it."

I clapped my hands together. "I have so many plans. I'll have an office, but I know I can't be here every day."

"Correct. You're still the wife of the Don."

"I know, baby."

We kissed and made our way home to eat dinner and hang out with Gaspare.

Once we made it to bed, I slipped off my nightgown, trailed my lips across his jaw and down his neck. It had been a long day, touring the building and meeting with our men.

"I love you," I murmured.

"I love you, too."

Axel moved the phone toward me. "Last thing to handle before we're finished."

"Okay." I nodded in understanding.

I smiled and handed the phone back to him, staring at the pictures of Connor and Mendoza.

Chapter 19

Axel

Turin slipped the crates open. He picked up a Glock and looked it over before replacing it and motioning for the guys to seal it up.

The minute I announced I was taking over the cartel, there was nothing stopping me from making my rounds to every person we had business with. I promised Gigi I would be home soon, so this was the final stop of the day before heading home for the afternoon party.

Gigi and I never had a baby shower for Gaspare, so Janice and Sabrina had decided to throw a little gathering. At first, I wasn't onboard as we'd have a house full of people, but Gigi complained about tradition and how we should be able to do normal stuff like other couples with newborns. Rather than get in a shouting match, I gave in and left the planning to her and the girls.

"All solid," Turin announced.

"The minimum is ten crates." I glanced at Chauncey, a local gang leader in the city.

"I want twenty," Chauncey said.

I looked at Turin, who nodded. He'd heard of Chauncey and knew how he did things in the Bronx. Antonio had sent word that he was clean and never had problems with his team.

"Twenty," I agreed.

"Monthly," Chauncey expressed.

"Long as you can pay the fee." I slipped my hands in my pockets.

"Money is no problem."

I removed my hand and stuck it out for him. "Then we have a deal, Chauncey." I gripped his hand tight and made eye contact. "I expect no problems."

He nodded and snapped his fingers for his team to bring the bags of money.

"Anything else will go through Turin. This is our first and last meeting," I announced.

"We're clear," Chauncey replied.

Turin and I strolled out of the building and headed toward the car. The car ride wouldn't take long, and I replied to a few emails on the legit businesses we had in the Carrington fold. The twenty minutes went fast and when I saw the red, white, and blue balloons outside our house, I knew Gigi had gone overboard with decorations.

Inside, I watched my son as he played with his toys. He had no clue why all these people were in his face. It wasn't his birthday, but Gigi thought gifts, music, and an ice sculpture made the perfect pick for a post baby shower.

"Ice sculpture?" I asked in disbelief.

"I love it. Look at the cake. They made it look exactly like Gaspare."

"He has no idea and won't remember this party."

"We have a videographer and photographer."

I picked up my son and nuzzled him close. "How much did it cost?"

Gigi wiped Gaspare's chin. "Not too much."

"How much?"

Gigi rolled her eyes. "Thirty thousand."

I chuckled. "I know I didn't hear thirty thousand."

"Axel, memories will last forever."

"Whatever you say, dear."

Gigi didn't need the stress of an argument, so I dropped the subject, but I would let Janice and Sabrina know to come to me next time when they got the idea to throw a party.

"Are you hungry?" Gigi asked, changing the subject.

"No. How are you feeling?"

"Fine."

"Have you eaten?"

"Not yet. I've been running around getting the party together."

"Come with me." I grasped her hand and walked us out of the living room to the backyard, where tables were set with food. I picked up a plate, filled it with food, and handed it to her.

Janice and a few kids were playing in the pool.

"You home for the rest of the day?" Gigi asked.

"Yeah. I finished my business."

"How did it go?"

"Nothing for you to worry about." I looked pointedly at her plate. "Eat."

"I can see how you'll be once the new baby comes," Gigi grumbled and dug into her salad.

"I missed the first pregnancy. I'm not missing the second one." I grinned and rubbed her stomach.

"Come sit with me." Gigi took my hand, walked over to the cabana at the side of the pool.

Gaspare reached for his mom while she ate, but I tucked him in my arms and let him play with the toy bear. "Who are these people?"

"Friends and extended family on my mom's side."

"You didn't tell me you stayed in contact with that side of the family."

Gigi shrugged and lifted her fork toward me to eat.

"You eat."

"I want Gaspare and this new baby to have as much family as possible. Have you thought about contacting some of your family?"

Gaspare bounced in my arms. "Never paid it any mind. A few people sent condolences, but no one stayed in contact. I needed an escape, and I did that when I became a part of the cartel."

"Well, Gaspare will have something neither of us got when we lost our parents."

"What?" My brow hiked up.

"A family full life of love and happiness." She leaned over and kissed me.

"How much longer is this going to go on?"

"So grumpy."

"Happy. You and my son are having fun, but I have work to do."

"It can't wait?"

"Not this."

Gigi tried to take Gaspare, but I stood up. "He's coming with me to the office."

"What about his party? We still need to open the gifts."

"Enjoy the party, Gigi. Gaspare only cares about putting his hand in his mouth." I bent and pressed a kiss on her forehead. She muttered, and I smiled at her pout.

I left the party and shut the office door behind me.

Gaspare fiddled with my cell phone as I turned on my computer and checked my emails.

The phone rang, and I took it from Gaspare's mouth. He whimpered, so I rocked him back and forth. *Probably should have given him to Gigi,* I thought.

"Everything set?" Antonio asked.

"Set and cleared."

"Chauncey won't be a problem?"

"No. Turin is back to full health and can handle the meetings."

"I hear congrats are in order."

"Gigi and the girls love to gossip."

Antonio chuckled. "My wife loves Gigi like a little sister."

"They've been supportive, and I appreciate the kindness with those other tasks."

"Don't mention it. New York is my home, and I welcome the Carringtons."

"Thanks."

"The mayor would like a meeting."

"Mayor?"

"A businessman like yourself could do great things in his city, and he'd like to schedule something for the future."

I sat back and pondered his statement. "The mayor knows I'm not foolish or naïve like Mendoza?"

"We've had a conversation." Antonio replied.

"I guess we'll have a sit down."

"Money moves in New York, and the mayor won't interrupt."

"Glad to hear it."

"I just got a text from my wife. She's on her way home."

"So that means I can have my wife back." I chuckled.

"Indeed." The dial tone served as a goodbye.

I looked at Gaspare asleep in my arms and ran a hand over his head. "One day, this will all be yours."

I finished reading over paperwork and emails. When I finished, I took Gaspare to the living room to find Gigi watching TV. "Party over?"

"Yes," Gigi watched as I placed Gaspare in the play pen to nap.

I sat close to her on the couch, reaching my arm around her and she leaned into my chest. "You have fun?"

"Fun as can be expected for a last-minute shower."

"The next baby will have a real one."

"Do you want a girl or boy?"

"I don't care so long as you're both healthy."

"Same." She yawned.

"I'm meeting with the mayor."

She jerked back at my statement. "Mayor? Why?"

"Business."

"Is he trying to do something?"

"Antonio arranged it and said he comes in peace."

"The mayor wanting to meet could be good for us. Help establish my business and you running the legit businesses on paper."

"More at stake."

Gigi placed a finger under my chin for a kiss. "He's not stupid enough to mess with you. How about we go out tonight?"

"The nanny?"

"She's asleep, but we can let her know we're going out. I want to go to Ryde tonight and dance."

"You know I'm not a club person."

Gigi rose from the couch. "But you promised to cherish your wife and spoil her, correct?"

I frowned. "That had nothing to do with going out to the club."

She grinned, wrapping her arms around my waist and standing on her tiptoes for a kiss. Our tongues danced, but before we got carried away, Gaspare started crying.

Gigi pulled back and picked him up. "See? Even he knows how to get what he wants from us."

***

It wasn't too crowded at the club. Ralfie turned off the engine, and I opened the door to help Gigi out. I held her close as the bouncer motioned us inside, and our private bottle girl walked us over to the VIP section. Antonio didn't get out much anymore, but he'd set us up and Carlo tagged along with Janice. Turin came without a date for protection, but Gigi kept trying to hook him up with women. Antonio and Sabrina stayed home to enjoy a night as a couple. In a few years, that would be Gigi and me when our kids went off to college and left the two of us alone.

My phone buzzed on the table and I lifted it to see the time and date of the meeting with the mayor. I extended it to Turin, and he noted it on his phone, then went to drink his beer.

"Are you going to sit here all night or will you dance with me?" Gigi spoke in my ear.

She was wearing a black halter dress with cut outs on the sides that showed off her full breasts and thighs. I wanted to burn it when she put it on, but she begged to keep it, telling me I could rip it off her when we got home.

"Baby, I don't dance."

"What if another man asks me to dance?"

"That won't happen."

She grinned. "How do you know?"

"Everyone knows who you belong to, *Mrs. Bresciani*."

Gigi bit her bottom lip. She slid her hand down my chest to my groin and squeezed.

I stopped before she could go further and lifted her hand to my lips, kissing each finger. "You know I love you, right?"

"*Mi amore*," she whispered.

She stood when Janice came over, snapping her fingers to the music. I watched the crowd as Ralfie escorted the girls down to the dance floor with the other guards. She was protected at all times, but I had my hand on my gun as a precaution.

She did some number with her hips twisting to the side and turned around to face me. I knew she wanted to rile me up and get a reaction. I winked and continued to listen to the song playing from the DJ booth.

"Janice asked me about Gigi's birthday and if you're doing something special," Carlo said.

"We haven't had time to sit and discuss it."

Carlo clapped me on the shoulder. "Women's birthdays are important."

"You're right. My head's been deep into the cartel."

"My advice?" Carlo looked at the screens of the club.

"Go ahead."

Carlo tipped his beer and took a sip. "Happy wife, happy life."

We still had a few weeks before her birthday. I planned on making her feel special and aware of how much Gaspare and I needed her in our lives. I had time to get something planned.

Dance after dance, Gigi enjoyed herself until she was ready to go home. She straddled my lap in the back of the limo, her palms on both sides of my face and her tongue down my throat. I slipped my hand under her dress and caressed her smooth skin. Her moans filled the car and my dick was ready to slide inside her hot pussy.

I gripped the back of her neck and pulled her head back to stare into her warm eyes. "You're pregnant."

"I am," she purred.

"My wife is pregnant with my baby."

She grinned. "Make love to me."

I buried my nose in her neck and smelled her perfume that drove me wild. "Fucking ready to taste you."

Gigi moaned when I squeezed her breast.

Chapter 20

Gigi

My plans came along great. I wanted each room to be a different theme, with security cameras inside and out. Being on the go for my new business felt good. I envisioned my schedule; up early to take calls, plan events, and visit with Gaspare so he could make friends. This could mean so much to families, and there was media interest in my new business venture. I enjoyed giving back and proving that a woman that could be a mother, wife, and business owner.

I turned to leave, and Ralfie opened the door. I took my cell out of my purse saw to see that Axel had sent a few messages while it was on silent.

Axel: Meet me at the boat dock at one.

I flipped my wrist to see the time was twelve-fifteen.

Me: Baby, I just got your message. I might be a few minutes late.

Axel: Bring your sexy ass. Be safe getting here.

I nibbled on my bottom lip and leaned forward in the limo. "Ralfie, take me to the boat dock at Waverly."

"Yes, ma'am," Ralfie answered.

A few months ago, Axel had rented a yacht for a night trip under the moon, food prepared by a chef, and a live band. It was the most fun I'd had for a long time. I was blissfully in love with a man who wasn't afraid to show me his flaws and his love for me was all-consuming.

Ralfie made it in a short time and passed through the gate to park. I looked out at the boats and saw the yacht he'd rented last time called Sunshine. Not waiting for Ralfie to open the door, I stepped out and darted down the boardwalk. The crew stood with a glass of cider, and I smiled as I took it from the brass tray.

"Thank you."

He smiled.

I headed up the steps and looked around. The place was decorated in gold signs that read *Congrats on Your Business*. I grinned and went inside to see the chef placing trays of food on the table.

"Mrs. B, how are you?" Sandy wiped the counter clean.

"Hi, Chef Sandy. I'm good."

"Please call me Sandy." She laughed.

"Call me Gigi, and we have a deal."

"You got it, Gigi."

"Everything looks amazing, as usual." I picked up an olive and popped it in my mouth.

Sandy laid out more food, from salad to a seafood bowl and cupcakes. "Mr. B said you'll be eating shortly."

"I'm going to go find him."

I grabbed a piece of shrimp and a napkin and went to look for Axel. Rose petals were scattered on the ground floor and I smirked as I went toward the bedroom on the next level. I heard music coming from the bedroom as I wrapped my hand around the door handle. I pushed it open and gasped.

Tears pooled in my eyes when I saw the large sign on the wall.

Congrats to the best wife.

I set the drink down on the dresser. "You did this for me?"

Axel stood from the bed, holding a rose, and his eyes heated as he approached me. Our eyes connected as I latched onto his shoulders, and he held the flower under my nose for me to smell.

"Anything for you."

"Thank you."

"You deserve this and more."

"Nothing is worth having without you."

"How did it go?"

"Good. I decided on the color scheme and security setup."

"Do you need me to look over anything?"

"No. I made sure to get people who believe in what I'm trying to do with building. This isn't just a daycare center. I want a place for parents to know their kids are a priority."

"Today is about you relaxing with me."

He flipped me around and massaged my shoulders. I moaned and tipped my head back.

"Was Gaspare asleep when you left?" I asked.

"He's fine. Relax and let me spoil you." He kissed my jaw as his hands roamed up to my neck. Hungry and horny, I faced him again. I looped my arms around his neck and kissed him.

"Before we get into bed, I want to go on deck in my bathing suit."

"I have a bag for you with a change of clothes."

"You"—kiss—"are"—kiss—"amazing." I giggled and patted his chest.

I moved around him to grab the bag off the floor and went to the bathroom to change into the one-piece black bathing suit with a high slit on both sides. I wrapped the shawl around my waist and came out to him waiting for me.

"Ready."

He lifted me in his arms bridal style, and I felt like a school kid with a crush as he carried me out of the bedroom. The yacht captain announced we would start moving out. Axel placed me on my feet and grasped my hand to walk me to the front deck, where a blanket and a glass of apple cider were laid out.

"What made you decide on a boat ride?"

Axel picked up the bottle and poured a small amount for him and me before replacing it in the ice bin. "A small celebration of us. I know my schedule will get hectic with the meeting with the mayor. I never want us to get off track."

I clinked our glasses. "Promise?"

"Promise, baby." He leaned in and took my lips in a soft kiss.

"Beautiful out here." I looked around at the backdrop of New York and felt content.

"Our new normal."

"New normal."

Axel pulled out his phone and showed me a few pictures of Gaspare making different faces.

I laughed. "He's your twin." I took the phone out of his hand.

"Spoiled like his momma."

"Next time, we have to bring him out here."

"Him and the new baby." He placed a hand on my stomach and I rested my hand on top.

Axel let me lean back against his chest and we watched a few young people jump off their boats. The sun would go down in a few hours. I locked our hands together and kissed the back of his palm.

My stomach grumbled. "I'm hungry."

"Sandy made all your favorites." Axel helped me to stand.

I wrapped my arms around his waist and we went to eat.

"We need to make sure we do this once a month," I said as Axel pulled out my chair.

He winked at me. "*Mi amore.*"

We spent the afternoon laughing and reflecting on how much we'd overcome. He'd gone from my best friend to my go-to person, no matter the situation. I believed this was what love was truly about.

Chapter 21

Axel

I had the entire world in my hands with a beautiful wife, a son, and a new baby on the way. When Gigi decided to retire, I supported her and knew how strongly she wanted to have the family business under the leadership of someone she trusted who would carry on Laurent's legacy.

"So, there'll be two kids running around the house soon," Turin joked.

"You know, she started acting weird. I felt she was off, but never imagined she was pregnant."

"I could tell she didn't want to give up."

"I'm glad she didn't. She's pregnant again, and this time I won't be out of the picture in a hospital bed for months on end.

"Bro, she just gave birth," Turin said.

I chuckled. "I missed too much time. Had to play catch up."

"I know she's pissed at you. After she gives birth, let her relax for at least five years before you get her pregnant again."

"She's talking about her charity work and opening her

business. The more time she spends on building a business and kids, the better. I think we'll both be occupied."

Turin laughed. "Well, let's go in and handle this business. If I get you back to your pregnant wife in one piece, she won't kill me."

"I missed so much being in a coma. I'm gonna make sure I put her first, and my son is why we're here in Chicago."

Almost all the threats had been straightened out. The bigger problem was the one I was looking at right now, sitting outside Mendoza's home. The minute it was taken care of, we could get back home on our private plane.

The chief set Raymond up with internal affairs on bogus charges. He'll be back on desk duty for a while. I planned to put a tail on him.

Mendoza was another story. I wanted to see his eyes when I killed him.

The compound doors flew open once we turned the power off. Luck was on our side with them living out in the middle of nowhere. No neighbors to see us creeping around in the middle of the night. Turin had some men come through the back, and we approached from the front. We had a layout of the floor plan to get to his room. I screwed on the silencer and crept up the stairs to the bedroom on the right. The guards were dead out front at the gate, and the security cameras had been scrambled to replay the night before, for when the police investigated.

"How many cameras?"

"Counted three, all running on repeat," Turin relayed.

"Let's go."

I pushed the door open slowly and saw Mendoza and his wife asleep in bed. I tapped the gun against his cheek and he opened his eyes.

"Oh my god!" his wife screamed as Turin dragged her out of bed. "Please don't kill me."

"Shut up. Do you know who I am?" I removed my mask.

Mendoza's eyes ballooned in fear.

"You thought I wouldn't come."

"You don't understand. This is business," he murmured.

"Mendoza, you disrespected my wife."

"We can work something out."

I chortled. "Too late."

"Please! I don't know what my husband does for work," his wife begged.

"Shut her up."

Turin shot her in the back of the head.

"My wife!" Mendoza screamed and tried to scramble to her dead body.

I shoved him back against the headboard. "An eye for an eye, Mendoza."

Mendoza tried to reach for his gun on the side table. I hit him with the butt of my weapon and pulled him out of the bed.

"Please, don't kill me. I will do anything you want! I'll give you Chicago."

"Already have Chicago. Everything you own will be transferred to us. Here, type in your code."

His brow dipped in confusion.

"You won't need the money where you're going. Look at it as a donation."

"Then I live?"

I wiggled the phone in his face. "No."

"I am the head of the Mendoza Cartel. Kill me and nothing will move in Chicago or with the Casella family."

"Casella won't be happy with you anyway because of your ties to getting Dario killed."

"Fucking son of a bitch. You killed my wife."

"This is business."

"I have people who will avenge me."

"Should have thought of that before you went against my family and me." I shoved the phone in his chest, pushed the gun to his temple. "Transfer all of your money to that account. Now."

He typed in his information and dropped the phone on the bed. Turin picked it up and confirmed with a nod.

"At least you'll be buried. Unlike Dario." I pulled the trigger.

Turin and I ran out of the house and jumped into the car to head to the airport, leaving the cleanup team to remove all traces of evidence.

* * *

I slept deeply on the return flight and fell into bed next to a sleeping Gigi as soon as I got home. I woke the next morning and turned over in bed, smiling when I saw my son and wife staring at me.

"Did you get him from bed?" My voice was groggy as I rubbed his hair.

"He was crying, so I brought him in here."

I kissed the back of his hand. "Gaspare likes to sleep with us too much."

"Where did you go last night?"

"Handled some loose ends. I think it is time for a little vacay to Italy. Maybe we'll tour Europe.

"I'd like that," Gigi said. "Ebony cooked breakfast. You want to go down?"

"Not hungry. I want to stay like this forever."

"We can't stay up here forever, sleepy pants." Gigi tapped me on the nose.

Being the Boss now took priority over being the Enforcer, and I had to delegate some things to other soldiers.

"Now that I'm pregnant again, I just want to be a mom and a wife. I want to enjoy my pregnancy without stressing over stuff that pertains to the cartel. I don't want to be always looking over my shoulder for someone trying to kill us."

"I'm all for that. Whatever makes you happy."

"Hard to cope with knowing Dario and my mother killed your parents."

"We'll leave the past in the past."

"I can go for that."

She placed Gaspare on top of the bed. I stood and went into the bathroom to freshen up. A huge weight lifted off my shoulders as I stared at the man in the mirror. I'd become a husband, father, and cartel Boss in a matter of months. It could be overwhelming, but seeing the two most important people right next to me smiling and happy gave me strength to do what Laurent Carrington trained and mentored me for, what I was ready for. To be a leader.

I finished with my shower and grabbed clean pants and a shirt. I kissed Gigi as she stood with Gaspare and passed him over to me.

"We should go to the beach today."

I turned back to look at her. "We haven't taken Gaspare to the beach."

"No, but I want to take him to the one back home."

I paused. "Italy."

"Yes. What do you think?"

"Right now?"

"Please? We can be back in the states in a few days. I want him to know his family history."

I hadn't thought about Gaspare knowing where his parents come from. Maybe I'd blocked out that part to focus on what I could control. "Pack a few bags, and I'll call the pilot."

"You make me happy."

"That's my job."

She grinned and turned to go back upstairs to get things together. I went into the kitchen and grabbed a bottle for Gaspare and took a seat to feed him and me. Ebony talked on and on about Gaspare and his feeding habits.

A few minutes later, Gigi came into the kitchen with a phone to her ear. "We'll be in Italy for a few days."

"Who is that?"

Gigi covered the receiver with her hand. "Janice and Sabrina on three-way."

I should have known she would be on the line with those two. Once they met a year ago, they became a sisterhood.

I removed the bottle from Gaspare's mouth and burped him. Placing him in his chair, I picked up the house phone and made arrangements for the flight.

* * *

Italy

The condo looked the same from when we left it a year ago. I still kept cameras and a detail on the place for security, but being back here came with memories of the first time Gigi came to my place and spent the night.

She sat on the couch and covered up with a blanket. The flight had been long and Gaspare's crying had kept us awake. We finally got him comfortable in the guest room that would become to his room while we were here. All it took was money and a phone call to get what you wanted.

"Are you going to call a meeting with Casella and the other families while you're here?" Gigi asked.

I stood at the large window in the living room and stared out at the night lights. "No. We're here to show Gaspare our roots and take him to the beach."

Gigi rose from the couch and stood next to me. "Never thought we would end up back here."

"You had it in your mind to never come back."

"I truly hated what it represented."

My arm automatically went around her waist, drawing her close. She wanted to go by her family home and I'd tried to talk her out of it, but I supported her choices.

"We need to get going first thing in the morning if you want to check on the place."

"Gaspare will sleep during the drive, so we're good." She dropped the blanket on the couch and went to the bedroom to sleep.

I pulled my cell out of my pocket and dialed Turin's number.

"How's it going?"

"Please! We won't get involved!" a voice pleaded in the background.

"All good over here. How is the family?" Turin asked cheerfully.

"Gigi's in bed and Gaspare finally went down."

"Are you coming to the farm?"

I rubbed my chin. "You have any problems?" I heard a buzzing sound.

"The Carringtons can have all the money. We'll give it all up!" another voice begged.

Gigi asked if I would attend a meeting with the Casella family and bring all five families to the table to negotiate. No longer did I feel the need to include anyone in my decisions.

Casella's people were pissed about me taking out their man and had good reason. Now I would wipe out the entire bloodline. As soon as they got back to Italy, Turin had kidnapped them and killed the top Bosses in the family one by one. The territory they owned was now under Carrington rule and soon, every cartel family would know not to play with me.

Turin answered, "No, it was an easy pickup."

"Make sure not to leave anything for a burial." I finished the call, and a smile came across my face. Everything had fallen into place.

I headed to the bedroom and stood in the doorway, watching my love sleep with the covers across her bottom half. She wasn't showing yet, but I wanted to be extra cautious with this pregnancy.

I moved close to the bed and pushed the covers further up her body. I sat on the bed and removed my clothes before climbing in next to her.

Gigi rolled over and reached for me. I took her hand and kissed her palm. "Finally, we have peace."

"My peace has always been with you."

I positioned her so we were spooning and rubbed her stomach. She clasped her hand on top of mine and we fell into a deep sleep.

Epilogue

Gigi

Two years later

I carried Antonella in my arms in the banquet hall and smiled at a few of our close friends and family members I hadn't spoken with in a few years. They'd all come to visit and celebrate the grand opening of my new business.

It had been a gradual change for me to not ask about cartel business. With Axel and Turin managing things, it never popped in my head to question anymore. My days were filled with sippy cups and watching cartoons with the kids.

As soon as the issues were handled with Dario and Hugo, I'd realized I needed to be more intentional with my life and cherish my family, rather than prove I could be the Don of a cartel. As a woman, it was rare to be put in that position, but I learned I didn't need to prove anything to anyone. My kids and husband came first over everything else. They brought me peace and joy every day. Gaspare loved being a big brother to Antonella, and Axel made it a point to travel less to be here for the family.

Antonella fussed in my arms and wanted to get down and play with the other kids.

"Be good, Nella."

Axel wanted me to pick a location that would be close to our home so I could check on the kids and oversee the business, so I found a new place not too far from the city. We ended up extending our property because I wanted more kids and Axel liked privacy.

"The Aurora Children's Center looks fabulous, Gigi." Janice stood before me with her oldest kids and Sabrina.

"Thank you, babe. I can't wait to get more buildings opened."

Sabrina joked, "That degree came in handy."

I finished online for college. I wanted to tell my kids that their mother, despite everything she went through, had gotten her education. Axel and I debated if we'd allow our children to be in the business, but ultimately it was their decision when they got older. The thought of my daughter being manipulated into an arranged marriage pissed me off. I knew Axel would never entertain the idea whenever he told me about meetings he attended with other made men who wanted to secure a future in the Carrington Cartel.

I smiled as Axel started toward me with the phone glued to his ear and Turin right behind him.

"Remember, you already have two under five years of age," Janice teased.

Axel ended his call, wrapped an arm around my shoulder, and kissed my forehead. "Sorry I'm late."

"You okay?" I brushed a finger across his bottom lip and he smiled.

Antonella rushed over with her arms in the air for him to pick her up. Axel bent and scooped her up, kissing her on the cheek. "Everything is fine."

I poked Axel in the chest. "Turin, is he lying to me?"

Turin raised his hands and smirked.

Axel placed his hand on my hip and whispered in my ear. "Be good for me."

Something about his deep voice as his lips grazed my ear gave me the chills.

"Aurora would be so proud of what you've built, Gigi." Sabrina commented.

Aurora was a wonderful house manager, friend, and nanny. I watched more families come in and sign up. The place had a low-cost fee for the application, and all operating dollars came from me and a few donations from friends. Any parent who needed a place to drop their kids off for a few hours while they worked and couldn't afford an arm and a leg could come here.

"We need to plan the next family vacation," Janice said.

I pointed at her oldest kids, and Sabrina's son, AJ. "Before the kids go off to college."

"I hate that I make pretty babies. These little fast tail girls keep calling the house," Janice fussed.

I held in my laughter as she glared at her son across the room talking to some girls who looked older than him.

"I'm glad I don't have that problem." I tickled Antonella's stomach.

Axel placed her on the floor and held out his hand to me. "Come with me."

"Where?"

"A surprise."

"What did you do, Axel?"

He avoided my question and walked toward the door of the building. This man spoiled me so much, I couldn't understand how I got so lucky. He showed me every day that I was priority number one in his life. The breakfasts in bed, the calls throughout the day to check in, and nightly lovemaking showed me a side of Axel I never knew existed when he was my bodyguard. He had always stayed quiet and avoided my questions.

A few people followed us out of the building, and I told Sabrina to watch the kids for me. We stepped outside and a brand-new Ferrari with a red bow on top sat out front with Carrington inscribed on the side.

"When did you do this?" I covered my mouth in shock.

"I wanted to surprise you and had it in motion for a few months. They call it a push gift," Axel answered.

"Baby, you didn't have to give me a gift. Besides, Antonella's not a newborn anymore."

"I know, but we're making up for lost time after Gaspare was born and doing things differently. So not only did I get you one..."

My brows dipped in surprise as another Ferrari pulled up with Ralfie behind the wheel, this one in white.

"You got me two cars?"

"Turin talked me down from buying you one for every day of the week, so I compromised with two. I want you to know how much you mean to me and make up for the times I tried to push you away."

"Axel, you could never push me away. We've been through difficult times, but how we overcame them is what matters most." I rubbed the tattoos of Antonella and Gaspare on his neck while I kissed him over and over.

"Please break up the love fest. We already have these two barely a year apart," Janice joked.

I couldn't resist my husband and how he made me feel every day.

I moved toward the car, opened the door, and sat in the warm seats, playing with the steering wheel and radio. Even with me being driven around by Ralfie, I found a few times to go out and drive myself, though still with security behind and in front of me at all times. Axel didn't take any chances. Our staff was trained to check all guests who entered our front gate.

I was happy to let go of the past and move toward a brighter future. No more pain or distrust. No more lingering doubts as a wife and mother.

I shut the door and threw myself into Axel's arms, thanking him passionately for each gift. As usual, his hands went to my ass, and I had to pull back and remind myself we had kids with us.

I smiled. "I'm ready for an official honeymoon."

"Your wish will be granted, Mrs. Bresciani."

"I'm thinking of the Dominican Republic."

"I'll have the plane ready in an hour."

"You spoil me, Mr. Bresciani."

"That's what happens when you claim the most beautiful girl in the world."

* * *

I hope you enjoyed Gigi and Axel's story. Check the sneak peek of "**Achille Cartel**" on the next page. Follow my standalone, opposites attract, age gap, military romance "**Exposed**" https://books2read.com/u/bQyYZe. Are you a fan of sports romance? Then download one-night stand, billionaire romance "**Refuel**" https://books2read.com/u/boDyDA. Also, follow it up with workplace, sports romance "**Pressure**" https://books2read.com/u/3Ly1r7. If you love romantic comedy, fake relationships, enemies to lovers, find it here, "**Something Gained.**" Click the link here https://books2read.com/u/baGLYy. My stories of friends finding love started with the Heart of Stone series that includes a host of characters and family. "**Broken**" book 1 Emery and Jackson a sports, one night stand, workplace romance is here: https://books2read.com/u/3LoelX

Then you can continue with a fun side story of Emery and Jackson with "Valentine's Day short here: https://books2read.com/u/4jAypY

Jordan, her best friend's story, continues here in "**Rebirth**" book 2 a single dad, widow billionaire romance here: https://books2read.com/u/ba2OMx

* * *

Please also check out a second-chance workplace romance here, "**Renew Book 4**" https://books2read.com/u/4NXyPG with a host of characters intertwined.

Follow Desiree and Gabriel in **"Temptation"** a stand-alone contemporary, sports, curvy girl romance. Check it out here https://books2read.com/u/mle1Vv

Check out dark mafia romance here that started my journey with Antonio and Sabrina in **"Ruthless Book 1"** https://books2read.com/u/4AxKLo

The relationship continues in "**Savage**" book 2 as they get to know each other and their families: https://books2read.com/u/bpED6g

Antonio and Sabrina have more work to do in "**Beast**" book 3 right here: https://books2read.com/links/ubl/4AxKOd

* * *

Did you know Janice and Carlo have a book? Well grab this dark mafia romance with emotional scars, and betrayal right here: https://books2read.com/u/b6je6M

Any fans of forbidden romance, political? Check out **"Mutual Agreement"** https://books2read.com/u/mgzzWX a steamy romance. Pre-order the full novel of **"Nasir"** click the link here.

Have you checked out **"She's All I Need"** click here https://books2read.com/u/49lkeW a sports, opposites attract romance. What about dark romance that has everything from steamy romance, opposites attract, suspense, thriller, celebrity, and more **"Stolen Book 1"** https://books2read.com/u/mvZlgV Don't miss the follow up Joaquin and Sofia's story in book 2 **"Saved"** https://books2read.com/u/4DWwLd

The conclusion for Joaquin and Sofia comes full circle in **"Betrayed"** here: https://books2read.com/u/4A5LGp

* * *

Catch up with favorite characters in this holiday short romance which includes spoilers. **"Holiday collection"** here https://books2read.com/u/bzd59G

For small town, single mom stories check out **"Until Seren**a" https://books2read.com/u/mej8vr. Always fun when you love billionaire romances so check in with **"Cocky Catcher"** a sports romance, enemies to lovers here: https://books2read.com/u/bOxNgJ. Some familiar characters show up in **"Bossy Billionaire"** a workplace, enemies to lovers romance here: https://books2read.com/u/mvZoDq

All curvy girl, plus size romance lovers get into **"I**

Deserve His Love" a standalone, second chance romance here: https://books2read.com/u/mVrGwP

The fantasy romance readers look no further than a **"Red Light District"** a curvy girl, fling romance here: https://books2read.com/u/m2RQ6G

Reader Questions

1.Do you think Ginerva deserved what happened to her?

2. Should Axel and Gigi wait before having another child?

3.Would Gigi go back on her word and get involved in the business again?

4.Will the Mendoza Cartel come after Gigi and Axel after the death of Hugo?

5.Do you think Axel should retire?

Coming in 2024: Achille Cartel

Coming in 2024: Achille Cartel

Priya

I know my way home. I could get there with my eyes closed. But when I take a shortcut, I end up in unfamiliar territory. What I stumble upon shakes me to my core. Now, I'm firmly in the sights of the Achille Cartel, New York's infamous and brutal mafia family, and Dante, the most sinfully sexy man I've ever seen.

Dante

I call the shots. I make the decisions. I have to deal with the consequences when my guys screw up. The last thing I need is a witness, but now it's happened, it's me who has to clean up the mess. But Priya isn't just any woman. She's sweet, innocent, and too damn irresistible.

What does a mafia boss do with a beautiful schoolteacher who was in the wrong place at the wrong time? Can we get this right?

Heart of Stone Universe

Broken 1 Emery and Jackson
https://books2read.com/u/boWPAV
Heart of Stone Book 1.5
https://payhip.com/b/kWg7
Rebirth 2 Jordan and Damon
https://books2read.com/u/ba2OMx
Heart of Stone Book 3.5 Bottoms Up
https://payhip.com/b/HGP1
Reveal 3 Angela and Brent
https://books2read.com/u/31rx9l
Renew 4 Jessica and Joseph
https://books2read.com/u/4NXyPG
The Early Years-A Prequel
https://books2read.com/u/49Zjnw
Ruthless Struck In Love Book 1
https://books2read.com/u/4AxKLo
Savage Struck In Love Book 2
https://books2read.com/u/bpED6g

Beast Struck In Love Book 3
https://books2read.com/u/3LpgdJ
Janice and Carlo Captivated By His Love
https://books2read.com/u/b6je6M
Brutal Struck In Love Book 4
https://books2read.com/u/4NQyE9
Stolen-Fuertes Mafia Cartel Book 1
https://books2read.com/u/mvZlgV
Saved-Fuertes Mafia Cartel Book 2
https://books2read.com/u/4DWwLd
Redemption Struck In Love Book 5
https://books2read.com/u/b5kZ8O
Betrayal- Fuertes Mafia Cartel Book 3
https://books2read.com/u/4A5LGp

What's Next?

Want to know what happens next?

Follow me on my website to catch the next release.

Reviews are the lifeblood of the publishing world. They're read, appreciated, and needed.

Please consider taking the time to leave a few words on your review platform of choice.

Sign up for updates and sneak peaks at the site below. www.chiquitadennie.com

Acknowledgments

I want to dedicate this to my team that helps me behind the scenes, from my editors, proofreaders, test readers, graphic designers, and especially Crystal. Truly appreciate each of you for keeping me on my toes.

304 Publishing Company

We showcase authors writing African American, Interracial, Women's Fiction, Urban Romance, Erotic, and Contemporary Romance novels. Along with Thriller, Suspense, Poetry, Beauty, and Style Books. Thank you for taking the time out to visit. Join our mailing list to stay updated with new releases and blog posts.

Catalog Releases

Catalog Releases
    By Chiquita Dennie:
    The Early Years-A Prequel Short Story
    Ruthless: Struck in Love 1
    Savage: Struck in Love 2
    Beast: Struck in Love 3
    Brutal: Struck In Love 4
    Redemption: Struck In Love 5
    Broken Book 1 (Emery & Jackson)
    Heart Of Stone Book 1.5 Emery & Jackson A Valentine's
Day Short
    Janice and Carlo: Captivated By His Love
    Rebirth Book 2 (Jordan and Damon)
    Temptation
    Reveal Book 3 (Angela and Brent)
    Cocky Catcher
    Bossy Billionaire
    Bottoms Up Heart of Stone, Book 3.5 (Jessica and Joseph
Short

Love Shorts: A Collection of Short Stories
Stolen: Fuertes Mafia Cartel Book 1
Exposed (Salvation Society Novel)
Saved: Fuertes Mafia Cartel Book 2
Refuel (A Driven World Novel)
Pressure (A Driven World Novel)
Until Serena (HEA World Novel)
Renew Book 4 (Jessica and Joseph)
She's All I Need
Red Light District (A Fantasy Romance Short)
Aydin: TN Seal Security Book 1
Nasir: TN Seal Security Book 2
Betrayed: Fuertes Mafia Cartel Book 3
Something Gained (A Romantic Comedy Book 1)
Torn: The Carrington Cartel Book 1
Claim: The Carrington Cartel Book 2

Thank you so much for reading and if you enjoyed the crazy ride and decide to leave a review, we'd truly appreciate the support.

About the Author

Chiquita Dennie is an author of Contemporary, Romantic Suspense, Erotic and Women's Fiction.

Chiquita lives in Los Angeles, CA. Before she started writing contemporary romance, she worked in the entertainment industry on notable TV shows such as the Dr Phil show, Tyra Banks show, American Idol, and Deal or No Deal. But her favorite job is the one she's now doing, full time writing romance.

A Best-Selling Author and Award-winning Filmmaker, her first short film "Invisible" was released in Summer 2017 and screened in multiple festivals and won for Best Short Film. She also hosts a podcast that showcases the latest in Beauty, Business and Community called "Moscato and Tea." Her debut release of Antonio and Sabrina Struck in Love has opened a new avenue of writing that she loves.

If you want to know when the next book will come out, please visit my website at http://www.chiquitadennie.com, where you can sign up to receive an email for my next release.